If man loved woman as much as he loved football, there'd be no such thing as divorce.

Knee High To A Grasshopper

By

Steph Lawton

authorHOUSE®

AuthorHouse™ UK Ltd.
500 Avebury Boulevard
Central Milton Keynes, MK9 2BE
www.authorhouse.co.uk
Phone: 08001974150

© 2008 Steph Lawton. All rights reserved.

No part of this book may be reproduced, stored in a retrieval system, or transmitted by any means without the written permission of the author.

First published by AuthorHouse   7/25/2008

ISBN: 978-1-4343-9063-9 (sc)

Printed in the United States of America
Bloomington, Indiana

This book is printed on acid-free paper.

To Robert Andrews, Simon Watson and Robin Wood, better known simply as Rob, Splodge and Woody.

"I never had friends later on like I did when I was twelve. Jesus, does anybody...?"

Stephen King, The Body
From the motion picture, 'Stand By Me'.

**To Gary Robinson. Not a workmate; a real mate.
Thanks Gary.**

Finally, last but in no means least, to each and every Newcastle United supporter past, present and future. The real hero's at a football club are rarely those on the wage bill. Ha'way the lads…

**Front Cover: Ritchie and Nathan Johnstone.
Father & Son.**

Part One

FATHER AND SON

1. *Ashington*

"This is the bairn then?"

"Aye, this is Keiron," he said, roughing the lad's hair a little.

"Keiron?" I asked him with raised eyebrows.

"Well I didn't know he was going to be injured every week did I? Besides," he smiled, "it could have been worse; I nearly called him Nobby."

I laughed a little in the warm pre-season Ashington night. His Dad, my Dad, resumed.

"Then I thought about the Hall's that lived in our street when you were just a bairn. Remember them? And their poor soon Albert? He's gay now you know. No bloody wonder if you ask me. Your Mam used to call him the catheter kid he had so much piss taken out of him."

"Dad!" I said, making the word last three syllables, "The bairn," I added, disapproving of his swearing.

My Dad, Keiron's Dad, just smiled; I think he liked it that I was already looking out for the kid.

I looked at the poor lad, standing on a terrace at Ashington FC but still in a world of his own. He was knee high to a grasshopper, perfect blond hair that I used to have at his age and a Newcastle shirt sporting most of his pop.

Dad – our dad – chuckled to himself as he blew upon his Bovril.

"If Keegan hadn't walloped a couple past McFaul back in '74 you'd be called Willie. Can you imagine that: two sons called Nobby & Willie!"

I'm not sure whether I was going to laugh or to cry, but looking at the little blond bairn smiling up at me I felt *something*. He put one arm above his eyes to protect from the setting northern sun and with the other he jutted his salt & vinegar upwards and offered me a crisp.

"No thanks, Keiron," I told him through the lump in my throat as I spoke to my brother for the very first time.

For a moment time stood still.

Dad was checking his match programme; I was checking the rumblings in my heart that carried back fully twenty-four years, and Keiron was checking where the smell of hot-dogs was coming from.

It was one of those summer football nights where you could close your eyes and all your senses just tell you that you're at a match.

There was the smell of hot-dogs and Bovril, the sound of banter and debate and turnstiles clicking in the background. And it was warm banter; wrapped in the dialect I know and love. I love the sound of the Geordie accent in a football ground, especially one like Portland Park. It was a warm July night and there was a cool Ashington breeze rolling down the terracing, not seats, terracing.

When my eyes were open I could see the beautiful sight of all that makes a football ground special: a North-East setting sun, people – real working class people – terraces and crash barriers and goal nets blowing in the breeze. I could feel the grass-roots romance as the tannoy announcer read out the teams and the players took to the field amidst the warm, if not the rapturous, applause.

There in the centre of it all was what we came to see: the players, the pitch, the goal-posts and the ball; there all around it – the supporters and spectators – was what makes all we came to see special.

Dad picked Keiron up and sat him on the barrier we were stood in front of. A million memories came flooding back like the Tyne along the Quayside. Watching the way Dad scooped my brother into his arms and sat him there safely with a better view; watching Keiron smile at our Dad and watching his eyes widen as his heroes (Newcastle United's Reserves – God the kid was in for a long few years) took to the field I could have been looking through a window in time and seeing myself.

I looked at Keiron's excited face and I couldn't help but wonder what the next 25 years would bring him now he was enlisted in the Toon-Army. What games would he talk about twenty years from now? What would be his highs and lows? Who would be his favourite players? And would we ever win a damned trophy.

Though I hoped his years would be blessed with more silverware than mine I doubted they could be filled with better memories or better friends. Football is like life: it's not always where you end up that matters, but who you travel with.

Then one of those awkward silences drifted over us. We were making small talk but there was a big talk looming and little way of avoiding it.

"I'm glad you turned up tonight," Dad said, not looking at me, just looking at the pitch. "He's useless," he added as a sub-commentary to our tentative family reunion.

"Yeah," I said, in reference to neither and both of his previous statements.

"I didn't think you would, you know. I thought maybe you'd be stuck at work, or didn't fancy the traffic, or maybe you just weren't ready to meet the little 'un yet," he added as a stray pass made its way into the stand. "Seriously, what do they do on the training ground all week?"

"It's hardly his fault is it?" I said.

"I blame Roeder. His job, his backroom staff, his fault."

"No, I mean the bairn! It's hardly his fault is it?"

"Aye, you're right," Dad said, his eyes on the pitch and gesticulating furiously for an offside.

I'd barely seen my Dad in years. Well, with the odd exception of Service Stations, Central Station, Wembley, Milan and Stanley Park. That was a weird one. I hadn't seen him in ages and then bang; he turns up at the same Burger Van as me yards from the San Siro just like he did on Wembley Way.

We came close to burying the hatchet a few times, but each time I fell short. Eventually I found out about him becoming a father again and I did what it took to cut the ties completely. The empty seat at St. James Park said more than my words ever would. I know it hurt; it was meant to. It's hard to describe how I felt about what Dad did. The best I can do is to say that it was like a family version of Gascoigne going to Spurs or Beardsley to Liverpool.

Basically, he left.

We weren't good enough for him. Just like Gascoigne and Beardsley wanted trophies and medals, Dad wanted love and happiness. And just like Gascoigne and Beardsley couldn't get the former on Tyneside, Dad couldn't get the latter from us. But when he left his wife he also left my mother. And when he left my mother he ultimately left me.

And I guess when you can't *have* the one you love, it's all too easy to *hate* the one you love. So just like I'd boo and throw Mars Bars at Gazza, and just like I pulled down Beardsley's poster that once sat pride of place on my bedroom wall, I did the same to Dad. Our house was no longer his home games. He had a new club, and every time he came back I booed like he was Chris Waddle and access was a Cup-tie.

Then, one day, he stopped coming back.

Beardsley came back and I loved him again, although I'll be honest it took me a while. It was the goal at Oldham in '93 that did it, live on Sky's Monday Night Football. I resented the fact that his best years were with someone else and he only came home when they no longer wanted him. Then he dropped his shoulder, beat the Oldham Centre-half, Richard Jobson I think, and bang! Beardsley's back and all is forgiven!

Waddle never came back, and he even ended up playing for Sunderland, which to me was punishment in itself. Gazza never came back, but it's hard to hate Gazza I find. Besides he did bugger all when he left so I wasn't that bothered.

But Dad, well, Dad never came back, and he *did* find success. And finally, with little Keiron sitting on the barrier watching his first ever match, Dad had his trophy. And like the pride I felt watching Waddle, Beardsley and Gascoigne playing for England, I couldn't begrudge him his success or his happiness.

"I've bought him a season ticket," Dad told me.

"Poor little bugger. What did he do to deserve that? Couldn't you have just grounded him or stopped his pocket money?"

Dad didn't respond; he just resumed. "I've bought you one too," he told me boldly.

Silence.

"Will you come back?"

"Jeez, Fatha" I said slipping into my broadest Geordie, the same that I'd picked up by his side all those years ago. "I don't know."

"Will you think about it?" he asked me fairly.

I said nothing. I had a thousand words hammering around my heart and head but none would organise themselves into a sentence that I could form in my mouth.

He ruffled Keiron's hair and the bairn turned and smiled at him. "You enjoying it son?" he asked.

Keiron answered in big eyes and wide smiles: he was loving it.

"Wigan will be his first game" Dad told me. "Remember your first game, son? Jeez, you were just knee high to a grasshopper," he said.

And did I remember my first game? Hell, I'm a football romantic. Your first game is like your first kiss; if you love the beautiful game it's something you should never forget.

"Yeah," I said, "I remember my first game. I remember it like it was yesterday…"

2. *Keegan*

It was August 1982. It was hot like summers used to be. Maybe summers are always hotter in our memories. We lived in Wallsend. It was summer holidays and school was out for what seemed like an eternity. I was seven years old. We played knocky-nine-doors, kicky the can, and hide & seek and we kicked a casey around the street from half past nine every morning until ten o'clock every night when the sun went down.

The sun never seems to set when you're a kid.

There was a gang of us that used to hang around our street and the community was alive and united. Someone's mother was always knocking up bags of chips, wrapped in yesterday's newspaper and covered in salt & vinegar; someone else's was dishing out ice pops and screwballs and cider lollies.

We ran around in shorts and T-shirts and had water fights with Squeazy-Liquid bottles not ten quid water pistols like kids have today.

That takes me to the Friday night before it all happened; the night before my life was changed dramatically and irrevocably in ever so nice a way.

It was nigh on 10 o'clock and the sky had gone Coventry blue I guess you'd call it now. It was the same colour as the Man City shirts, the ones they wore in the 1981 Cup Final.

There was barely cloud in the sky and the heat was finally starting to subside.

My mates were Adam and Dave, Julie and Mandy, the young lass from our street that I used to have a crush on. We lived in a long line of terraced houses, all sloping down a little towards the Tyne. There was a main road at the top and a smaller road at the bottom, both running horizontally. In between there were twelve streets sloping vertically. That's where our gang lived.

That little corner of that little part of Wallsend was where we all grew up. The Tyne ran proud at the bottom; the shipyards towered tall above us, and everywhere you went Newcastle United was never more than a heartbeat in a conversation away.

The Chronicle was our bible, the working mans clubs were our churches and St James Park was our Mecca. Men smoked cigarettes, drove cars like Cortina's and Capri's, and worked for a living; women wore perms, raised families and talked over the garden fence; and kids, well us kids played out from first thing 'til last, respected our parents, feared the local bobby and dreamt of pulling on the black & white shirt.

I knew nowt about football before the summer of 1982. Wembley was a Fraggle, Villa was an ice-cream and the only Bolton I knew of would go onto ask us how we could be lovers if we couldn't be friends. Then the '82 World Cup caught my eye and the twinkle and the interest was noted by my father.

It's funny; I spent so many years just wanting his attention, so much of my time just wanting some of his. But he was always too busy, too tired or too drunk. He never had any time for me and I guess by time I was seven I took his lack of interest for granted. Then football came along and everything changed.

I remember him looking at me curiously one morning as I hammered Adam's casey against the chalk sketched goal on the end house wall, raised my hands aloft in triumph and yelled "Brooking!" at the top of my voice.

That end house caused us no end of bother. The man that lived there was a right mean old bastard. We used to call him Hitler. I guess when you're seven there ain't much difference between someone moaning that your ball keeps whacking off his wall and genocide. In fact, if someone had asked me what genocide was I'd have probably said 'that band that Phil Collins was in'.

Every time Dad came out of the house or appeared at the top of the street we'd quit in fear of a rollicking. Then when he'd gone we'd welly that ball off the end house wall and its chalk goal all day, all night long.

That's how it was when that magical Friday night arrived.

Streets of Mam's were at their respective scullery doors and yelling that it was time to come in. In unison every kid in the street yelled back a plea for "Five more minutes!" All these *five more minutes* added up to nigh on quarter to eleven and soon a new record for staying out late was looming. The light was on behind *my* Mam and it turned her into a silhouette in a doorway. She was busy working in the kitchen, she came out to call again, and then she got drawn into a conversation with Mandy's Mam, our next-door neighbour.

Slowly but surely Mothers gathered at the gates and we knew they'd talk for hours. As conversation went we continued kicking the casey off the end house wall, celebrating every goal under streetlight and feeling every minute as 11 o'clock loomed, arrived, and then passed.

In the end it wasn't the goals we were celebrating but the minutes.

Finally, with the threat of my Dad's imminent return from the Club growing large, I, like Mandy, Julie, Adam and Dave traded streetlight for kitchen light and called time on one of the best days of the summer. Jackie, that's my Dad, was home around 11:30, with a swagger and a stagger, a song and a smile, and three packets of fish n' chips under his working mans arm.

Even though I was tucked up in bed when he came home he knew I was only pretending to be asleep and soon I was whisked off in his merry arms and rushed downstairs for my supper. I never really thought about it at the time, but Dad used to be a bit nasty when he'd had a drink. We always used to give him a wide berth. But that night he was magic. He was a happy drunk. He sat me downstairs and poured me a Dandelion & Burdock, handed me my fish n' chips and told Mam and me all about how things would be different now.

He reeled off what I'll always remember as a Geordie fairytale, told a Geordie way: fish n' chip supper, Dandelion and Burdock, a terraced house in Wallsend and hero coming to save us and make us proud once again.

Dad told me how the barren years were over, the sleeping giant was awakening, and I would be there to see it.

Newcastle had signed Kevin Keegan.

The furore surrounding Keegan is still a haze in my memory up until that night. I went to bed too excited to sleep. I awoke early and a little confused. Dad had said a lot of things in his drunken excitement and I wasn't too sure what that Saturday would bring.

As I climbed out of bed, got dressed and made into the street to call on Adam & Dave I had no idea that Saturday would bring my first ever visit to St James Park.

I was chasing the casey all over the street, drilling shots off the chalk wall goal when Dad came out of the house.

"Terry!" he yelled, "Get a shift on!"

I looked at him bemused, Adam's casey at my feet.

"Well are you coming or what?"

"Where?" I asked puzzled.

"For trombone lessons you plonker!"

"What?" I asked him, my stupidity testing his patience to the yield.

"To the match you daft bugger!"

Adam's casey rolled away, I ran off towards my Dad, and as we made our way towards the bus stop on Wallsend high street father & son took the first steps on the road to friendship.

On the bus going to Town Dad and I started to bond right from the off. Basically I said nothing and just hung off his every word as he explained everything that had ever happened in my life – and more importantly – in Newcastle United's life since day one.

He explained the clubs history and he summarised the first 90 years in a matter of minutes. As the bus made its way into the busy town centre he told me to memorise the years we won trophies. Despite repeating '10, 24, 32, 51, 52, 55' or '5, 7, 9, 27' under my breath the facts and figures went over my head. Still, the principle was well and truly taken aboard.

"There's not many high numbers is there Dad?" I asked him innocently.

He didn't reply with words; he replied with one of those stern looks that normally got my little legs going in any direction but his.

I got the gist anyway: great club, great place, great fans and great people, run by idiots for way too long and have slipped into the wilderness. He made Division Two sound like some God-forsaken nether world in a child's fairytale.

There were four Divisions; I didn't know that.

We were in the Second Division; I didn't know that, either.

Divisions Three and Four were not worth even thinking about they were so dark and cringe-worthy. Although Dad did still hold out hope that our enemy, Sunderland, would one day end up there.

Sunderland were in Division One. That was the best division. Seemed logical.

We were in Division Two, but we were (always had been and always would be) better than Sunderland, who were in Division One. Okay, now I was confused. I thought about asking but didn't wish to provoke my father's wrath with my stupidity so I let it go. Time would have a way of answering it for me.

So, we were in Division Two, which was bad. And we wanted to be in Division One, where we belonged. And because people kept making stupid mistakes (vaguely I remember a tirade of abuse that included names such as Lee, McGarry, Dinnis and Westwood) we had fallen behind.

Dad used one of his now famous metaphors to describe our predicament.

"Right, imagine we're on a bus yeah?"

"We *are* on a bus."

(Clip around the ear-hole)

"And the driver's taking us to Newcastle?"

"He… Okay"

"But he's an idiot and he gets lost and we end up in Gateshead, yeah?"

"Yeah," I said slowly, not certain I knew what he meant, not daring to risk another clip around the ear-hole and ask.

"So we end up in Gateshead, Okay?"

"Okay" I said, thinking *'so are we going to Newcastle or Gateshead?'*

"Well that's not where we want to be!"

So we are *going to Newcastle!*

"Is it?" he asked.

"No!" I said assuredly, "We want to be in Newcastle!"

"Exactly" Dad said, and roughed my hair. Whatever I'd said I got it right.

"Now just like a bus driver's job is to get the bus from say Wallsend to Newcastle, the Managers job is to get the club, our club, into Division One," he explained.

Hearing him call it *our* club sent shivers down my spine.

"Now putting petrol into the bus is like putting money into a football club. Finally the board has put some money up, and we've bought ourselves the best damn petrol money can buy: Kevin Keegan is five-star fuel lad!" Dad said excitedly.

"So who's the bus driver?" I asked, finally grasping his metaphor.

"Arthur Cox, son" he told me assuredly.

"Arthur Cox is taking us to Division One," he added as the bus made its way to the Haymarket, "And it's going to be a hell of a ride."

That's one of the things I love about my Dad: he always had a story to tell.

3. *Home*

It was August 1982. It was hot like summers used to be. Maybe summers are always hotter in our memories. We lived in Wallsend. The Tyne ran proud at the bottom and the shipyards towered high above us.

I know it's a massive world, later years following The Lads to Holland and Milan would teach me that. But back in 1982, when Kevin Keegan signed for Newcastle United, my world was condensed into about a half-mile radius that included our home, my work at Swans, and the social club.

Our home was at the bottom of one of twelve rows of terraced houses sloping towards the Tyne. My work, the shipyard, towered above us and stood tall overlooking our little part of the world. In a way seeing work towering tall from my bedroom window was depressing, in a way it was reassuring. It was early mornings, long hours and more than a man's share of sweat and oil. But it was also a reminder of my roots, a promise of a wage packet, and a place where more friendships were forged than pieces of metal ever were.

I'd apprenticed there when I was 16 year old, back in 1971. My first day was Tuesday July 6th. Working in the shipyard was a natural progression for me; my Dad had done so, and his Dad before him. Life was work hard play hard. It's the way we do things up North. And I did work hard. From the crack of dawn when the sun crept over the horizon and lit this working man's world, to the 5 o'clock whistle that sent us out of the gates and off to the pub, I did my graft and I did it well.

There ain't anything wrong with a hard day's work. I'm not going to sit here and bitch about kids today or when I was a lad but I will tell you one thing: a little more hard work for the things you want and a little less expecting them for free would see this world of all generations be a far better place.

And there ain't anything wrong with playing hard either. Life ain't a dress rehearsal and life sure ain't a spectator sport either. Life is there to be lived, so make your memories and take a bounty of them to your grave. I know I'm quoting a song here, but I know I'm going to die so my revenge is living well.

We work hard for our money, we deserve to see every penny of it go towards making us happy, whatever that happiness be.

To some it's flash cars; to others it's big houses. To others it's holidays. To some it's the nest egg and the bank account, to others it's waking up on Saturday morning and just hoping there's enough left in their wallet to go drink their damn hangover away.

Me, well my first car was a hand-me-down Ford Corsair, my first home was a crammed little terrace right here in Wallsend and the only bank account we ever knew was the notes my Mam stuffed into the biscuit barrel to stop my Dad from pissing it away before the Provie Wife could come collect it. And the only holiday I ever had was a chalet in South Shields and one July week in Morecambe.

Mind, I did like a pint after a hard day's graft. There's a certain satisfaction about putting your dirty hand around an ice cold pint glass and sinking the first lager of the weekend and knowing that you earned every penny that paid for it.

But to me – a young man who cherished the fact that his elders thought he worked hard – my play hard was neither beer nor banking nor holidays, cars or homes. To me my play hard was only one thing: football.

And if you come from these here neck of the woods football means only one thing: Newcastle United.

The club was in my blood since I was a bairn myself. I was born in 1955 and my Dad had only one name in mind, whether I be boy or girl: Jackie. I was eight years old when my Dad, Frank, took me to my first match. It was Manchester City if I remember right. I can still remember being passed from the back of the Popular Side to the front and watching the game with every other bairn who'd just surfed the Geordie Dad Wave.

I never forgot how much going to those games meant to me, and how it bonded me to my Father in a way that nothing else in our lives ever did.

I saw a few good times in the years that followed, and as a Geordie I saw a whole load of rubbish too. But win lose or draw I loved it. I loved being one of those fifty-odd thousand and I loved learning my football lessons amidst such wonderful, witty folk.

I hadn't thought about those things in years… and then one in 1982 day I walked out of our house and saw the bairn, our Terry, kicking a casey off old Hitler's wall and running off shouting 'Brooking!' at the top of his voice.

And I knew.

And amidst the furore of Kevin Keegan's signing and standing at the back door and watching the bairn growing up in front of my eyes I decided that it was time.

Before he knew it we were on a bus into The Haymarket and off to see the lads play QPR. I can barely remember *my* first game, but I bet the bairn always remembers his.

4. *The Haymarket*

The bus pulled into Haymarket Bus Station and my Dad put out his cigarette and ushered me down the aisle to the doors in the middle of the bus. The bus was hot, it was ram-packed and everyone around us had black & white on. Well, everyone but me.

Dad took me by the hand and led me through the crowd. I don't remember every little detail but there's a poignant memories dotted all over my mind when I recall that day. When you join those dots together you see Kevin Keegan's first game, *my* first game, and QPR at home.

I remember eating a burning hot mince pie from what I presume must have been a Greggs or a Carricks somewhere near the top of Northumberland Street. Everything about that day was hot. But it wasn't just the temperature, it was the atmosphere. The place was electric. I think that for the very first time I began to understand the bond between a football club and its City, a football club and its people.

There was, well, not white noise, but *black & white* noise behind everything my father said to me and everything we did. There was a buzz around every street, every shop, and ever person on every corner. I'd been to Town shopping with my Mam countless times – most of which against my will – but I'd never seen anything like match day.

I was absorbing positively everything.

I learned what *debut* meant for a start. When I went home that night I impressed myself that I could now speak French.

Times have changed so much over the years, not least of all in terms of equality, human rights and political correctness. Excuse me if what I say next contradicts that and rolls back the years not only in terms of my memory but also in terms of my ignorance. But there was just something so different between the feminine oestrogen Newcastle – where my mother shopped and bought shoes, handbags & glad-rags and groceries – and the male testosterone Newcastle – where my father bought me mince pies, sneaked me into pubs and sat smoking and swearing with other men.

The differences were subtle. With my Mam I would hold her hand, cross at the crossings and wait for the green man. With my Dad I would be dragged along or guided with his strong arms, we'd cross anywhere we liked and as long as we didn't get killed then all was well with the world.

Another thing I was beginning to understand was that a great match and a great day were two different things. It wasn't just about the 90 minutes where – as my Mam would willingly tell you – 22 grown men would run around like kids chasing a football. It was about everything. It was about everything from the first minute you woke up to the last thing at night where you lay your head on your pillow and dreamed of the match you'd just been to, and all the emotions and memories the whole day had created.

Football by and large *is* about twenty-two grown men kicking a ball around. It's also about twenty-two men that are probably total strangers to you. But if you fall in love with the game, you realise that it's about so much more than that.

Just like the Tyne isn't just about the water, football isn't just about the match. The water in the Tyne means nothing; it's probably the same water that was in the Wear a day before and will end up in and out of the Great North Sea for as long as it exists. The Tyne is about all of the things that the river creates and all of the things it carries through.

The Tyne is about the Sunday market that sits on its banks, the shipyards it was home to, the bridges that cross it, and the people and buildings that stand beside it. In the same way the football isn't just about the match; it's about the day. It's about the people you meet because of the match; the places you go, the friends you make and the feelings and the memories that the whole day induces. It's about building a bridge of it's own, between a Father too busy or too drunk to make time for his son and a son too young to understand why.

Of course, I *was* too young back then to understand, and thoughts such as these are ones that I have formed with the blessings of both hindsight and experience. Back then, on that sunny August day I was just an excited bairn going to his first ever match.

I remember sitting in a pub drinking a coke-cola while my Dad drank a few pints and talked to some other grown ups. This, time would tell, would go on to become our match day ritual. We'd get the bus from Wallsend to Town, get off at the Haymarket, get a mince pie from the bakers and then head to The Farmers where we'd meet Dad's mates.

That particular Saturday I was perfectly behaved and sat quietly and respectfully, sipping coke, dangling my legs off the edge of the seat I was perched on and simply taking it all in. Despite my well-mannered exterior I was going crazy inside. I had butterflies, I was nervous, I was excited, I wanted to talk about everything that had happened so far and everything that was going to happen next and I could barely wait to see St James Park.

My Magpie education was continued while we sat in The Farmers. The jukebox played hard in the background, the atmosphere and the banter was everywhere and pockets of singing would break out at random. Cries of "United" and "Keegan, Keegan" and even *Come on Eileen* would vibrate around the bar.

Dad's mates seemed to revel in my company. Dad was narrating the Newcastle United story in a way that 8 years later Roger Thames would struggle to do with half of the passion. Dad's mates seemed enchanted by it all. They were almost competing with each other to teach me something more, or mention something, be it a match or a player that the others had neglected to mention.

Basically I think it came down to two things: firstly they genuinely did welcome me to their footballing family, a new member of what would later be referred to as the Toon-Army. Secondly, they simply just loved talking about Newcastle.

The Newcastle story was a pretty simple one: we were class but we were shite. Dad's friends simply reaffirmed what Dad had told me. We were great, we had been great, we were crap right now, and it would take a miracle to make us great again. But as one of Dad's mates told me, Jesus stopped working miracles a long time ago; football can do them every week.

Our miracle was the astonishing signing of Kevin Keegan.

Now, it wasn't astonishing to me. I barely understood what happened on the pitch let alone the things that happened off it. The likes of transfers and contracts were concepts I was not ready to take in just yet. But I would, in time.

One thing that did baffle me was the love for Keegan. I understood why they loved Imre Varadi; he played for Newcastle and he scored lots of goals for them. Fair dues. I understood why they still loved Malcolm Macdonald; he had given them wonderful memories and scored a load of goals for them. Even though he had left, he left on good terms with the fans and there was a bond that time and moving to another club would not break.

But I couldn't quite understand why they loved Keegan. He'd never played for them, he'd never scored for them, hell, he'd even scored against them, including two in the FA Cup Final. But without kicking a ball, without playing a single game, they loved him, they adored him and they took him to their hearts.

They didn't wait to see if he was any good. They didn't give him a few weeks to prove himself. They didn't even wait until the end of that afternoon's match with QPR. They simply loved him because he had joined them. Of course, it wasn't just any player that had joined them; it was one of the greatest players in the world.

They were stunned that he'd chosen them. They thought it was all a publicity stunt, another false dawn at the hands of a club that they had come to know as a permanent under-achiever and source of disappointment. But this was real, and they loved it.

Arthur Cox' role in all this cannot be under-estimated. As years went by I would learn to love and look up to Arthur. He was strong, determined, powerful and ambitious. He made an astonishingly bold move, and the football world was shaken when Cox & United pulled off the Keegan signing.

Of course, I learned all this in retrospect. Years of reading old programmes, buying United DVD's, reading books by the likes of John Gibson and Paul Joannou as if they were nothing short of the Holy Grail. They all added up to teach me what I was experiencing right there and then but that I was too young to comprehend.

In hindsight I understand why the love for Keegan was so unconditional and given in what basically amounts to emotional credit. And Keegan, quite probably the greatest signing this wonderful club has ever made, went on to repay all that credit and more.

He began that very afternoon.

5.   *QPR*

The bairn was like a cat on a hot tin roof all day long. I tried to teach him all about the clubs tradition but he had so many questions of his own that I'm not sure he took anything in. The only time he was quiet was when I took him to Carricks and shoved a mince pie in his mouth. His gormless, happy wandering here and there was reminiscent of the time I accidentally got him drunk when he was about 3. There was half a box of liqueurs, a low kitchen tabletop and a lapse of concentration on my behalf. But that's a whole other story for a whole other time.

"Has your Mam dropped you on you head or something?" I asked him as we left the bakers and made towards Percy Street.

"I fell off the wall last week," he told me.

I just shrugged and presumed it had been head first.

Still, I reminded myself, I was probably the same when I was his age.

Although I can barely remember my first game, I do remember the bond it forged between my Dad and me. That was something I wanted to replicate with Terry. I taught him the essentials, including a little of United's history and how we came to be where we were the day he joined the ranks of what would later be known as the Toon-Army.

Essentially we were shite. But Kevin would change all that for us.

I also taught him some family stuff too. I taught him things about his Granddad, God rest his soul. My Dad, Frank, was allegedly named Frank after United's legendary centre-half Frank Hudspeth of the 1927 League Championship side; the *last* Championship winning side I hasten to add.

My Dad, Frank, then went on to have a son of his own, me, in 1955. I was always going to be named Jackie, no matter what sex I'd been, but you can rest assured Dad was over the moon when I came out of that particular tunnel a boy.

I carried the tradition on with my son. At the time everyone was calling their son Malcolm and born in May 1975 I could quite have easily done the same with the bairn. Like I say, I almost called him Willie! I loved McFaul, I think he was a far better 'keeper than he ever got the credit for being. He was unlucky to have Pat Jennings blocking his way to more International Caps. I remember standing on the Leazes End years ago, back in the early '70's trying to hit Jennings with bits of broken concrete from the terrace as he kept goal in a match against Spurs.

At least two efforts whistled past his ear. Another one, I think, accidentally struck Tommy Cassidy.

If I could have just caught him square on the bonze I could have maybe got Willie a few more caps. Unfortunately I had the shooting capability of the likes of Bobby Shinton and the opportunity for both Willie & I passed us by. Sorry Willie.

Sorry Tommy!

So, as soon as none other than Kevin Keegan rattled a couple passed McFaul in the '74 Cup Final that name was ruled out. When Sheila told me she was pregnant late in 1974 I began deliberating on the bairns name. If he were a girl, well, he wouldn't be a girl so there was little point worrying about that. If he was a boy, and he would be, then his name would be Terry.

My favourite players of that era were Supermac (which I toyed with the idea of calling him after one drunken night at the Wallsend Social), Tony Green (whose injury cut short his stay at United and gave me an uneasy superstition that naming the bairn after him would result in the bairn dying young or something), Terry McDermott and Terry Hibbitt.

So, Malcolm, SuperMac and Tony out of the way it left just Terry as his name. And Terry it was, although I still maintain that *Supermac Scott* has a certain ring to it.

I promised him one day I'd teach him the real origins of his name, in far greater detail than I could do sitting in a boozer up The Haymarket on the opening day of the '82 / '83 season.

We left The Farmers and went to the old supporters' shop in them little cabin things up The Haymarket. I bought the bairn his first scarf. Then I looked at the tatty mess I was wearing and I swapped mine for his. He wasn't impressed. I just smiled at his frown. Poor bugger. The thing is, mine was the one my father bought me many moons ago. And I wanted to pass it on to the bairn… in the name of tradition. So I did. And I kept the swanky new one. Bless him.

He wanted to buy a match programme and he clutched it hopefully in his little hand. I took it off him and put it back on the shelf. For a moment his pet lip started curling up; like that was going to work. Then I explained that we *would* buy a programme, but it would have to come from my usual programme seller. Superstitious folk us football supporters aren't we?

We walked along Percy Street, stopping once for a pre-match Hot-dog. Recalling all this suddenly brings Keiron flooding to the forefront of my thoughts like a Terry Hibbitt through-ball. We turned off Percy Street and made through Gallowgate amidst a barrage of questions about where we'd be standing and would the bairn be able to see and would there be more Hot-dogs on sale in the ground and where *was* the programme seller and…

And then there it was: St James' Park. The bairn had his head down while he was walking, occasionally lifting it to ask me another stupid question (would Keegan be there yet, and would we see him… would *he* see us?).

Then he lifted his head and time stood still. Someone pressed the pause button on the VCR of life and suddenly everything went frame-by-frame, just like David Kelly's goal against Portsmouth all those years later, all those years ago.

In the moment that time stopped the bairn clocked St James' Park with his own eyes for the very first time. In a heartbeat I saw the place a whole lot different. Suddenly a part of me grew up.

I wasn't a kid anymore; I wasn't one of the lads anymore; I was a Dad; I was his Dad.

We walked up through the car park squeezing past Cortina's, Escorts, Capri's and Granada's. The club's sponsor, Scottish & Newcastle Breweries was to our left and the famous blue star stood modest and proud in the sunny Tyneside match-day sky. The famous blue star had been integral to the whole Keegan signing. Basically, as club sponsors, the brewery put the cash up and sorted out a bit PR work to go hand in hand with Kev's wages. There was all kinds of talk about how much the fella was getting, but of the 35,000 homing into St James' like it was Mecca on that beautiful August Saturday I can tell you now how many cared about the mans wages: none.

So what if Keegan's wage was linked to the gate?

So what if he had get out clauses and such?

So what if he wanted assurances from the board that they would add to his prestigious signature?

Hell, that's what *we* wanted!

We'd had enough of empty terracing and players getting paid next to nothing for one simple reason: they were crap. We'd had enough of a board of old men sipping whiskey in the old West Stand and talking about the good old days while keeping the purse strings tightly closed with our hopes locked in that very purse.

We wanted superstars, great players earning great wages and showing why they got such great wages by turning it on week in week out in front of a full house. We wanted a *return* to the great days. And in signing Kevin Keegan not only did we have someone to bring us that, he also seemed to know what we wanted and hold the board to ransom so that we got it.

He wasn't a man for the directors and the wages, no matter how smart he was with his contracts. He was a man for the supporter, the punter, and the fan. He was a man, a great man, who never lost the common touch and to me he earned every penny that we put in his pocket.

Dreams rarely come true, and when they do they rarely come for free. We paid Kevin well, and Kevin would go on to deliver.

He began delivering those dreams that very afternoon… with the winning goal.

I normally stood in the West Stand Paddocks with my mates, but I had a hankering to get behind the goal and find our Terry and me a little place on the Gallowgate. I knew a fella who knew a fella and as was the norm I queued at the adult turnstile with the bairn in front of me. The queues were huge, but basked in the sunshine we didn't care. Rather it be busy for a great reason than empty for a bad one. When we finally got to the front and squeezed in through the tight black turnstile I slid my money under the mesh with a little extra to boot and simply lifted the lad over as I squeezed through.

These were the days before Valley Parade, Hillsborough and Heysel, and whatever the official attendance was ever recorded there'd be another two thousand bairns who got in free to be added to that.

The Gallowgate steps were in front of us: little lines of steps that lead us from the turnstiles up high to the entrance to the back of the Gallowgate End terracing. The bairn could have bounded up them in seconds if I'd let him. But it was packed, heaving, chocker block man, and he was pressed to my side with the mass of people around us.

The steps went up side by side with another set, then they split; one went left, one went right and there was a little square of grass and bushes and trees in the middle. Then the steps re-emerged side by side again, and – with a metal barrier between them – they lead the supporters on to the top of the Gallowgate.

The Leazes End had been the place for die-hards until it was demolished in 1978. Even as we were walking up to the ground I wasn't sure where the bairn and me should go. We couldn't afford seats, besides, seats were for the posh people; we were terrace people. The Gallowgate was pretty much the cheapest at £4 for adults and £1.50 for kids. It was also set to become the new home for die-hards and I wanted the lad to be part of that.

His first day there, his first memories and his first match would do so much to cement him emotionally into the actual concrete and cement that he would be standing on for years to come. I knew that *first* spot would become *his* spot.

And it did. I never really thought about it that deeply at the time, but I wanted his first day, his first game to be a special one. I knew he'd fall in love with football and I wanted his first date with Newcastle United to be memorable.

All in all QPR was a wonderful game – a wonderful day.

If I'm honest I don't remember that much about the match itself. The day I will never forget; the game I remember for just a handful of things.

Not least of those was the bairns face when Keegan lead the Lads out of the tunnel.

6. The Gallowgate End

Dad was like a cat on a hot tin roof all day long. He tried to teach me so many things but he had so many stories that I'm not sure I took anything in. He was in a constant hurry and when my little legs couldn't keep up with him he simply dragged me along such was his excitement. And I kept getting these flashbacks of a Christmas when I was about three and I found a box of sweets on the kitchen table.

Anyway, we went to a pub and he sneaked me in. That was fantastic! He took me to the club shop and bought me a brand new black & white scarf. Then he nicked it off me and gave me his crappy old one. He tried telling me that he was doing something nice for me, and it was tradition, and his Dad had done the same for him.

I tired milking the sympathy cow and getting him to buy me a match programme. He refused. I even tried pulling the pet lip that nearly always got me what I wanted. It got me a clip 'round the earhole. Dad is so much different than Mam. She'd have taken one look at the quivering lip and I'd have had a programme in no time... and a nice swanky scarf.

Nevermind.

I chanced my arm with a request for a Hot-dog and – bracing myself for another clip – he whipped a pound note and bought me one.

I wanted a programme because I wanted a memento of the day; something to remember it by in the years that were to come; something I could pick out of an old shoe box twenty years later and feel the rush of the day coming back to me. I know they say that the memory is the keeper of all things sacred and I believe that, and so I just wanted something to spark that memory off and turn on the streetlights down memory lane.

I needn't have worried: it's not the match programme that brings the memories flooding back like a roar down a terrace, it's the smell of those Hot-dogs. I know that might sound strange but it's true. Fact is nearly always funnier than fiction. Once I smell those Hot-dogs (and I mean match day Hot-dogs, the kind that somehow smell different than any tin you can cook in your own kitchen, or throw on at a BBQ; the kind that just have a unique smell of their own) I can close my eyes and live that day – and every match day since – all over again.

That said, the game itself is a blur.

I remember walking up to the ground and feeling the anticipation and excitement grow inside me. And suddenly the bond that I'd felt towards Dad all day began to spread. Suddenly I felt connected to, bonded to, and linked to everyone else around us.

Suddenly I wasn't just my father's son; suddenly I was a Geordie too.

I was part of something. I was a part of something special. I was one in a crowd of over thirty thousand people and I was like a soldier in an army. Everywhere I looked I saw people, predominantly men, but a few women and of course plenty boys too, and we were all there for one reason: we were going to the match.

From that very day there has remained something wonderful about that one simple thing and all the various routines that go along with it: going to the match.

I felt the bond to these people, this place, this City, and this football club so forcefully. And I recall how proud I was to be part of that.

These thoughts swirled around my head and heart alike as the sun hung high above St James Park. And with every step we took the blue sky became smaller and the back of the Gallowgate End, with its bright grey concrete wall, its little gap and then the dark wood of the back of its advertising boards, and the huge back of The Scoreboard became more prominent.

It was taking up my view like it would go on to take up my life.

I remember queuing for what felt like ages and I remember this pulsating in my stomach with nerves and butterflies as my Father ushered me into the darkened little entrance to the turnstile and promptly lifted me over it as he clicked through.

Suddenly there I was, inside St James Park for the very first time. I don't know why or how I knew, but something told me that something special was about to begin, and I didn't want to forget the moment. So I closed my eyes and felt the sunlight on my eye lids and my face and I told myself to cherish that moment because I knew that what would follow would be something I'd think of for years to come.

I was right.

Dad dragged me up the steps and my feet almost lifted off the ground such was the rush of the crowd beside me. And then there we were, on the Gallowgate. We must have been quite early because it was still pretty empty on the terrace, but it was filling up fast. We were right behind the goal, on The Scoreboard, to the right hand side. We walked towards the centre and the metal aisle that ran between the two middle sections. Dad sat my on a concrete barrier about 2/3rds towards the back of the terrace and he stood behind it.

That spot became our spot for years.

I know that change is a vital part of life, and I know the stadium today is a vast improvement on what it was then. No matter who you are, no matter which club you support, the way the stadium is when you first meet with it is the way you'll always most fondly remember it. St James' of '82 is *my* St James', just as Roker Park will always have a place in the hearts of Wearsiders who first knew it as Sunderland's home; just as those from Teesside will so fondly recall Ayresome Park.

It was breathtaking being able to see the actual pitch itself through the big metal perimeter fences. I could see the goals, the nets, the white lines of the 18-yard box, the penalty spot, the advertising boards, the scoreboard, the little Hot-dog stand in the corner of The Corner (damn, why weren't we in The Corner!) everything. Behind the other goal was The Leazes, or what was left of it. To my right was the 'new' East Stand that is still there today encompassed in the redevelopment. To my left was the great old West Stand, built in the early 1900's and dated though it was it maintained certain majesty.

The ground continued to fill, the atmosphere grew, the singing was incredible and then it happened: then I saw the players.

I was miles away, just gawping around the ground looking at everything and nothing and trying to digest with my mind all the things my eyes were feeding me. Then I heard the roar of the crowd and I looked up. There was the players running out in their tracksuits on to the pitch and clapping as they did it.

And that really struck me: they were clapping *us*. They warmed up, they stretched, they kicked balls around and then they were gone.

The ground filled to bursting point, the singing was deafening, the atmosphere was electric and as 2:55pm came the players took to the field for real and the whole place just went off like a rocket. And there were the players, amidst this magnificent roar, running on to the pitch and clapping us again. With that another bond was forged; one between supporter and player, and the standard was set for all that I expected a player to be and to give in all they years that were to come.

The first of those special players was of course Kevin Keegan himself. The first special team was still a year away.

Keegan was everything a seven-year-old starry-eyed boy could need in search of a role model and a hero figure. Some kids had Disney and its fairytales, some kids had bedtime stories of dragons and castles and princesses and battles. I had only one castle: Newcastle. I had a battle: to get this wonderful club back into the First Division. And I had a knight to do battle: Special K.

And caught up in my first Newcastle fairytale Keegan would write the happy ending that all our heroes need and all our greats can surely do.

Keegan scored the winning goal.

To me, life seems to mirror and parallel football so beautifully. And just as it tends to do in life it did in football, and the best thing came from something seemingly innocuous. We had a throw in, down by the West Stand, just shy of the halfway line. I've no idea who took the throw but I'm guessing it was our right back. Before I was really paying any attention the ball had been flicked on a couple of times and suddenly one touch would put Keegan of all people clean through on goal.

The flick duly came... and Keegan was in.

Before I'd registered with head & heart alike what was about to happen the ball was in the net, Keegan was running to us, to the fans, and well, I was going to say all Hell broke loose but that would be inaccurate: all Heaven broke loose.

Dad grabbed me and we hugged and rejoiced and went daft and celebrated and shouted and roared and just let everything out. My first Newcastle United goal was one of my favourites. In the carnage that followed I found myself stepping as far out of my shell as I had ever been – especially in front of my Dad – and there I was doing some kind of jig on the barrier. All my inhibitions were gone, and to cap it off there was some bloke I've never met before or since who was holding my T-shirt and stopping me falling arse over tit back off it.

Suddenly I knew what a huge part of football was all about: goals... and how you never celebrate a goal with a stranger, just a friend you've never met.

The celebrations seemed to last for ages as Keegan struggled to get free from the adulation bestowed upon him. Watch the footage of it on your DVD's and VCR's and you'll see the way he clenches his fists and shouts out something like 'Come On!' as he finally makes his way back to the halfway line. That's not a man thinking of money. That's a man thinking of winning. That's a man thinking of football. That's a man thinking of goals. That's a man falling in love with a very special football club and it's very special football supporters. And those supporters were very much falling in love with him.

Standing there on The Gallowgate End as the match played up to the final whistle, and as we won our first match, I realised I was one of them.

And as Keegan's love affair with Newcastle United began so too did mine.

7.   82 / 83

1982 / 83 brought lots of wonderful things. Promotion, however, was not one of them. It brought Rocky III (*Eye of the Tiger* was number one when KK made his debut), The Steve Miller Bands *Abracadabra*, and a little ditty about Jack & Diane.

It also brought a lot of bad things. It brought The Human League's *Don't You Want Me* (and no, quite frankly I didn't), it brought ET The Extra Terrestrial (which somehow I ended up seeing no fewer than five times thank you very much Terry) and it brought Culture Club and *Do You Really Want To Hurt Me* (and yes, quite frankly, yes, I did).

By time Michael Jackson was telling us to beat it so too were the Police and the Stewards in The Gallowgate End. And by that time the season had brought us a fifth placed finish and ultimately another year in Division Two.

Keegan had been injured and missed a few games; the young 'uns didn't really find their feet and even though (for me the personal highlight) Terry Mac returned the season failed to live up to all that sunny August day had promised.

The Cup competitions exposed our shortcomings even further. I was at Leeds the night Imre Varadi gave us a wonderful 1-0 first leg lead; I was also at St James' the dour night when Leeds walloped us 4-1 to turn that road to Wembley into a cul-de-sac. The Leeds game, along with the FA Cup tie with Brighton ensured that our 14-year wait for a trophy would stretch to at least fifteen. Yeah, fifteen and counting.

The Brighton game I can't quite recall. I'd had a good few New Year's beers with the lads and we'd been in The Farmers and The Gateshead Arms from pretty much the minute the doors were unlocked. To put that into context the Brighton game was a replay and a 7.30 kick off. In the drunken blur that surrounds the game I remember Newcastle having a small handful of goals disallowed (sobriety and newspapers later confirmed it was in actual fact 2), a couple of blatant penalties turned down, and lost to a right spawny goal to boot.

But the season brought quite a few highs too. Of course the QPR game – captured by the cameras as well – was a major highlight. But there was also the fabulous 5-1 away win at Rotherham, also in front of the cameras, where KK scored four belters and United hit the jackpot.

It brought a great trip to Oldham, where we had two players sent off in a 2-2 draw. The fans were going mental and threatening a riot. I did the decent thing and calmed my lads down. Then one of the lads pointed out that Terry Mac was one of those red-carded and I singled handedly tried to get everyone on to the pitch. We got lost on the motorway on the way home, the exhaust fell off our car and we ended up rolling back into Wallsend after 3am… and that from a 2 to 3 hour drive.

82/83 also brought a strong end to the season, and a promise of better times to come on the footballing front. Our promotion push came too late to land us a return to Division One at KK's first attempt, but it did provide a backbone of form that gave us confidence that May for what was surely to come the May after.

And Keegan – apparently on a one-year contract – stayed.

Football is all about opinion and I can't quantify or qualify the remarks that follow but they're what I believe so to hell with it. To me Keegan stayed for one reason and one reason only: the supporters.

He didn't stay because the board wanted him to stay.

He didn't stay because of the money he was offered. He could have got that anywhere.

He stayed because he wanted to go out a winner. He *was* a winner and he wanted to end his time in football *here*, as a winner. He wanted to make *us* into winners. I've no doubt that had anyone other than Arthur Cox been driving our bus then Kevin would have got off in May 83. But he didn't. He stayed on.

And he knew, just like we did as we savoured the entertainment and the results, that glory was only a year away.

But while the footballing front was building up to glory the home front was starting to go the other way.

8. *Hero's*

1982 / 83 brought lots of wonderful things, including me getting to see ET the Extra Terrestrial 3 times (thanks Dad). Paul McCartney & Stevie Wonder taught us that ebony & ivory could indeed live side by side, Michael Jackson still was black and if you had a problem, if no one else could help, and if you could find them, maybe you could hire The A-Team.

It brought a lot of bad things too. It brought endless nights of my Mother playing Jennifer Warnes and Joe Cocker's *Up Where We Belong* and waiting for Dad to get back from the club or some away match down south. It brought Toto and their rain down in Africa, and it brought a bloody load of it to Wallsend.

Not that something like that mattered to me and the gang. We were out there in the street every opportunity we had, come rain or shine, and all we ever played with was footballs, bikes, and our imaginations. And if there was time left before sunset, football again.

Some people had Colonel John Hannibal Smith as their hero, others had BA Baracus. Some people played on the new Commodore computers (not anybody my neck of the woods I can tell you), others played on their parents nerves. Not me, not us. We played football with chalk goals and jumpers for goalposts. We played on Raleigh Strika's, Grifters and Choppers; we wore T-shirts emblazoned with Arthur Fonzerreli, we danced like the kids form Fame and we bounced 6 miles a day on a Spacehopper. No wonder I was almost 17 before my balls dropped; I spent half of my childhood hammering them back up there on 100lb of inflated rubber.

There was no Xbox or Playstation; the posh kids in our streets simply had breaks on their bikes. The rest of us stopped whatever we were peddling with the sole of our trainers.

My hero's weren't from TV shows; they were from Newcastle United.

Firstly there was Keegan. I loved Keegan. But his magic wasn't restricted to just him. Like all true greats in any walk of life the ability to touch others with their magic is paramount. Being magic is one thing; spreading magic is another. It's one thing to beam a light from within yourself; it's another to ignite the light in others.

And Special K had that; perhaps that's a pre-requisite to being special.

So, alongside Keegan, more stars began to shine. Although he seemed to struggle at first Chris Waddle soon became a real crowd favourite. Waddle was one of those players who set a sense of footballing romance in you that you never lose. From seeing Waddle play for the very first time I fell in love with the notion of wingers. It's such a shame that they are becoming a dying breed these days.

Wingers were pure theatre, pure excitement, and pure entertainment. No defensive responsibilities; just shear attacking flair. If scoring goals is Christmas then wingers are Christmas Eve. They're the foreplay to the great sex that is seeing the ball slam into the back of the net. If great strikers were great boobs then great wingers would be those great boobs with the bra still on. Chrissy Waddle was my first romance – in a heterosexual footballing kind of way mind you.

I was mesmerised watching Waddle dribble. He was probably my favourite player. Dad's favourite player was Terry McDermott. He was Keegan's sidekick and Dad had loved him since before I was even born.

Terry Mac was the Starsky to Keegan's Hutch, the Bo to Keegan's Luke, the Bodie to Keegan's Doyle. Terry Mac was to Keegan what jewellery was to BA, or what cigars and crocodile suits were to Hannibal.

But my A-Team was just one Team: Newcastle United.

After the first wonderful day at St James Park I went home and told Dave & Adam and Julie & Mandy all about it. I talked from around 7 o'clock when we got home until around 10 o'clock when I ran home to watch my first real Match of the Day. Dad was drunk – or well on the way to it – by then but still he sat me on his knee, cracked open a can of McEwans Export and proceeded to hold it in one hand, a Marlborough in the other and perch me in between.

We watched the highlights of the day's action and as I sat restlessly waiting for United to come on I fell in love with something else that magical day: football highlights.

I went to bed too excited to sleep, too exhausted to stay awake. I dozed off asking just one question: when would I be going back...?

9. *Sheila*

April 1983 also brought my 8th Anniversary with Sheila. I was born and raised a Wallsend lad. I went to two schools my entire life, one junior school and one senior. I had one job my whole life through and I had just one woman.

I knew Sheila from school and we courted for a few weeks when we were about fifteen or sixteen years old and then – after that had fizzled out – we met up again and dated properly – and permanently – from being 17 years onwards.

I was born in 1955. I met Sheila when I was 11 years old at our senior school. That was the September following England's World Cup win. As the Jules Rimet made it's way to Wembley or wherever the hell they kept it, I made my way to Wallsend's Senior School.

I was football daft and a bit of a rogue so I fitted in real well. Being a Newcastle fan – and such a fervent one at that – made it easier. I knew all the players' names, I knew the scores and the fixtures, I knew the whole kit and caboodle. I had a lot of friends from my old junior school and I was soon very popular with the rest of the kids from the other junior schools too. The main reason for that was football, or to be more accurate Newcastle United.

I'd been going to games since I was 8 years old and standing in the Popular Side, basically where the East Stand is now, with my Dad. England's World Cup glory came with United surviving a relegation battle in their first season back in the top flight after promotion in 1965. I was at a load of games in that promotion season; it was brilliant. We only lost one home game all season and although it was only Division 2 it was still fantastic to see The Lads win a trophy.

My Dad took me to a host of games the following season too as football gripped England and Newcastle alike. It was a great time to be a football supporter, and a great time to be a kid starting a new school, especially a kid who went to almost every Newcastle home game.

Most of my school days were spent playing footy, watching footy, being lucky enough to be going to footy and talking about footy. We played footy in the street every night, come rain or shine. And come rain or shine we played footy every day at school.

I was never *that* into music back then – how things have changed. I was too young to get caught up in flower power and if for one moment my parents had caught me taking drugs then this story would have been about the Wallsend boy who was murdered by his Father just as Joe Harvey's boys were coming back from Hungary with the Fairs Cup.

I remember my Dad catching me smoking a cigarette when I was sixteen back in 1971. He made me smoke the entire packet one after the other right there and then in front of him. I often wonder what would have happened if he'd caught me shagging.

'*Right, go get all the girls in your class and…*' Okay, I'll stop there.

Football was different back in them days, and for me, in a million ways it was better. Not that we knew it at the time mind you. Hindsight is a wonderful thing isn't it?

Anyway, I made it through secondary school to take my apprenticeship at the shipyard in 1971. During those formative school years I'd seen United win the Fairs Cup, I'd seen the open top bus that greeted their return, I met Joe Harvey one day by pure accident when I bunked off school to go get me & Dad tickets for the Glasgow Rangers semi final and I met Sheila.

Sheila and I went to school together. She was brainy; I wasn't so much. She was in the top classes; I wasn't. But we were in the same year and in the same Tutor group. Basically we met first thing every morning for assembly and registration and every lunchtime in the bikesheds and the tuck-shops and we clicked. When it became fashionable to smoke, Sheila's gang smoked. When it became fashionable to wear makeup, Sheila's gang wore makeup. And when it became fashionable to get a boyfriend Sheila's gang went and got boyfriends... and Sheila went and asked me out. And I said... "Aye go on then". Not exactly Ross & Rachel is it?

Truth was, I wasn't arsed. I had football, I had football and of course I had football. I had taken a keen interest in smoking and was applying my spare time to saving up for / scheming for / blagging and / or pinching cigarettes. I used to sneak off around the bikesheds at school – as cliché as that may sound – for a quick smoke. I used to have a nice little match day routine too; one that let me sneak a smoke away from my fathers disciplined eyes. By that time the East Stand was built and the Popular Side, sadly, was gone.

It was the first time St James Park had really changed since I started going and it was sad. I know it was the future and development and modern and all that bullshit but it was sad. They bulldozed the place where my Dad and I first stood watching Newcastle United and they replaced it with this empty, soulless concrete stand with crappy cheap plastic seats.

People seeing St James in the last 5 years will barely recognise it from that which it once was. I know the stadium is far better now, but sometimes what you gain in facilities you lose in atmosphere; what you gain in comfort you lose in tradition.

When the East Stand replaced The Popular Side Dad and I went and stood on The Leazes End. It was magical. We'd get in, he'd stay in the back third, I'd go to the front, and when I fought my way to the front few steps I'd light up a tab with all the others kids right behind the goal and hanging over the advertising board.

By that time I knew I wasn't going to be a footballer; I was enthusiastic about it, but I was basically just crap. And I've never been one to kid myself, not at anything in my life, ever. Maybe that's where it started.

So life for me was football and cigarettes. And when Sheila asked me to be her boyfriend life became about football, Sheila and cigarettes. And football.

We went out for a few weeks. We held hands, we kissed, we even went to the pictures a couple of times. I'd walk a little out of my way every morning and walk her to school and I'd carry her books home for her every night. Everyone else was doing it so why shouldn't we.

We never got carried away, we never made it to anything physical, and the closest we ever came was one time at Tynemouth Pool where she wore a bikini and I couldn't leave the pool for over an hour. Hell, if I'd done the backstroke you'd have thought I was a sailing ship. Her form, her curvy womanly hourglass form left me dumbstruck.

Suddenly Sheila wasn't a girl, she was a woman; suddenly I was no longer just a boy, I felt like a man. The seed of all that is the mystery and the muscle of love was sown and although it would take a few years to grow into a bud, it was planted that day for sure.

We were just kids, of course, and like most relationships formed in the playground and the bikesheds we 'broke up' after a few weeks. Looking back you wouldn't really call it a relationship, even if I did indeed call her a girlfriend. But something happened during that short spell that Sheila and I went out.

All of her mates were getting boyfriends and Sheila wanted one too. So she asked me out. And we went out. And despite some poignant little moments that I will always treasure, like our first kiss and that day at the pool, we split up a few school weeks later when all of her mates did.

That's all Sheila and I ever were.

I'm not sure why she picked me; maybe I was just walking through the classroom door at the right time, or chasing some kid around the playground at the wrong time when she happened to gaze my way.

But she did choose me, and it was only when we broke up that I really started to feel something. There was no big yellow taxi's, even if they had just paved paradise and put up the new East Stand, but Joni Mitchell would have known how I felt.

Sheila went back to her crowd; I went back to my mates, from school and The Leazes End. But after that little flirtation with romance, after jump-starting a heart that I was sure would only beat for those in black & white, suddenly there was something else in there too.

Though we had nothing in common beforehand, curiously, after that little venture as kids into the adult world of relationships, there was always something between us.

That something lingered throughout our remaining school days. I remember our last day, watching Sheila walk away across the school field to go home while I was set to turn and walk the other and an awaiting apprenticeship at the Shipyard. I couldn't help feeling that a chance was passing me by. If romance was football then it seemed like an open goal was right in front of me. But for whatever reasons the shy hide behind I just couldn't get the final touch to put he ball in the net.

That was in May 1971. Wow I wished I were Pop Robson that day. (Actually he top scored that year with a meagre 9 so perhaps it would have wound up just the same). A year later Malcolm Macdonald slammed in 23… and when the next opportunity presented itself to me I banged the ball home with just the same aplomb as Supermac.

I lost my heart twice that season, 1971 / 72. The first was with a cockney with as much swagger as ever graced the St James Park turf; the second was with a familiar faced girl who walked into the local one Friday night.

I'd been to work all day, and in true tradition I was off to the local afterwards with all the lads – my new shipyard family – for a couple of after work wind downs and weekend wind-ups. It was a fine day, one that had held that special Tyneside Friday vibe all day long. Friday to Geordies is like Christmas Eve to kids.

When you've grafted all day, when you've earned every penny you're about to waste, probably on beers, birds, cigarettes and football, there's a special vibe that is the privilege of the working class. By clocking off time you're ready to blow off all that steam you've been working up all week.

And love them though you do, everyone of them – beer, birds, cigarettes and football – is as bad for you as the last, especially if you come from these here neck of the woods. If I didn't have enough bad addictions in loving a pint, a tab and a football team that just made you pull your hair out, suddenly I had something else to pine over: Sheila.

She walked into the pub looking a million dollars to coin a phrase. The jukebox was playing, and that tingle I used to get walking through the Leazes turnstile, that tingle I used to get watching Macdonald pull the trigger, that tingle came flooding through me in ever so much a familiar, ever so different a way.

Roberta Flack's *The First Time Ever I Saw Your Face* had just replaced *A Horse With No Name* at number one in the hit parade and in so many ways the song seemed to sum up just what Sheila meant to me.

And just like Supermac took every chance that came his way, so did I. Sheila and I said our surprised *hellos*, I bought her a drink, and the shipyard family took the piss. I sat at a table and talked to her, and the shipyard family took the piss. Finally, an hour later, as she was finishing her drink and getting ready for the door, I asked her out. And she said, "Aye go on then…". Tom Hanks and Meg Ryan had nothing on us.

When Sheila left the shipyard family applauded to a man like I was John MacNamee swinging on a crossbar.

This time there *was* chemistry, magic, passion, romance, and plenty in common. And this time it did get physical. I lost my virginity to Sheila and she in turn misplaced hers with me.

Also a number one that year was Chuck Berry's *My Ding A Ling* somewhat ironically. It could have been worse: a band called Black & White had a hit with *Three Dog Night*…!

It wasn't Romeo & Juliet; it wasn't Robin Hood & Maid Marion either but for a year and a half we went out and for a year and a half we were pretty happy. Then in November '74 things changed. Sheila told me she was pregnant. And my world collapsed.

And if you like irony, then try this. Sheila must have conceived in August sometime – and what was number one in August '74…? *You're Having My Baby*, Paul Anka & Odia Coates. It was followed by *I Shot The Sheriff, I Can't Get Enough Of Your Love Babe,* and *Rock Me Gently.* And while everyone else entered Christmas '74 *Kung Fu Fighting* I entered it despondent. The last two number ones of '74: *Cats In The Cradle* and *Angie Baby.*

That was my last Christmas at home. I moved out when I was just 19 year old and joined the other members of the shipyard family having babies. The '74 Cup run had a major effect on the Tyneside birth rate.

The things is, the others were either adding to their family, or just simply older than us.

As for Sheila and me, well we were young – too young – and we knew we weren't ready for it. For a week we thought it over, and we wondered and we pondered and I don't think we even seen each other more than once. Nobody said 'abortion' but we both knew I was thinking about it. It was a mistake, and I wanted to go back and undo it. But it was too late for such flights of fancy.

Yeah, I'd scored all right; a great big bloody own goal.

And so I thought about those I respected as I searched for what to do. I thought about the lads, especially the older lads, the men and the mentors I had found in the shipyard family. I thought about my own family. Hell I even thought about Joe Harvey!

In some ways adversity shines a light on your fortunes that good fortune never does. In such distressing circumstances I really came to appreciate the integrity of the good folk in my life. And I knew, in the light of the overwhelming respect that I felt for those people, what I had to do.

So I asked Sheila to marry me. And she said, "Aye go on then…" And as I took the biggest step forward with my life, I took the biggest step backwards with my heart.

Sheila and I weren't that strong, we weren't that close. What we did have would go on to be crushed by the weight of the mistake we had made. But we had enough to build on, and we promised we *would* build upon it. We promised we'd work hard together, put each other first, and make our marriage work. There'd be sacrifice, no doubt. She'd have to give up some things and so would I. I'd have to give up a lot of football, a lot of Newcastle United, and a lot of matches.

And I was prepared to do it.

The things we do for family.

And so Sheila and I were married in 1975, a few months before the bairn, our Terry, was born. We made our promises and we made our vows, for better for worse, for richer for poor. But where in those words do we ever vow to be happy…

10. *Screaming Varadi*

Dad took me to exactly eight games that season, 82 / 83. And looking back, I think I learned the first of countless lessons about life that football had to teach me. Part of my love affair with football is that it compliments, reflects and matches life itself so very fittingly. Part of it is that I just love it when Newcastle score.

The first thing I learned was that football, just like life, has an uncanny knack of kicking you square in the knackers just when you're walking tall.

Hand in hand with that is the fact that things rarely turn out the way you expect them to. And kicks in the knackers or not, there's a beauty to that which makes both football and life so enchanting and intriguing.

For all the twists and all the turns, for every kick in the knackers and every blessing that falls upon you, so often it's the unpredictability, the spontaneity, and the surprise that makes life so exciting.

Just like life itself, as the game nears the final whistle the outcome becomes clearer. And just as you would with your own team, you've got to do everything you can to keep the chance of winning alive for just as long as you can.

Those are all of course lessons that have revealed themselves over the many years, many seasons that I've followed Newcastle

United. The first lesson, well that was a bit of a shock to the system.

Signing Keegan was a fairytale. Not that I fully appreciated it myself at the time, but in hindsight I can see why my Dad was so excited that wonderful August of 1982. We still have The Chronicle from the day that he signed, the one with Keegan freezing his bollocks off on the tarmac of Newcastle Airport.

My first page in this fairytale was of course the day my Dad took me to *my* first match, *Keegan's* first match, and I realised I was part of something special. Not only was I a Geordie, I was a Geordie who went to the match.

Going to bed that night wondering how many more times, if any, I would be back in St James' Park that season I never thought for a minute that United would fail to win promotion. Surely that's not how the fairytale would go. Fairytales, of course, have happy endings. Therefore we *would* win promotion. We had to. If we didn't then what was the point of all the hullabaloo in the first place?

As April 1983 came and went, and as Michael Jackson tried to convince us that Billie Jean wasn't his lover, reality began to hit home and I began to at least contemplate that Newcastle wouldn't win promotion.

A week later Cox's side lost to lowly Cambridge and contemplation turned to concern turned to fear. By time Irene Cara was flashdancing (and say what you like about Flashdance; fair play that girl can dance, but that weld is never going to hold) my only feeling was despair.

Newcastle finished 5th, and they didn't win promotion.

That's when I learned another valuable lesson: to truly enjoy the highs you need to suffer the lows. What good would a rollercoaster be if it went straight to the top and stayed there? What fun would the League Title be if one Team bolted straight to the front and won at a canter? To make something interesting, entertaining, it needs highs and lows. A rollercoaster needs ups and downs. A truly great race needs to see the lead changing hands a dozen times. In a way it's all about the rise and fall. It's rags to riches. It's about bouncing back. It's about losing but then coming back to win. It's about being down but fighting your way back up. The further those extremes the better.

Perhaps it's an appreciation thing. Perhaps it's just about good story telling, be it by pen, keyboard, or just simply by the hand of fate itself.

Newcastle missing promotion in 1983 was the painful side of that lesson. What I learned the year later was sweeter side.

The following year, 1983 / 84 Newcastle *were* promoted.

I learned that promotion in May of '84 would not have tasted anywhere near as sweet if I hadn't tasted the bitter pang of my dreams fading away a year before.

That was just the point: May '83 wasn't the ending, May '84 was. And then it *was* happy.

I love the Rocky films. But it's easy to forget that Rocky loses in Rocky I. He gets beat. Apollo wins on points. But that just serves to make Rocky II so much sweeter. To me, Keegan was very much the same. We lost in '83, and you might say that was on points too, but the sequel was the next season, 1984, when we won.

And just like Rocky sent Apollo to the canvas to stay, Keegan sent United back to the First Division.

I turned nine in the May of '84 and promotion was the best present I could ask for. I was 8 years old when the season kicked off in August '83 and it didn't start well. For reasons beyond comprehension to my tender mind (and that of most United followers) Arthur Cox kicked Imre Varadi off the bus just as it was set to finally make its journey back to where it belonged, and to where Dad had promised it was going a year earlier when he took me to see Keegan's first game.

Varadi was a crowd favourite, a goal-getter, passionate about the shirt and about the people who came to see him in it. I was shocked when he was sold. But I learned another valuable lesson at that point: if you trust someone, then trust them. It's easy to trust them when the going is good, but stand your ground and trust them when the rain starts to fall too.

I remember my Dad saying to me, "Arthur moves in mysterious ways." He chuckled when he said it. I didn't understand at the time. But it has lived with me since.

Dad was right. Cox was right. He replaced Varadi with Peter Beardsley and the first lines of another fairytale began. Saying this off the cuff right now I'm not sure if I have ever seen a better player play for Newcastle United than Peter Beardsley. Maybe after 8 pints and a pack of cigarettes in The Anson I'd disagree. But here and now, I'd be hard pushed to name a better one than Beardsley, and that includes Alan Shearer and Keegan himself.

So by time Billy Joel told us to tell her about it the only thing that Tyneside was talking about was Keegan, Waddle and Beardsley.

It was a new United, an improved United, and they were a joy to watch. I missed the first couple of games. Dad went with his mates again and I had to settle for Doug Wetherall or whoever it was announcing the scores and reports at 4:50 on BBC North East.

But Newcastle didn't start well, and Dad got all superstitious with me. It was Saturday October 1st and Newcastle were playing at home to Portsmouth. Dad had seen us lose at home to Shrewsbury, and he'd seen us fail to win at Middlesborough, Grimsby and then Barnsley. He'd been to the home win over Oldham but missed Palace's defeat on Tyneside just after.

He tried going to a different programme seller, he'd tried buying from a different hot-dog van. He even swapped the bloody scarves back and once again wore his grotty old one on his shoulders.

But nothing worked for him.

So he tried one more roll of the dice: he took me.

And we never looked back.

Newcastle exploded. The football was pure theatre, pure entertainment, and pure excitement. I think too often in the modern game we forget that although football is a competition it's also an entertainment industry. The football I was weaned on from that day was pure thrill. To me, it was the way football should be played. United took off. As father and son our relationship took off too.

It started with me kicking my ball off Hitler's wall and screaming 'Varadi, GOAL!' every time the ball flew beneath the chalk line crossbar. Adam, Dave and me took turns in going in goal, unless Mandy or Julie were out and about and we got the chance to coax one of them to do the honours.

So there I was, cracking left footers passed someone or other off Hitler's wall in our little corner of Wallsend. The Shipyards stood tall and expectant; the Tyne ran long and proud, and there, in the street, with my jacket in his hands and two scarves over his shoulder, was my Dad.

"You coming or what?" he asked me with begrudged warmth.

"Where to?" I asked him naively, nervously, hopefully.

"For trombone lessons you plonker!" he yelled at me.

I'll never forget the feeling inside as I ran towards him. I don't think I'd ever felt more optimism in my entire life either before or after. I was going to my favourite place in the world with my favourite person in the world to do my favourite thing in the world. And no matter what your favourite thing is well that takes some beating.

The next thing I can recall with any real clarity was the old West Stand, where the Milburn Stand now proudly resides. The old stand epitomised what going to the match was all about to me. I could close my eyes and breathe in the air and the atmosphere alike and I could tell you exactly where I was. The smell of the brewery heavy laden in the air, the sound of cars, horns, and people *shouting 'Programmes, get your match programmes'* over the buzz of banter that centred around the match. The rustle of thousands of feet shuffling their way towards Gallowgate. And then you'd lift your head and there it was: the metal side of the West Stand, with it's curved roof taking precedence over everything else on the Tyneside's skyline.

The West Stand, wooden and metal, with its grandstand arch in the centre and its giant NEWCASTLE UNITED F.C. painted high and boastful on the back. The sight of that stand triggered something inside of me, something magical, something that brought all of the excitement of being at the match rushing through me. More than that, it made me realise I was there, and that which I had been waiting for for so long was finally now mine. I liken it to Geordies who leave the area, if only for a day, and who travel back on the train. Something happens as your pull into Newcastle, not the station as such, but when your train slows down and you catch your first sight of the Tyne Bridge, for example. It sets a warm homely rush off inside of you. It makes you feel like you're home again. And you feel proud, and strong and tall and safe.

The sight of the West Stand did just that to me. To me that stand was home, even though I never actually sat in it.

I had waited for that particular day for a long time. It was my first game at St James In ages, and the first time I had been that season. The close season was bad enough, but when football resumed and my Dad didn't take me back to the match I was gutted. I didn't moan, I didn't complain, and I never pestered him about it. I never even had the nerve to ask him to take me, as much as I wanted to go back.

But that day – totally out of the blue – Dad took me back to see Newcastle play Portsmouth. And we won 4-2. When the next home game came around it was a midweek Milk Cup tie with lowly Oxford. It was a school night and although I know Dad toyed with the idea of upsetting my Mam and her golden rules the bottom line was that I was tucked up in bed long before United had been held to a 1-1 draw.

Three days later and I was whisked off to St James Park to see my second game in 7 days: the visit of Charlton Athletic. It pissed down all day and Dad's superstitions seemed to be ill founded when United found themselves 1-0 down with little time remaining. Then Keegan banged in 2 goals and we won 2-1!

Three weeks later Newcastle, by now out of the Milk Cup at the hands of the aforementioned lowly Oxford, were at home to Manchester City.

Dad, as superstitious as ever, dragged me along. It was a 5-0 win, a Peter Beardsley hat-trick, and one of the best Newcastle performances for years and years. As little Pedro slammed in his third, and as Chris Waddle slammed in United's fifth that was me pretty much guaranteed to be at every home game for the rest of the season.

Just like the wonderful football (including a thrilling 3-2 win over Malcolm Macdonald's Fulham) my relationship with my Dad blossomed too. We became more than father & son; we became friends. He was 28 years old; I was eight. But football united us and gave us something that helped our relationship develop away from just being parental. He'd ask me about my favourite players and I'd ask him about his. He'd give me history lessons on what the club had achieved in the past. He'd show me old programmes and talk about great games he'd been to. We'd guess the score of the next game and put a little silly bet on it, just between us. And I loved every minute of it. I was supporting my Dad's favourite team and they were now my favourite team too.

I went to 17 league games that season. I missed the Blackburn game on Boxing Day, when we drew 1-1. I had a family thing that my Mam insisted I go to with her, as opposed to going to the match with Dad. Failure to win meant Dad pulling me out of any New Years family do and carting me merrily to Gallowgate for the Barnsley game and true to form, United won 1-0. It was like a family version of club versus country.

I saw only two defeats: Grimsby & Sheff Weds both by 1-0. Kevin Keegan's Newcastle losing 1-0 at home to Grimsby on the way to promotion. Funny how things come around.

As the season drew to a climatic conclusion only three home games remained: Carlisle, Derby, and Brighton. I had endured another harsh lesson when my hopes had been crushed by Liverpool in the FA Cup. That was pure romance and I got caught up in it. I over estimated United and underestimated Liverpool. We were crushed 4-0 and my hopes and dreams took a right wallop. That Anfield hiding did damage to me; it made me fearful of getting my hopes up, fearful of disappointments. I wrestled with that as the season drew to its climax.

It's important not to let the past stop you from believing in the future. Love like you've never been hurt, so they say. Part of me didn't want to get carried away again in case United missed promotion and broke my heart again. Fortunately it was a battle that I won. Because if I had let that fear stand in the way I would have missed out on being a part of, and fully emotionally invested in, what was to become one of the finest parties Tyneside has ever seen.

11. *Farewell*

My life changed dramatically when I moved out of home and moved in with Sheila. She was heavily pregnant by that time, the turn of the year 74 / 75, and our marriage was imminent. I didn't officially move in with her until we were wed, such were the wishes of our respective families.

I said farewell to my home with my parents, where my Mam still took mighty good care of me, and I said hello to life with a pregnant girlfriend, where I did almost everything for her. I worked long hours, hard hours, and I earned the bread that we put on our table. To me, at least, it was what a man should do. I'd made my bed and I was prepared to lie in it. But I'm man enough to admit that it sure as hell was uncomfortable.

I'm not a man who cried easy and I'm not trying to be big or hard or clever in saying that. That isn't my style, end of story. But I'll tell you that I cried that year, and not just once either.

I lay in our bed in our tiny terraced house while Sheila, the size of a house end we could never afford, lay beside me carrying our child. And I cried. Why? Well for one I wasn't ready to be a father, and it scared me. And for two I didn't love her, and that scared me more.

All that was familiar to me was slipping away. I missed *my* bed, *my* home, *my* window and *my* view from it. I missed my Mam and her cooking. I missed having my ironing done and I missed having just a little bit of time to come home, get a bath, grab the Chronicle and read about United.

I'd screwed up and I felt like the walls were closing in on me. It was like a nightmare and all I wanted to do was wake up... wake up and be home.

But *I'd* screwed up and *I* had to fix it or live with it. I was up the junction. I had to take my medicine, and bitter as it tasted I guess in the end it did me good. Basically, I grew up. Hell I was just a bairn when I was expecting a bairn of my own. But I had Sheila to think of, and that's what I did. I rolled my sleeves up and I made the best of it for her, and for the bundle of *joy* she was carrying around.

I worked hard all day and I worked hard all night. I had neither time nor money left to spend with my mates down the pub. I barely had time left for the football. But Newcastle and St James Park was something I just wasn't prepared to say farewell to and I think Sheila understood that. She didn't agree with it, but she knew I needed something to hold on to, something familiar, somewhere to go and blow off some steam.

And I thank her for that.

But life at St James was about to become just as disconcerting.

When I needed stability in my life, when I needed something familiar to hold on to, something else new and unsettling came along: United parted company with Joe Harvey.

Harvey had been in charge since 1962 / 63. He'd been the only manager I'd ever known. He was my footballing father figure so to speak. He'd given me the Fairs Cup in '69 and all the memories that still go hand in hand with it. He'd given me an FA Cup Final (though I watched it on the tele' with my friends and family) and he'd given me someone to look up to and respect.

I loved Harvey. He had history and tradition; he had links with the club; he had the club in his blood and he'd been the captain in the legendary cup winning teams of 1951 and 52. I respected him, I felt safe with the club in his hands, and to me, just a kid, I didn't want him to go, especially at a time when I was going through so much change at home.

As my son, Terry, was born and I became a father for the first time at just 19 years old the crowd began chanting 'Harvey out'. And when the season ended Harvey was gone. It was a dark time.

Now let me just say one thing now for the record: I love this football club. I love the club, the ground, the stadium, the stands, the players and the fans. I love all the wonderful things this club has been and I love all the wonderful things I still believe it can, if maybe never will, go on to be. I love all the legends that have helped make this club as special as it is. And I ain't just talking players nor managers there neither. Not all the hero's at this club are on the wage bill. No one makes a club more special than its supporters. And I class myself proud to be one of those supporters. The size of this clubs support is staggering. If the club is indeed a giant – awake or asleep – then the supporters are the giant's heart. And no matter how many times we *get* beaten we *keep* beating.

To this day, while this club has flirted with success, gave us moments and matches that will reside in the hall of fame that is our memory and our reminiscences, I maintain that the route of the clubs mistakes began with the sorrowful departure of Joe Harvey, or Sir Joe as I like to call him.

Appointing a new manager is always a bit of a gamble. Those that have followed United for only a few years will understand that; those that have followed the club for decades will know it only too well.

United's appointment as a replacement for Joe Harvey was a brave one; I'll give them that. It had future echoes of Arthur Cox appointment five years later. It was the same sentiment: take a lower league manager who had enjoyed relative success, but who was a young man with a hunger to fill. It was the recruitment of a man who would see Newcastle United as a step up. It had a lot of common sense for a lot of reasons. But the appointment of Gordon Lee was not the one to fill the hunger of the Geordie faithful.

Talk was ripe of Clough or McMenemy. I was intrigued and seduced by talk of big names and wonder as to what they may do with my club. In the end, like most of the then still to be titled Toon-Army I was a little underwhelmed by the appointment of a man who had just guided Blackburn Rovers to the Third Division title.

Good God, taking Managers from Blackburn has been a kiss of death to us.

The hardest thing for me to accept was that Lee was a man with absolutely no connection to our club. Gordon Lee was an outsider. And from the off, although results and even the quality of the football tried to coax me otherwise, I never warmed to the stranger in Sir Joe's seat.

I was always trying to convince myself I liked Gordon Lee, while truth was, my heart was always whispering that I didn't like him one bit. To me at least, it just never felt right.

The echoes from my heart were similar to the ones that flowed at home, my other home, with my wife and our newborn baby. Though I tried to convince myself otherwise, I knew I didn't love her. The heart can be fooled, but never does it lie.

Terry, this gurgling, crying, shitting machine wrapped in a black & white baby-grow was the impressive results of what was fundamentally a mistake. Beating high-flying QPR 3-1 at Loftus

Road, hammering little Southport and not so little Coventry City, and ultimately making the League Cup Final after beating Spurs was pretty much just the same.

So many things were good, but something just felt wrong. There were rumblings of discontent at all levels of the club. Directors seemed split, players told us they were split by their body language alone, and supporters, well the Gordon Lee reign certainly split us. There was something off with Lee & SuperMac and bottom line was that SuperMac was the bollocks.

The man wasn't just a goal machine, he was a swaggering, stylish and charismatic goal machine who not only appeared to love what he did but who he did it for. He seemed to understand just what it meant to play for this club. Some people are crushed by that famous number 9 shirt; some people raise it up and make it great. Macdonald wore it like a black & white flag. He took it and waved it loud and proud and I loved him for that.

He connected with the Geordies and he understood in simple terms what we wanted: someone to bang in a boatload of goals. And he did that. But not just that, he did it with style.

In the back of my heart I always felt that whatever rift was between them it would eventually lead to SuperMac's departure and I almost hated Gordon Lee in advance for that. I resented him for what I feared he would do. To younger supporters it's akin to the Gullit / Shearer thing. Only in this case Gullit won and Shearer was forced to leave. And every goal, every memory, every record that he broke would never have happened if Gullit had won. Back in 1976 Gordon Lee did win, and SuperMac was destined to leave.

I was at the Bolton Wanderers game in the FA Cup in around February or March '76 when Lee had just been named Bells Manager of the Month. He took his huge bottle of Whiskey and had it reduced to miniatures to hand to the crowd as a good will gesture. I took one. And I held it in my hand for ages. I wanted it. I wanted to want it. But I felt like I was selling my soul if I even sipped it. I felt like George Bailey shaking hands with old man Potter that famous Bedford Falls Christmas Eve. So I tossed it onto the concrete in front of me – and probably half down the leg of the kid in front – and I snubbed it.

The daft thing is that I felt sorry for the man that I'd done that. I wanted to like Gordon Lee but I couldn't. And in a way it hid some pretty good football, and some pretty impressive results. There was method to what Lee was doing. We were going well in both Cup competitions, including that – our first – appearance in the League Cup Final, losing of course to Manchester City on the day.

The FA Cup took us all the way to the 6th round when Derby County knocked out a depleted Newcastle 4-2 at the old Baseball Ground. Had it not been for injuries and a cold epidemic we could so easily have gone to Wembley in both of the 75 / 76 Cup Competitions. But as the season went into its final stages, and as the walking, talking, shouting and shitting machine that was our Terry neared his first birthday, the dream ebbed away.

United finished 15th and won nothing. In those final weeks of the season a lack of money and time and the demands of my young family made it increasingly hard for me to keep making the games. To my devastation, just as my own place at St James Park came under question, SuperMac lost his. I saw it coming and I hated it. When it happened I went numb. For that, and that alone, my relationship with Gordon Lee was done. Selling Macdonald was a cardinal sin.

So after saying farewell to my home and my parents and moving in with Sheila, and after saying farewell to Sir Joe, I was saying farewell to SuperMac.

About a week before the new season started SuperMac was sold to Arsenal. And sitting, watching the news come in that August from the relative discomfort of our second hand sofa with the bairn on my knee I had never felt so alone and so unhappy.

I wasn't ready to be a father. Hell, I was still a kid myself. I missed going out at a weekend, I missed having a pint with the lads, I missed having the freedom to go to the match and not have to worry about what time I was coming home because the bairn, my son, needed a bath or a sitter or just that my wife needed company. Jesus I had a wife! And I wasn't ready for that. My life felt as good as over at the tender age of 21-years old.

When every other twenty-one year old was getting birthday cards and keys that were meant to symbolise their freedom my key seemed like it was locking me behind a cell door that I wouldn't get out of for at least 18 years. I'd blown it. It was over. My life was finished. All I had left was Sheila, who try as I might I knew I didn't love, the bairn, who offered me little more than something to clean up after and feed and then clean up after again, and football. Without Macdonald the football just didn't seem the same anymore.

But somewhere, from out of the blue, the United of 1976 / 77 clicked.

Sitting in 3rd place as we entered a cold and bitter December of 1976 I began learning a sweet reminder of how football and life go hand in hand. Just when I expected the worst, things suddenly looked better. But the flip side to that lesson is just when you think things are going to be all right you get that good old kick in the knackers after all.

To me it happened big time. Just as the decorations were coming down so were United.

Gordon Lee had defied the critics and the odds and even his own popularity by leading United to the brink of a genuine title race. And all of this without Macdonald. My attachments to the club are emotional, mental, physical and spiritual and I make no apologies for that. My life runs in parallel with the clubs. When they're up, I feel up; when they're down I feel down. When things go well for Newcastle United things also seem to go well for me. Conversely, when things go wrong for Newcastle things seem to fall apart in my life too.

So with United edging into joint second in early winter and with the FA Cup again looking like it would offer us a decent cup run, things looked brighter. That good mood carried to my other home and hence I started thinking that maybe life weren't so bad after all.

After all, I was a father. And I'm not sure what can be written with mere words that would do justice to such a unique bond. The link between father & son is one that cannot be broken, by time nor by death, by stubbornness nor by fall out's. I learned that one the hard way.

Time had weaned me away from my home with my parents and by early 1977 I was no longer referring to their place as 'home'. Suddenly, and without realising it, the place where I grew up was 'My folks'; the small 2 bed terraced with Sheila and Terry was home.

As Mickey Burns and Alan Gowling slammed goal after goal I realised that even without SuperMac life still went on. It wasn't the same, but it was a goal nonetheless. Just like coming home to a burned hot-pot and a flustered wife wasn't the same, but after all, it was home. I missed my Mam & Dad, and I missed all the comforts that living there gave me. But I had a new family now, and in their own way they gave me comfort too.

Yeah, I had to wash dishes, iron shirts, change nappies and all that, but there was nothing, nothing in this world, that could make me feel the way the bairn did when he grabbed my finger and said 'Daddy'. And more than my Mam's cooking or the quick read of the Evening Chronicle before Dad could nab it, I found it was the bairn and the moments he gave me that got me through the day.

Once I got used to that way of thinking, my home life, just like United's results, took a surprising up turn. I worked hard hours, I worked long hours, but I loved the lads I worked with and when I wasn't with my real family I was with my shipyard family. Sheila and I started to recover from the impact that having a kid had upon our social lives. For the first time in nigh on two years we began dating. We had something new in common, something that we didn't have when we met and when we first went out; we had the bairn. In its own way that – finally – began to draw us closer together. Hell, even the sex life got better… though we did take a lot more precautions this time around.

To some having a kid is their dream, their fairytale, their hearts desire. And I'm not one to knock that. There's something wonderful about having a kid, but Newcastle will win the Champions League before I find the words to describe it. I love being a Dad. But as wonderful as it is, those with kids will sharp advise you, it's hard work too.

It isn't all cuddles, first steps, first words and birthday parties. It's nappies, tantrums, sleepless nights and flying Heinz baby-food. It's learning that certain pieces of Lego will make their way through a toddler's digestive tract in less than 12 hours. It's learning to always look in the oven before you use it, and that any toy that goes missing can almost certainly re-appear in said oven. But as any of those with kids will tell you, it's worth it.

Learning along the way, I got used to it. I mean hell, I was far from a great father. Have you ever seen a drunken baby? Well thanks to a box of rum liqueurs, a low kitchen tabletop and a lapse of concentration on my behalf I can honestly say I have. At first it was fun watching the poor little bugger bounce off the walls, but before I knew it he had a bucket on his head and he was heading straight for the TV. Man that was a scare; it was our first colour set. These were back in the days when the Chronicle was about the size of a billboard, milk came in proper bottles with silver foil on, and die-hards stood on the Leazes End.

That was my life. And as strange as I found it at first, there was a spell where everything worked out. It was strange, it was unusual, and it was new but I got used to it and it for a while I bordered on being happy. Sheila and I worked at our relationship and we made it work. Relationships are not always rainbows and butterflies; it's compromise that moves us along, so the song goes.

So we did compromise. I gave up a lot of social time in the social club and spent less time with my shipyard family in preference of my real family. And in turn, Sheila understood just how much my football meant to me and although she never encouraged my love affair with Newcastle United she no longer complained when I donned my scarf – the one my father once owned – and made my way to St James Park to see my black & white mistress. Then, as the bairn passed 18 months, as 1977 saw United challenging in the top 5 of the First Division and as Manfred Mann was blinded by the light, so too was Gordon Lee.

And along came the kick in the knackers...

United faced Manchester City in the 4th Round of the FA Cup. Part of the rebuilding of my relationship with Sheila was her consent to go to the match. I was so excited all week long. All the lads at work were talking about was the match. I was like a kid on Christmas morning come Saturday. Sheila offered to be a single parent for the day so I could go back to being a big kid. The only condition was that I was back in the house by 8pm and I was I wasn't a menace to sobriety.

I was up earlier than both her & the bairn, I was sizzling bacon and reading The Journal by 7.30am and I was in the pub to meet the lads by 11. We booked a taxi – a big Granada like the one The Sweeney had – and by 12noon we were in The Farmers. The Farmers was a real pub with real music, real ale and real atmosphere. But that day, although the beers tasted sweeter than seeing Sunderland in 80's Teletext magenta, the atmosphere had a bitter twist.

Talk was rife that Gordon Lee was about to quit. The controversy the man created and the resentment many fans were harbouring for him seemed to spice up that talk. It all contrived to turn the pub, the day, and the ground into a cauldron of bad feeling.

Some rumours you know are just rumours, just talk, and just bullshit basically. Some rumours, other rumours, well they're different. They carry a vibe about them and more substance. Some rumours you can just feel – for good or for bad – are true. And that's how it turned out with Lee.

The talk on the terraces must have been repeated in the dressing room. United were well below par and we all knew why.

A few hours, a 3-1 defeat, and a pitch invasion (that I may have accidentally started) and Lee was gone. He bid farewell and buggered off to Everton with 18 months still to run on his contract. That's gratitude for you. Bastard.

That night I got drunk: really drunk. By time I rolled in well after marital curfew Sheila – having a terrible night with the bairn – spat her dummy at me and a huge row erupted. I was too drunk to remember it well, but whatever was said that night it did damage. Just as everything was starting to look bright again the repercussions of that Man City defeat spilled into my personal life and that night brought a storm cloud that Sheila and I never emerged from. Just like some players never recover from a bad game, some couples never recover from a bad argument, especially one that is fuelled by drink.

Following that defeat the leg continued to swing towards my footballing nuts so to speak.

Lee's number 2, Richard Dinnis took over for the remainder of the 76 / 77 season. The board weren't keen to hand the job to basically a PE Teacher who had never played above the level of reserve team football. The players, however, were. They liked Dinnis, and went public in support of him. In a sorry series of events the players got their wish. And although their hearts were in the right place quite frankly they only ended up making arses of themselves.

In the summer of 1977 Dinnis got a 2-year deal based on finishing 5th with what Lee had left behind and on his popularity with the players if not with the board of directors. But the boat had been rocked and the mess United had tumbled into would go on to cost them, ultimately with the loss of their First Division status. After less than 5 months in charge Dinnis was sacked as the 1977 / 78 season went from bad to worse.

Despite dreadful domestic form the place in Europe that Lee's former number 2 had gotten United kept him employed. But when that dream ended against little Bastia it cost Dinnis his job. In truth the board could hardly wait to get shot of him, and in fairness Dinnis did little to coax them out of action they'd wanted all along.

This time the board went and got the man *they* wanted: a disciplinarian to haul the players back in line and sort out the shambles that the club had become. He wasn't their first choice and he wasn't popular with fans but the 'lucky' man was Bill McGarry. Fans of the latter years and the Graeme Souness era might think this all sounds familiar. The disciplinarian, McGarry, made an arse of the job and United were stranded in no mans land with a poor squad, no direction, and even less hope. Bet it sounds even more familiar now.

I once read in a book that there's no such thing as irony; it's just that fate has a sense of humour. And in such light McGarry's first taste of football in Tyneside's home dugout was against Arsenal… and SuperMac.

United lost 2-1; The Leazes End gave Macdonald a standing ovation, and Macdonald then told the press what we all already knew: Newcastle had no chance of staying up. McGarry took charge midway through the 77 / 78 season and amidst the mess the club had become he was unable to stop United from tumbling out of the First Division. It was the first time I'd seen Newcastle relegated, but sadly not the last. Finally the deathknell fell before the final home game with Norwich City when me and the lads were joined by less than 8,000 others in seeing United say farewell to the First Division.

But the hardest thing to say farewell to that year was The Leazes End.

The Leazes End was closed to make way for further development of St James' Park. The demolition of our footballing home was only worsened by the clubs pathetic failure to actually go on and carry out that redevelopment. The fact that The Leazes End was bulldozed in 1978 and wasn't built upon until John Hall's Magpie Group took charge of the club some fifteen years later tells all you need to know about how our club was run.

I remember standing there that last home game. Even the police seemed sad. Most of them had patrolled that terrace for years. Me and the lads and a host of die-hards stood there long after the players – most of who weren't fit to wash the shirt let alone wear it – had trooped dejectedly down the tunnel.

And I cried. Not big whaling girlie tears that can only be soothed by a giant tub of ice cream, a chick flick and a pamper night with friends. I cried man tears: one or two solitary tears that spill from the eyes and roll silently down the cheek. No words are spoken; just a friends hand on the shoulder to say it all.

To me, watching the bulldozers make there way through The Leazes End was akin to watching them dismantle the Tyne Bridge or pull down your local, your old school or the home you grew up in. The Leazes End had been 'constructed' around 1929 / 30ish. For nigh on 50 years it had been the Kop to United's hard-core, United's die-hards, United's grittiest of faithful. Even when I used to go to the Popular Side as a kid there was always a part of me, a little devil in black & white stripes that longed to be amongst the lads on The Leazes. When I started going to that such hallowed part of St James Park I loved it. I was nervous and excited and scared and enthralled. And I loved it.

Saying farewell to The Leazes End left just a bit of a crack down this black & white heart. The only solace was that I was privileged to share that pain with thousands of great folk who felt exactly the same. There really is something wonderful about unity; there really is something wonderful about United.

Plans were afoot to build a stand, a little like the East Stand on the space where our beloved Leazes had fallen. Arguments between club & council and ever tightening purse strings meant no such development took place. The club could barely afford the repair work needed to bring the old Leazes up to scratch, so they opted to pull it down and invest the money in the new stand. The new stand appeared… some 15 years later.

As my home life and my supporter life seemed so intrinsically locked hand in hand, as one tripped and fell, so too did the other.

United failed to gain promotion in the 1978 / 79 Second Division; their first attempt ended with an 8th place finish and a 14-point gap to third. The first half of the season saw much promise; the second half saw the team and the dream fall apart. In that time United lost to McGarry's old club, Wolves, in the FA Cup and also succumbed to a 4-1 home pounding to a Gary Rowell inspired Sunderland.

The following season brought more derby dismay. Newcastle & Sunderland met in a two-legged League Cup tie with the season in its infancy. I was at Roker Park for the first leg, a 2-2 draw where United outplayed the auld enemy. That was the first time I ever went to Roker Park. Oh but it wouldn't be the last.

The second leg was much the same; United again played the better stuff; the scoreline again finished 2-2. In the penalty shoot-out that ensued the spot-kicks kept on flying past the respective keepers. Someone was destined to miss; and in such circumstances fear always seems stronger than belief. The crowd were fantastic; in voice more than number, but when jinxed jock Jim Pearson stepped up I held my breath. United were out by time I inhaled again.

The moral victory was scant consolation to Sunderland's actual one. Come the turn of the year, and the turn of the decade, both sides were battling for promotion. Newcastle looked the stronger of the two North-East contenders and emphasised that with a 3-1 revenge win over Sunderland on the first day of the 1980's at St James Park.

But from then on in United went on to snatch despair from the jaws of glory in quite spectacular style. First there was the FA Cup defeat to mighty Chester and some scrawny little Welsh kid who looked like Bert's mate from Sesame Street. The kid went on to join United, but not before he'd made a legend of himself at Liverpool alongside Kenny Dalglish. Ian Rush' goal that killed off our Cup hopes for one more year also seemed to kill off our promotion push. That defeat marked the beginning of the end. By time Easter had arrived Newcastle's form was more in line with a team leaving the Second Division the other way. An Easter Saturday trip to Roker was my second venture into the enemy's back yard. Stan Cummins headed a late winner to seal Newcastle's last ever defeat at Roker Park, some 17 years before the old ground was closed.

That 1-0 defeat went along way to ending Newcastle's promotion hopes and an equally long way to sealing Sunderland's. The tension between the two sides, the two clubs and the two sets of supporters simmered viciously. That period of time and those pivotal and frequent meetings altered the tone of the Tyne-Wear rivalry in a way that would remain for almost 20-years.

It was a hard summer on Tyneside, 1980. A few miles down the road Wearside was jubilant with the sunshine of promotion. Newcastle's summer sunshine felt more like a footballing desert.

Fortunately, in football as often in life, the end is merely the prelude to a new start. The summer sun was still high in the sky as McGarry led United into the 1980 / 81 season. But to put it blankly it went tits up by time August was out… and thus so too was McGarry. Again fans talked of a big name, but again United went down the Gordon Lee road, only this time with far more success. In my opinion, the difference wasn't so much in the quality of the manager, but the quality of the man.

In September 1980 Newcastle United appointed Arthur Cox from Chesterfield.

And although it took Cox time to turn the club around, just like a bus driver trying a U-turn in a high-street, he knew where he wanted to be and he would go on to get us there. But not before he lit the fuse that blew this wonderful box of fireworks that is Newcastle United sky-high with the signing of Kevin Keegan.

Keegan came in August 1982. I was stunned. And the beauty was that I was privileged to share that sensational feeling with thousands of great folk who felt exactly the same. There really is something wonderful about unity; there really is something wonderful about United.

I remember it was August 1982. It was hot like summers used to be. Maybe summers are always hotter in our memories. We lived in Wallsend. The Tyne ran proud at the bottom and the shipyards towered high above us. I came home drunk one night, with Fish & Chips for me, Sheila and the bairn. I think I promised to take him to the match, so next morning I did just that. And Keegan's first game was our Terry's first game. Hell, he was only knee high to a grasshopper at the time, and he loved it.

Although we missed promotion the first year we were set to make it the next. By April 1984 Arthur Cox' Newcastle were on the brink of a return to First Division football. Only three home games remained, and the bairn, who had become our lucky mascot, was going to be at every one of them.

It didn't impress his mother much but I didn't care. For the first time in my life I was enjoying being a father, even if I wasn't enjoying being a husband. Or more to the point I wasn't enjoying being *Sheila's* husband. Not that I noticed at the time. You see, after years in the wilderness suddenly, thanks to Keegan and Cox, we had something to be proud of.

So as Van Halen jumped, as Frankie told us to relax, and as Kenny Loggins got footloose, my son became my friend and my marriage began to fall apart. Not that I cared: Newcastle were on the verge of saying farewell to the Second Division and I was too caught up in what was to become one of the finest parties that Tyneside has ever seen.

Part Two

TRANSFERS

1. *Crush*

When I was bearing down on my ninth birthday girls were just ceasing to be icky. For the first time in my life I began to notice girls. For the first time in my life I *liked* a girl. That particular girl was Mandy Robson.

Mandy was just one of the gang from home. There was me, Adam and Dave who used to play knocky nine-doors and hide & seek and tuggy and hell even football with two other kids our age: Mandy Robson and Julie Clark.

The differences in sexuality never mattered a jot when we were kids; it's a shame it matters so much in adult life. Hell I've seen Mandy & Julie running 'round our street topless a dozen times a summer when we were just bairns. But then you stop being a bairn and you start noticing things that your innocence and your childhood never let you notice before.

Suddenly Mandy was different to me. All girls were different to me but Mandy, well, Mandy was especially different. I liked her. And by time I was baring down on my ninth birthday I had developed my first crush.

It wasn't sexual; hell it wasn't even physical: I just liked spending time with her. It's a pity that we tend to lose that sentiment as we grow up.

We were in the same class at school, Mandy & me. Actually all of the gang were in the same class. We used to gather outside

Dave's house at 8.30 in the morning and we'd all walk to school together.

We used to head out of the street, call at the corner shop, get some sweets, kick a penny-floater around and meander off to our little Junior School. We'd talk football and neighbours and teachers and football.

We'd swap our Panini football stickers and we'd climb over walls and into gardens to get our ball back. They were happy days. It was April 1984. It was spring, it was sunny and it was warm. Newcastle were odds on to win promotion. There was only three home games to go, and United, Keegan and all, were on the brink of what to me was the holy grail: First Division football.

As the Easter Eggs that had gathered on our wood-stain sideboard were opened and devoured Newcastle took on Carlisle United – outsiders for promotion – at St James Park. And in similar fashion to the way an 8-year-old devours Easter Eggs, United devoured Carlisle; but it was so much sweeter than chocolate could ever be.

We stood on the terracing at The Gallowgate End, centre, slightly to the right of the barrier than ran down the middle. When I went to Town with my Mam I was made to wear a jacket and invariably a hat or scarf or even gloves for crying out loud. When I went with my Dad all I needed was a T-shirt and my lucky black & white scarf. That summed up the differing levels of freedom in my respective relationships with my parents.

I loved going all the way to Newcastle in nothing but my T-shirt. It felt liberal and outlandish. I loved it the warm Tyneside sun beaming down upon the St James Park terracing and my shoulders alike. Mixed with the smell of hot-dogs and onions and the brewery in the air, the sound of the banter, it all added to the magic of match day on Tyneside.

Every time you went to St James Park you had reason to believe that Newcastle would win. More than that, every time you went to St James Park you knew it would be exciting. Every time you went to St James Park you knew you'd be entertained. But more than the excitement and the entertainment, for those rare few months in a lifetime of following a club like Newcastle, every time you went to the ground you had reason to believe that you were on the verge of being successful.

When Carlisle United rolled into Town – only about 2 places below United in 5th – success, just like hot-dogs and sunshine, was very much in the air.

I remember Newcastle being 2-0 ahead and cruising. Then a moment happened in the St James Park sunshine that seemed to sum up the whole magic of the entire season: *we* scored from *their* penalty! Alan Shoulder, one of Dad's favourite ex-Newcastle players, took the kick at The Leazes End. He was a master of spot-kicks in his Newcastle days. Fair play, I thought; 2-1, game on. But Kevin Carr saved it. And then someone rushed on to the rebound (Poskett) and Carr saved that too. Dad and I were going mental! Everybody was jumping around and celebrating and hugging each other. It was brilliant. Then suddenly amidst the mass of arms waving around I saw Chris Waddle raring down the right wing.

There was a one-two between McDermott and Keegan, then the ball was fed into Beardsley who had made it to the by-line. Beardsley then knocked it over his head to the back post. And there was Keegan again, winning the header to send the ball ballooning into the Gallowgate End net. Amazing! I never stopped celebrating from first to last, and my heart never stopped racing from dead ball to goal, from spot-kick against to Keegan on his knees in front of a loving Gallowgate. Keegan's goal pretty much sealed what went on to become a 5-1 win.

Watching Newcastle play is a wonderful thing. Watching Newcastle win is… well at the time I was too young to say *better than sex* but it sure was better than a crush.

The wins kept coming and ultimately promotion drew ever nearer.

The schools went back after the Easter Holidays, the sun continued to beam down on Wallsend as it did on Tyneside as a whole and being nine years old never felt so good. It didn't matter that it was only the Second Division, it didn't matter that we weren't rich, and it didn't matter that it was only a crush; the bottom line was that I was happy. And no matter whereabouts in life you find yourself, there's a lot to be said for being able to wake up in the morning and simply think, 'I'm happy'.

It wasn't just what we had that made us happy; it was the bright future that tomorrow seemed to hold. I think happiness is a complex thing. To me, to be truly happy, I need to enjoy my life in the present, I need to have reason to believe that the future will be bright and joyful, and I need to have as little as possible to worry about. As my ninth birthday loomed I had all of that and more.

I loved my life. It was all schooldays, football and games in the street as the '84 summer drew ever closer. It was going to bed at night dreaming of crushes; the one I had burning in my heart for Mandy, and the ones that I enjoyed on The Gallowgate with my Dad as Blaydon Races rang through the Tyneside afternoon.

Just as it should be when you're barely 9 years old, I had nothing to worry about.

After that wonderful result and performance against Carlisle, Newcastle had only two more home games to go and promotion was so very much in our black & white grasp. I looked forward to those two games more than I'd looked forward to anything ever before in my short little life, Christmas' included.

Knee High To A Grasshopper

Next up was Derby County. Newcastle demolished them 4-0. Derby were leaving Division 2 one-way, we were leaving it another. So with Derby destroyed and sent packing Newcastle travelled to Huddersfield for the final away game needing only a point to seal promotion. The bitter sweet lessons in life that football was sure to keep teaching me continued with that game.

I was delighted that the finish line of Promotion was there within our reach. But as a kid I was just a little sad that I wouldn't get to see it. The game was away, and *my* appearances at away games were still a few years down the touchline. Dad went. And I think he toyed with the idea of taking me. Still, it would be 9 more years before I would enjoy all the magic that is seeing a Kevin Keegan inspired United travel a few hours south and win promotion. It would prove worth waiting for.

But while Grimsby Town and Blundell Park was still a date with destiny too far for Geordie eyes to see, Huddersfield Town and a Peter Beardsley inspired 2-2 draw was just around the corner.

Beardsley's two goals were buried in front of my father's ecstatic eyes. I, like an injured Kevin Keegan, missed the game.

But there was still two special pages left in what was to be one of the greatest chapters in this wonderful clubs story.

The first was the final home league game of the season, with Brighton & Hove Albion. And the bittersweet lingered: for this was Keegan's final ever league game.

I'm a man, a supporter, and a person, who believes that football isn't all about silverware and league positions. There's more to win in football than just trophies. Being a Geordie I guess it's a bloody good job I feel that way. Football is about entertainment. Football is about theatre. Win, lose or draw I go to football to see a game. I go to football to support my Team, my Club. I watch thousands of games on TV – especially since the wonderful conception of Sky

– and I hope to be entertained. The only difference is that with Newcastle it's something that I'm emotionally attached to.

Newcastle didn't win a trophy that season, but they did win Promotion. More than that they won back some pride. Along with that they entertained us, and countless others. They epitomised all that makes football wonderful: they were a joy to watch every week, they always played to win, they always attacked, and icing on the cake, they were successful.

It was wonderful: every heart-racing, tear-jerking, gob-stopping moment of it. And though I have no trophies in my memory – except the Title that Keegan himself went on to give us after that wonderful night in Grimsby – I have a 'trophy' cabinet in my heart with all the footballing things I treasure. None of them means more to me than seeing Kevin Keegan's last ever league game with my own two eyes. I was honoured to be there, and win, lose or draw, I will always have that.

As it happened folklore of course tells us that United did win. The 3-1 final day victory over Brighton was a day that every Geordie will treasure, especially those that were there that sunny day, May 12th 1984, 3 days before my 9th birthday.

Better yet, those that were there had a little place in their hearts touched by all that day brought: Waddle's header, Beardsley's wonder goal (chipping an 8ft 6 goalkeeper after a sliding tackle that most centre-halves would be proud of) and of course, Keegan's last goal.

I remember the crush as I fought my way to the front of the Gallowgate with my Dad, climbing on to the metal perimeter fencing that was erected in the early 1980's and brought down within a week of Hillsborough, to get a better view of our heroes. There's a point on the history video where someone throws a scarf and Keegan stoops to pick it up. You can see my hand in shot as Kev struggles to get the knot loose.

Those who did indeed have their hearts touched with all that day brought were destined – little did they know – to have their hearts touched again by a very special man some 8 years later.

But before Kevin Keegan could return, he had to say farewell.

2. *Auf Wiedersehen, Kev*

On 10th February 1984 Dennis, Neville, Oz and the boys boarded a ferry and headed back home to Blightey. Their adventure building bricks on German soil was over. It was the end of one of the best drama series ever seen on TV. It was, of course, popular all over England but *Auf Wiedersehen Pet* held a special place in the hearts of Geordies all over the world.

When it ended we all hoped that another series, another instalment, another adventure would follow. It would… in time.

But as Dennis, Neville, Oz and the boys were heading home another man close to our collective Geordie hearts was heading the other way. Keegan was retiring; his send off would be Liverpool at home in a farewell that would put tears in my eyes for the first time since they pulled the old Leazes to the ground. Only this time the tears were different; this time the tears were full of pride, thanks and gratitude.

Me and the bairn stood on The Gallowgate, just to the right of centre, in our place. And we all had our place didn't we? They say the heart is left of centre; to Terry and me I'd say it was always just to the right. We were under the glow of the Scoreboard and the 'Newcastle-BlueStar-United' logo and the dotted illuminous letters that so often danced 'GOAL!'

The bairn had no real concept of Liverpool. "They're just like the successful version of us, son," I told him. "They're everything we could be if we got our act together."

"So why aren't we as successful as them?" he asked innocently.

I was going to start telling him, but the game only lasts 90 minutes and the kid had school in the morning.

Still, I knew he was excited at the prospect of locking horns with the Reds, not just that night, but in the season that was to come when Newcastle once again stood in the elite division of English football.

But before we could go down that road – without Keegan – we first had to say Goodbye to him. A 2-2 draw, a standing ovation, the man himself bowing to us, his faithful, and another tear-jerking wave to the crowd culminating in Keegan leaving St James' just as spectacularly as he arrived, in a helicopter and still in his black & white.

When it ended we all hoped that another series, another instalment, another adventure would follow. It would… in time.

When he left I had a tremendous sense of the *better to have loved and lost* about it all. It was an amazing feeling, and as I walked away from Gallowgate with the floodlights beaming and my heart still pounding it made me wonder; it made me wonder about loving and losing and being brave enough to fall in love… and being braver still to let go of that which you know you're not in love with.

3. *Big Jack*

My birthday came and went and, having already borne witness to promotion, I got the present I wanted the most: the Newcastle United away kit, the silver kit. That was *the* kit. To this day it's my favourite all time Newcastle strip: silver shirt with thin black stripes, silver shorts and silver socks with black Umbro logo.

And of course, it wore the famous NUFC badge that I still adore.

I was 9 years old. I was growing up. And as I did football continued to teach me valuable lessons that I could use in everyday life – the first was one that, sadly, most of us can relate to: sometimes we lose the ones we love.

First to go was of course Keegan.

I cried. I was happy, but I cried.

Second to go was Arthur Cox.

I cried. I was absolutely slap-me-six-ways-from-Sunday dumbfounded, and I cried.

Cox' departure made absolutely no sense at all. Stay with me here; you're nine years old, your team has just won promotion back to the First Division, you've succeeded, everything is good, everyone is happy, the world is spinning like it ought to and then bang… the man who just drove the bus to the hallowed ground he was tasked with ups and buggers off… to little Derby County who's bus had just left the Second Division the *other* way.

Dad tried explaining it to me, but he got angry in doing so and nothing he said really made sense. He said 'bastard' quite a lot, which was unlike him because he was under strict instruction not to swear in front of me in case I picked up bad habits. All I could gather was that it was the boards' fault.

Mam used to put a lot of strict instruction on Dad. It was only years later I realised that, long after they'd split and the damage was done. The poor bastard.

Appointing a new manager was strange. Arthur had been driving our bus since I first got on it. Appointing someone new was a bit weird. It was like waking up, coming downstairs in your pyjamas and finding your Dad is gone and a new fella is taking on the role of *father*.

Little did I know it but that was something I'd later learn for myself.

When Arthur Cox took over at Derby it was like seeing your father move in with another family and watching him become their Dad.

Little did I know but I'd get a fair crack at seeing that one for myself too.

But ultimately, as much as we love football, and as big a part as it plays in our life, it isn't as important as life. Someone once said to Bill Shankly that football was a matter of life and death to him. Shankly replied famously, "It's more important than that".

Of course, that's bollocks. In a world of deaths and murders and aeroplanes crashing into tower blocks then maybe 3 points isn't so important after all. Next time your wife, your mother or even just your friend gets taken to hospital after an unusual smear then ask yourself how much that home win really means.

So, while losing Arthur Cox *felt* like losing my father, ultimately time would tell that it was of course nowhere near as painful. Same road, just nowhere near as far – emotionally – down it.

And while I never did, never *could*, replace my father, United, of course, would replace Arthur Cox. And in, with some sort of call-a-spade-a-spade love about him, came the one, the only, Big Jack.

Jack Charlton arrived with a big reputation, and by and large everyone seemed more than happy with his appointment, even though they were all at a bit of a loss as to the loss of Arthur Cox.

Cox had quit because of a dispute with the board. He was a good man Arthur, a man of great principle and someone to look up to. He was the kind of man anyone would be better off for knowing or having in their lives. He had morals and standards and honour. Sadly, in life as much as in football, that seems to be an ever-decreasing quality.

Dad tucked me in at night and told me all about Big Jack. It was indeed a black & white fairytale and it spouted many spin off tales of Geordie Knights. I learned so much about Newcastle's history and the road that had lead from the West End & East End of the 1890's to the United that were braced for First Division football in 1984 / 85.

I learned about England in '66 and Big Jack's part in all of that. I learned of Jackie Milburn. I learned the ups and downs, the highs and lows, the success and failure that had lead my club, our club, to where it was there and then.

But one thing I didn't learn was tactics. And by the end of the season, although the feat of keeping United afloat in a tough division should not go underestimated, the fans were questioning Jack's tactics too.

I've got to go on record as saying I like Big Jack. I don't know why or what for specifically but he just seems to be my kind of fella. Jack did a great job at other clubs I have since learned, and did a great job for Eire afterwards, but at Newcastle it didn't happen. And in Jack's departure I got my first lesson in how quick the sweet can taste so bitter.

With the blessings of hindsight at our disposal it saddens me just how many times this club has come so close to something magical just to piss it all away for nothing. How many managers will come here with great track records and then walk out the door with a huge pay off and the club in a shambles…? How many times will we make ridiculous decisions – and I mean at boardroom level here too – and ruin in months what has taken years to create.

Running a football club is like Jenga. It takes ages to build something special, and sadly one stupid move and the whole lot comes tumbling down. Big Jack's reign was the first time I've seen it, but sadly not the last.

Incredibly United started the 84 / 85 season by going top. Bryan Adams was reminiscing about his first real six-string, Tina Turner was asking us what love had to do with it and Michael J Fox was hitting 88mph and waking up in 1955. And Jack Charlton's Newcastle were in their highest league place since lightening struck the old clock tower. Tactics smactics I say! I didn't understand jack shit to be honest. I went to the pictures, the old Odeon in Newcastle just up from the Fire Station on the Friday night to watch Ghostbusters and then on the Saturday to watch Newcastle thump Aston Villa 3-0. Life was brilliant! I didn't have a clue about long ball, I didn't have a clue about round pegs and square holes and all that, I just knew Newcastle were winning First Division games just as convincingly as they had done Second Division games a few long months before.

To this day I still get a wonderful feeling when Newcastle win.

However, by time Stevie Wonder was just calling to say he loved us and we were waking Wham up before we went went,

Newcastle, under Big Jack's guidance, had sank to the brink of the relegation battle. By then the fans were calling to say anything but they loved Jack.

For me, I just didn't understand. I fathomed out it was a higher level of football and hence a harder one. And from that it didn't take a rocket scientist to deduce that results would probably not be as good as last year. Not that I wanted to be a rocket scientist. And strange as it seemed I didn't want to be a footballer either. Well, I did, but I knew I wouldn't be. I was crap. I could trap a ball further than most kids my age could kick the bloody thing. But hell, I was a realist. I actually wanted to be a journalist. I wanted to write about football. I wanted to follow Newcastle all over the country (the idea of getting out of the country and into Europe never even crossed my mind. Funny how expectation works isn't it?) I used to make up my own articles from cuttings I took from The Chronicle, The Pink (remember The Pink?) and Shoot!

Fair dues my articles were a little less than impartial, they were stuck on with Prit-stick and most were written in crayon or pencil but they were frequently more accurate than Alan Oliver's.

What I really couldn't understand was the change in style.

For two seasons – and all I had ever known – we played football the way I believed, and still believe, that football was meant to be played. I think it was the great Brian Clough who said that if football was meant to be played in the sky God would have put grass up there. Fair point, Brian. God never did put grass in the sky; he put Sky on the grass and they televised positively everything.

I had seen United dazzle and attack and entertain and play neat little fast little triangle football that saw the ball fizz all over the St James Park turf. Suddenly all United did was whack the ball from the back to the front, bomb it into the opponent's 18-

yard box and battle like beggars on a street corner to pick up the scraps. Surely Newcastle United were about more than scraps. I thought so; my Dad thought so, the fans thought so and Beardsley & Waddle thought so too. Sadly, Big Jack thought not.

It was like watching a Harley Davidson being used for scrambling; it was like watching a Jaguar being used as a rally car. I rarely looked at the St James Park turf that year, but I grew mighty familiar with the Tyneside skyline. We'll never know what would have happened if Cox had stayed, if Newcastle had approached the First Division in the manner they conquered the second. What we do know is that Big Jack's style of play kept United safe. A 14th place finish tells half of the story; a First Division average gate five thousand lower than the previous years Second Division gate tells another.

But as Jack brought in players suited to the long ball he lost players suited to the beautiful game.

A-ha wanted us to take them on and Chris Waddle felt the same way about Spurs. When Waddle left in the summer of 1985 it started the clock ticking on Jack's time in charge. A few weeks and a poor pre-season later and Jack had climbed through that famous split at Newcastle and left the club managerless on the brink of the 1985/86 season. He wasn't one to stay where he wasn't wanted, Jack. When the crowd turned on him, he turned and walked away.

He took with him some great memories: the News Years Day victory over Sunderland, with a Peter Beardsley hat-trick to boot, the 3-0 win over Villa that put us top and even the incredible 5-5 draw with QPR at Loftus Road. But he left some sorry state of affairs: not least of all some sorry players in the likes of Gary Megson, Pat Heard, Tony Cunningham and George Reilly. Reilly once hit me with a ball while taking a shot at The Gallowgate End. I wasn't even at the match! I was in Eldon Square with my Mam!

We just came out of Mothercare and then wallop! Smack, right on the head.

Of course, I'm kidding, but he was that bad. No offence, George.

Yeah, when Jack left he left a mess. But ultimately we were all just pretty happy that he left.

4. *Slippery When What...?*

By 1985 / 86 I was landing on my 30th birthday. Did I have a mid life crisis…? No. And by no, I of course mean yes.

It started with a new look, a new image, including a swanky haircut that was the result of a big money transfer (one pound seventy-five pence) from Dave's The Barbers to Harkers.

It incorporated a new car: a second hand Ford Escort Mk I. I still remember the registration plate: GDC379N. It was a beige 2 door with maroon Heart of Midlothian seats and a 1.3 engine. It had one careful owner… and of course, as the joke goes, about 5 that weren't so careful. Hey, the old ones are the best. Not with cars they're not. And not with cars that I buy I can tell you.

1985 and my 30th birthday also encapsulated a change in my musical taste… and a venture into my own business.

Basically, I got into the whole rock scene. I'd been into the punk stuff quite mildly in the 70's. I liked the music, but unlike football, where I wore my clothes to show the club I represented, I never dressed punk. I think my change in music as the mid eighties came to play was possibly – like all good punk or rock – about rebellion.

I wasn't happy in my marriage; I hadn't ever been truly happy; the heights I'd reached were probably *contentment.*

I was subconsciously toying with wild notions of a life where I hadn't made such mistakes and hadn't been sentenced to a life with Sheila. The thing was that I loved the bairn so very much and I wouldn't have changed the past for the world. It wasn't about going back and undoing the mistake; that would have undone the birth of my son. No, to me it was becoming about moving on, moving forward, and changing the future as opposed to regretting the past.

I was upset, I was frustrated, and I felt crushed by the weight of my marriage to Sheila. And bless her for all her sins and all her beauty but I tried. I really, really did. I tried to make it work and to keep it romantic and passionate and happy and I did all things that a good husband or hell just a good boyfriend should do to make it work. My heart wasn't in it, but I didn't quit and I didn't just let us wallow into misery. But for all her beauty and all her sins, Sheila never tried back.

From that grew resentment. We'd screwed up; I accept that. We'd made our bed; we'd lie in it. But lying in it was one thing; dying in it was another. And I wasn't ready to die. Sheila seemed happy to. My *life* had years left in it, why should the *love* die now. My lungs and my kidneys would keep working; why shouldn't my heart?

From those sentiments resentment grew further. And in that resentment flourished rebellion and my sudden inkling to some good old fashioned rock music.

Rebellion is a powerful thing; accompanied with loud guitars, heavy drums and a good melody it's even more powerful. I'm a simple man; I have simple pleasures. I like my beer cold, my guitars loud and my football entertaining. I always get a warm feeling watching a teenager fall off a skateboard and I like to be with people who like to be with me. Sheila wasn't one of those people; my friends were. So I spent more time with them and less time with her.

Sheila and I had so little in common. That might sound strange because we grew up together, we went to the same school, we lived in the same Town and we had shared so many things – not least of all our lives – for ten years and rolling. But what we lacked in common was that we were essentially two very different people. We both grew up to be people that weren't really suited to one another. If we didn't have the kid then we would have just stopped going out with each other years earlier and moved on. But because of him we were bound together. That was fine in 1975 when we were similar, but a decade later we tethered and dying. If we'd never got together in the 70's but instead met up in 1985 we wouldn't have went out; hell we wouldn't have been friends. We'd exchange pleasantries, as old acquaintances do, but then we'd pass at the bus stop and go off our separate ways.

Our characteristics, our personalities, our interests and our beliefs were different. If we were colours we'd be colours that didn't go together. We'd be white trainers on a black suit, or a red shirt on brown chinos. I've never understood what chalk & cheese was all about but maybe that was us. We barely liked each other anymore, let alone loved each other. We didn't enjoy each others company, basically. And being trapped in that environment made us both tetchy and both defeated. There were times when I felt that the pressure was so intense that I was suffocating; there were times when I was just so emotionally bored. When I felt like that I just had to get out and let me heart and my dreams get some air. Hence, I didn't have a problem seeing less of Sheila, but unfortunately seeing less of the bairn was an unavoidable consequence.

It started to show as the 85/86 season began to get into flow. By that time Jack Charlton was gone. Sadly, so too was Chris Waddle. The managers' seat was temporarily filled with Willie McFaul. He'd been at the club since about 1892. In fact I think he actually made his debut for East End he'd been there so long. He'd had a little spell in charge before United appointed Arthur Cox, and although his brief was again as a caretaker manager it ended up being anything but brief.

McFaul was a loyal and loving servant of United, an Irishman black & white to the core. A former player, he understood what Newcastle United were all about. He'd been signed by Sir Joe in the 1960's and by time he took the managers chair from Big Jack he had been at St James for 20 years and worked from Reserve Goalie to Gaffer.

McFaul had seen wonderful highs, such as the 1969 Fairs Cup win, but he also endured painstaking lows. He's the despairing keeper flying in vain to stop Ronnie Radford's equaliser in the infamous Cup defeat against Hereford, or Bastard Hereford as I like to refer to them. He lost in both of those mid-70's Wembley Finals, conceding 5 goals and collecting only two runners up medals. Like SuperMac whom he played alongside McFaul too was a casualty of the turbulent Gordon Lee era, or Bastard Lee as I like to refer to him.

Ultimately Willie McFaul understood our club and I don't doubt for a second that he loved it. You don't always have to be a Geordie to fall in love with Newcastle United. In McFaul's case the Irishman was the ideal pair of safe hands to leave the teams affairs with after the sudden departure of Jack Charlton.

But as affairs at Gallowgate started to calm with McFaul's settling hands, fortunes at home were becoming intolerable.

If my marriage was a football team then we were losing week in week out. If my marriage had been a football game then it would be the equivalent of being 2-0 down and the heads dropping. I didn't let my head drop; I battled on. Sheila's head went down (no, not *that* way) and she gave up. I was a better player than that. I was working hard and although I didn't love Sheila I gave her

100% week in week out. I bought the girl some flowers, I took her to nice restaurants, I tried to be affectionate and loving and I tried talking – and listening – to her. And yes, hell, I even tried to make love to her. After all, McFaul wasn't the only Willie in my life.

Sheila and I slept in opposite sides of our marital bed and it reached the point where I began sleeping in the spare room, the one that we once planned to fill with a brother or sister for our Terry.

Relationships are hard. It takes effort to make them work. We'd all like to think that it all just happens by magic, and while falling in love maybe *is* magic, staying in love takes a whole lot of hard work. I just think that if the person you're with is the right one then that effort seems effortless. It should be a labour *of* love, not a labour *to* love. I tried to save it, to give it CPR and the kiss of life, but Sheila wouldn't kiss back. By the 85 / 86 season CPR was out, QPR were in and I knew that our relationship was circling the drain.

A failing marriage is difficult. It hurts. It's complicated. It's messy. It's rare that both parties with no kids come to an amicable decision to go separate ways no hard feelings no ill will and remain friends always. Life doesn't work that way. If life was that easy I'd be married to Wincy Willis, Sheila would be married to Tom Jones and the bairn would have been writing match reports on the Willie McFaul glory years.

In reality when a marriage – or any relationship for that matter – fails it comes down to just how damaging it is. Damage limitation they'd call it in footballing terms. You know you're going to lose; it's just a case of how heavy the defeat is going to be.

Suddenly West Ham away springs to mind. Late on in the season Newcastle crashed 8-1 at Upton Park, with Peter Beardsley ending up in goal. 'Keeper Martin Thomas was clearly unfit from the off but with no fit reserve he had to play. His injury worsened early doors and by 4-0 down he left the field. I recall Chris Hedworth – an outfield player – going between the posts and amazingly (and in hindsight almost comically) getting injured. And I was thinking *Okay, we're clearly going to lose, just please keep the score-line at least semi-respectable.* I think I'd have settled for 5 or even 6 quite happily. In the end circumstances helped to conjure up 8 in what Ron Atkinson would have called the onion bag.

Circumstances soon after would be equally damaging when my marriage did finally end.

But before I came to that decision – or more accurately before I had the courage to act upon the decision I had made around the end of the 85 / 86 season – I threw in the towel and I quit. I went through the motions, even if I didn't go through the *e*motions.

Firstly I went where I was happy. Happiness was a rare thing for me around that time and my only outlet was football. I needed to blow off some steam. I needed to be away from the home and the family and I needed some space to either forget about my problems or even just think about them from an impartial place. Sheila was so cold I just needed to be around people who were nice to me and those people were only at work and at the football. Hell, it was the same people. We were united. We worked together, we went to football together, and in my friends I found a crutch to help me through some of the hardest times of my life.

I'd be sad and depressed all week – well apart from those halcyon days where Sunderland slipped towards wonderful Second Division trap door at the hands of Lawrie McMenemy – and I would only come to life on a Friday morning.

Friday – or LagerFriday as the lads called it – became my lifeblood and my salvation. But having alcohol as a saviour is a dangerous religion. The lads from the shipyard were many, and each one of them a legend in his own way. I enjoyed every pint and every cigarette I shared in the company of all of those lads. But the three lads I had grown closest to were Tom, Garry and Hopper.

By time LagerFriday came around I was positively buzzing. I felt like a kid again, when the thrill of your first weekend pint was whetting your thoughts all the working day long. I never smoked at work. I was strictly a social smoker. But by Friday morning, by the 11 o'clock break I was ready to crack a packet open. I was excited just buying them at 7am on the way to the Shipyard. There was a warm little newsagent on a corner in our street and no matter what the season, what the month, what the weather it was always a warm and cosy place to be.

7am on a Friday morning, dawn just a few moments away and the morning full of the promise of the rising sun. The warm orange glow from the newsagent's window, the hustle of newspapers and milk bottles being unwrapped and unbound and placed to sell. The counter full of chocolate and sweets and buying a Fruit & Nut for the bairn because I knew it was his favourite.

There was the warm hello from old Mr MacMilligan or his wife who were always there bright & early to get their day – and countless others – under way. We'd make chitchat and a quip about Newcastle and I'd buy a packet of Marlborough Lights and the bairns Fruit & Nut. I'd grab a paper, the Journal of course, and off I'd go to work. Garry, Tom and Hopps would meet me around the gates and in we'd go to a cacophony of jokes and banter and anticipation of all that the weekend would bring. I felt free and I felt happy.

I have so much to thank all my friends for. The Lads have all been great people to drink with, great people to go to football with. I hope they know how much they mean to me. Friends are the family you choose for yourself so they say, and I feel honoured to call these lads my friends, my family, my LagerBrothers. Maybe one day they will find out just how much I mean that.

But living like that, so socially, can be dangerous. Our Friend*ship* sailed in such social waters that a tide of recklessness or alcoholism was always an undercurrent that threatened to carry us away. And sadly, without knowing it, I began to sink. There's no salvation at the bottom of a bottle of vodka; trust me, if there was I would have found it.

And no matter how great your friends or your family are, there's only one thing that can save you from that: love.

For me that love was so much closer to home than I knew, but still a few more seasons down the line.

I think that many of things that kept Garry, Tom, Hopper and me so close was our home lives. Whereas the other lads all had happy home lives with relatively happy families, we didn't have that. For differing circumstances and differing reasons we found ourselves in the same boat, so we slapped friendship on the side of it and we sailed off into a crazy, smoky, lager, vodka and brown ale haze.

And the camaraderie was amazing.

I needed my friends every weekend, not just every home game. For a side like Newcastle that would normally be 21 league games and about 3 cup games a year. Even if we got a good home draw we'd barely play more than 3 times before seeing our Wembley dreams pulled down a little like the old West Stand that was soon to make way for the new Milburn Stand.

If the fixtures were cruel I wouldn't see the lads outside of work for 2 weeks. Away game Saturdays (and back in those days football *was* played on a Saturday) saw me shopping with the missus, doing DIY or cutting the grass (or just sitting getting drunk in the garden shed with Metro Radio on listening to The

Lads play away). The alternative to that was actually *going* to the away games. And what a fine idea that turned out to be.

We'd been to many away games over the years and I could spend the next week regaling a thousand stories that these jaunties produced. Match specials, Tranny Vans, Box Vans, and a convoy of cars; we'd done them all over the years. The things is that we football fans take our obsession seriously. It starts with going to home games. Then you want to emulate the hardcore, the diehards and prove your commitment by going to away games. Away games are a million times better than home anyway. You get the real true supporters, the diehards with generations of football behind them. They know all the songs, all the words and they sing their hearts out every away trip just to back the black & white.

From there it becomes competitive in a nice way. Everyone is keen to prove how ardent their support is, and the group almost dares one another, to raise the bar, set a new standard, and see who will go the furtherest to follow United. One week it's a trip to Yorkshire to see the lads play Bradford. The next you go all the way to London on a Saturday afternoon and make your first trip to Upton Park. Finally you're off to Norwich on the Saturday and Portsmouth on the Tuesday night just to keeping raising the bar.

You keep on looking for the daftest, the craziest, the most testing way to prove your loyalty and your dedication to the cause. Every footsoldier wants medals. Then you become obsessed with not just getting to the away games but with never missing one. It becomes your duty, your destiny to play a perfect game to the beautiful game, and be an ever-present at every game in a season. One minute it's a Moordale coach from Haymarket to Bramall Lane, the next it's 6 lads in the back of a Ford Escort estate doing Shrewsbury on a winters night.

After marriages and babies and unwanted pregnancies and B&Q and DIY suddenly your away trips lay in your memory and your Saturday's lay in cutting the grass, mending the fence and maybe getting a tinny down while you watch the nipper and she goes to her mothers.

But my need for my friendship fix led me back to the finest of the finest; I was once again an away supporter of Newcastle United. Hello! I was a Geordie Boy. We might not win the Football League, we might not win the Cup, but we will follow United.

Dire Straits were installing microwave ovens, custom kitchen deliveries, and I was at The Farmers, banging on Aerosmith, Bon Jovi, Van Halen, and Europe.

While Sheila was dragging the bairn around Wallsend to help carry the groceries I was living on a prayer, having a permanent vacation and asking why this couldn't be love.

The notion hit me in a moment of brilliance never quite matched by the John Cornwell's, Ian Stewart's and Billy Whitehurst's of this world. Away games were expensive; there was petrol, tickets, food and drink to pay for and there was the inconvenience of either two of the lads volunteering to drive or going on the supporters coaches, which by & large were okay at best.

The supporters' coaches meant we had to fit in with what everyone else wanted to do. We were at the mercy of the local police of wherever we were going and invariably we didn't get to drink on the coach and frequently got where we were going too late to find a boozer down there.

Also, we couldn't listen to the music we were all into: rock music. We actually went to one away game where the coach driver played nothing but SuperTramp all the way there, all the way back. Before that trip I used to like SuperTramp. Now if I so much as hear a minute of SuperTramp *I* feel like taking a dive.

So, in a fit of brilliance so often matched by the Gascoinge's, Beardsley's and Waddle's of this world I came up with the idea of hiring a mini-bus to take us all away. We could go whenever we wanted and do whatever we wanted, including drinking. We had no constraints other than getting to wherever we were playing a good few hours early so we could get pissed before the game, which when watching Newcastle during the 80's was usually a good thing.

We all had too many restrictions at home to have them placed on us with our football. It was rebellious and it was beautiful. There were no women, no bosses, no police, no arsey coach drivers and jobsworths and no hassle.

While Dire Straits were moving refrigerators and colour TV's we were getting picked up from the Shipyard gates, drinking lager by the crate full and blasting out Skid Row, Motley Crew and Poison 'til our hearts content.

We left as early as was needed to beat the traffic, avoid any police and get to some boozer near to that days opponent in good time. Frequently we would stop somewhere on the way there and invade some little village in the middle of Yorkshire and drink enough to sink a ship. Actually there's a pub in Ferrybridge whose landlord and lady retired on the back of the profits we made them.

I can still see us parked around the corner from the Wetherby Whaler while one of the lads was sent in to buy 18 large cod and chips.

Soon word got around and other lads, good lads, wanted to join the trips. We began advertising at work with a few posters made with the bairns felt tips and then we put a few more in the local boozers and the working mens club.

Before we knew it a mini-bus wasn't enough and we were booking 52-seat coaches. Soon after that the numbers had climbed to 52+ and we needed a second coach and then a third and eventually a fourth. And Garry, Tom, Hopps & I saw a business opportunity.

We accidentally launched our own supporter's club travel. Soon not only were we travelling for free but we were also making decent money every away game.

The only problem was that people were calling us at home and asking about Jackie's coaches or Garry's bus, Tom's Travel or the Hopper Clipper. We needed to make it more official and more professional. We needed a name. And as all the lads travelling with us were not just Geordies or Toon supporters but also predominantly rockers we picked a theme based upon that.

After toying with a few other names, such as Motley Toon, Geordie Satellites and Jef Leppard Travel we opted for *Slippery When What…?*

It came from Bon Jovi's album release. We were sitting on the coach heading to one of the away games and one of the lads – singing away to *Living On A Prayer* and *You Give Love A Bad Name* – mentioned the album release.

"What's it called?" I asked.

"Slippery When Wet," Tom said.

Garry looked confused. "Slippery when *what*?" he asked.

We all laughed, and the name picked itself.

That was it: *Slippery When What* was up and running, making it's debut in the 1985 / 86 season. We used it to get to enough away games to back Willie McFaul's side to a commendable 11th place finish in our second season back in the top flight. I was proud of *Slippery When What*. I shared it with Sheila. I remember being so exited when it took off and I remember telling her all about it and showing her the coaches and how we were hiring them and we were going to invest and buy them and so on and so on…

I remember thinking she'll be proud of me, pleased for me and happy for me.

I remember she was so underwhelmed. She was so uninterested.

"This is it, Hon, this is how it works," I told her standing in Cassidy's yard showing her the coaches like a child on a Christmas morning excited at a new toy.

"Hmm," she said, adding, "they're a bit dirty aren't they?" and "They're not very new…"

"Yeah," I said, trying to maintain my excitement, "But we'll get better ones when we get more money" I told her.

"You'll need some of that money for the garden fence mind you. That reminds me, the bairn needs some new shoes for our Margaret's wedding next month" Sheila went on, raining heavily upon my parade.

I felt so downhearted, so disappointed, so sad and so deflated.

"And you'll need a new suit for that too. I'm not having you going in something tatty and showing me up," she told me.

It was Thursday teatime and I trooped dejectedly out of the coach yard and back home with my wife walking a pace ahead and berating me like she must have done the bairn when he lagged behind her during shopping trips to Newcastle or Wallsend.

Then the following day, LagerFriday, something happened that changed everything.

5. *Blue-tack & Blue-Star's*

By time the 1986 / 87 season got under way Ferris Bueller had had his day off, Huey Lewis was happy to be stuck with us and Newcastle had enjoyed two relatively successful seasons in the First Division. Dad was anything but happy to be stuck with us and as Madonna was telling her Papa not to preach mine was slowly drifting away.

By August '86 rumours were starting to surface that Peter Beardsley wasn't happy to be stuck with us either. I was constantly worried and unsettled. I desperately didn't want Peter to leave. He was my favourite player and surely if we were to be successful we needed to keep him. I had this awful feeling in the pit of my stomach that Peter would sooner or later leave us. I wanted the rumours to end, I wanted clarity to the story and I wanted some form of commitment from both Newcastle & Beardsley himself.

None was forthcoming and my fears stayed with me.

At that time, September 1986, Dave, Adam, Mandy, Julie and me were settling into the town's Comprehensive School.

My crush on Mandy remained all the same. Years had passed and not one word had left my lips about my feelings. My eyes adored her, though I never laid a hand on her. Still waters run deep and all that. And just like I would go to bed at night and dream that Peter Beardsley would stay on Tyneside and Newcastle would win the FA Cup I also dreamt that Mandy would one day be my girlfriend.

But I didn't have Mandy. And I was sure I was losing Peter. Worse still, I was sure I was losing my Dad.

In the FA Cup that season my dream made it as far as Round 5. Dad was one of over 10,000 Geordies crammed into White Hart Lane as Newcastle went down 1-0 to a very controversial goal and a Chris Waddle inspired Spurs.

"We were robbed, son," Dad told me. It was a feeling that was ever more familiar to me as the season rolled on.

I was constantly worried and unsettled. I desperately didn't want my Dad to leave. He was my favourite Dad and surely if we were to be happy as a family we needed to keep him. I had this awful feeling in the pit of my stomach that sooner or later he would leave us. I wanted the rumours to end, I wanted clarity to the story and I wanted some form of commitment from both my Mother and from Dad himself.

None was forthcoming and my fears stayed with me.

Just as Beardsley and United seemed to grow a little further apart so too did Dad and us. So too did Dad and *me*.

For starters, he stopped taking me to the matches. I was gutted. I loved going to Newcastle home games. Suddenly and without warning Dad stopped taking me. And he never told me why. That was the kicker. If he had sat me down and explained it maybe I would have understood. I would surely have had a better chance than him just saying nothing.

He took me to Reserve games to see the stiffs whenever his shift permitted and I enjoyed being in the main stand at St James, somewhere we could never have afforded on more orthodox match days. But no matter where we sat, it just wasn't the same. Reserve football and first team football are two entirely different words. Dad later described them as 'like a relationship with love and a relationship without'. Only years later did I begin to understand what he meant.

The happiness that I had enjoyed when I was just 9-years-old and watching Keegan's United stroll the Second Division and win promotion with such emphatic style was sadly over. Summer had passed. Suddenly everything was dark and cold and autumn had set in quite ominously. There was the new school, no more football and even though I wasn't there I still loved Newcastle United and I lived in hope every weekend that Dad might tell me to go get my scarf, grab my jacket and come back to Gallowgate.

I mean, it was not like they were setting the world on fire without me.

But what was I missing…? Well, just like the clouds had formed on my previously sunny horizon, the same had happened with United. After 2 years in the First Division Newcastle were in relegation trouble and I feared that McFaul would take us down.

As much as I liked him and as much as my father loved him he simply wasn't as big or as strong as Arthur Cox had been and I worried that we needed someone like Arthur to save us.

Dad used to come home and tell me all about the games. He never seemed to have a problem in that respect, but he never took me to another game. He was going to home games without me and suddenly started going to away games too. He was spending all his time with his mates and none with his me.

He opened up his own business – I think. I'm not sure how legitimate it was but low and behold he was proud of it, and so was I. I was proud of him. He called it *Slippery When What*, which at the time made as much sense to me as Jack Charlton completely changing our style of play a few years earlier. It was something to do with music, and hence in a desperate attempt to close the gap between Dad & me I began listening to the same stuff he was listening to.

Maybe I should've learned to play the guitar; I should've learned to play them drums.

I did get my hands on the likes of Van Halen, Meatloaf, AC / DC, Bon Jovi and Europe. And I liked it. I learned the names of the band members and the instrument they played and I learned about their songs and I tried to talk to Dad about it but he just wasn't listening anymore. He didn't seem to like me and I didn't know what I'd done wrong.

I felt like my world was caving in. I missed going to the match with my Dad. As good as it may be as an *addition* to your Geordie footballing week Reserve Team football was quite frankly bollocks as a replacement for it.

The famous Blue Star was gone from the Newcastle shirts, and that pissed me off too. I loved those shirts and I loved that Blue Star. The blue star and the black & whites were but one to me. It seemed like every partnership, every team, everything I cherished was going separate ways.

The blue star was the brewery. It was Scottish & Newcastle. Dad loved them too. For one it was beer and for two it was their backing that brought Kevin Keegan to Tyneside those few short years before. I didn't want the brewery to leave us. Everyone it seemed was leaving us and as petty as it might seem I was upset when the Blue Star was replaced by Greenalls. I mean, who the hell are Greenalls anyway…?

United rallied towards the end of the season, and with new signing Paul Goddard in particular Newcastle pulled themselves clear of the relegation trap door they'd been tipped to fall through. Every week Dad would come home, come into my room, wake me up – whether it was Sunday morning or Saturday night he wasn't bothered – and he'd tell me all about the match. And even though he wore a heavy scent of cigarettes and booze I didn't care, I was just happy to be by his side.

As the season wore on and my 12th birthday approached Dad spent more and more time talking about a new player from the youth team who might well go on to be better than Waddle, maybe even better than Beardsley. And better still, he was a Geordie too. Paul Gascoigne had arrived, and for all his sins and all the things that the world has gone on to say about him, Paul Gascoigne was one hell of a player.

Gascoigne – or Gazza – was brilliant. He played the beautiful game the beautiful way. But better than that he played it with an air of fun and pleasure and love that is sadly invisible in so many players. And Gazza played with just a little bit devilment too… although always in a cheeky way, never in a malicious one.

*(Gary Charles disclaimer needed here).

"He's worth the admission money alone" Dad told me after a 2-0 win over Southampton in March 87.

"Will you take me to see him then Dad?" I asked him, my heart thumping like a big fat butterfly in my chest.

"Aye, he's due a reserve game soon. I'll take you then eh?"

I was about to protest, to request a proper game, but Dad just stood up and bounced off the doorframe as he left my room. A few minutes later the voices got louder, the doors got slammed and the argument began. Then the front door slammed and there was silence, with the exception of footsteps thumping up the street towards the pub.

Every time I heard that door slam it was like reading another Chronicle headline about Peter Beardsley and Liverpool's alleged interest. I hate Liverpool. That night I remember the blue-tack that held up my many Newcastle United posters (free in this weeks Pink! God rest its soul) came loose and Peter Beardsley fell from the wall.

I pinned it back up in the morning, but time and again it came loose and threatened to fall from the wall. To me, a good old superstitious football supporter, there seemed something ominous in that.

A few short months later and with United safe in 17th place the Beardsley poster came down again, this time ripped from the wall with my own two hands. It followed The Evening Chronicle into the bin, the one with the photo of Beardsley and Dalglish at an Anfield press conference.

6. Kenny Wharton Is Not From Argentina

By time the 1987 / 88 season got under way U2 still hadn't found what they were looking for, Michael Jackson was bad and sadly Newcastle fell into both categories quite nicely. Beardsley had buggered off to Anfield and as pissed as I was that he had I couldn't really blame him.

You see, leaving home because you're just not happy, nor can see yourself finding that happiness is a big and painful decision. Peter's professionalism and ambition wasn't matched by Newcastle's, and although he loved us (and lets face it he might have been flattered and all that but he couldn't have *loved* Liverpool) he got a better offer and he left us.

Beardsley's replacement was a bit of a surprise. We replaced the kid from Tyneside with a boy from Brazil. And Tyneside went just a little bit nuts in the process. Mirandinha arrived from Palmeiras and he took a bit of getting used to. Mind you, for all his critics, and for the fact he never really made it on Tyneside, he did bring with him some incredible moments. He swore in English – Gazza taught him most of his swear words and passed them off as niceties, including one amazing moment in Wimpy where he left two teenage autograph hunters absolutely gob-smacked – he allegedly drank vodka at half time and the guy shot from pretty much everywhere. One word Gascoigne didn't teach him was 'pass'. Basically he was crazy.

He was the first Brazilian ever to play in the Football League. I was there at Carrow Road when he made his debut and I was there at Man United when he scored his first goals in a black & white shirt. It was one of the rare occasions where we didn't go to Old Trafford and get a pasting. And Mirandinha (*his name is Mirandinha, he's not from Argentina, he's from Brazil, he's fucking brill...*) smacked in a first half double. It ended 2-2. He wasn't brill; he was Okay; but since when have terrace chants had to be factually correct?

Example: *'And it's Oxford United, Oxford United FC. They're by far the greatest team, the world has ever seen...'*. Your witness.

We travelled on one of three coaches from Slippery When What and by that time the money was starting to rake itself in. That was the time I tried to share it with Sheila. She wasn't interested.

Six days after that trip to Old Trafford my world was turned upside down. It was LagerFriday. I woke early, I hadn't slept much anyway, and I left for work without waking Sheila. I put on my big thick donkey jacket and I made myself a cuppa and some toast. It was dark, around 06:50 in the morning and a September morning at that. I left the house via the front door and stepped straight on to our street. It was a muggy, misty Tyneside morning. There was dew in the bluey-grey Wallsend air. It wasn't raining, but it was wet.

I folded my collar up and munched the last of my toast as I walked toward the warm glow of MacMilligan's Newsagents. The light shone through the large square windows either side of the door that was situated right on the corner. As I approached, a man with a small dog on a leash was leaving, untying the leash from the corner fencing as he did so. I stepped to the side and let him out first. Then I stepped inside and shivered my shoulders as I made towards the counter.

"Cold out?" she asked.

And I just looked at her, stunned. She was gorgeous. My tongue tied, my mind went blank, my speech totally deserted me and I found myself as lost as Kevin Scott was when Martin Thomas yelled *'Clear it'*.

"Cold out?" she smiled with big brown eyes and a smile that could make a man need a calendar to have even a clue as to what time it was.

"Yeah, yeah," I said stuttering. "Sorry, was in a world of my own!" I explained.

"Not quite awake yet?" she asked.

"No, no, been up a while. I work at the Shipyard. Clock in anytime from 7am" I told her, not knowing what to say to be honest.

I'd turned 32-years old just weeks before but suddenly in the blink of an eye, the beat of a heart, I was just a little boy again. I'd never *really* been in love before and what was happening to me that morning was new to me, whatever it was.

"So what can I get you?" she asked me warmly.

I didn't have a clue. What did I normally buy? What day was it?

The fog cleared in my mind a little like that drifting from the Tyne up to our little Wallsend streets and Wallsend newsagents, where grown men of 32-years-old could walk in to buy cigarettes (yes, damn it, that's what I wanted, cigarettes!) and end up losing their hearts.

"Eh... 20 Marlborough Lights please... and a Fruit & Nut."

She served me, I smiled, she gave me my change, I looked gormless, Tom turned up, and we left.

"Who's that Tom?" I asked him.

"Aye," he says, "She's the new lass they've hired now that they've got their second shop down in Easington I think. One of the them [Mr or Mrs MacMilligan] will be based down that way and the new lass will cover here. She seems nice, a drop of canny eh…"

"Yeah," I said, already well past such a casual thought.

Rachel was absolutely gorgeous in my eyes. She was girl next door gorgeous. She was pretty, she was sweet, she was nice and she was warm and approachable. And I was smitten. In fairness that was quite a lot to get from one 2-minute meeting but you get where I'm coming from.

Sometimes in our lives we meet someone who we just click with; someone who just steals our heart in a heartbeat and sometimes that happens right out of the blue. Sometimes in life, just like in football, the most amazing things are borne out of something innocuous.

Sometimes in our life there's just chemistry. I'm an old romantic. I like the thought that there's someone out there for everyone. I like to think that some people are destined to be together. I'm not sure how accurate that thinking may be, but the sentiment has always kept my heart a little warmer than my marriage ever did. There's a certain beauty, a certain feeling, like pressing on a bruise, that wraps itself around you in the time between falling for someone and them finding out how you feel.

It's the going home at night and dreaming about them, waking up in the morning and thinking about them, and hoping all day to run into them. They're the backdrop to everything else that's going on in your life.

It's not a sexual thing. It's not wanting to get someone into bed or anything like that. It's an emotional thing. It's about just wanting to be with someone, to share their company, their time. It's what kept us watching Friends for almost 10 years.

No matter which roads we walk in life, sooner or later we all fall in love. When Rachel (my Rachel, not Jennifer Aniston) walked into my life – or I walked into her shop – it happened to me.

To describe her physically she was about 5'6 tall, very pretty, collar length brunette meets blond hair and with the most amazing brown eyes I ever did see. She was a bonny lass and her smile warmed my day like walking into that shop from the murkiness of a midwinter street. But to describe her physically would be doing her an injustice. Her looks were just part of who she was; who I really fell in love with was the girl she was behind those beautiful eyes.

And day after day I couldn't wait to see those beautiful eyes and get to know the girl behind them better.

I started popping into MacMilligan's Newsagents every morning, not just LagerFriday. I started popping into MacMilligan's Newsagents every night too, just as soon as the shipyard gates had closed behind me and I began my short walk home. It was Autumn, and you can say all you like about foreign lands and beauty spots but I'll tell you this and I'll tell you this for free: Tyneside is beautiful.

And like true beauty, it's beautiful all year 'round.

Wallsend, this hearty and established River Tyne spin off Town, steeped in industry and elbow grease, in history and in tradition is as beautiful in summer as she is in winter. When the sun rises and the terraced houses of a working man's Town are blessed with the same summer sun that tans the English on the coasts of Spain Wallsend looks beautiful to me. She looks just as beautiful when the frost bites and the snow falls and every cobblestone and every chimney is coated like a Christmas card.

When the leaves fall from the trees and California Dreaming echoes through every Tyneside street and every local park I still love this place. And when Spring comes around, the way that the flowers start to bloom and the skies once more turn blue is a wonderful contradiction to the steel and the iron, the pit and the shipyard.

Real beauty is timeless and effortless.

To me, Rachel was exactly the same.

Autumn was gathering pace and the nights were cutting in. Winter was but a few stops away on the calendar. The mornings were wet even when it hadn't rained.

It was the time of year to wrap up warm in a morning, and maybe even carry a bacon sandwich or a slice of warm buttered toast on the short journey to work.

It was autumn outside but it felt like spring in my heart. Every morning I would wake up excited and nervous and full of butterflies. I'd get up, get a bath and then get dressed in the sanctity of our spare room. My wife lay sleeping in our marital bed. Our marriage lay dying beside her. But for the first time since the days of Joe Harvey and Malcolm Macdonald my heart was alive. For the first time since the days of the old Leazes End and the newly constructed East Stand my heart was pumping not only blood but optimism around my veins. For the first time since I learned that life was inside my girlfriend I felt life inside of *me*.

And there was one reason and one reason alone for that change in feeling. It wasn't attributed to Kenny Wharton *'his name is Kenny Wharton, he's not from Argentina, he's from Cowgate, he's fucking great'*, it wasn't attributed to Johny Anderson or Davie Mac and it wasn't attributed to the all drinking, all swearing, all shooting from all angles Brazilian either. It was all because of Rachel.

I would leave my room, sneak down to the kitchen, peaking in on the bairn and watching him sleep for just a minute. I'd rustle up a bacon butty or tea & toast and I'd dress up warm in my big donkey jacket and off I'd go, with a spring in my step, to MacMilligan's Newsagents.

I'd step out on to the street at the foot of our front door and I'd turn left towards the shipyards. At the bottom the Tyne ran grey and proud. Lights were coming on in living rooms all along our street and some of the houses were too spawning men just like me on their way to work. I'd meet friends amongst my neighbours, colleagues amongst my friends and we'd all meander a few hundred yards down the street to our place of work.

But the brightest light of them all was the one from the newsagents, and the girl behind the counter. Not to sound too REO Speedwagon but she really was a candle in the window on a cold dark winter's night. Or a cold murky autumn morning if you want the cap to fit.

I began going in earlier too, to miss the crowd, and to talk to her a while. Those 5 or 10 minutes in her company in a morning got me through 7 or 8 hours of hard graft… and 11 or 12 hours of a loveless marriage.

One morning, October '87, I popped in nice and early for one of our little chats. I had a bacon butty with me. As soon as Rachel spoke I promptly got all nervous trying to buy a 'paper and dropped my butty. Luckily my Journal broke its fall, and although the back page was no longer legible my bacon sarny was still in tact.

Rachel laughed, heartily. I blushed like a kid at a school disco asking a girl to dance. Maybe a girl he's had a crush on for years.

She insisted I take a free Journal – a clean one – and she rested her hand on mine as she did so. We laughed together but it was one of those moments, you know, where both hearts are talking to each other and your eyes are just spectators in the emotion. I held her gaze, she held my hand, and something deep inside went off like a Catherine wheel or a Leazes End roar.

For all my life – all 32 years of it – I was falling in love for the very first time.

7. *School Boy Errors*

Dad's an idiot. Firstly, he didn't blame Peter Beardsley for leaving us; I did. He tried to explain how it was the club's fault, and that something to do with a lack of ambition, a lack of professionalism and the club being a *selling club* had inspired Beardsley to better himself. I just called him a Judas and went back to playing my Wham cassette. Choose Life…? How about Choose loyalty you little…

Secondly, he'd stopped taking me to matches and despite my best and subtle hints (standing there on a Saturday morning in my jacket and scarf) he maintained his new match day ritual of going to St James with his mates… and coming back drunk.

And thirdly was the drink. Dad was drinking a lot. I rarely got to see him at weekends and when I did it was even more rare that he'd be sober. From Friday night he'd be in the club, he'd roll in drunk long after my bedtime, and then Saturday he'd either be at St James Park or travelling the length and breadth of the country to watch the lads. And when he did get back he'd be plastered. There were times he'd even roll in singing Jingle Bells and it was only autumn!

By then the drinking had become a sticking point. It seemed to coincide with an increase in arguments with my Mam. I don't know who was right and who was wrong but it's difficult to side with the one who was drunk and shouting and bawling at the top of his voice. So, invariably, my allegiance was to my Mam.

He started wearing a Brazil shirt, and that baffled me somewhat. I got the Mirandinha thing, but I failed to see the significance. And to cap matters off he had his car stolen. And he didn't know how.

He sold his old car, the N-reg. Escort and bought a spanking new Ford Capri. It was bright white, like Minder's, but more modern. It was a 2.8 Ghia. It was lovely. He looked like something from The Professionals.

In order to look after it he rented a garage.

Behind our house was a set of 'terraced' garages, sloping down from top to bottom in line with the street. There are about 40 houses in our street and only eight garages. To get one of the garages you have to have your name on the list, and when one becomes available you get it as a matter of first come first served. Dad had been on the list 2-years and finally got the opportunity when three of the families in our street moved out.

It came at a time when money was starting to come in thick & fast courtesy of *Slippery When What* so as well as taking on the new garage Dad decided to put a new car in it. He had the garage two weeks before he got the Capri and he refused steadfast to put the old car in its new home. He traded the Escort and collected the new Capri on Saturday December 12th 1987, just hours before Newcastle played (and drew 1-1) with Portsmouth at Gallowgate. He came home from the match, got a bath, jumped in the Capri and went back off to the club. He got drunk and drove home, as he'd been doing for months. He'd dented the Escort dozens of times and I figured – and Mam hoped – that the Capri would mark the end of the drink driving.

In fairness he only ever did it once with the Capri.

It was stolen the same night.

He claimed on the insurance for it, and they paid up, but his story was sketchy largely because he was pissed when he last had it.

He'd driven home from the club any time between 11.30 and midnight depending on how late the lads were allowed to keep supping. Lock-ins were common enough in those '80's days of drink and disco and domino dancing at the Wallsend socials.

His version was that he'd driven home from the club, put the car in the garage, and then walked the short distance around the corner to home. The next day he went to get the car and it wasn't there. He opened up his garage, and nothing. Just thin air and a handful of tools (and my old BMX) hanging from the wall. The Capri was nowhere to be seen.

"At least they didn't take my bike eh Dad?" I reassured him.

He didn't say anything but I suspect that the good old slap around the ear wasn't too far away.

By New Year the car hadn't *turned* up and hence the insurance *paid* up, not knowing Dad was hammered when he drove home. And contrary to what he says I know he went back to the club to check that he hadn't indeed walked home and left the damn thing there. He hadn't, and it wasn't.

The Policeman told us it was likely to be the victim of a region wide scam on stolen cars that was rife at that time. Local villain David Rutherford was suspected but the police couldn't quite nail him and they never found Dad's new Capri. The Policeman was called PC Goddard, which I thought was quite funny because Newcastle's striker and number 9 was Paul Goddard. I thought it was a good omen. But while PC John Goddard didn't come up with the goods, Centre forward Paul certainly did.

1988 started well. The Lads won 2-0 at Nottingham Forest on New Years Day and then dumped Crystal Palace out of the FA Cup when Gazza scored a belter from about 40-yards. His – and

United's form – carried over to the next game, a 2-0 win over Spurs at St James' where Gazza scored twice. Dad was suitably impressed. So too were Spurs.

And in what I look back on as the most pivotal point of my whole life a chain of events came into place that dictated the outcome of my entire childhood.

For starters, Gascoigne's display in that win over Spurs prompted the Londoners to take note. A few months later and Gascoigne would join Waddle at White Hart Lane, and his poster would join Waddle and Beardsley's in my rubbish bin.

Then came the Swindon game in the 4th Round of the FA Cup. We won 5-0. But incredibly although that game went on to see United go no further than the Fifth Round (and defeat to eventual winners Wimbledon) it would go on to see Sunderland promoted… and at our expense. The game sparked a betting scandal involving the Swindon hierarchy and the pending investigation lead to an illegal payments scandal. The eventual outcome was to impact right back where it started, on Tyneside, 2 years down the touchline.

But the Swindon game did more than that. You see, it wasn't just half of the Swindon Town Board and Management (allegedly, allegedly) that were betting on it; my Dad did too. Every week *Slippery When What* used to run a correct score competition. Dad went for 5-0 and won it. First prize was two tickets for the Milburn Stand and a pre-match meal and all that.

Dad offered the spare ticket to my Mam and suggested they both go to the next game and make a bit of an occasion of it. I sat in the living room listening to the conversation taking place in the kitchen.

"So do you fancy it Sheil', we can make a day of it, free food, free drink, nice seats, it'll be lovely!"

- *Damn it, that should have been my ticket…*

- "The only Wimbledon I want to see is the tennis, thank you" Mam told him bluntly.

- *Nice one Mam, looks like I'm going after all…*

- "Come on love, we never do things together any more. It'll be good for *us*."

- *Stand your ground Ma' stand your ground…*

"I'm not going. I don't want to. I don't even like football."

"It's not about football, it's about you & me spending some time together. It's a meal and everything. The football's barely half of it, tops,"

"It's like talking to the bairn! I don't want to go, Okay?"

"So what am I meant to do with the extra ticket?"

- *At that point I wandered casually into the kitchen…*

- "Seen the Cup draw Dad?" I asked him.

- "Not now Terry, not now…" he said as he stormed out.

- I know he wasn't mad at me, he was mad at her, but like any kid in a breaking marriage I got caught in the crossfire.

It's like being in no mans land; both sides are shooting at each other and invariably while they duck down in the trenches and seem to avoid getting hit the kid in the middle almost always gets gunned down.

In hindsight the repercussions were comical.

Dad didn't give me the spare ticket, despite me spending two solid weeks hinting for it. I washed his new car – an 'X' Reg. Ford Cortina 1.6 – and I even took my BMX out of Dad's (then empty) garage and went looking for his Capri. I never found it, but I was closer than I realised.

And I was a damn sight closer than PC John Goddard ever got to finding it…

The ticket eventually went to some woman from the Newsagents down the street. It didn't seem so bad at the time. I was a bit pissed about it, but Rachel, the shop assistant, must have felt quite guilty about it because soon after Dad took her to the match I started getting 20p mix ups for 10p and a free Fruit & Nut whenever I was in the shop alone.

To confound matters, I then made one simple mistake, one that many of us would have made in the name of shyness, and it cost me more than I could ever imagine.

When the big Wimbledon FA Cup clash came around I desperately wanted to go. I was pissed that Dad was taking someone else other than me and I got the notion into my head to go myself. I'd been talking big about it for ages, showing off, and Mandy, the best friend I ever did have in the world, was the only one to support me. For weeks I'd been bragging on the walk to school that we should go to the match, all of us, the gang together. I said we should bunk off school and go get tickets.

In the end, none of the others took me up on it, but Mandy said she would. And as much as I wanted to, as much as I still wanted to be with her, I bottled it. I was scared, I was shy, I was nervous and I bottled it. I was worried I'd have to act upon my feelings and I wasn't ready for that. I'd been living with the security of the safety of the dream, and stepping up to make your dreams come true means you run the risk of your dreams falling short. For years I had lived by the motto *what if I did ask her out and she said 'no'*. Yeah, she might have said yes, and I'd have loved that. But she might have said no and the dream would be over. Safer, I thought, to say nothing and keep on living in hope.

Besides, maybe one-day fate would deal the cards straight to my ever-willing hand and I'd win without trying. To be honest that's a pretty piss-poor way to live your life. Sadly, I was too young to realise that back then. Actually, scratch that, because I *did* realise that, I just lacked the courage to change it.

Destiny by and large doesn't offer us things on a silver plate; it offers us opportunities. It is up to us to grab those opportunities.

Back then I was too shy, too weak and not brave enough to do that. And it cost me.

Mandy put me on the spot and asked me if I wanted to go. She'd bunk off school with me and we'd go get tickets. It was everything I'd wanted. But – despite the fact we were great friends and I was as close to her as anyone – I was acting all weird because of these feelings. She gave me a funny look, a smile that I still treasure, and the opportunity passed me by.

It was Okay, I thought, there'd be more opportunities along the way. That's a very dangerous doctrine to live by. And it's one that ultimately broke my heart.

It's a little bit like a striker too scared to shoot in case he misses. He wants either a tap in, or he passes the ball even though he's in a good position and hopes someone else has the courage to do what he hasn't. In my case someone else did.

There was a kid called Grant in our year at school. I'd never liked him since I met him when we went to senior school. For one he was a Man United supporter and that really pissed me off. He wasn't even from Manchester! He liked them because they were good supposedly. I'd seen him plenty of times with a Liverpool shirt on too, I can tell you. Bastard. And he'd always like Mandy, I could tell. I knew all the telltale signs of a boy with a crush; I saw them every morning when I looked in the mirror and put on my school tie.

But deep down inside I knew that part of the reason I hated him was because he was the me I wished I could be. Well, not the glory hunting Man United git but the confident, go-get-it part.

Grant did go get it too. He asked Mandy out the day after that Wimbledon game and she said yes. How could she? She was supposed to be mine. I just never got round to telling her that. That easily, Mandy was gone.

The poster I had of Mandy – in my heart, not on my wall – stayed there regardless, but she had another team now and I had another space where once my hopes and dreams had been. Sadly, it made me bitter. Just like I wanted Beardsley & Liverpool and Waddle & Spurs to lose, I wanted Mandy & Grant to break up. I wanted to be with her, and I rued sitting *waiting* for the right moment, when I should have been *making* the right moment.

All I had to do, on any of the many times we hung out together, was do my best Tiffany, tell her I think we're alone now, and when there didn't seem to be anyone else around, ask her out. All I had to do was tell her that she sent me clear to the moon, that I thought she was fantastic and that I'd love to be her boyfriend and then walk away. So what if she said no. So what if the other kids in the street or at school took the piss. So what. At least she would have known. Then if she felt the same maybe something would have happened.

But instead the fear of my dreams not coming true lead me to hiding behind the hope that one day – effortlessly – they magically would.

It was a top-flight mistake, a schoolboy error and I got punished for it the same way the Norman Whiteside's, Clive Allen's and Ian Rush's of this world were punishing the likes of Peter Jackson, Glenn Roeder and Kenny Wharton. It was the same way Terry Gibson and John Fashanu had punished us in the FA Cup. And the result was the same: broken dreams and broken hearts.

The ultimate twist came when Wimbledon went on to beat Liverpool (and Peter Beardsley) in the FA Cup Final. The ultimate kick in the knackers came when Grant moved away (fantastic!) three months later. Unfortunately he kept going out with Mandy (thank you very much Tyne Wear Metro) and unfortunately his new estate had remarkably cheap house prices (thank you very much Wimpy Homes).

By time the 1987 / 88 season had closed – with a trophyless Newcastle in a respectable 8th place – Mandy and her parents were off to Walkergate and a swanky new home. They moved into the same estate that Grant and his family had some weeks earlier.

That summer Paul Gascoigne, Spotty-McDonald and Paul Goddard all departed, and Dave Beasant, Andy Thorn, John Hendrie and John Robertson arrived. I missed Mandy very much, and as the summer transfers poignantly highlighted, there are some people you just don't replace.

8. *Appetite For Departure*

The Friday after I dropped my bacon sandwich in MacMilligan's Newsagents Rachel surprised me by making me one.

"There's a kitchen in the back," she told me. "I felt a bit sorry for you when you dropped your butty last week; and I felt even sorrier for laughing!" she added.

"Thanks Rach'" I told her.

"Just the way you like it too; crispy bacon with brown sauce."

The last time Sheila made me a bacon sarny she used red-sauce. I don't like red sauce.

The chemistry was there between Rachel and I from the off. I liked talking to her. It was nice to have someone ask me about my day, and it was nice to ask about hers and get an answer. *'So how are you'* might seem like a simple enough question, or *'How was your day'* but when it ain't been asked (sincerely at least) in a dog's age it's remarkably nice to hear it again.

87 / 88 was a bit of a strange time. Guns N' Roses rocketed to popularity with Appetite For Destruction and while St James Park was anything but Paradise City, I thought about Rachel every time I heard Sweet Child O' Mine.

I bought a swanky new Ford Capri – but it was stolen straight away and I never got it back. Newcastle started badly, teased us with the FA Cup, and then rallied – albeit trophy-less – to a respectable 8th place. It was our highest in eleven years since Richard Dinnis led us into the UEFA Cup with Gordon Lee's starless wonders.

The 87 / 88 team did have stars, including a very bright one born and raised right here on Tyneside: Dunston's Paul Gascoigne.

Last time United were that successful the most famous Gascoigne was either in The Gentle Touch or hosting University Challenge. This Gascoigne – Gazza – was anything but gentle. And in truth he was anything but university. But he had balls... as large as Vinny Jones' hands... and he was the maestro behind United's resurgence up the table.

But by the end of the season Gascoigne would be on his way. And I wouldn't be too far behind.

It started with the car. Sheila disapproved of me buying the Capri. I was only going to get a cheap 1.6 laser but once I realised she was pissed at the idea I thought 'bollocks to her' and I went and bought an even faster, more expensive one.

Then the bugger got nicked and Sheila revelled in the luxuries of 'I told you so'. Next time I got a Ford Cortina, because it was all I could afford. If I could have rallied the cash to get an Opel Manta I would have. Sadly, I was stretched to the limit to get the Cortina and Sheila took my step-down in motor as a sign of her victory.

Thanks to Don Johnson I got caught up in the 5 0'clock shadow fad – although supporting Newcastle it was more like a 4:45 shadow – and the boys and me went to the club and the disco dressed like the lads from Miami Vice. I had the pastel suit, the white shoes, the vest top, the lot. Sheila just mocked me – justifiably so in hindsight – but that just pissed me off further.

By this time my relationship with Sheila was equivalent to negotiations between United & Gazza. I wanted to stay, but I wanted to be happy, and I wanted a better deal. I wanted some sign of commitment and ambition from her, just as Gazza did United. But none was forthcoming on either front and soon a split became inevitable.

Of course, by then I knew exactly who I wanted to be with… Rachel.

In hindsight I didn't leave Sheila for Rachel, although on the surface that was how it looked. In my experience, however, rarely is infidelity the reason for a marital split. More commonly infidelity is the result of marital unhappiness. That unhappiness often leads to infidelity. And in the end the infidelity often carries the can for the break up, where in most cases it was simply the final straw.

There's a difference between cause and symptom.

For me, infidelity is rarely the reason a marriage fails; more often the result of a failed marriage.

And I certainly didn't turn to Rachel when Sheila and I went through a hard time. Sadly, I turned to drink.

There's an inherent danger in drink. Nobody offered me the opportunity to become an alcoholic; if they had I would have read the small print and seen that it would cost me my health, my money, my family, my friends, hell even myself, and I would have declined. But nobody did; all they offered me was a drink. And another one. And another one…

The crux of the matter wasn't that I loved the taste of the lager or whiskey or vodka I was swilling around my mouth. It wasn't that I loved waking up in the morning feeling like shit with a head that sounded like the away end when Newcastle conceded at Gallowgate. It wasn't checking my wallet and seeing I was broke and it wasn't having Jack Daniels on speed dial.

No, the crux of the matter was simple: I had problems in my life and I wasn't ready to deal with them. So I hid behind drink. And ultimately that only made all of my problems worse.

And then one night something happened to change everything.

The summer of 1988 had been a hard one; it had been one of broken promises. I pleaded with Sheila to come on holiday: me, her and the bairn. She promised she would, and then after stringing me along all summer long she bailed. People can say all they like about the highs and lows of life but there's something about a broken promise that really does feel like a football blasted straight against your nuts. Perhaps part of it is because the promise itself is like the green light to build your hopes up. Then when the promise is broken your hopes tumble from a greater height. Or maybe it's the conflict you feel inside when you doubt that the promise will be honoured. You want to believe it, you're told you're safe to believe it, but still you try and quell your hopes so you don't get too hurt should it all go tits up.

For me the summer of 1988 was a summer full of broken promises.

It started with the holiday that never was.

It ended with me packing my bags and following Paul Gascoigne's example and leaving my home.

I think the holiday was the straw that broke the camel's back. Pat Benatar said that love was a battlefield. Well, soldiers don't always fall where they're shot. Sometimes they're stumble on a few more steps after the mortal wound had been delivered. Just like players don't always fall where they're tripped. Sometimes they make a few more yards towards goal before they tumble.

The holiday that never was became the foul I couldn't ride, the trip that brought me down, the clip on the matrimonial ankles that brought me to the turf.

From that point on I resigned myself to the fall. I kept going a few more yards but that was more down to my momentum than any desire to stay on my feet.

That summer saw the departure of not only Gascoigne but also Spotty McDonald and Paul Goddard too. But in untypical Newcastle United style they actually invested the money they received back in the team. And in so many ways I feel heartly sorry for Willie McFaul because they players he brought in seemed pretty decent buys.

McFaul employed the *if you can't beat them join them* policy to the best of his ability and – having struggled badly against Wimbledon in both Cup competitions as well as the two First Division games – he signed Cup Final hero and penalty saving goalkeeper Dave Beasant. It doesn't matter how old you are reading this; the truth is for as long as you've been around we've probably had a crap defence. McFaul, to his credit, then went out and bought Beasant's Plough Lane colleague Centre-Half Andy Thorn to shore up that particular shortcoming once and for all.

By time Hearts free-scoring striker John Robertson and exciting winger John Hendrie had joined from Bradford Newcastle looked all set for a decent year, despite Gascoigne's departure.

And along with *'till death do us part* another major verbal gaff on my behalf was sitting with the lads on the Coach on the way to Goodison Park for the opening day exchanges of the 88 / 89 season with Everton and confidently stating *Well at least we won't get relegated this year.*

Ahh bollocks.

We arrived at Goodison Park in fine spirits. We drank – which was nothing new to me – and we poured buoyantly into the away end. And within 34 seconds we were 1-0 down. From there we went on to get pummelled. I remember thinking to myself, as Everton went in 2-0 up at the interval, that the promise the summer had shown had just been broken in the finest of style. It wasn't until May 3rd, standing on the Gallowgate End watching 19th place Newcastle lose to 20th place West Ham – a defeat which condemned Newcastle's fate and saw the club relegated from the top division for the 4th and to date final time – that I realised the extent of that broken promise.

I came home from Goodison drunk. I needed the season video and the 'highlights' to recall anything other than Dave Beasant digging the ball out of the net with his second touch in the United Goalie's jersey.

The drink, the defeat, the broken promise and the unhappiness all spilled out in a sorry episode. Sheila and I had a blaring row. It was a humdinger. And worse still, the bairn was there to see it all. It must have woken him up, and he came downstairs to see for himself a sight that I will always regret putting in front of his tender eyes.

But there's some things in life you just can't take back, no matter how much you wish that wasn't so.

I was like a player who had been given the red card but then just loses it. You know you're only making things worse, but it doesn't stop you. The red mist had descended and I was really going to Town. That was, fortunately, until Tom came to the door because of the noise. He took me outside and sat me on the wall of our little terraced house as the August sun set and the days broken promises set with it.

I made to go to the pub and he stopped me.

"Do you think that's wise kidda?" he asked me.

I just mouthed some drunken obscenities in his general direction.

"Come on, we're going to mine" he said, leading me across the street and 3 doors down.

A day later I left his settee and went home. A week later we were at St James for the first home game of the season. I once read in a book that there's no such thing as irony, it's just that fate has a sense of humour. That was very much the case as Newcastle entertained Spurs… and Gazza made his Tottenham debut.

I think seeing Gascoigne running around in Tottenham yellow, trying to beat his beloved Newcastle, further increased the sense of disorientation I was feeling. It was surreal. We sat in The George & Dragon after the game – a 2-2 draw with United chucking away 2 vital points – and we talked.

Tom looked at me with sincerity. "Look, it's none of my business," he said turning on his charm, "but imagine *you* were Newcastle United, yeah? The team is your life, and you're in charge of it, you're the Manager of your own life, Okay?"

"Okay," I said, making a short-list of new Centre-halves.

"Are you making the right decisions, are you Managing the club right? No, you're not are you? Or are you ducking decisions you know you need to make and hoping the booze is going to keep the wolves from the door?"

"And just like this lot," he said casting eyes over his Spurs match programme, "If you don't sort it out fast you're going to go down."

I learned my lesson there and then, before it was too late. Sadly Newcastle United didn't.

9. *Cottee, Raleigh Burners, Anfield and Dad*

August 1988 was a bit of bastard by all accounts. Taylor Dayne wanted you to tell it to her heart, Michael Jackson was with Dirty Diana and the Communards never could say goodbye. Sadly, Neil McDonald, Paul Goddard, Paul Gascoigne and my father could.

I mean at the time I didn't really know that. I knew Goddard had found Derby County (and Arthur Cox) and I knew that Paul Gascoigne had found Spurs (and Chris Waddle). Of course I knew that Neil McDonald had found Everton; we were playing them first game of the season, but I had no idea that Dad had found this Rachel woman.

It was a strange time, the 88 / 89 season. Liverpool had Sesame Street's Bert & Ernie up front, Brian Clough was punching pitch-invaders at the City Ground and if you didn't drink milk you'd only be good enough to play for Accrington Stanley.

There's things in life that you learn as you grow up; things that you discover as you become an adult that sometimes come as a shock to the once all-believing, all-innocent child. For example, the Toothfairy doesn't exist, neither, sadly, does Santa Claus. Your favourite players kiss the badge and the shirt one week and then sign for another club the next. Your favourite Dad, your only

Dad, can suddenly pack his bags and up and leave and Berlinda Carlisle isn't actually from Carlisle even though Hebburn is indeed a place on earth.

And of course, you can spend millions on new players and somehow, somehow, you're still shit.

For reasons I can only attribute to childhood innocence I genuinely thought we'd do all right that season, 88 / 89. We got relegated. And even after all these years I never cease to amaze myself how wrong I can get my predictions. From that first occasion in August 1988 when I confidently predicted a top 5 finish I have gone on to systematically prove that I really do know fuck all about football.

Newcastle and their four expensive summer signings opened up at Goodison Park against Everton. Dad went to the match. I took my Raleigh Burner from his garage and rode around the streets all morning with Dave & Adam. We were so excited. Like every kid in Wallsend we were Newcastle fans. But I was the pioneer; I'd been to the match. Mind you, not for a while.

We bought the Journal and we sat on the wall at the bottom of our street and read it. We bought The Chronicle and we sat on the wall outside MacMilligan's Newsagents and we read every Newcastle related article. Actually, that's technically not true. I went in to buy The Chronicle and I got it for free, as well as a Fruit & Nut and a nice smile from Rachel, the girl behind the counter.

"Maybe she fancies you?" Adam said.

"Maybe..." I said. It's funny in hindsight.

I do have my father's eyes they tell me.

We took Adam's sisters ghetto-blaster, ditched the compilation tape that she'd recorded from Sunday's Charts and we hung around old Hitler's house at the bottom of the street pulling wheelie's and listening to Graham Courtney or whoever reading out the teams.

I was gripped with adrenalin and excitement. Finally Newcastle had spent big. Finally Newcastle were a decent side. Finally Newcastle were about to do well. The build up to kick-off seemed to last an eternity. Finally it arrived… and suddenly Newcastle were 1-0 down.

Tony Cottee – on his Everton debut – scored after 34 seconds. I mean for the love of all that is black & white 34 bloody seconds! After all the summer waiting, including the thrill you get when the fixtures come out right up to the team news appearing on Ceefax and Teletext on the Friday. After all of that built up and hope and expectation and excitement, there we were, pulled smack back down to earth in just 34 seconds. Eventually the score would roll up at 4-0. 4 bloody 0! Cottee, bless him, went on to get a hat-trick. Newcastle by all accounts were lucky to get nil.

I'm not sure why but I wasn't too despondent. For some reason I thought it was a setback, a fly in the ointment, a bad start to a good season. I never realised it was the sign of things to come; I never realised it was the beginning of the end.

It was a bit like the row Mam & Dad had when Dad finally got back – drunk – from Goodison a few hours later. I was tucked up in bed, and given that it was the summer school holidays it must have been around 10.30 at night. I remember the sky out of my bedroom window was a wild array of orange's and blues, purple's and red's. The flame red sun was setting on Tyneside and Geordies all over were reeling at the opening day defeat. I was replaying the commentary in my mind and wishing things had been different. Newcastle's results still had the capacity to ruin my whole weekend.

I was wide-awake when Dad arrived home. His voice was loud to say the least but putting alcohol passed my fathers lips was like putting a loud-speaker in front of them. His deep hassy voice carried and echoed downstairs and even though most of the words weren't evident the sentiment most certainly was.

It was a bad argument, I can tell you that. It was one of the ones that hurt my ears. I pulled the covers over my head – with my NUFC duvet cover of course – but the quilt offered about as much protection as the back four had earlier that day.

Dad's angry words and my mothers sharp piercing retorts cut through them like Cottee himself had.

Then someone else joined the affray and my curiosity led me downstairs. I was 14-years-old the day I saw a side to my father that I had never seen before, and it was a side I greatly didn't like. For the first time in my life I didn't respect him. I probably still feared him, but he didn't look like my Dad; he looked like a drunk. He looked angry and bitter and silly and embarrassing. I think a part of the boy in me died looking at my Dad in such a light, and the early steps of the man I would become was born.

When Tom – one of our neighbours – took Dad away I was happy that he'd left. Tom just ruffled my hair and told me it was going to be Okay. He mentioned the result and said I should probably go back to bed. I did as he told me. That was because I respected him. For the first time in my life I had been in a room with someone I respected more than I did my own father.

It's a strange sensation that one.

For the first time in my life I looked down at him. For the first time in my life I felt I was better than him. I wouldn't have let myself get into that state. Yeah, and it's easy to think like that when you're fourteen years old.

I'm not sure why but I wasn't too despondent. For some reason I thought it was a setback, a fly in the ointment, a bad episode to a good home-life. I never realised it was the sign of things to come; I never realised it was the beginning of the end.

The turbulent home life went hand in hand with Newcastle's results. And just like 1 win, 2 draws and 3 defeats spelled the end for McFaul, the 6 weeks of constant feuding between Mam & Dad spelled the end of their marriage.

Newcastle crashed week after week, including a shock 3-0 first leg Littlewoods Cup defeat away to then Third Division Sheffield United. The next game – and the one that we expected a complete hammering in – was the trip to Anfield. But just as life throws up the most unexpected, so too does football. Newcastle won, somehow, 2-1.

All hope was reborn!

If we could beat a Liverpool side – who were then still at their 80's prime – at Anfield we could beat anybody anywhere! Mirandinha's penalty at The Kop will live long in my memory and my heart alike, not least of all because Peter Beardsley was in the Red's side that memorable October afternoon.

But my personal joy was short lived. Dad returned from Merseyside a lot sooner than he had the last time. And this time he was sober. He & Mam had been bickering all week because Mam had some family do to attend and she wanted Dad by her side. He wanted to go to Anfield. A compromise was reached whereby he'd be back by 8pm to meet her and go to the club – somewhere in Tynemouth – that the do was held at.

He arrived at about 5 past eight at home. Mam had gone without him. He dashed in and got a bath and re-dressed. He sat me down on the sofa and told me a story about the game, about how we bravely fought back from 1-0 down to win 2-1. He told me that he was proud, and that I should be proud too. And he told me that sometimes people are stronger than we realise. He told me that sometimes people underestimate themselves. And he told me that sometimes when you overcome fear you're capable of greater feats than even you yourself believed.

That night – inspired by Willie McFaul and the boys – Dad did the bravest thing of his life: he left my Mam.

10. *Divisions*

The trip to Anfield in that year, 88 / 89, was a cantankerous one for one simple reason: Sheila didn't want me to go. She had some family thing lined up and it landed on the same day of the game. She knew how I felt about such things; my football always came first.

Still, when the do was arranged, she was adamant I attend. A compromise was agreed; I would go there as soon as I got back from Merseyside. It meant inconveniencing a full coach load of lads who I hurried back from the game, and given the unlikeliness of our victory the inconvenience was only worsened.

Nobody in their right mind gave us a prayer of anything other than defeat, or at best, the luckiest 1-1 you ever did see. But John Hendrie netted on the half-hour to get us back on level terms after we'd conceded at The Kop in less than 5 minutes. Being bottom of the table and one down at Anfield with 85 minutes to go normally marked the onset of a hiding. When the first – a Gary Gillespie header – flew past Dave Beasant I, like the majority of those in the Anfield Road end, feared the worst.

But Hendrie netted on the half-hour and despite being slapped around the park like a sparring partner out of his depth we showed the kind of guts they make glory out of and we hung on in a way that would have made Rocky proud. And when the final whistle went it was Liverpool who ended up all Dolph Lundgren and face down on the canvass.

Mirandinha slammed home a penalty with just seven minutes to go; the players to a man did the shirt proud did and Newcastle held on for all three points. Beasant in particular had a game that showed why McFaul had shown such faith and investment in him that summer of promises.

Normally any trip to Merseyside – and especially to Anfield – incorporates hours upon hours of supping in The Arkles, a grand little boozer with mixed support just a few minutes from Anfield and smack on Stanley Park. This time – one of the rare times we have had any reason to celebrate – we had to dash back to the coach and celebrate on the way home. I had fifty lads on Coach 1 all coming back early while everyone else stayed and partied or stopped off en route. I gave every one of them a fiver discount on the way home – setting me back a sweet £250 – and I didn't have more than 4 cans myself all the live long day, and all of that was for one reason only: to keep Sheila sweet.

In the end it didn't matter, because I was 5 minutes late.

In the end the straw that broke the camel's back was no more than five minutes thick.

I got home, I was dropped off at the top of our street, I dashed down the doors, and I opened the door to my home – her home – just 5 minutes after eight o'clock.

Sheila had a taxi booked for 8pm and she left right on the dot with no room for reprieve, no room for redemption, no room for reason. I found out later – from the bairn ironically – that she left at 7:45pm. That's how sure she was that I'd let her down. All the effort I put in and even if I'd made it she'd have been long gone anyway.

Somehow that told it's own story.

And speaking of telling stories, I couldn't resist sticking around a few minutes longer and telling the bairn all about our shock win at Anfield.

"Was Beardsley shit Dad?" he asked me enthusiastically.

"He wasn't a patch on Mirandinha son," I lied to him. Sometimes we lie to our children; sometimes it protects them more than the truth ever would.

"What time are you coming back tonight Dad?" he asked solemnly. "Will you bring me something from the buffet?"

"Sure son," I told him, "Sure." And sometimes we lie to our children; sometimes it protects them more than the truth ever would.

I'm not a big fan of making decisions in the heat of the moment. Sometimes the adrenalin, the fire in our bellies and the red mist conspire against us. In cases such as those we snap and only serve to make matters worse. Ask Paulo Di Canio about his push on the ref' (who then moonwalked 80 yards before he fell over) that day at Hillsborough. Or ask Eric Cantona about his Kung fu kick at that Palace fan that fateful / extremely funny night at Selhurst Park. But other times I think that adrenalin, that fire in our bellies and that sheer determination serves us well. Ask any of the players who donned the Newcastle shirt at Filbert Street in 1992, or any of the United side that won at Anfield that day in October 1988.

When I went out that night I had such a fire burning in my belly. I had the embers of rebellion and survival smouldering like a smoky November 6th morning when kids just can't resist poking the fire with a stick.

I went to the club, down in Tynemouth, and I took my own taxi there too. I smiled when I went in and made my pleasantries to all and sundry. I didn't want to be there, but I put on a brave face and made the best of it. You see, to me, that's what husbands do. Actually, it ain't about husbands or wives is it; it's about partners. Doesn't matter whether it's the man or the woman, the girl or the boy, it just ain't fair if one of them is trying and the other one, sadly, isn't.

In our case Sheila, sadly, had stopped being a wife a long time ago. Finally, that night, I stopped being her husband.

I was upset from the minute I arrived. I had rushed the lads back from Anfield and took some stick for it too, despite the two hundred and fifty quid it cost me. I was annoyed at Sheila for not waiting for me when I had only been five little minutes late. I was fired up because of Newcastle's 2-1 win and not least of all I was there at a party I didn't want to be at with a woman I didn't love when the woman I did love was out at the club – my club – with all the folks from back home.

Rachel had mentioned during the week that she hoped to see me on Saturday night. She'd been talked into a rare night out with friends. Rachel had never married but had two daughters to a fella she no longer seen nor had any desire to. Being a single parent curtailed pretty much any social life she might have had but in true sods law the one night *my* girl was out was the one night I wasn't.

I guess in hindsight that inspired me more.

Man can nearly always overcome in adversity what he struggles to in the name of freedom.

If Rachel hadn't been out I would have sat and wasted another night by a loveless partners side and I would have hidden behind the fact that there was always tomorrow, always tomorrow. Newcastle United have been hiding behind that – there's always next year, there's always next year – since 1969.

If my life *was* Newcastle United I was making all the wrong decisions. And sitting there in some smoky function room with in-laws I never got on with and a wife who barely spoke to me all night I was making another wrong decision. That bad decision was only worsened by knowing that Rachel was sitting somewhere in the club at the top of our street probably being tapped up and maybe snapped up by some other man.

I likened it to the transfer market. Rachel was a free agent. If I didn't sign her up then somebody else surely would. But I couldn't be with her because I was with Sheila. The adrenalin, the alcohol, the frustration and the desire all boiled up in me like a magic potion in a cauldron. All night I kept asking myself why I didn't just break the chains holding me back and go. All night I kept daydreaming of a fantasy world where I got up and walked out on Sheila, where I could go and be with my mates any time I wanted, where could get back from the match whenever I wanted and where I was free to ask a pretty girl with a pretty face if she'd like to go out with me one night.

The clock made it to ten past ten with me still sitting contemplating the division that had grown so much between Sheila and I. Time spent thinking is time that could be spent doing, my Dad used to say. Then it happened. I'd bought about five rounds in the time I was there and Sheila went to the bar when I nipped out to the loo. When I came back she'd bought drinks for everyone, everyone bar me.

"Where's mine?" I asked her bluntly.

"You've still got some," she said, pointing to the dregs left at the bottom of my pint glass.

"Keep my seat, I'm going to the bar," I told her disgruntled.

When I came back just 2 minutes later my seat was gone. Some fella was sitting in it talking to Sheila and the rest of a circle I clearly wasn't part of. And then it hit me; it wasn't a circle I *wanted* to be part of. But there I was buying drinks and making conversation and trying to be what she wanted me to be.

To really be true to others you have to be true to yourself. So to hell with the consequences, I did what I felt like. I left.

I unhooked my black leather jacket from what used to be my chair and slipped it over my shoulders. It was time to stop being what other people wanted me to be; it was time to be what I wanted to be. And I wanted to be free. I wanted to be in the club at the top of our street. And I wanted to be with Rachel.

So I turned around and walked out, and you know, Sheila never even noticed I was gone. Nobody did. *"Was Beardsley shit Dad?" he asked me enthusiastically.* Well, almost nobody.

11. *Barriers*

It was Wednesday by time they sat me down to explain. Not that it mattered; I'd pretty much figured it out by then. Dad never came home from the do on Saturday night, his clothes were gone and Mam had reverted back to smoking. Oh, and I got bugger all from the buffet.

By time they gave me their communal speech I'd already deduced that they were splitting up. Hell, it didn't take Spender to figure it out.

Ahh, Spender. He could jump on the tracks at Monkseaton Metro and come out at Central Station in 2 minutes flat. I loved Spender, hence that brief stage in the early nineties when I wanted to be a Detective. Well, a Detective come rhythm guitarist.

Anyway, their speech had a lot of *it's not your fault*'s in it and quite a few *sometimes people just grow apart*'s but it lacked any real reason or substance. I wasn't condemning their decision; hell a blind man could see they weren't happy and hadn't been in ages. It just would have been nice if they could have treat me like an adult and told their kid the truth. Perhaps if I could have found an un-plugged Zoltar machine and dropped a quarter I'd have grown up as quick as Tom Hanks did and my parents might have told me the real reasons they were splitting up.

In hindsight the clues were there all along. Sadly, I missed them. What happened was I took everything on surface value.

It was a bit like not seeing the game just seeing the score and deducing who was to blame for defeat. *We conceded 4 so it must be the keepers.* Maybe we missed chances when it was still 0-0 and maybe in the end our keeper had a blinder but just couldn't keep the score down enough.

All I knew was that Mam was crying a lot and smoking and generally just being upset whilst Dad had been shouting, fighting and drinking. And ultimately it was he who was packing his bags and walking away.

Bottom line here: Dad left *us*. That was the result; I just never looked closely enough at the game to understand why.

So to me that was it; I blamed Dad.

Mam & me were Newcastle United and Dad, well, Dad was Chris Waddle, Peter Beardsley and Paul Gascoigne. It's bad enough when a great player leaves this club; it's harder still when that player is a Geordie. You never like to see one of your own leaving you behind. And effectively that's what Dad was doing.

So I pulled down the Dad poster I had deep in my heart, my soul, hell, even running through my very veins and I threw it in the bin alongside Waddle's, Beardsley's and Gazza's. And just like we'd boo any returning player who we deemed did the dirty on us I gave my own Dad the same frosty reception normally reserved for the worst of the visiting player: the one that used to be your own.

I saw him that Wednesday but that was the only time in the whole week. My mates were great, as mates, true mates, always are when you're going through a hard time. Mam was so busy that suddenly the reigns were off me a little bit. And being a 13-year-old kid I did what all good 13-year-old kids should do when their parents split up; I took advantage of it.

In fairness it was a shallow silver lining on a pretty big grey cloud but I made the most of it. I stayed out late at night, I got away with things I generally wouldn't get away with and my pocket money almost doubled on the spot. But there were a lot of mixed emotions building up in side of me.

I loved Dad but I hated him. I didn't want to see him ever again but I missed him so much.

I loved my Mam but I didn't really like her. I wanted to be there for her but she did my head in so much I just wanted to be out of the house and somewhere I could breathe. I wanted to be home, but home wasn't a nice place to be.

So, when Saturday came around, I went to the one other place I had ever considered home: I went back to St James Park.

Newcastle were at home to Coventry City, October 1988. I wasn't allowed to go to the match and I had no one to go with but given the circumstances quite frankly no one was going to stop me. The game itself was suddenly more than a game; it was a gesture, a marker, something symbolic that the boy inside me felt I had to do to start the process of becoming a man. St James Park was somewhere synonymous to me & my Dad and to our relationship. As his marriage to my mother had began to sink the first thing thrown overboard had been me. Well, the bit of me he took to the match anyway. I didn't want to see him again but I wanted him to see me. I wanted to snub him like he had snubbed me. I wanted him to see me so I could ignore him. I wanted to prove a point. If Dad was walking out on Mam & me then fine; but I was man of the house now, I didn't need him anymore, and I'd prove it by donning my old scarf, scraping together a few quid and making my own damn way to the match. All that was left was to find someone to go with me.

I tried Dave and Adam and they both said they'd go if the other one went. In the end they both bottled it. They weren't allowed to go to the match, and in truth neither was I, but as they rightly pointed out, I was far less likely to get grounded than they were, what with my Dad doing off and all. What it lacked in tact it made up for with common sense.

By 11 o'clock I'd pretty much given up on anybody coming with me. It didn't bother me that much in truth. The thing is, I was feeling all rebellious and wound up and ready to take on the world so going on my own was just another barrier to break through.

Sometimes there's barriers in life that hold us back and prevent us from doing what we want, from doing what makes us happy. You can accept that and be miserable or you can smash through those barriers, whatever the cost, and chase that happiness.

The best teams, the most successful teams are ruthless and they don't let such barriers hold them back. Where second place teams and runners-up fall short winners smash through regardless. In the end, it's the winners that are remembered, not the cost nor the consequence.

To hell with them all, I thought, I'd go to the match on my own. After all, there'd be about twenty-thousand other people there too and I can't help but feel – to this day and beyond – that if you're a football supporter than you're never really on your own.

And then it happened, right out of the blue.

"I'll go with you," the voice said from behind me.

I turned around and there she was: Mandy.

"I'm here all day while my folks drop in on all the old neighbours, not least of all your Mam," Mandy said. "I'm sorry your Dad's left and all that," she added, warmly, sincerely, kindly.

That silver lining suddenly got a little brighter.

"Thanks," I said. "It's good to see you. The old street, the old gang, it ain't the same without you."

Mandy just blushed. "Come on," she said holding out her hand, "Let's go to the match."

"Won't you get in trouble?" I asked her.

"Yeah," she said. "But I figure some people are worth getting in trouble for."

I blushed. And then we left.

All day long we talked and none of it was about football. We talked the way I always wanted us to do when I wanted her to know I had a crush on her, the way we always used to before my crush started messing up my behaviour.

We talked on the way to the bus stop, we talked sitting upstairs on the old yellow and white double-decker. We talked all the way to Town, all the way to the Supporters Shop at Haymarket and all the way to the Hot-dog stand. I dropped brown sauce on my chin and Mandy wiped it off and laughed. In hindsight, the way she smiled at me and delicately dabbed my chin with her napkin, the look in her eye as she did it, well that's the moment I realised I loved her.

You can rain on the parade all you like in the name of just being kids and puppy-love but the truth is that there's an innocence and integrity about your first love that doesn't exist when puberty takes hold, sex gets in the way and you let your genitals make all the major decisions in your life.

That moment, at the hot-dog stand up at the Haymarket, was one of the few times all day that we stopped talking. For a moment all we did was feel. I love moments like that.

Newcastle v Coventry in October 1988 was the first game I ever went to without my Dad. It was a match that will live long in my memory, not for the result (a 3-0 hiding that saw Willie McFaul sacked) but for the occasion. Sometimes it's not the result that matters; sometimes it's about who's standing by you no matter what the result is.

That day was spent with Mandy. So win, lose or draw, I'll always treasure it.

We paid our money – I actually paid a fiver and got us both in, and that felt amazing – and we made our way up the Gallowgate steps to The Scoreboard. I didn't pay her in to impress her; I paid her in to maker her happy. The feelings I had for her weren't about me; they were about her. When we reached the terracing we walked a few steps down and leaned on one of the concrete barriers. And we talked. We sang *Sack The Board* together, we booed Coventry together, we laughed at childish jokes together and as the October afternoon got colder we huddled closer together.

And I can tell you to this day I will never forget just how hard my heart was thumping. There's something almost spiritual about standing that close to the person you love, especially when that person doesn't know you love them.

After the match we wandered slowly through Town and got the bus home together. And we talked all the way home. We got off the bus on the main road and we made our way back to where the old gang had hung out since we were just toddlers. It was the same street that Dave, Adam, Julie and I still lived in, the same street that Mandy moved out of the summer before.

When we reached the top of the street and our farewells became imminent I finally allowed my heart to start talking as opposed to my big Geordie gob.

"You still going out with Grant?" I asked resignedly.

"Yeah," she replied sympathetically. She was always a very emotionally diligent girl, Mandy.

"Won't you get in trouble?" I asked her, "for going to the match with me?"

"Yeah," she said. "But I figure some people are worth getting in trouble for."

I blushed, but before she could walk away I told her "I wish you'd never moved away, you know."

"I know," she said. "I wish I hadn't too."

"What I mean is… well… I always liked you, you know."

"I know. I always liked you too."

"No, I mean, I always…*liked* you."

"I know," she said. "That's what I meant. I always *liked* you too."

I blushed again. Then she walked over to me, took my hand and thanked me for taking her to the match.

"Thank *you*," I told her sincerely.

"I've got to go," she said. Then she kissed me softly on my lips. And I kissed her back. And the peck on the lips grew into a real kiss. It was a proper kiss too, like the ones on Dallas and Dynasty that my Mam made me watch every Friday night after The Fall Guy.

Mandy was my first kiss, and I'll never forget that.

"I'll see you later," she said when the kiss ended.

She did and she would.

For the rest of that sorry season I lived off the back of three things: one, the lack of discipline that emanated from the break up of my parents marriage; and two, the bad-boy image I earned from buggering off to the match behind my parents back with someone else's girlfriend and three, that kiss. In Dave & Adam's eyes at least, my stock went up.

I used that rise in regard and influence to finally persuade the lads to come to St James Park with me. They had wanted to for ages; now finally they were brave enough to do it.

I had a very simple system that got all three of us to and from St James Park for any Saturday match without issue. We all told our parents / parent that we were going to buy computer games from the little shop in The Grainger Market. We showed them the money we had on us, we left, and we sneaked a computer game we already had out of the house with us. We went to the match, came home, hid our Programmes under the scales in the bathroom and showed our parents / parent the 'new' game we'd bought. Convinced our money had gone on new games for our respective Amstrad CPC464's no questions were asked. Harrier Attack, Chucky Egg and Football Director; I have so much to thank you for. No one was any the wiser we'd been wasting our money standing on the Scoreboard leaning on the barriers and watching Newcastle's First Division life slowly ebb away.

By time McFaul had been replaced by Colin Suggett and Colin Suggett had been replaced by Jim Smith Newcastle were screwed. Jim, God-bless him never realised how big the club was nor the size of the mess it was in and somehow became addicted to the transfer market and swapped players like most kids do Panini Football Stickers.

Life moulded itself into a pretty mundane routine, which I largely attribute to the Grunge Rock phase I was wandering into, Newcastle's piss-poor results and the hormones of an angry, sensitive teenager embarking Dad-less into puberty. I lost interest in school, became interested in Grunge and cars, I would see my Dad every Thursday and then go to the match most other weekends. As for Dad and me we'd barely speak, we'd do something like play pool or go to the baths and the relationship was badly damaged. The only relief I got from the hurt that him leaving had caused was by being a prick for the one night a week I was with him and blocking him out as much as possible. It was a lame attempt at revenge and independence. I was bottling all of the pain and the rejection up inside and the only way I could express it was by, once a week, trying to make him feel the same way.

As for Newcastle and me we'd turn up at St James most home games, we'd do very little and we'd go home with another defeat and a chilling chorus of *Sunderland, here we come, Sund'land, Sund'land here we come* ringing in our empty ears.

Aah, the auld enemy awaits. It was the only thing that excited me all season.

It was good to be back at St James although it was sad – and somewhat poetic – to go back in such sorry circumstances. I missed being there with my Dad. And I never once seen him from that first game with Coventry right up to our fate being decided. I didn't even tell him I was going back, and the way he talked to me on those awkward Thursdays I can only presume he didn't know.

From that October against Coventry I made it to at least half a dozen games as Newcastle were sucked into a relegation battle they never looked like getting out of. I don't know whether it was the divorce and the home-life that had me resigned to the drop, or whether it was the results and the football but either way I accepted Newcastle's fate long before it happened.

The Goalkeeper's jersey went from Dave Beasant to Tommy Wright to Gary Kelly but the goals kept going in; the 9 and 10 shirts went from Mirandinha to Michael O'Neill, from Rob McDonald to Frank Pingel, and from finally Andy Thorn to Anth Lormor but the goals never came. Kenny Sansom, Ray Ranson, Paul Sweeney, Bjorn Kristensen and Liam O'Brien joined the ranks and although O'Brien's goals almost kick-started an Easter revival the side never seriously moved clear of the trap door.

Then, as United crashed 1-0 at Highbury, news soon filtered through of an incident at the FA Cup Semi-Final between Liverpool and Nottm Forest. That incident of course was later simply known as 'Hillsborough'.

I know kids at school that made jokes about it. It sickened me. I got in trouble for fighting with the kids that did so and I don't regret any punch I threw, and I'm not a brawler by nature.

There's little point in speculating on things I know so little about. But I will add that those fences never killed anyone;

cramming people behind them like animals most probably did. It took the deaths of 96 Liverpool supporters to force the government and the authorities to see that and to pull those barriers down. Football supporters to this day still get treat like animals, especially away from home and even more so in Europe.

We're not animals; we're people, and lest anybody forget that. It shouldn't take another tragedy to remind those in power of such a fact.

United kicked off at 3.06pm the week later when they entertained Luton Town. It was the first time I had stood on the St James Park terrace without barriers and fences penning us in. It was strange, but nice, but sad because of the reason behind it. I had a clearer view of the match, and that clearer view gave an even clearer view of the Second Division that we were plummeting tamely towards.

That game ended 0-0. We had a chance to win it late on but Mirandinha sent his diving header so far wide it spilled pints in The Strawberry and that was that for Newcastle.

A 4-0 hiding at Plough Lane pretty much wrapped things up, but as much as I no longer connected to my Dad I still remembered the Geordie way by which I was raised. And the bottom line is that even when the ship is sinking you stand on deck and you go down with it, because unlike players there is nowhere else for us to turn.

A club can get relegated and half the players can bugger off to a new club. Supporters can't. Supporters don't get transferred. Supporters just get stick.

The final nail was placed nicely over our First Division coffin and in a bittersweet little footballing quirk who better than the Hammers to... well... hammer it in.

Newcastle v West Ham was a midweek match, and that put the cat amongst my parental pigeons so to speak. I wasn't allowed to go to the match. I got away with it on Saturdays. That little scheme wouldn't work on a Wednesday. I'd promised my Mam I wouldn't go to the match. But then again she had promised to stay with my Dad until death do they part and to the best of my knowledge – and to my happiness – no one had died. Adults break promises, get used to it. So what if I did?

To me it was a matter of loyalty. And my loyalty lay not with my Mother, nor with my Father. It didn't lie with the talentless and gutless players of Newcastle United and it didn't lie with the Manager or the board of directors either. It lay with the club, the 97-year-old club, and the wonderful supporters who I had stood beside when Kevin Keegan had made his debut, when Newcastle hammered Carlisle, Derby & Brighton to win promotion, and all the games since until my Dad had abandoned me.

Football is about thick and thin and if the supporters of this wonderful club were about to get a slap in the face in the name of relegation then as strange as it may sound I wanted to be beside them when it came.

And so I went to the match.

I knew I was going to get caught but to hell (or to the Second Division) with it, I was going anyway.

It was a strange night. Gallowgate was resigned and defeated long before kick off and the terrace was as devoid of hope as it was of supporters. I paid my £2.50, clicked myself through the old black thickly painted turnstile and walked up the steps to the top of The Scoreboard. I wandered down a few sets of steps and I leaned on the old concrete barrier that Dad and I used to stand beside. It was the first time I had went to a match on my own, that May night, but strangely I didn't feel the least bit lonely. Every face around me wore the same look, every joke, every laugh, every *for fucks sake lads* echoed of my own.

Three victories – against West Ham, Millwall and then Manchester United away – would possibly see Newcastle stay up. And despite Anth Lormor putting us 1-0 ahead after about 2 minutes Newcastle could have played 20 more times that season and they wouldn't have recorded three wins. They were awful.

When West Ham – the only team in the Division that were lower than us – equalised it just underlined that fact quite neatly.

It stayed at 1-1 until after 9 o'clock, pretty much as late as I could leave it before having a prayer of getting home and getting away with it. The ship was sinking slowly but I figured in for a penny in for a pound, so I stayed until the end.

With 15 or 20 minutes to go – I can't remember now to be honest – West Ham scored again and that was it. I hung my head over the barrier and spat my Hubba Bubba on to the concrete below.

"Your Mam's going to kill you, you know?" came the voice to my left. There was a metal gangway running down the centre of the Gallowgate providing an aisle for supporters. I was on the East Side; at the other side, on the West, leaning on a concrete barrier, was my Dad.

Two seconds later the Policeman manning the gates opened one up and Dad ushered me through. I went and stood beside him for the first time in years. It was fitting that Newcastle should fall with father & son standing together, or united if you will.

When the whistle went and Newcastle were relegated Dad turned to me and gave me advice I will never forget.

"Look at these people," he said as his eyes surveyed the Newcastle fans making their way dejectedly out of the ground. "Football is like life, son; there'll be highs and lows, ups and downs. Ultimately the be all and end all isn't whether you win or lose; the important thing is the people you share those losses and those victories with."

My mind was deep in contemplation when he added, "These people that are here with you tonight, watching us get relegated, they're the best of the same people that stood beside you when we won promotion. And son, they'll be the same people standing beside when we win promotion again. Be proud to be one of them, and never, no matter what life throws at you, never lose your faith."

I stood at the top of The Gallowgate just where the exits lead down the steps to outside. I turned and looked across St James Park. Suddenly I realised that relegation, just like divorce, didn't change anything. I loved this club just like I loved my father and that, I finally understood, would never change.

Part Three

FOUR DAYS IN ONE SEASON

1. *August*

August 1989 was a good month for me. Like most football supporters I don't class January as New Year; I class August as New Year. My life doesn't really change in January. The last two digits change every time I write the date; 87 becomes 88 and 88 becomes 89 but that's about it.

The League table doesn't change. We might end a calendar year having played 21 games and we resume in January with the 22nd. No, my New Year, my fresh start, my clean slate is, and always will be, August.

I measure all the things in my life by football. If someone asks me to recall something from the past I won't say 'Yeah, that'll have been early 1987', I'll say 'Yeah that'll have been around the time we played Preston in the FA Cup'. If someone asked me when I left Sheila I wouldn't say 'That would have been October 88', I'd say 'That was the season when Newcastle won at Anfield but still went down'.

When the season closes in May so too does a chapter in my life. I have a few summer months of reflection, contemplation, and a little time to recharge my batteries and consider what I want for my future. Then the 'new year' opens up with the new season. It's not a countdown from a cold shivery winter midnight to the first seconds of a new year which is just as cold, shivery, dark and wintry; it's a few months of sunshine, warmth, contemplation and consideration.

Everything Zen.

I love the build up to the new season. No matter how bad the year before was the year coming starts with played none, lost none and I like that. Of course, World Cup's and European Championships help to pass the summer months, but in truth I'm not a big England fan. I remember the Hand of God and all that but my love is Newcastle United, end of story.

I love reading the Chronicle all summer when there really is bugger all to write about. Alan Oliver, bless him, has some job of filling that back page in those close season months. That summer, 1989, was a bit easier mind you thanks to Jim Smith's obsession with the transfer market.

Then of course comes the thrill when the fixtures are released. And the first three games get leaked to the press and the radio stations and then finally The Chronicle has the lot. The lads from the Shipyard sent one of the apprentices up to MacMilligan's as soon as news broke. He was under strict instruction to come back with 22 Chronicles and not one less or not to come back at all. I told him to speak to the pretty brunette behind the counter who would have all 22 neatly reserved and put to one side.

When he brought them back we sat out in the Wallsend sunshine eating bacon butties and ham sarni's and drinking flasks of tea and bottles of juice. The Tyne ran proud at the bottom; the Shipyard towered high above and there in the middle was us, the working class Newcastle United fans covered in grease and oil and debate and discussion.

The biggest topic was whether to follow the supporters for change and boycott home games in favour of forcing the board out of the club and allowing someone else to take the club forward. Newcastle United were in a mess on & off the field and as Jim

Smith made seemingly endless changes to the playing staff debate raged as to the need for change in the boardroom. John Hall's Magpie Group were growing in number and in power.

Me, well, I was all for the change. I wanted the old board, the Gordon McKeag's of this world out of the club and I wanted John Hall and his forward thinking, ambitious Magpie Group in.

When those fixtures came out that summer I had no idea whether I'd be there to see them unfold. Walking away from that which I loved was not my style but – as leaving Sheila proved – sometimes you have to take drastic action to force a change for the greater good.

And in the case of Sheila and I, leaving had proven to be the right choice. Not that the bairn saw it that way mind you. In fairness I didn't blame him; he saw it the way any thirteen-year-old would see it, the way I would have probably seen it if it had happened to me. I just hoped that he would see things differently when he grew up.

The hard part was staying in his life until he reached an age where he was able to do that.

But while my relationship with Terry was strained, and while my marriage to Sheila was being undone courtesy of overpriced solicitors, my relationship with Rachel was as fresh and as new as August is to us football fans the land over.

I'd gone to the club the night I left Sheila and true to her word Rachel was there. She was with two other girls, all dressed up in their finest Madonna attire. I met the lads, had a pint, and waited for my chance to go and talk to her.

Our eyes met, our lips mouthed 'hello' but sadly Rachel was with another man and with only a little time left I feared my chance to ask her out would not come. The fella was called Andy. Though we weren't friends, hell, barely acquaintances, I knew who he was and we all knew him as a bit of a ladies man. As last orders were called I cheated a little bit. Tom sent one of the lasses across to interrupt Rachel and Andy. With Rachel free I plucked up my courage and approached her.

"Walk you out?" I asked her as midnight made its way to the clock.

"Sure" she said, letting me put my hand on her back and escort her safely through the drunken crowd.

When we got outside we just stood face to face. And I can tell you to this day I will never forget just how hard my heart was thumping. There's something almost spiritual about standing that close to the person you love, especially when that person doesn't know you love them.

I didn't know what I was going to say, so I just blurted it out. "You shouldn't get involved with that Andy, you know."

"Why's that?" she asked me.

"Because you deserve better than him. I know him. I know what he's like. He's had tonnes of girlfriends and then when he's got what he wants he just messes them around and leaves them. You deserve better than that." I told her.

She smiled at me regretfully. "And what is it that he wants, Jackie?" she asked me.

"Come one, cut me a break here! What do most men want?"

"And what do you want, Jackie?" she asked me softly, but tinged with sadness.

"I want you…" I told her. And once it was said I had to continue; there was no going back by then.

"Look, you know how I feel about you; or maybe you don't; I don't know. But if you don't well I'm telling you now. Jeez this is not coming out well!"

Rachel took hold of my hand and just smiled at me. It was all that I needed. Suddenly the words made sense.

"I want you to be with someone who wakes up in a morning and realises how lucky he is to wake up beside you. I want you to be with someone who knows how lucky he is to be with you when you go to bed each night. You should be with someone who knows how beautiful you are, someone who will take care of you, respect you, and someone who spends all of his days just thinking about you. I guess I just want you to be with the someone you're meant to be with."

Tears welled just a little in here eyes.

"And where do I find a guy like that?" she asked me poignantly.

"Right under your nose," I told her and stepped a little closer to her pretty face.

"And what if a guy like that already has a woman?" she asked me.

"And what if he doesn't Rachel, and what if he doesn't…"

That night, fresh from a wonderful win at Anfield and an echoing of separation from my wife of 14-years the man Rachel wanted *didn't* have a woman, because that man was me.

Nothing happened between us that night other than words and feelings, but when you think about it, in relationship terms, words and feelings are a lot more important than just sex. That night was October '88. It was almost a year later before anything did happen.

Actions speak louder than words, I guess, and while cheap local solicitors untied my matrimonial knot, Rachel and I kept building up the romance in a way that Tom Hanks and Meg Ryan would have been proud of.

In all that time there was nothing more than a Christmas kiss, a couple of Valentine Cards and a pint of Guinness on St Patrick's Day, because, as Rachel whispered in my ear, 'Good things come to those who wait'.

By time August 1989 came around Newcastle and Jim Smith were ready for a new future, and so too was I.

2. *Whatever Happened To Yellow Monster Munch*

The day was incredibly sunny; it was a proper warm summer's day and the kind of day that football seasons were meant to be launched on. Newcastle, care of Jim Smith's rebuilding, went into the new season in good spirits and with a side that was unrecognisable from the one that went out of the First Division with such a tame whimper.

I think the change was good; it was sure as hell needed but it brought freshness and newness to something that had become so old and worn. One Newcastle United side had died; another was being born.

The change with the football club helped me close a sorry chapter in my own life and open up a new one. It seemed like I had been a kid all my life and then in the last 12 months I'd suddenly had so much growing up to do. Change does that; it makes us grow. One minute I was buying pegs and CW's for my BMX, pulling the stickers off Rubix cubes and trying to convince everyone I'd finished it and watching Michael Knight and KITT go on to prove that one man really can make a difference. Well, one man and a talking car. The next I was sinking my second straight can of Top-Deck shandy and wondering whatever happened to Yellow packets of Monster Munch.

The change at home went hand in hand with the changes at Newcastle. And I guess they were needed, too. Dad had left, Mandy had left, and life at home was a whole new scene.

David McCreery left, Glenn Roeder left, Kenny Wharton left and so too did Michael O'Neill, Darren Jackson, Frank Pingel and of course Mirandinha. There were probably loads more that left too but it was kind of hard to keep track with Jim Smith in charge.

Coming in were six new faces. They were Kevin Dillon, Mark Stimson, and Wayne Fereday (who all turned out to be crap), John Gallacher who did well until he was robbed by injury and there was Mick Quinn and Mark McGhee who turned out to be absolutely fantastic!

I was a kid, I was impressionable, and I needed a hero. And in the shape of Scouser Mick Quinn (no pun intended) I found one. I'd seen great players before, and I had shared with my Dad the love for the Keegan, Waddle and Beardsley's of this world. But part of the resentment I felt towards my father was expressed in my desire to have my own heroes.

I needed someone *I* could believe in. I needed someone who was *my* hero. I needed someone who gave me memories of my own, not ones I shared with a Dad who had buggered off and left me.

In Mick Quinn I found that.

To me Quinny was everything a Newcastle number 9 should be. He was irrepressible, he was funny, he was hungry (again, no pun), he loved the shirt, the fans, the club and I guess in the simplest form the man just loved scoring goals. More than that he loved the people he did it for and the shirt, the prized number 9 shirt that he did it in.

Against Leeds on the opening day of the 1989 / 90 season Mick Quinn started the way he would continue, with a big bag full of goals.

Quinn signed his full debut with no fewer than 4 goals in an enthralling 5-2 Newcastle win over promotion favourites Leeds. That was some day. I think it was 3-2 with about 4 minutes left and the crowd nervous as Newcastle hung on. The sun beamed down, the green-dot clock on The NEI Scoreboard was broken and victory was within our grasp. Leeds were pressing. Then Newcastle broke away and John Gallacher walloped home the fourth to seal the win. Two minutes later and Quinny had broken away into the Tyneside sunshine and fired his fourth and Newcastle's fifth into the Leazes End net.

It was the first time I had seen Newcastle win in years, and the first time I had seen them win without my Dad by my side. I didn't know where he was and I wasn't bothered. Football was no longer something I needed my Dad for; I was growing up, I was independent, and I could make my own way to the most cherished part of Geordieland. A new chapter was opening up in front of me and Mark McGhee and Mick Quinn were writing Goals Goals Goals all over the pages.

I had found my hero.

3.   *Talk Of The Tyne*

August 1989 was our first date.

It'd had been around 10 months since Sheila and I had separated and divorce proceedings were well under way. Time is a healer they say, so I left a fair bit of it between leaving the woman I had never loved and loving the woman I would never leave. I guess everyone concerned needed a fair bit of healing, so I gave it a fair bit of time.

For Rachel and I well I think those ten months were the foundation that our love was built on, and I have to say it was built on solid stuff.

Somehow, popping in to see her twice a day and running into her in the social club every other weekend was enough to keep the fires burning.

There was something unspoken in every glance, every shared touch, every lingering moment that held us together until the day came to finally ask the girl out.

Finally, as Mick Quinn made his Newcastle debut alongside Mark McGhee and about twenty others I felt a new season and a new chapter open up in front of me. I wanted it to be a happy one and I knew that without Rachel by my side it wouldn't be. Life is too short to be unhappy.

Life's not a league whereby you get 42 or 38 chances to win; it's not a case of not minding if you lose one week because there's always next week to try again. Too many people live that way. I used to live that way. Not any more.

To me life is a cup-tie, where you get one chance and one chance only to make it through. Finally, I started living like my life was a cup-tie; I was up for it, and I was out to make the most of every opportunity that I was fortune enough to stumble across. One of those opportunities was the chance to fall in love and better yet to be with the person I loved. There's a difference there I can tell you, and my heart goes out to those who know what I mean. Not everyone gets to be with the person they love, not everyone loves the person they get to be with. I got that chance and I'd have been a fool to pass it by.

The team that wins the league is invariably the team that treats the season like it's 38 cup-ties.

And in winning a date with Rachel it was like winning the Cup Final itself.

One Thursday evening, in the summer sunshine, I went to the newsagents, bought my Chronicle and hung around Rachel like a love struck puppy. I'd done the same thing for almost 2 weeks – each night planning to ask her out, each night being interrupted before I could get the words out.

The same thing happened that Thursday. But I thought about my new outlook on life and I figured to hell with it. I was half way out of the door when it hit me: no more wasting time. So I just turned around and walked back in. And even though she was serving about 5 other people I just shot straight from the heart and said what I'd been bottling up for weeks.

"Look, Rachel, you send me clear to the moon. I think you're fantastic and I've wanted to tell you that for ages. There's never been a good time, so I'm pushing in front of all these good people and I'm making this a good time. Would you do me the honour of coming out with me one night…?"

Rachel beamed and blushed and beamed some more. "You mean like on a date?"

"Yeah Rach' I mean like on a date. A real date. Just you & me…"

She smiled and beamed again: "I'd love to," she said, "Yes… a million yesses!"

And that was that. That was how easy it was. I think there's times when we let our minds or our circumstances build barriers that stop us from doing the things that would make us happy. Whenever that happens you just have to remember that you can drive right through them.

I remember our first date. Rachel looked beautiful. More than that, it was that she had made such an effort to dress up so nice for my benefit. She had gotten ready for a night out with me. I was touched that she had even bothered to come out with me, let alone that she had taken time to make herself look so wonderful. That said, she'd have looked good in rags she was so pretty.

I was so happy to be with her and so proud to have her on my arm. Rachel was younger than me, by a good few years. But despite the years in her favour we had so much in common. We were taking the relationship to a new level, but there was tremendous comfort in the friendship that we had built up while the fires of our affection had smouldered in every glance, every look, every word.

I was nervous, a little, and I don't think that was a bad thing. But because I knew Rachel so well I was so comfortable with her and found our date so easy and so enjoyable.

We talked about our favourite films, and I told her my top three: It's a Wonderful Life, The Time Machine and… Rocky II. No, Rocky I. No, II. One. Two! One of the Rocky's!

We talked about our favourite songs.

"What's your top three?" she asked me sincerely.

That was easy: Mama's & The Papa's; California Dreaming; the theme from Auf Wedersehen Pet of course, and Van Halen; Why Can't This Be Love. I always thought their greatest hits should have been titled *Why Can't This Be Van Halen*. It never was. I can't help but thinking that a fine marketing plot was well and truly missed.

We knew each other so well, but we had so much more to know. Talking about all of our favourites was such a fun way to do that.

We talked all night. We talked about our favourite meals, favourite place, favourite colour, favourite actor, actress, everything. I learned that Rachel loved autumn when the leaves turned golden brown and fell from the trees and the nights cut in. I learned she loved rain against her window when she lay snuggled up warm in bed. She learned I love summers and the sound of a turnstile clicking in the August sunlight. She learned I love winter when you wake up at 3am and sit by your bedroom window, wrapped in the blankets with a cup of tea, watching the snow get deeper and deeper, thicker and thicker.

I learned that she longed to come home from work and have an adult to talk to, as opposed to a three-year-old girl with a bin liner for a parachute and a sprained wrist that needs a taxi to the General. She learned that I longed to watch the sunset abroad. We agreed that bin liners *don't* make good parachutes for young children and that we *should* see the sun set abroad.

I found out that her favourite food was a proper Sunday dinner and that she reckoned she was an awful cook. She found out that I love pasta in spicy tomato sauces and that I long to cook it for someone I'm in love with while we share a bottle of white wine and all the romance that goes along with the cliché.

We talked about home, we talked about houses, and we talked about which bridge was our favourite. Rachel said hers was the

Tyne Bridge, I said mine was the High Level. It has more tradition and character than anyone really notices and from it I can get a pure view of the Tyne Bridge and appreciate all the beauty that it is.

We talked about ambition, dreams, goals, and all that you hope for when you lay down to sleep under the lamplight and the rain, the blue sky and the promise. We talked about how sooner or later we all sleep alone. And how sometimes all you want is someone to fall asleep beside you, someone you know is as much in your heart as they are in your bed.

We did the serious stuff too, such as discussing our ex-partners. I never think that's a good thing to do; the past is the past and in matters such as love and sex and all that I think the past is best left buried. But in our case it was relevant and needed to be discussed – not submerged in or obsessed over, but discussed.

After all, I had a 14-year-old son and Rachel had two young daughters. Millie and Emily were 4 years old and 6 years old respectively and if things worked out there was every chance I'd become a big part of *their* lives.

Rachel had never married their father, nor truly loved him either. They were both very young, and in his case – though he was never around to defend himself – he was also very thoughtless and very immature. He had left Rachel when they shared a small flat in Easington, where he was from and where they were based. He moved to Sheffield for work and never asked nor wanted Rachel and the girls to go with him.

Eventually, as I found out the night that Rachel and I shared that magical first date, Rachel decided that she had endured enough of heartaches and heartbreaks and decided that she wanted a better life for her and her girls. That included finding a better father for her kids and a better husband for herself. She slammed a Tom Petty cassette into her sister's car and made her way up the A19 to the sounds of American Girl.

She settled on Tyneside. She swapped MacMilligan's of Easington for MacMilligan's of Wallsend and she met – and dated – a man who cared nothing for her past, loved her spirit and defiance, and was falling in love with her more and more with every word that drifted from her pretty lips onto the surrounding banks of the Tyne where we sat and talked on our very first date.

She asked me if having the kids made any difference to '*us*'. It never could, never would. She called it baggage. To me that sounded harsh. Baggage is something that you drag around with you; kids are something wonderful that – drive you mad as they do – you love and cherish for every precious moment spent with them. I never knew a man who loved a suitcase; I would go on to be a man who would love four children. I would go on to be a man who would love four children as if they were his own, when only two of them shared my blood.

In time Rachel's girls, Emily & Millie, would go on to call me Dad. They welcomed me into their lives in place of the man, the father, who had walked out on them and who would go years without seeing them, forgetting birthdays and all. Sadly, however, while Rachel's daughters would go on to welcome me into their lives, my son would go on to force me out of his.

4. *Just Like Watching (Gary) Brazil*

There's things in life I will never understand. Such as why the cancelled ALF, why Volvo's always have their lights on and whatever happened to that bloke from the Manic Street Preachers. I never understood Jim Smith's addiction to the transfer market either, and I never understood why – despite United being slap in the middle of a promotion race all season long – 1990 just didn't feel the same as 1984 did.

Firstly, there was no romance, and without romance there can be little happiness when it comes to something you're supposed to be in love with. Dad was gone again. In 84 we stood side by side. In 1990 I stood without him. The brief encounter standing beside him the May night West Ham relegated us felt like 15 minutes with his ghost.

Maybe it was just being a teenager; maybe it was the divorce. Maybe it was Mandy or maybe Kurt Cobain's lyrics, but as much as I supported United that season, 89 / 90, I had this knawing in the pit of my stomach that there would be no happy ending. That wasn't to say that the story itself wasn't enthralling; it was. But all throughout that year something felt wrong. And I kept looking over my shoulder at the places below us and at one team in particular: Sunderland.

I was there when we won promotion in '84 with Kevin Keegan. It felt warm and magical and special and right. I was there week in week out during 89 / 90 but – challenge in the top three as we did 6 years before – it didn't feel the same. Six years on it felt cold and dark and muddy and it just didn't sparkle as it had before.

Both seasons were riffled with away defeats; both seasons saw United challenge for the final promotion spot as opposed to the title. Maybe it was just the quality of the football; maybe it was just that I saw the past through magical black & white coloured spectacles, but the Jim Smith team of 1990 didn't have the chemistry that the 84 side ignited.

But I kept my hopes and my support up all along, despite the inability to shake off the shadow that cast itself unerringly across it. And that shadow shouldn't hide some wonderful days following the lads. I saw my first away game that year – at Roker Park against the auld enemy Sunderland – and I made it to every single home match.

The trip to Roker was amazing. The adrenalin rush being marched from the Moordale Coaches up to the Roker End was exhilarating. It was like staring the devil in the eyes and I loved every single minute of it. Seeing the lads play in a change strip, being on someone else terrace – and not just anyone else neither, but Sunderland's terrace – made my heart race. As a teenage boy such an aggressive and electricity charged environment stirred emotions in me that were hard to control. I was high on aggression, passion, pride, defiance, love & I dare say hatred.

I was high on atmosphere and I loved every minute of it. A nail biting 0-0 did little to quash the emotions firing through my black & white veins.

The rest of the games I seen were at home, and they too produced some wonderful days and wonderful atmospheres.

There were strings of home wins in a row, there was Mark McGhee's goal-of-the-season against Bradford City, and there was the epic cup clashes with Reading. I turned up to the second leg of that Reading League Cup tie late and didn't know Mick Quinn had missed the game through injury. When the famous number 9 shirt rammed home a Leazes End penalty I broke into chants of *'Micky Quinn'*. About 4,000 Geordies stood pissing themselves as Gary Brazil ran off in celebration.

There was Roy Aitken's debut and the amazing 5-4 win over Leicester when United went into the last 13 minutes 4-2 down. There was the boisterous atmosphere in the FA Cup 5th Round clash with Man United live on BBC. And of course there was over 60 Goals from Quinn & McGhee.

I think my favourite Mick Quinn goal was against West Ham in the last home league game of the season. We'd fought back from 1-0 down to 1-1 and then piled the pressure on the Cockney's. Quinny turned and hit a shot, it bounced loose in the box and both Quinn and McGhee smashed at it. I was in The Corner – another testament to my teenage angst – and from where I was standing I couldn't tell which of the two had walloped it home. Then Quinny ran of arms aloft and his 36th of the season was chalked up.

Sadly, even though the First Division was in reach, the shadow loomed large, the omens came to pass, and Quinn's 36th was his last. That result was the brightest of our season and the closest we came to glory. But as they say it is brightest before the dawn it is also true that the sun shines the most just before she sets.

The clouds broke over St James and the blue skies on the black & whites went grey in our very own back yard. The season ended in that terrible North East sideshow as Roger Thames gleefully described it and Newcastle again snatched tragedy from the jaws of glory.

The final game of the orthodox calendar was at Ayresome Park against the Boro. If Newcastle won and either Leeds or Sheffield United – the only two teams in the league above us – lost then that would see promotion clinched. That win – regardless of what it did for us – would have sent Middlesborough crashing back into Division Three to boot.

Another trip away was beyond me, try as I did to pull it off. So instead of making my first visit to our other local rivals I settled for joining 14,000 others and watching it unfold from the big screen at St James Park. The screen was at The Leazes End; we were stood on the Gallowgate. The view varied depending on sunlight from poor to non-existent. So amidst cried of *'Norman is our leader'* we made our way en masse onto the St James Park turf behind a pitch invasion that lead by the afore-mentioned Norman.

There I sat, with the lads, with my arse on the Leazes End 6-yard line watching the dream die: a 4-1 defeat and an awful performance did the trick. Boro crushed Newcastle and then sent what was left of our team just 20 odd miles back up the A19.

That brought us face to face with none other than Sunderland themselves. The auld enemy had finished 3 places and 6 points below United. As in 84 Newcastle finished 3rd. Although this time that coveted third place brought no promotion, only a Play Off game to earn a trip to Wembley and a bite at promotion against the other Play Off winner.

The dream that had died against Boro was well and truly buried over two legs against the red & whites. At Roker Park Newcastle held on to a creditable 0-0 not least thanks to John Burridge penalty save in the last minute at The Fulwell End, which was indeed full that day. The Fulwell End is always full though isn't it? Yeah, full of what…

At home everyone said we were favourites. But I went to St James that night, a rainy 16th May just a day after my 15th birthday a very worried kid.

My fears proved well founded.

Newcastle lost 2-0. Sunderland went to Wembley. Newcastle went back to the Second Division, and despite a few thousand angry fans – largely kids my age trying to replicate the Forest Cup-tie of '74 – every Geordie went home with a broken heart. It was one that took me over 2 years to recover from. It was one I knew the team never would.

Newcastle had an old side and Jim Smith had gambled – understandably – at experience getting the club back into the First Division at the first attempt. I don't blame Jim. In fact I like him an awful lot. I met him once at Benwell. He's a really nice guy. He's still got my pen though after he signed my autograph book and then buggered off. Never mind. Anyway, like Jim as I did, I knew going home that night that there was no bright future anymore.

Hell, I was a teenager and we all know how stroppy and moody teenagers can be, will be, have been and are. I certainly was. The defeat that rainy night was so much darker, so much gloomier than even relegation had been twelve long months before.

Relegation had been like putting a dying side out of its misery; the Play Off defeat was more of a shock, a surprise, a cruel and personal blow that came at the end of a by & large previously successful season. The prospect of facing all those crap Second Division sides again, the sound of the Mackem's singing aloud on the Leazes End, knowing they were going to Wembley in our place and suspecting they were going to Anfield, Old Trafford and Highbury too was more than my heart could take.

There was no hope, no light, no heroes, no dream and in truth no justice. It was galling that the side could get done by

Sunderland of all people, especially when they had finished so far behind us.

The promotion dream was over and I knew it would get worse before it got better. I knew that it would be more than just one more year until we were promoted. Suddenly, walking out of St James through the Tyneside rain and Tyneside tears and sounds of sirens and Sunderland singing, I missed my Dad so very, very much.

Though I was surrounded by thousands of people who felt just the same as I did I still felt ever so, ever so lonely.

Patrick Swayze and that lass were having the time of their lives (what is it with girls and that film…?) and Demi Moore and… Patrick Swayze (wow, busy year, Patrick) were making horny pottery, using Whoopi Goldberg as a medium and trying to say something other than '*ditto*'. I was having anything but the time of my life, getting a stiffy every time I so much as looked at Demi Moore (it took GI Jane to put that particular problem to bed) and trying to say something other than '*for fucks sake Dillon*'.

And just as teenagers can feel they have the weight of the world on their shoulders when really its just hormones pulling the smiles into frowns, I got angry. In my youthful naiveté I acted like a kid. In fairness I was a kid! And all the things that I felt sad about I suddenly felt mad about.

I loved Newcastle and I hated Sunderland. I missed my Dad, but as much as I missed him suddenly I was so mad at him. While my world was falling apart his was apparently going pretty well. While Sunderland were off to Wembley, Anfield, Old Trafford and Highbury we were off to Fratton Park, Boundary Park, Twerton Park and Vicarage Road. That only made me angrier.

Then something happened that pushed my anger too far, and I reacted the way a blinded and hurt teenage kid was always going to react. It was bad enough when he left us, but Dad hadn't just left us; he'd joined someone else's team, someone else's family, and that took a lot longer than just two years to get over.

5. *The Kids*

Life really is just like managing a football team; if you get decisions right you'll have more chance of being successful, if you get them wrong you'll most likely not.

One of my biggest decisions was whether to tell Terry the truth about my new life. I had a good track record of getting such decisions right since I grew myself a *Y* chromosome and plucked up the stones to leave Sheila for Rachel. I handled meeting her kids right too, which was a major plus. And the reward for getting these decisions right: I was happy.

The next tricky one was Terry.

He knew I had left his mother, of course he did, what am I stupid? But he was wrestling with the notion that I had also left *him*. I mean, I had, but he wasn't the reason. Hell if it weren't for him I'd have left years ago. That said, if it weren't for him I would never even have married her. But he couldn't see that. Telling him I had a new girlfriend was inevitable. I wasn't sure how he'd take it. Telling him about her kids never even crossed my mind.

Newcastle & my life had always gone hand in hand. But since the split with Sheila I had also broken the cycle that tied my fortunes so intrinsically to the clubs. I would never split from Newcastle United; hell that *was* a marriage that would stand the test of time; for better or worse, rich or poor. Truth was I loved Newcastle United – still do. Truth was I never loved Sheila – still don't. But in breaking free from her I also broke free from tying my fortunes to those of the club. In 1990 / 91, whilst the club was going through a torrid time, I was embarking on a particularly happy one… football aside.

Music was crap, with the exception of Jon Bon Jovi who was going out in a blaze of glory, but as 1990 faded to black Newcastle United were going out anything but a blaze of glory. Jim Smith's team was an old one, riddled with experience but tiring legs and not enough heart to take another year in Division Two. He had built a side geared to get promotion or bust in 1990. It didn't get promoted, and as the debts began to mount there was every chance it would actually go bust.

Everything around Gallowgate just seemed darker than before. I'd seen some crap in my time, the late 1970's and early 1980's and I was wise enough to know that – despite the bairn being adamant it was the end of the footballing world for Newcastle United – the darkness would break and day would indeed follow night. It always does.

Maybe it was Richard Gere finding love with a prostitute (I never actually thought that Julia Roberts was *that* pretty), maybe it was Patrick Swayze and that lass having the time of their lives (what is it with women and that film…?) but I never lost faith that as dark as it got a hero would one day emerge and the club would rise again in his black & white glory. Somewhere out there was a man who would save us, enchant us, make us fall in love again and make our great club proud once more. Somewhere amidst the darkness of defeats to Millwall, Bristol City and Hull there was a new day waiting to break.

It would, but not before the night got a whole lot darker first.

So there I was, turning off the radio every time Vanilla Ice came on, making so much money from Slippery When What that

I was contemplating making it my full time vocation and building a strong relationship with the love of my life – well the other love of my life – and her two beautiful daughters.

But as my skies were sunny and blue, those that my son standing on the Leazes End were under grew darker by the week. He'd moved from The Corner to The Leazes to avoid seeing me and so he could vent that anger by taunting the away fans in that poxy little section of the terracing. I saw him once a week officially and we did something like go swimming or play pool down the arcades at Tynemouth or Whitley Bay. He frequently called to say he couldn't make it, too. I hated it. I missed him so much but what could I say? Could I complain? Hell no. He'd already made it perfectly clear that my right to feel sorry for myself or my right to miss him had been forfeited the day I packed my bags and went about buying a 2-bedroom a mile away from our once-family home.

The only one that could feel sorry for himself was indeed him, and in fairness he did enough of it for both of us. I had wronged him, deserted him, left him and let him down. And he was in no mood to let it be water under the Tyne Bridge.

It didn't help that he was unhappy at home. Hell, I knew what life with Sheila was like and I didn't envy the kid that at all. But he wouldn't turn to me because I was the bad guy. And he wouldn't throw himself into his schoolwork because, well, he was a kid and not many kids do throw themselves into their schoolwork. So his life became football. His life became Newcastle United. And to be perfectly honest that was a pretty piss poor life to have.

Newcastle were awful. I remembered how my own unhappiness of the late 70's tallied perfectly with the clubs demise and it only made me feel worse. I could see the same thing happening to him as 1990 drifted coldly & darkly towards 1991. The team were languishing in the lower reaches of the Second Division with old, crap players, and no money. The ground was cold and half-empty and worse, there was no reason to believe that this would change.

As happens too often in these here neck of the woods when your team isn't performing you focus on your rivals shortcomings rather than your own. The bairn became consumed with hatred for Sunderland. They had robbed him, stolen from him, took his place at Wembley, and took his place in the First Division. He was as engrossed in their defeats as he was in Newcastle's victories and for a time I'm not sure what meant more to him. He would celebrate Sunderland conceding more than he would Newcastle scoring even though they were one division and sometimes hundreds of miles apart.

A lot of that hatred was manifested from my break up with Sheila. But he loved me in his heart and so he refused to let that out. It broke free in little petulant outbursts but that's bairns for you. He bottled it up the best he could and he tried not to put into words what was ricocheting around his cavernous cauldron of a teenage heart.

And then one fateful day it happened.

It was December 29th 1990 and Newcastle ended the year with the visit of Notts County. I had barely seen the bairn over Christmas but he had agreed to forsake his usual pre-match ritual of going with Adam & Dave and come to the game with me. Like his old man he was superstitious, not that it was doing us much good. But he still bought his programme from the same spot I had bought mine all those years ago and he still wore the scarf I bought for him that very first time together.

We got the bus together from Wallsend, just like we had when we went to see Kevin Keegan's debut some 8 years before when the bairn was barely knee high to a grasshopper. Suddenly Keegan — and my son — seemed so long ago, so far away. We went early;

it must have been no later than 11am when we hit the icy streets of Newcastle.

We went to McDonalds, we drank Milkshakes, ate fries and we talked. And somewhere in the conversation I told him about Rachel. He took it relatively well. I mean he wasn't enthralled by it but there was no great reaction. I told him the truth too. I told him that I was moving in with her and we were going to 'give it a go'. Hell, I even told him that I loved her. He just nodded and sighed and slurped strawberry milk.

The gulf between us was killing me and all I wanted to do was hold him and tell him I loved him and I missed him and being without him all Christmas had been agony. And I so desperately wanted to tell him that I was worried who this was turning him into. He wasn't growing up to be the young man I always thought he would do if I had stuck around. But then I reconsidered; I hadn't stuck around; so if anything it was my fault. And even if I had plucked up the courage to tell him that I had little doubt that he'd be quick to remind me why he had changed over the last few years.

Finally, with that difficult conversation piece out of the way we made our way to the ground, together. It was a cold, dark, miserable winter and though the lights up Northumberland Street and throughout Town sparkled and shone, sadly no such luxury was bestowed upon the frosty St James Park. Newcastle were God-awful and lost 2-0. Everything about the defeat and the manner in which it occurred seemed to sum up the demise of this once great club.

The crowd that day was 17,657. You know how I know that? Because despite there being 17,655 of them around us somehow after the match Terry managed to see me meeting Rachel in the Gallowgate End car-park. He made to come over and he even smiled and waved at us. Then Emily & Millie threw their arms around me and his face turned. I could see his heart breaking. I hadn't not told him deliberately; I just genuinely never thought.

There by the St James Park floodlights and the velvet blue winter sky he shook his head and took off the scarf I bought him 8 years before.

"Terry, look, this is…" I stuttered.

"Oh it's Okay, I get it," he said.

"Terry, wait," I pleaded.

Then all of the things he'd been bottling up started coming out, along with his tears.

"Look at this mess behind you," he said, gesturing to the sorry embers of what was once a great club. "This is what's left when the ones you love up and leave you. Gazza's happy, he's got Spurs. Waddle's happy, he's off to Spain."

He was off to Marseilles of course in France but it didn't seem like the time to point it out.

"And do you think Peter Beardsley gives a shit anymore? No, I'm pretty sure he doesn't. But they're all happy, and this is the mess that's left. And look at you, you're happy. You've got her and these two and what have I got? You're their Dad now, not mine," he said.

I tried to reason with him. I tried to explain. I can't remember what was said, I can't remember how it ended up where it ended up, but suddenly he looked at me like he'd been stabbed through the heart and his face froze cold in the Tyneside winter floodlit night.

In a heartbeat I closed my eyes and realised what I'd said. The poor bugger had never done the maths before. He never tallied the time between our wedding anniversary and his birthday. He never realised, until I said something stupid and the penny, bitter and truthful, dropped like the programme that slipped from his hand

"I'm a mistake...?" he said, tears welling in his eyes.

"Terry, look..."

He shook his head. He was devastated. "I'm a mistake," he said again as the tears fell over his cheek.

And there by the St James Park floodlights and the velvet blue winter sky he took the scarf I bought him 8 years before, threw it on the car bonnet and walked away.

I saw him only twice more that season.

Jim Smith duly departed the club in March and Ossie Ardiles soon came in. Before long Smith's old and tired team was dismantled and discarded and the bairns of the Newcastle squad were given their chance.

Steve Watson, Robbie Elliot, Matty Appleby, Alan Neilson, Steve Howey, Lee Makel, David Roche and most notably Lee Clark were soon in the team. Newcastle rallied well and ended the season strongly. The club had put its faith in youth and there was independence about these kids that boded well for the future.

Terry took to them immediately. He was inspired by the youthfulness of the team and by the fact that these kids were now being asked to become men. It brought a more independent side out in him too. He duly pointed that out when we ran into each other after the 3-2 home win over eventually promoted Oldham.

"We don't need oldies anymore; the kids can stand up on their own now Dad," he told me as I tried again to rebuild the bridge that I had burned when I left his mother.

The next time I saw him I didn't speak. He was running around the pitch sliding onto his knees on the St James Park turf and kissing the heavens. It was the final game of the season. He was celebrating like we had won promotion. We had lost 2-1 to bottom of the table Hull City. Sunderland had been relegated.

I knew then that the bairn was wrong. The kids needed guidance and help; they needed 'oldies' or at least some experience.

They needed a father figure; and so did he. Without it I wondered how they would turn out. Less than a year later – and after some incredible experiences on and off the pitch – Ossie Ardiles was sacked with his kids staring the Third Division in the face.

6. *Keegan Returns*

It was the 1991 / 92 season. Extreme wanted more than words, Bryan Adams was number one for pretty much the entire year and Michael Jackson – looking paler by the day – told us it didn't matter if we were black or white.

In truth it didn't matter whether everything we did *was* for love as long as we were black *and* white the only words we heard were 'and another defeat for Newcastle…'. Then John Hall added his words, to the effect that if we were indeed relegated we'd probably go bust. Great, no pressure then lads.

By time Right Said Fred were too sexy, Mr Big wanted to be with us and Vanessa Williams was saving the best to last, Newcastle were too desperate, Special K wanted to be with us and the Magpie Group had indeed saved the best to last.

I was at school. I was in 6th form. I did a B-Tec in Business & Finance. I was in my maths re-sit at the time. My locker was number 19. I picked it because of Gazza's number in the Italia 90 World Cup. It was covered in posters and pictures and cuttings from the Chronicle & Journal. There must have been about 12 of us in 6th form that played 5-a-side every night and went to every Newcastle home game. All of our lockers were the same. But mine had the classics on them. Every other locker had pictures of Lee Clark or David Roche or Gavin Peacock. Clarkie was especially popular because he was a Wallsend lad.

But my locker had old pictures from old programmes I had bought from the old Supporters Shop that used to be at the Haymarket. I had pictures of the promotion side of '84, the silver stripped legends that staved off the drop with Big Jack in '85 and the side that finished 8th with Willie McFaul in '88. I had pictures of John Anderson, Kenny Wharton, Jeff Clarke, Glenn Roeder and Davey Mac. I had pictures of Kevin Keegan and Terry McDermott, whom my Dad said I was named after. And though I would never admit it to anyone else, there tucked in the corner on the side wall were pictures of Gascoigne, Waddle and Beardsley.

I'd be at school by 8:15am every morning. I'd be one of the first in; I'd have a bit craic with John the cleaner, I'd bang the lights on, line the balls up on the table and me and the lads would play pool and talk Newcastle United to lessons started.

I couldn't understand what was happening. The youngsters were basically getting pasted week in week out and as injuries piled up – not least to my hero Mick Quinn – the dreaded drop loomed large on the spring horizon. Newcastle had never been in the Third Division, my Dad, the wonderful Paul Joannou written *United: The First 100 Years* and basically just Geordie folklore informed me.

Sunderland had. Losers.

The football Newcastle had played was exciting and attacking but the notion of defending had never crossed Ossie's mind. If Ardiles had been in charge of the Argentinean military the Falklands would have been over in less than 90 minutes. There was countless 4-3's, a 5-2 and even a 6-6 draw at one point.

Ultimately the 5-2 defeat was at Oxford United, who were the only team below Newcastle in the 24-team league table. It followed fast on the heels of a 3-4 home defeat to Charlton in which Newcastle had led 3-0 and then lost agonisingly to a Liam O'Brien own goal. Newcastle were doomed. It was arguably the darkest time in the clubs entire history. The year, January 1992, opened with a 4-0 away defeat to Southend United. I thin part of Newcastle United died that day. And although that was arguably the lowest ebb somehow it continued to get worse from there. Newcastle were in the second worst league position in the clubs history and never had they occupied such a perilous position at such a late stage of a campaign. Add to that the circumstances they were in, injuries, a team full of kids, an inability to defend, no money, potential liquidation, then basically they were fucked.

This might sound strange, but for me there was no anger towards the team. The club was a mess but everybody was pulling the same way, right threw the club. From John Hall, Freddie Shepherd, Freddie Fletcher and Malcolm Dix in the Boardroom to Lee Clark, Steve Watson, Robbie Elliot and Alan Thompson out on the pitch everybody pulled together to try and save this dying club before it was too late. Maybe I remember it better than it was, because it was God-awful. But there was camaraderie and a will to battle. These weren't overpaid, over-hyped primadonnas; they were kids, our kids, Geordie kids.

And so as Geordies what did we do? We stood by them and we faced the drop together. If United faced the end then we would face the end united. There looked to be nothing to save us. We needed a hero, but in such dire straits where would we find someone able to save us so late in the day...?

Then one of the teachers walked into my maths class and whispered to Mrs Freeman.

"Terry," Mrs Freeman said seriously, "You're Dad's on the phone; he says it's important."

My heart tied in knots, my face flushed red and nervously I made my way to the Head of Sixth Form Office. I had put quite a distance between my Dad and me since that awful home defeat to Notts County. I lifted the phone from the desk and said "Hello?"

"Terry?" Dad asked.

"Yeah…"

Then there was silence for what seemed like an eternity.

"Ossie's been sacked… Keegan's in charge."

Goosebumps flooded my arms and my neck, my eyes welled and a tear spilled over my cheek. Two teachers stood looking at me worriedly. I took a deep breath, cried a little "Thank you Dad…" down the phone and then bolted out of the Teachers Room, into the Common Room and let out a mighty and primeval roar that could have been heard the length and breadth of Tyneside.

I arched my back, clenched my fists and shook my arms at the heavens and roared out loud. People from all over the 6th Form, hell from all over the school came running in to see what all the drama was about. I had an audience of about 20 plus people; teachers, kids, the cleaner, two photocopier engineers all looking at me with eyes and words saying '*What, what…?*'.

I took a deep breath, felt a tear of pride run down my Geordie cheek and I told them boldly "Ossie's been sacked… Keegan's in charge."

They looked at me in disbelief.

Then I yelled at the top of my voice "Keegan's back! Keegan's back! KEEGAN IS BACK!"

One of the engineers nodded, jumped up, hugged his mate and then hugged me.

"He is! He is! Listen, it's on the radio," he said turning up the little wireless he had next to his tool kit.

All of a sudden the Common Room was a tickertape parade. Dave & Adam, Splodge, Rob, Woody, Mel, Pete, Forbsey, they all came bolting in a few minutes later.

"Is it true? Is it true?" they asked like kids wondering if Santa has been on Christmas morning.

I just smiled and hugged them like we were right there on the terracing. It was true: Keegan was back.

7. Not Tino; Sarsaparilla

It was February 1992. I had never been happier, perhaps in my whole life. I had hope. Sometimes that's all we need. Anything without hope can easily become nothing. Anything with hope can easily go on to be something.

There and then, hanging up the phone with Terry's "Thank you Dad" ringing in my ears, I had hope. I had the hope that one day my son and I might be reunited, just as Newcastle United were busy announcing that they had been with Kevin Keegan.

Some people are just born United.

At that time we needed a hero; in Kevin Keegan we had one. I know Keegan came out and said it was the only job in football he ever wanted, but in truth, he was the only man I ever wanted to get the job. I never really saw Ossie getting sacked; I didn't think the club could afford it. But if I had then there wasn't any man, any manager, any anybody that I would have turned to in order to save us other than Keegan.

The man could master the media, inspire the supporters, rally the whole damn club and ultimately he could get results. Messiah seemed a bit over the top; I mean I never saw him cure the lame or give the blind back their sight and the last person in this country to roll away the stone was Mott The Hoople. But I never doubted for a second that Keegan would succeed. He brought feel-good to everything he did. He said all the right things, he did all the right things, he turned average players into good players, and more than that, he let you go to bed at night and feel that finally your club was in safe hands.

His first *miracle* came with his first game in charge; a 3-0 win over Bristol City at St James'. There was a bumper crowd, I was in it, and the boys played brilliant. And it just snowballed. A week later we went to Kenny Dalglish's expensively assembled Blackburn Rovers who were well on the way to promotion.

We went a goal up and about 7,000 Geordies behind the goal went mental when David Kelly smashed home the first. We sang as always, we shouted as always and we took the piss as always, in the most humorous of ways. Chants questioning the fidelity of David Speedie's wife rang out around Ewood Park, booming from the buoyant away end.

Speedie to his credit rammed in an equaliser. So we sang louder and longer. Speedie to his credit rammed in a second... and then proceeded to run up to the 7,000 Geordies and give us the V-sign. To our credit we tried to kill him. The flimsy red fence and the hordes of police and stewards thought it best we didn't but we gave it a good go. Speedie, to his credit, smashed in his hat-trick and promptly ran off to the Newcastle fans and gave them the finger again.

To our credit we tried to kill him, again. And when that failed we promptly smashed up Blackburn after the match. I'm not an advocate of football violence by any means but I must admit I got caught up in that and loved every window that went out, every bus that rocked, every fan that got chased and every chant that we sang. I especially loved the guy with the Milk Float full of crates of pop.

He made the error of driving into Blackburn Town Centre just as 7,000 Geordies made their way – thirstily – back to their cars and coaches. One lad reached over as the float got stuck in traffic and helped himself to a bottle of pop. The chap driving was just about to go ballistic when everybody else thought *Mmm, nice idea; I'm a tad thirsty myself…* A few threatening gestures went his way before he locked his cab, tried to muscle through the traffic and watched a weeks worth of profits make their way into Geordie hands and down Geordie throats.

When we got back to the Slippery Coaches it was like playing swaps with the old Panini football stickers. Everyone was swapping a Dandelion & Burdock for Orangeade, or two Cola's for a Sarsaparilla. Very refreshing.

On the journey home the pop turned to something more adult and the upbeat mood that KK had created was carried on.

That was the thing with Keegan; even in defeat the atmosphere remained positive; defeats were a setback not a way of life. Keegan seemed to galvanise the players he inherited and suddenly they were playing with structure, confidence, belief and ability. Suddenly a group of players became a Team and we, the supporters, suddenly had a team to be proud of.

Kevin Sheedy and Brian Kilcline were added to the side: father figures to our kids.

The side continued to pick up points and the crowds continued to swell at St James'. Then came the game we had all been waiting for: Sunderland at home. We had met them at Roker in autumn, on a sunny, misty day with a twelve-noon showdown. We earned a 1-1 draw with a team of kids, and a midfielder in Liam O'Brien who would go on to write his name all over this fixture in the years to come… oh yeah, and our Teesside neighbours too. O'Brien's equaliser – a chip over the Sunderland Goalie right in front of us at the Roker End – would take some beating in our black & white hearts. He would beat it almost a year later at the very same place.

Anyway, I digress: to the first home meeting between the two sides since that infamous play off night almost 2 years before.

So with one point and the moral victory in the bag the two sides met again at Gallowgate in March '92. It was a typical local derby, with both sides scrapping for what was on offer. Newcastle were clearly the better side; all that remained was to make that difference count in the score-line. Then, from a corner at The Leazes End, David Kelly scored a header that he called *'a spawny arse goal'*. Spawny arse goal my arse, it was one of the best I ever did see! I mean, it was scrappy, but it was the winner against Sunderland and no goal that ever wins us a match against that lot will be seen as *spawny* in my eyes or my heart.

We won the game 1-0 and I was one of the last to leave the Gallowgate terrace. I just stood savouring the moment, watching those in red & white behind the Leazes End goal, standing just where they had that fateful night in May 1990, but in ever so differing circumstances. And I felt something shift: a power, a balance, a superiority. It would take time to reveal itself and prove me right but there and then I felt the two clubs jolt and I knew that fate, that destiny, would see them go in very differing directions.

To my right, oblivious to my eyes upon him, standing victorious on one of the concrete barriers, the same one we stood at all those years before when I first took him to the match was the bairn. Hell, I say *the bairn*, but he was fast bearing down on his 17th birthday.

He clocked me, just as he was about to jump down (under police advisement I might add), kissed his badge, waved his fist at me and yelled, "We did it Dad! We did it!"

As I sat in the Three Bulls Heads after the match, savouring victory and feeling content that the club – in the hands of John

Hall & Kevin Keegan – were set for a prosperous future I couldn't help but wonder what lay ahead for my fatherless son.

8. *Teenage Kicks*

I kissed my badge and waved at Dad. I was so emotional at that time. I was so happy. He smiled at me and we just held a glance for a moment. I love my Dad. I wonder if he knew that. He must have done; after all, he was *my Dad*. He always would be my Dad. Then a copper told me to get down and, using Adam & Dave as support, I jumped from the same barrier that Dad and I used to stand at years ago and I rejoined the last of the jubilant crowd leaving Gallowgate.

I missed Dad. I was being an idiot about things but I was just too young to see it that way. I was hurt, my pride was hurt, my heart was hurt and I was sad without him. It was Okay for him; he had a new girlfriend and he was being a Dad to her two little girls. I didn't begrudge them – they were lucky to have him. I just wished I had him too.

It didn't seem fair. These two girls had a Dad and presumably he'd buggered off. And now they had my Dad to replace him. That meant I didn't have a Dad; not a one I seen anymore anyway. Why should I miss out, I wondered? And anyway, he couldn't love them like he loved me, could he?

I mean, using football as an example: Peter Beardsley was a Geordie. He wasn't a Scouser; he was a Geordie. But there he was playing for Liverpool and then Everton. Why couldn't they get a Scouser to do that? Why did they have to pinch someone that was mine, ours, a Geordie, a Newcastle player? Neither Gazza nor Waddle were Cockneys, they were Geordies. Well, Gazza was, I'm not sure what Waddle was. I called him Judas from the day he left to the day he retired, including one sorry episode at the Masters at the Arena when I called him a little more than that and I was asked to leave.

So anyway, Gazza was a Geordie, but the Cockneys pinched him and Newcastle United – his football family – were left short. Why couldn't Spurs get their own bloody genius instead of pinching ours? Waddle, well he was off to Marseilles and that made no sense! Why couldn't they get their own Spanish winger instead of pinching one of ours?

(I was 24 years old before I realised Marseilles was in France…)

And the same that had happened with the football had happened with my family. This girl didn't have a husband so she pinched my Mam's; her kids didn't have a Dad so they pinched mine.

Now as fucked up as that might sound it's how I saw the world when I was bearing down on my 17th birthday.

And all I wanted for my birthday was for Newcastle to survive their Second Division relegation battle and avoid the drop into Division Three for the first time in their history.

9. *United We Stand*

What followed the marvellous derby win over Sunderland was five straight defeats that left the club right on the very verge of the drop. There was a 6-2 mauling at Wolves, ironically, and then two straight 3-2 defeats to Tranmere at home and Ipswich away. John Wark scored. John Wark always scores. I sometimes think he spent his career just following us around waiting to piss on our strawberries. Oh, John Aldridge scored too; see *following us around pissing on our strawberries*, above.

The fourth defeat was at home to Millwall when a Malcolm Allen goal ensured the Londoners left Tyneside with three points that would have meant so much to our survival bid.

The fifth – and final – defeat came in a game that will reside for all time in my top three memory matches.

Newcastle travelled to The Baseball Ground to face Derby County. Derby's bus was heading for its Premiership stop and it was being driven by none other than Arthur Cox himself. The irony wasn't lost on any of us as we made our way – cans and Greggs in hand – down the A1.

It's hard to relay back just how desperate times had become that April, the Easter of 1992. Those that were at these games and remember them will understand the depth of the situation we were in. The way the club were talking, the way the press were peddling it, it was as if the clubs very life was on the line. That is probably true. The financial mess the club had wound up in meant that relegation might actually lead to that: being wound up.

One hundred years after the club was first formed its very life was hanging by a thread in the final weeks of an incredible season. And under Kevin Keegan's charismatic leadership we stood together, every man, woman and child, defiant and United in the face of such adversity.

That's the thing you see; if we'd stood a mass of individuals, all blaming each other, players, manager, boardroom and supporters all pointing fingers we would have been relegated. Divided we would have fallen.

But *United*, well, United we were always going to stand strong. And when you do that you really do have a hell of a chance against anything.

When we arrived at The Baseball none of us had any idea what was about to unfold. But the unity and the defiance that it brought out of every last one of us, every player, every supporter, Keegan and his staff, everyone, well even just thinking about it sends shivers down my spine.

After no more than 3 minutes Kevin Brock handled on the line from a Derby corner and along with the penalty, which was duly dispatched, came the red card. Down to ten-men, 1-0 down away to a promotion chasing team, with 87 minutes left to play was hardly what you'd call a game plan. But to a man every one of us was up out of our seat (in some cases launching said seat onto the playing surface) and vociferously backing the lads.

We've all heard the chant *Sing your hearts for The Lads*. Well this was the epitome of it. You could feel the emotion, the hurt, the love and the pride in every chant that was started, every *Ha'way* that reverberated from the away end all around the old ground.

A mistake at the back allowed Paul Kitson through soon after for the second. Maybe that's why I never liked Paul Kitson when he joined us years later. I feel the same about Nicky Butt. I remember the Batty – Butt square up at St James in the famous 5-0 take-that-you-Manc'-bastards pasting of '96. I wanted Batty to rip his head off. Never took to little Nicky when we bought him. And that was before his last appearance for Man United… against Newcastle in the Cardiff semi-final.

Anyway, back to The Baseball.

I remember Alan Thompson running into the back of the net, in front of the away supporters, to retrieve the ball after the second goal put us 2-0 down. Maybe it's clouded nostalgia kissed memory or maybe it really happened but I swear he was crying when he picked the ball – and our tattered survival hopes – out of the back of the net. Even if he wasn't he might as well have been. You see, it's because he cared about the club. See, *never liked Nicky Butt*, above.

As well as having a mountain to climb referee Brian Coddington (trust me, if I can find his address it *will* be printed in the back of the next book alongside Trelford Mills) decided to make things more interesting by giving us 3 less men to climb it. He started by sending off Kevin Scott for squaring up to / kicking over Marco Gabbiadini. Gabbiadini of course was of Sunderland fame and had scored the clincher in that fateful play off game 2 years before. To latter day supporters he was the pre-Kevin Phillips Kevin Phillips.

I can't remember what happened in what order but I think we made it to half time with 9 men and a 2-goal deficit. But we fought and we rallied and we gave everything we had. And I'm not just talking about those on the terraces (they had started off as seats but most had been sent flying in the direction of the ref / police / Tommy Johnson during the first 45).

No, I'm talking about the players too. I'm talking about players who gave everything for this club, for these supporters, for their shirts and for the colleagues. Those were players who knew that the shirt had a Newcastle badge on it and they knew that meant more than just damn good wages.

I remember the atmosphere being the best I had ever known it. It was love colliding with hate (not in a big wet Def Leppard way neither). It was pride entwining with defiance; it was seats colliding with stewards, and it was amazing. I remember Stan, one of the lads form the other Coaches walking past us at half-time. Stan was one of the most reliable, calming, steady-influencing people I ever met. He got to the row in front of us and yelled "If he wants a fucking riot, he's gonna get a fucking riot…"

It was electric!

As the second half got under way 9-man United (and they were *men*) pulled one back. The place went barmy. We really did go mental. He doesn't know it but the hand on the bairns back stopping him making a beeline across the Baseball Ground turf was actually mine. Maybe he was going to get his seat back… I'd seen him fling it about 30 minutes before.

Any lingering hopes we might have had were then cruelly and disrespectfully extinguished. The third goal was a killer, so too was the third red-card. This time it was Liam O'Brien for kicking out at Tommy Johnson. Bit of a cheap card in the end. He never even made contact. But the referee – the same one that once sent off 3 or 4 Gateshead players in one match – saw an opportunity to increase the drama – and the crisis – and reduce Newcastle to 8 men. Scratch that, 8 hero's.

Not wanting to risk having the game abandoned he then restricted his red-cards to the bench, where Terry Mac was sent of for something or other. But as the goals went in and tallied up to 4-1, and as Arthur Cox seemed to revel in it – which really pissed me off – the Toon Army grew in voice. While the old master savoured the victory his apprentice simply waved to the Geordie faithful from the dugout. And incredibly the faithful grew even more in heart and defiance, in voice and support.

I will never forget that day at The Baseball Ground, watching Derby milk it like older kids slapping first years around a playground. I will never forget the enormous wave of support and defiance that must have echoed through every black & white heart in that ground all the way back to Tyneside itself as we stared relegation to the Third Division and hell even extinction in the face without so much as blinking. And whatever the future holds, whatever trophies this club might one day go on to win, I will never in my life be prouder to be a Geordie than I was that day.

It isn't players that make a club special; it's supporters. But when the two, when playing staff and supporters combine that way, when they're United like that, that is the best thing you can ever win in football. Sometimes that kind of bond will bring trophies with it; sometimes it will bring survival. But whatever that kind of unity wins, it will never be worth more than the unity itself.

That unity was needed more than ever for the 2 remaining matches. Newcastle needed all 6 points without fail. First up was Portsmouth in our final home game of the season.

10. *That David Kelly Goal*

I will never forget it as long as I live. Two games to go, all six points desperately needed to fight off relegation and possibly extinction, and the green dot neon clock on The NEI Scoreboard down to 07 minutes left.

Jesus Christ in 7 minutes we were going to be a Third Division team for the first time in our history. There's needing to score a goal, and there is *needing* to score a goal. I was in the Paddocks in the Milburn Stand. I was just yards from the dugout. Everyone was down to the nerve ends. The skies were blue, the colours of the crowd were brilliant black & white & yellow & green. The roars had turned to screams. The support had turned to desperation. My fingertips had turned into my knuckles. Our dreams were turning into a nightmare.

06 minutes left.

Maybe it was my fault; maybe I should have gone to the Scoreboard like I used to with Dad. Maybe I should have gone to the Leazes like Dad used to. Maybe… maybe. maybe…

05 minutes left.

Ray Ranson knocks a long ball up the line. God the people were willing Newcastle to score with everything they had. David Kelly wins the header. This is a bit like Keegan's first goal, I thought obscurely. Mick Quinn flicks it on, I love Mick Quinn. David Kelly runs onto it. This *is* like Kevin Keegan's first goal.

Everyone holds their breath, the Gallowgate seem to suck the ball towards them and Kelly swings his right foot at it.

Then someone pressed pause.

I swear to God and Joe Harvey that everyone I have ever spoken to about that game, that shot, that goal says the same thing. The ball arced towards the willing wind blown Gallowgate net frame at a time, like fate was using the buttons off of a VCR to make the suspense even greater.

I could see the gap. I could see the net. I could see the flailing 'Keeper too far away from it. I could see it! I could see it! My heart was in my mouth. Tyneside stood still. Destiny stood still. Football stood still. Then BANG! The ball smashes into the back of the net and Newcastle have scored! Newcastle are winning! And David Kelly scored a goal – that goal – that will forever live in the top three Newcastle United goals of all time as by Terry Scott.

There was just this explosion of emotion that spilled over onto the pitch, terraces, everywhere. Everybody hugged everybody. Friends hugged friends. Strangers hugged strangers. There were no strangers; everyone was a Geordie that day, that moment. Players hugged coaches, coaches hugged players, players hugged fans and I hugged Steve Watson… and I think I scared the shit out of him!

Happy, happy days.

The last 4 minutes took as long as the previous 85 had. But the final whistle arrived and the ground just spilled with relief. All that was left was to go to promotion chasing Leicester City and win away.

I love how we do things the easy way.

11. *Filbert Street*

I will never forget that season, for a multitude of reasons. For Keegan returning, for beating Sunderland, for Liam's chip at Roker, for Derby away of course and for *that* David Kelly goal.

But perhaps the residing memory was the final day, at Filbert Street, then home of then promotion chasing Leicester City. A win and Newcastle were safe; anything less and we could go down.

Now, I'm not a cynic, but I don't believe they ever did put a man on the moon. I reckon they faked it in the desert. That aside, we live in a world where we can launch rockets into outer space, where we can save someone's life by giving them a new heart and where we can change the channel on the TV by sitting in the chair and just pressing a button on a remote. But still, despite such amazing technological advances, despite the ever-eager onrush of science, we are unable to convey football scores over the radio.

If I were at home, sitting in the living room or perhaps having a BBQ in the garden, I would be able to discover the score, the scorer, the minute the goals were scored in and the implications of said goals. If I were in the car, perhaps travelling to or from a football match, I would be able to tune in, listen to the commentator read out the scores, brief me on the details, and understand the state of play.

However, put a man in a football ground and something remarkable happens. Put a man in a football ground and the radio is unable to provide anything other than falsities, inaccuracies, rumours and plain old lies.

It is impossible to get an accurate football score through the radio to a crowd in a football ground. If Brighton – who were in the relegation mix alongside Newcastle – were to go 1-0 down through a disputed penalty that would come through to the crowd at other grounds as *Brighton are 2-0 up and have just been awarded a stone wall penalty*. If Plymouth Argyle (what kind of footballing 'surname' is Argyle anyway…?) who were also in the mix with us that fateful May afternoon were to equalise with 20 minutes to go, that would come through as *Plymouth are now 3-0 up, despite having only 9 men but kick off has been delayed by 20 minutes due to crowd congestion*. Crowd congestion…? At Plymouth…?

As far as Newcastle were concerned we entered the very violent, very charged, very aggressive Filbert Street looking to dodge relegation to the Third Division… and a boat load of coins that were thrown our way. Nice folk those Leicester lads.

Our fate was at least in our own hands, and we entered battle alongside Oxford, Plymouth, Brighton and Port Vale. Of the five of us only two would survive. If we won, then one of those survivors would be Kevin Keegan's Newcastle United. If we lost or even drew, then the clubs very life was on the line.

In a scrappy game there was very few chances and the biggest threat came from the hordes of supporters trying to kill us as we stood in our little pen in what really was a shit hole of a ground. The bairn had built better stadia out of cardboard boxes when he used to use his A-Team figures to play carpet football. Newcastle's plan did indeed come together and the lads went in 1-0 up at half time.

The score line remained unchanged as rumours and contradictions came and went about the games involving the other strugglers. I can't remember for sure any more – but I'm sure Tranmere and Blackburn Rovers were involved as opponents.

Then it happened. The Filbert Street Scoreboard had finally counted down to 00 minutes left, after what seemed like 4 or 5 hours of football, United were into injury time and their survival was all but guaranteed. Then I got this cold shiver as the ball broke forward. It was like someone was standing on my grave; or standing on Newcastle United's. Someone hooked the loose ball back across the face of goal and I knew what was going to happen before it did.

Some tragedies you see coming just a moment before they do, just a moment too late to do anything about.

I felt a hand on my shoulder. It was one of the lads. They'll always be like brothers to me, the lads. We've faced a lot of things together. That's what friends are for. Life's a journey not a destination. It's not always where you end up; it's about the people you travel with. And in the lads I have as friends I can honestly say I could not have travelled with better people. They know I love them; I'm sure they do. But if they don't well I'm telling them now.

We stood arms over one anothers shoulders. We all felt it as soon as the cross came in. We all knew before Steve Walsh, the Leicester Centre-half, leapt up to meet the cross. We all knew before his header flew past Tommy the Barman in the Newcastle goal. The home fans erupted. They spilled onto the pitch. They celebrated like they had won promotion. Maybe their radios were as fucked up as ours were. Maybe they thought they *had* just won promotion. I didn't care what it meant to them; I cared only for what it meant to us. And despite some fans saying not to worry, others looking bemused and confused, where we were standing the news filtered through that a point wouldn't be enough; results had went against us; United were down.

The shiver on my spine spilled over like a bucket of cold water and ice had been tipped down my back. My heart sank; it actually sank. A solitary tear rolled down my cheek as I tried to muster enough in my lungs for one more '*United.* The words wouldn't come. I couldn't speak.

About 5 to ten minutes later the pitch was almost clear, and although some spectators had taken up better defensive positions than I've seen Kevin Scott take the game resumed. I pulled myself up, surrounded by a mass of confused and devastated Geordie friends and family, and I watched the last few seconds play out. The ref would blow any second and then the funeral of this once great club could begin.

Tommy the Barman punted the ball forward. Someone – I think it was Ned Kelly or Gavin Peacock – chased after it. Steve Walsh (bastard) got in front to nod it back. The header was weak so Steve Walsh (bastard) ran on to slide it back. Then Steve Walsh (stupid bastard) toe poked it straight past his own keeper and the ball trickled towards the goal. Surely one of the fans would run on and whack it clear. Instead, the same people that took up better defensive positions than Kevin Scott went on to show the same lack of awareness as Scottie and the ball promptly ran over the line and into the back of the net.

The fans spilled back on to the pitch. The game was over. Newcastle had won 2-1! Newcastle were safe! Newcastle were SAFE! The place just exploded. Newcastle were back from the dead. They had won the game in the most amazing circumstances. The Leicester fans charged towards us. There were all sorts going off. It was chaos. But Newcastle had done it!

I have never celebrated a goal like it in my entire life, not before, not after. The players were caught up in the melee and some ran to the away end for safety. I remember standing on the side of the pitch with David Kelly. I put my arm around him and said "Thanks Ned…"

"My pleasure mate," he said in an awful Brummie accent, which surprised me because I thought he was Irish.

I love Ned Kelly.

He stood there, sweat dripping off him, the famous number 9 shirt soaked through because he had ran his heart out for the club… And for its supporters.

That shirt has seen some hero's. But in the heat of a Second Division relegation battle, in the ramshackle surroundings of a pitch invasion at Filbert Street, none seem to eclipse that image of Ned Kelly in my memory hall of fame.

Is there any greater glory than that in the face of adversity…?

Thanks Ned.

Part Four

NEWCASTLE, NEW QUEEN, NEW KING AND NEW PRINCE

1. *Every Rose*

I love the sunrise over Tyneside. I love it when the blue morning sky gets lighter with every passing minute and the horizon is a reckless brush stroke of yellow and orange. I love the mix of colours and magic above these gritty Tyneside streets, working man's clubs and muddy football fields.

I love the new day and all that it just might bring.

I went downstairs, had a cup of tea and an orange club biscuit and I waited for The Journal to land through the letterbox. I used to go and buy it, but now that my Dad was living with the girl from the newsagents Mam and I agreed to fork out for the paperboy. Every cloud, silver linings and all that.

I only ever read the sports pages. Scratch that; I only ever read the football pages. To me the back page is the front page.

The headlines were as warm as the Wallsend summer I was enjoying. Keegan had signed a 3-year deal. He was staying. Speculation had been rife ever since that game at Leicester that the Keegan wand had *been* waved and now all the great man would wave was Goodbye.

But the deal was done, and on the back of the 13-week verbal agreement for KK and Terry Mac to save the club the two were going to stick around.

Maybe it was the summer sun and the successful survival of the season before. Maybe it was the promise of the new season

225

that August would bring now that Keegan was staying. I don't know what it was, but there was a wonderful sense of contentment and optimism in the air. Alongside it another kind of wonderful came into bloom too: love.

Love is a strange thing. Or if you're Freddie Mercury I guess it's a crazy little thing. But one way or another, sooner or later it gets you and sooner or later your heart wanders off and plays on the dangerous side of the tracks.

I had difficulty coming to terms with Dad's love for this Rachel chick. He had my Mam; he loved her; why would he be greedy and want someone else? That I thought that was just underlined my lack of understanding of the mystery and muscle of love. It was only years later when that muscle flexed in me that I understood the great mystery: Dad didn't love Mam. Pity I couldn't have fathomed out it earlier. Dad and I would have saved a lot of years.

Another thing to spur on my meandering of all that is love was reflecting on my Mam's failed attempts at a romance since she and Dad had split up.

She's not good at being alone, my Mam, and no more than 6 months after Dad packed his bags and walked out she started *seeing* this new fella. His name was Derek. He was from Washington. She met him through a friend of a friend and they seemed to hit it off so fair play to her. I had nothing against the fella or the notion: after all, Dad walked out on her, just like Gascoigne, Waddle & Beardsley walked out on Newcastle. They all needed replacing, or else the Team would be short. Well, our Team was short now, so I guess Mam figured Dad needed replacing too.

That said, although I wasn't opposed to their getting together I wasn't exactly interested either. As Mandy, Waddle, Gascoigne and Beardsley had taught me: some people are just irreplaceable.

To continue the football metaphor I would rather have played with 10-men than have Dad substituted.

Anyway, while I didn't object to Mam & Derek I made no attempt to get to know the guy. I didn't cause any friction between them, or between him & me. I just went to my room when he came around, or called on my mates, Dave & Adam.

We've faced a lot of things together, my mates and me. That's what friends are for. Life's a journey not a destination. It's not always where you end up; it's about the people you travel with. And in the lads I have as friends I can honestly say I could not have travelled with better people. They know I love them; I'm sure they do. But if they don't well I'm telling them now.

Derek to his credit did make an effort with me. I mean, the guy was a dork, but he tried. I don't think he liked me (after all, I didn't give him much to like) but for my Mam's sake he tried to build a bridge to me. I made no such effort. Nice pier, Derek.

There was, how can I put it, a few misunderstandings, shall we say? You see, Derek was a bit of a Sandancer and he failed to grasp both the ferocity and the direction of my passion and my allegiance.

He made small talk with me one day about neither nowt nor something. He made some idle promise to, and I quote, *'Take me to Town one Saturday'*. Now to me that translated as *'Terrence, I am aware that you are keen on football; perhaps one Saturday when Newcastle are playing at home I may take you over to spectate upon the match'*.

To Derek it meant *'Look, it'll make your mother happy if you & me go down the coast one weekend'*.

So, one dull Saturday morning duly arrived.

"You fancy going to Town this afternoon then Terry?" Derek asked with false enthusiasm.

"Yeah, sure," I said with genuine nonchalance.

"Go on then, get your stuff, we'll get away in 10 minutes and beat the traffic."

Fifteen minutes later I'd gotten my stuff, pinched The Journal and was sitting in the front seat of Derek's Talbot Horizon. His dog, a snappy little Scottish Terrier or something, was yapping around the back seats. Derek got into the driving seat, put on his driving gloves – which said so much about his personality – and off we went.

Derek made small talk. I just buried my head in the 'paper. The traffic came and went, but I didn't pay attention. We weren't going the normal way, but I figured Derek just knew a short cut. Finally we parked up. I folded the 'paper closed and looked out of the window.

"What the hell…?" I asked sharply.

"What's the matter?" Derek asked.

"What are we doing here?"

"I thought a day at the seaside might be fun. We can walk the dog, get some chips…"

"What about the match!"

"What match?"

"What do you mean *what match*? THE match! The Newcastle match!"

"What about it?"

"Good God am I speaking French?"

"You *are* speaking out of turn," Derek added pompously.

There was an awkward silence while the situation sunk in.

We were parked in a car park down Cullercoats. I mean, Cullercoats… in March…when Newcastle were at home!

You said you fancied a trip to Town today." Derek reasoned.

"Yeah! To Town! This isn't Town. This is the bloody seaside!"

"Well why didn't you say you didn't want to come here?"

"I didn't know we bloody were!"

"So where did you think we were going?"

"Town! I don't know, call me stupid, but the cryptic clue was when you *said 'You fancy going to* Town *this afternoon then Terry'.* So I just presumed we were going to... Town!"

"Well, we're here now, let's make the best of it."

"Derek says what?"

That was my new thing. Whenever anyone said something I disagreed with I would always say, for example, *Derek say what?*

He sighed; no doubt regretting his attempts to get close to me, and tried again.

"Look, we're here now, let's make the best of it."

"Derek say what?"

"We can play pool..."

"I can watch football,"

"You can throw sticks into the water for the dog..."

"He'll drown!"

"You can go on the Dodgems..."

"You can fuck off!"

I braced myself for being chastised for the bad language. None was forthcoming. Stepfathers are lapse to check a child, let alone stepfather candidate elects. *Mental note, takes advantage of Derek...*

"So what *do* you want to do...?" he asked me resignedly.

"I want to go to Town."

"And what are we going to do in Town that we can't do here?"

I don't know – maybe it was me, but it didn't seem that complicated. "I can go to the match!"

I think Derek noted that I said *I can go to the match* as opposed to *we can go to the match*. He was a decent enough bloke Derek, for his sins. He drove me to Town and dropped me off at the match with a fiver to boot.

Mental note – stop taking advantage of Derek…

I went to the match. Derek took the dog back down the coast. Newcastle lost. The dog survived.

And that incident, sadly, wasn't a one off. The first time had been harmless enough; the second time posed a serious threat to my well-being.

Derek, bless him, tried to learn from his mistake. He went about establishing that my Saturday's were spent one way and one way only: at football. Now, I might have lead him astray a little, but purely by accident and anyone with any interest in football – which Derek didn't have – would surely have side-stepped the potential minefield Derek took us running into.

I *did* say that I went to football every weekend. The key here is the word *every*. Of course, I didn't go to football every weekend. What I meant was I went to every *home* game (be it midweek or weekend, Saturday or Sunday). What Derek heard was *I go to a football match every weekend…*

You can see where I'm going here can't you…

So, there we are one painfully long Wednesday night; me, Mam and Derek playing Monopoly or Game of Life or something. I made sure every time I rolled the dice I demolished most of Derek's hotels and as many houses as I could get. I was the top hat, Mam was the iron, and Derek was the little dog. Jesus, talk about stereotypes.

Derek said "How about we go to Town one weekend, maybe go to the football some time…?"

I interpreted that as *How about we go to Town one weekend – not the seaside – and, maybe, if Newcastle United are engaged in a home fixture, we can spectate upon the game*, hence I agreed.

I even checked. "We're not going to the Coast though are we…?"

"No Terry, we're *not* going to the coast."

Excellent.

A few Saturdays came and went and no such trip occurred. Then, one murky Wallsend Saturday morning Derek asked if I would fancy popping into Town with him. Newcastle were away, I'd have the radio in the car but to be sure I even said, "We will be in time for the match though won't we…?"

"We can leave at 12 if you want to be sure?"

"Yeah, cool," I told him. That seemed fair enough. Derek was of course a man – well, barely – but being a man shopping meant one-hour maximum including travelling time.

Shopping with every woman I had ever known had meant going on Saturday morning but not before phoning the school to explain that there was a 50/50 chance I wouldn't be there on Monday.

I ran upstairs, got dressed, put on my thick shell-suit jacket top and wandered down to the car. Derek clambered in alongside me and made small talk, which was my cue to go for The Journal. I read the football pages, I listened to the radio, and nodded at the nonsensical things that Derek was muttering.

"Okay, this'll do," Derek said, taking advantage of our early arrival and parking up the Horizon.

I put the 'paper down, looked out of the window at my horizon and froze. "Fuck me…" I said shocked.

"Jesus Christ what now?" Derek asked, sensing his latest attempt to bond with his girlfriends' son about to backfire.

"Get me the hell out of here… Now!" I instructed with a certain degree of panic in my voice.

"What's wrong? You said you liked football. You said you went to the match every weekend!"

231

"Not fucking Sunderland I don't…!"

"But you said…" Derek broke off, figuring out the error with no need for my panic-stricken voice to explain it.

I just sat there, ensuring my jacket was zipped up.

Then Derek did something that baffled me beyond comprehension and fuelled my suspicions that he was indeed from another planet.

"Look it's only one game, we're here now, let's just go and make the best of it."

"Derek say what! Are you mad? I mean, really, are you mad?"

"What. What now? What else have I done wrong? I mean Good God Terry it's only a football match."

"No. No! It's *not* only a football match; it's a *Sunderland* match."

"So," he said, "They're a local team, get behind them, support them. When I was a lad my Dad used to take me to Newcastle one week and Sunderland the next. He used to watch Jackie Milburn one week and then Len Shackleton the next."

"Geordie reject." I slipped in stubbornly.

"What?"

"Len Shackleton. He was a Geordie reject."

"What are you talking about?" He was one of Sunderland's greatest players ever!"

"Aye, but he was a Geordie reject. He made his debut for Newcastle in a 13-0 win over Newport, and he scored 6 goals. But he wasn't good enough. So we sold him. And this lot bought him. You see, Geordie reject."

The argument unfolded in a strange way. I took up my colours as a black & white and Derek began revealing a Sunderland tendency that basically ensured this would be our last attempt at bonding.

"Besides," I said, "this lot are crap…"

"Oh," he said, "Unlike the world beaters across the water that you're so proud of…!"

"Right, that's it," I instructed. "Take me home!"

Then Derek did something that really surprised me. I guess he'd just had enough.

"No." He said.

"What do you mean, no?"

"I mean no: as in the opposite of yes."

"Hmmm…" I pondered.

"If you want to go home Terry there's a bus concourse down by the shopping centre, you'll find a way."

"Okay, Okay. Hang about here. You're going to send me out there… into the land that time forgot? Jesus, Beamish is more modern. A bus concourse? A bloody bus concourse? If I hang around long enough someone might invent a tram that'll take me home…"

"Terry, I'm stopping. You can come to the game or you can go home, I don't care, I give up. But I am not driving you home until 5 o'clock. Okay?"

"But Derek, this is Sunderland. Do you know why they love Mr Bean around here? Not because he's funny, but because they admire his sense of grace and his standard of education. You can't leave me *here*."

"Take it or leave it," Derek said as his pier reached an end.

"But what about this…?" I asked him, unzipping my jacket.

"Good God Terry…" he said, eyeing my black & white top with the Greenalls logo stretched across and sown on by the woman who would never forgive him if he sent her only son out to get killed in the enemy's back yard.

Mental note, never get in a car with Derek ever again…

It wasn't long after that Derek stopped coming around. I spent a few sleep-overs at Dave or Adam's when Derek & Mam went out, but soon her relationship with Derek had passed and Team Scott were back to playing a man short.

Whilst Dad had been lucky in love, finding and ultimately leaving my Mam to be with his soulmate, his Rachel, then the woman he left behind had not been so lucky. I don't think Derek was my mother's soulmate mind you, but when Derek faded out no one else faded in. The curtain had seemingly come down on Sheila Scott's love life, and the play had ended a tragedy not a fairytale.

So that left just me.

As my heart expanded and I began to flirt with notions that I could love more than just football, football itself gave me something wonderful to love. And as Kevin Keegan's resurgent Newcastle got off to a storming start to the 92 / 93 campaign the first rose of my adult love life was just about to land in my hand, thorns and all.

2.   *When Cole Was King*

I love the sunrise over Tyneside. When the sky is dull and grey and loaded with raindrops and the horizon is like blanket of fog hiding the sun behind it. I love the sparkle of the grey above these gritty Tyneside streets, working man's clubs and St James Park terraces.

We build our dreams on steel around here. We keep tradition close to our hearts and we do things the way we always have. If you want to change the TV channel you get off your backside and you change it. The 'net' is something you cast into the sea and nuts, bolts and loyalty keeps things together.

It was August 1992. After our glorious survival of the season before we all needed some time to recharge and recover. Kevin Keegan's loyalty kept him with Newcastle United. Special K had decided to stay and rather than play down Newcastle's chances of promotion he came right out and said what we were all thinking: we should walk right out of this league.

Keegan wasn't wrong.

Newcastle went off like a train and never once looked back, never once looked like anything could derail them. Paul Bracewell – fresh from leaving Roker Park for St James' – got off to the perfect start with a 25-yard screamer to set up a 3-2 opening day win over Southend at St James Park. A week later we went back to the Baseball Ground and – in a 2-1 win – we extracted our revenge in an incredible atmosphere that carried over from the season before. Nine more wins followed to make it a famous eleven straight wins at the start of the season. But none were sweeter than where the last of those wins was achieved: Roker Park.

Newcastle had taken some stick over the years from their local rivals. There was the Play Off defeat still to avenge, of course, and there was the little matter of Middlesborough and the part they had played in it all.

Since the two sides were relegated together in 1989 Boro had almost slipped out of the Second Division trap door with consecutive relegations. That fateful day in 1990 we could have put the nail in the coffin and buried them. Instead they trounced us, buried our promotion hopes into the bargain and then went on to net a promotion the following year while we went the other way.

I was witness to a series of 2 and 3 goal defeats at Ayresome Park, including the Rumbelows Cup exit to boot. I hated losing at Ayresome Park. I hated seeing the Holgate End light up and celebrate and I hated hearing them mock us as we tried to cling to the tattered ribbons of 'big club status'. Every time I left that little away end at Boro with defeat I vowed that one day I'd return and leave Teesside victorious.

As Keegan and Terry Mac contrived to save Newcastle in 1992 Middlesborough were promoted. The League Cup then re-introduced the two clubs in autumn of '92. The 1st Leg at St James Park finished 0-0 and Boro made the mistake that so many teams do of thinking that the hard part was done and that the home leg was a mere formality.

The Second Leg came on October 6th at Ayresome Park. Boro were the favourites, but all the way down to Teesside I had this feeling in the pit of my stomach, this burning in my heart and this fire of adrenalin running through my veins. I knew that, despite

Middlesborough being in The Premiership and United being in the newly named Division One, Newcastle were going to slay those Ayresome Park ghosts once and for all.

And that is exactly what happened. Newcastle tore the Teessiders apart, hammering home a 3-1 win in front of 24,000 in Teesside, where at least 7,000 where Geordies, gallantly singing Blaydon Races so loud that they'd have heard back home on the banks of the Tyne.

I felt like a great big indestructible black & white giant. Whatever poor team happened to wander out in front of our all-conquering path were smashed beyond recognition by an all shooting all firing high scoring outfit that played awesome football and carried an army so big that everyone knew us and everyone feared us.

We took around 10,000 supporters to Peterborough and won 1-0 in the drunken autumn sunshine. We took thousands to Brentford – including Dave Beasant and Joe Allon – and we won again. Finally, we travelled to the one place we wanted to go the very most: Roker Park.

Sunderland stepped out in front of us and it was the most amazing feeling. The team I hated more than any other in the world were standing toe to toe with me, and I knew that we could crush them with ease. More than that, all the hate from that rainy Play Off night spilled through me as the two sides kicked off. I bayed with all I had in my heart that this Newcastle United, my Newcastle United, our Newcastle United, would avenge the defeat that May night and bray their opponents into submission.

Newcastle scored at the Fulwell End (which was full of course, but the Fulwell End was always full wasn't it…) after 12 minutes. The game rolled on to the last 15 minutes with United still in the ascendancy but the scoreline still at just 1-0. Then amongst a crowded goalmouth Gordon Armstrong sneaked an equaliser to bring Sunderland level at 1-1. The Roker faithful erupted. Soon, a boisterous chorus of *'Where's you bubble gone, where's your bubble gone'* bounced around the sunny Sunderland sky.

I was enraged, incensed, angrier than perhaps I had ever been. I knew we were going to get promoted, I knew we were better than they were and I knew they knew it. But I wanted the score line as proof so I could ram it down their damn throats and leave every last one of them with nowhere to hide.

Then United won a free-kick outside the box… the same one where Liam O'Brien chipped that wonderful equaliser a year before…

I was standing on the Roker End. I was with my mates and a couple of thousand Geordie brothers. We were just behind that guy waving the zebra around. Liam stepped up… Liam curled it… Tim Carter stepped to his left… the ball curled to the right and…

…THERE'S OUR FUCKING BUBBLE! THERE'S OUR FUCKING BUBBLE! THAT'S THE FUCKING THING THERE WITH *KEEGAN! KEEGAN! KEEGAN!* WRITTEN ALL FUCKING OVER IT…!

The hairs on my arms stood on end as we went – to coin a phrase – absolutely mental and Liam (I will never need to buy a drink in Tyneside again) O'Brien only went racing off to the Geordie's in the Clock Stand Paddock, the Sunderland end!

Only about 5 minutes later did my heart return to a regular beat and pace that didn't threaten my very life and I was able to savour the last few moments of what was to be our first win at Roker Park since 1956.

When the whistle went the celebrations began in earnest, despite the emotional exhaustion amidst the Toon-Army. The best way I can describe it is the way you feel after you've had the best sex you have ever had in your life. You're exhausted but so very,

very happy and all you can do is lie there in an afterglow and try and take in just how wonderful it was.

If that game was amazing sex then the week later we were clearly too spent to get it up again. We lost three games in a row. Not that it mattered. Tasmin Archer might well have peaked too soon with her sleeping satellite but Newcastle United had certainly not. We dusted ourselves down and then went on and walloped pretty much everyone and stormed to Promotion, and the Division One Title, including thanking Sunderland very much for the 6 points by beating them again 1-0 in the rain at a glorious St James Park. I love this club.

And there is nothing quite like taking your old enemy and giving them a right good pasting. Especially when they've had it coming.

Keegan was masterful that season. We hadn't won at Ayresome Park since 1964 and we hadn't won at Roker since 1956. But Keegan, he took us to both and he conquered them both in the space of just 11 days. And people wonder why we love him? He followed the whole buy-when-you're-winning philosophy and brought in three new players as we entered into the home straight. Mark Robinson came in from Barnsley, but injury prevented us finding out how good he could have gone on to be. Scott Sellars came in to become a crowd favourite on the left-wing. That status was furthered with the winning goal in that aforementioned rainy game at St James'. But if Sellars was to be a crowd-favourite then the next signing was to go on and be a legend: Andy Cole.

Cole was a 1.7million pound capture from Bristol City, where he was making his name following release by Arsenal as a youngster. He was lightening quick, shot at a flash, and after netting on his home debut against Notts County Cole went on to bag 67 more in just 82 more games. He was like the First Divisions Ian Wright… only in black & white eyes he was better.

That was an argument that was soon to be proven as Cole and United joined Wright & Arsenal in The Premiership and Andy gleefully outscored the Gunners legend.

Promotion was clinched with a wonderful Tuesday night trip to Blundell Park and Grimsby Town. Memories of Huddersfield and 84 came flooding back. If anything, Grimsby was even more special.

The season ended with a 2-1 Thursday night victory over Oxford United – who were clearly not the best team the world has even seen – and a 7-1 hammering of last seasons final day opposition, Leicester City. David Kelly – legend – signed off with a hat-trick, which was a wonderful way to say goodbye to those who adored him. Andy Cole also bagged a hat-trick, which was a wonderful way to say hello to The Premiership.

The papers revelled in the headlines: Cole to Newcastle and all that. The fans just revelled in the legend and the free-scoring antics of what appeared to a Keegan masterstroke. Andy Cole: when he got the ball he scored a goal, simple as that.

3. *670 Days I Will Never Forget*

The Premiership, Nirvana, Beardsley and Roxy. That was the spring of my adult life and it was heavy laden with beautiful sunshine and clear blue skies. Even the clouds were fluffy white ones. It started with Promotion lingering in the Tyneside sun.

After the wonderful derby win over Sunderland on a rain soaked St James' Newcastle waited 10 days to travel to Grimsby. The trip to Blundell Park was on a Tuesday night, May 4th to be precise. How do I know? I still have the programme framed in the house.

It was an amazing trip. We arrived in Cleethorpes around 2.30pm for an evening kick off. We took a mini-bus. We found a bar where we all managed to get served, despite having only 4 eighteen year olds amongst us. The bar was quiet, so we moved on. And then we found *the* bar; it was a cracking boozer that was jam-packed with Geordies.

The atmosphere was incredible. How we made it up to the ground sober is beyond me. Luckily we did or I would have missed a tonne of memories of seeing United promoted. A 2-0 win took care of that. Everyone piled on to the pitch; me and the lads included, and we all just went crazy. We'd done it! We were the Champions! We were in The Premiership.

Those memories will live with me forever, and strange as it may sound that night at Grimsby seemed to be the very dawn of my adult life. From that point on it seemed both Newcastle United and myself were in with the big boys. We made News At Ten, and we were introduced by Trevor McDonald to boot. Beneath the deep velvet blue skies of Blundell Park we sang and danced and ran all over the Grimsby Town pitch in our new blue Asics away shirts. We wore scarves and hats and we hugged the players and we put crowns on Kevin Keegan and we thanked them all for all they had given us. Players and supports were but one and when you have that kind of unity and that kind of class you have a force to be reckoned with.

In the final two games we beat Oxford 2-1 on the Thursday after Grimsby and then hammered Leicester – who threatened our very lives the year earlier – 7-1 at Leazes. We were 6-0 up at half-time! Cole scored a hat-trick, David Kelly scored a hat-trick and Tyneside partied and celebrated like it was Christmas, New Year, Mardi Gras and The Hoppings all rolled into one. It was Carnival. It was Festival. It was dancing around the Bigg Market at 1am under a great big black & white flag. It was watching some crazy daredevil Geordie drunks leap off the buildings next to the Beehive and slide down lampposts by the Bigg Market toilets. It was incredible. And it was followed a few days later by the open top bus and the Teams parade of the streets on the way to the Civic Centre. And it was followed by Carnival, Festival, well, you get the picture.

When the dust settled it was followed by a summer of anticipation as the weeks between leaving Sixth Form and joining College were filled with season videos, 5-a-side, Diamond White and driving lessons. And as if to sum up the clubs rebirth the famous Leazes End – that I had heard so much about – rose once again. The structure of metal was like a giant's skeleton rising from the ground. Soon it would have flesh and blood in the form of the concrete laid upon it; soon the completed stand would have a soul, in the form of the 11,000 fans it would play home to.

That really was a wonderful summer.

And that was the summer I met Roxy.

August rose brilliantly in a vanilla sky that saw July wave goodbye and the new season wave hello. To Newcastle United that meant saying hello to The Premiership. To me personally it had meant saying goodbye to Sixth Form and saying hello to College. I waved goodbye to the terracing and said hello to a seat in the new Leazes End and as United clocked up their first Premiership points under the stands mighty presence I waved goodbye to my heart and said hello to craziness. You see, love – like football – brings emotions you never knew the likes of and takes away the logic you always thought you'd have.

For me it all began on the day I enrolled at college. I was at a bit of a loss over what to do with myself. In the mix of a teenage mind I decided that I wanted to be a mechanic. I was still rebellious and if the world had said stand I'd have sat, if the world had said sit I'd have jumped to my feet. I was into Grunge music, and had developed a kindred ear to Nirvana, Pearl Jam, Stone Temple Pilots and Rage Against The Machine. I wore ripped jeans and tie-dyed T-shirts with *Nevermind* or *Fuct* plastered across. I had an earring and sported my first tattoo, a little Magpie taken from the ones The Chronicle and The Pink were sporting during the Promotion season of 92 / 93.

Based upon such notions of rebellion I made my decision to skip the Business & Finance courses that everyone I knew was taking and I opted for a B-Tec in Motor Vehicle Engineering. That meant skipping all the Tyneside colleges and going to Gateshead College.

Going to Gateshead was really good. Nobody knew me. It was like having a clean slate. For all they knew I might have been cool. At college I met my new classmates and I made new friends, including a really canny lad called Lee Gallacher. Of course, I was Newcastle daft. Lee, as it turned out, was Hughie Gallacher's grandson or great grandson or something like that. That was me sold! Lee was one of a number of good lads in our class, and a number of good lasses for that matter. However, by that time there was only one girl for me: Roxy.

I met Roxy the day I enrolled. I recognised her immediately. I had *first* met her on the day Newcastle signed Andy Cole, back in March of the same year, 1993. I remembered her face straight away. It was hard not to. Back in March I had been making my way to Barrack Road trying to catch a glimpse of the new signing. Then I caught a glimpse of this really bonny lass walking away from the ticket office. Actually, I think my heart spotted her before my eyes did. She was stunning. She was Roxy.

You know how every once in a while, maybe even just 2 or 3 times in your lifetime, you see someone who you just know, based upon only their looks alone, that you could fall in love with. I'm not talking about looking at someone and thinking you'd love to sleep with them; I'm talking about just by seeing someone's face you drift away and see a future together. Just by seeing their face you see kids and wedding bells and anniversaries and romance and holding hands along the beach and pretty much everything someone in love would desire. One look and it's like a Hallmark card or Meg Ryan film flashes before your heart. Sometimes the eyes are just a fuse and with one glance at the right person the fuse is lit and moments later the heart goes off like dynamite. Seeing Roxy was just like that.

She struck me to the core and left an impression on me that lasted for months. Whenever romantic notions or fleets of fancy took my head or heart alike they always wore her face. That beautiful brunette with the stunning eyes and angelic smile walking down the Millburn Stand steps was burned onto my heart and whenever I watched a romantic film or heard a love song that made me think, I always thought of her, whoever she was.

She passed me by in less than 10 seconds but it was a moment that flooded me with something I had never known the likes of before. Then she was gone, fading into the Strawberry Place crowd just as smoothly as she had emerged from it. Every match I went to that season, every time I went to St James Park to buy an away ticket or hand my application in I always hoped I'd meet her again. I never did. I met Mick Quinn once – and that came close – but it didn't quite top it for me.

On the day I enrolled for College I saw her again. She was standing in the bus stop right outside the reception as I turned up to enrol. I couldn't believe my luck. My heart raced for weeks from that day at enrolment to the day my course began.

On the day I finally made my debut at Gateshead College, dressed in my finest white T-shirt, blue overalls tied poser style around my waste, and my steel-toe-cap boots my heart was absolutely palpitating.

As Newcastle were storming up The Premiership and earning the label of *The Entertainers*, I was discovering that women were a little like The Premiership: I'd waited years to get there, I was nervous and excited, but ultimately it wasn't as scary as I thought it would be.

Every time Roxy and I passed each other by there was always a glance between us. Every time we passed in the corridor on the way to classes, every time we passed in the cafeteria getting lunch, every time we sat in the refectory during break we smiled at one another. And every time we did there was something there. The lads in my class teased me about her, in the nicest of ways, and it was obvious that I liked her. She would smile sweetly every time they teased me that way. Roxy was a few years older than me and although she was too mature to get drawn into playground games she still found it sweet the way my I tried to play down my crush and look cool while the lads in my class continued to both deliberately and accidentally embarrass me.

In the end it was one of the girls who bailed me out. Anya, a bit of a babe herself but so much better a friend, played the part of wing-man / wing-woman / wing-hottie. It resulted in a moment that somehow balanced itself beautifully between awkward and exciting, all you've wanted meets all you've feared. It felt like taking a penalty in an FA Cup Final. Anya basically went and sat next to Roxy in the refectory and told her all about me, including how much I liked her. I could see her pointing at me and the lads, sitting at our table a few rows away. Anya and Roxy talked, laughed, smiled and finally as Anya made her way back to us she gave me the thumbs up.

Anya reached our table and said, "She's nice. She says you've got to go and talk to her."

I didn't know what to say or what to think. Try *'Jesus'*, I thought.

I wasn't ready for it but there was no backing out now and still having any chance of a future with this girl. Some moments present themselves once and once only and if you miss them then you never get them back.

I felt like a centre-half that somehow finds himself clean through on goal.

I knew what I had to do: grab the opportunity with both hands ready or not. And so I did. And because Roxy was so wonderful and so special she understood my shyness and admired my bravery. Most importantly, when I asked her to go out with me on a date – she said 'yes'. And in the time it took her to smile, with her eyes as much as with her lips, and say "Yeah, I'd love to," my heart packed its bags, made its reservations, wrote my head a postcard and leapt on the first wild horse out of Dodge.

I had a date. And soon I would have a girlfriend. And soon after that I would be in love.

As summer shimmered in its twilight Roxy & I lit up like a sunset on the Tynemouth coast. She made me feel like Rock n Roll, Roxy. She was stunningly good looking, deeply beautiful, warmly enchanting, and – being a year or two older than me – she had a *show me the way* about her loving that would have made Frampton proud.

Life was good – when you're in love with someone who loves you back it often is. Life and football held hands and skipped merrily away together. To me, if my heart was the famous number 9 shirt, then Roxy was my Andy Cole. Now I know to most women being referred to as Andy Cole probably isn't going to constitute a compliment. But I'm sure that the Geordie faithful know what I mean.

Both were passionate, exciting, enchanting, successful and a thrill to be with. Cole was free-scoring his way to 42 goals that season, gleefully banging the ball into the net week after week. Roxy was gleefully sending me spinning deeper and deeper in love with her, mesmerising me with her charms and her personality and her looks and her love all along the way. The number 9 has a tradition, long and magical. Andy Cole did it justice. Love too has a tradition, even more magical than any a football shirt that ever there was. And Roxy, well, Roxy did justice to that too.

Life was good – when your lover is as special as your number 9 it often is.

Many a player has said that scoring a goal feels better than sex. Well that wonderful September of seaside sunsets I got my first chance to compare.

It was a hot summer night, and the beach was burning, there was fog crawling over the sand. Roxy and I had bunked off College early and went to Whitley Bay to just lay together on the beach and watch the sun set slowly. When I listened to her heart I heard the whole world turning, I could see the shooting stars falling through her tinted hair. We ate ice-cream, I spilled ice-cream and we cuddled up close on the beach. She was licking her lips and her lipstick was shining, I was dying just to ask for a taste. The seaside sun was setting and we were lying together in a silver lining by the light of the moon. As soon as it became secluded we knew there wasn't another moment to waste.

She held me so close that my knees were weak and my soul was flying high above the ground. I was trying to speak, but no matter what I did I just couldn't seem to make any sound. She leaned forward, pressing her breast against my body and asked me if I wanted to make love to her. She took the words right out of my mouth. It must have been when she was kissing me.

About seven of the best minutes of my life later I knew I'd never feel that way about anybody ever again. I was still trembling beneath the Cullercoats dusk 2 hours later as we ate CandyFloss and cartons of chips with loads of salt and vinegar on. And though that might sound like something for kids, which I guess we still were, still, she was my girl and the woman in her had made me a man.

That night, walking hand in hand along the sea-front as the summer sun set around us, being with her, being with Roxy, and loving her so much, well I'm not sure if I have ever been happier in all my life.

And just as Andy Cole went on scoring goal after goal, including that wonderful trip to Oldham where I forgave Peter Beardsley, Roxy and I kept on making love. Beardsley's return had at first been greeted with my teenage cynicism and spite. But Roxy's love was allowing me to love life as well. Love is funny like that; when you're without it the whole world is a glass half empty; when you're in love the whole world is a Champagne glass or a Brown Ale bottle always half full.

Newcastle were incredible that season. Everything just felt right. After years of waiting and under-achieving and being in the doldrums suddenly everything was magic and exciting and passionate. The team were fantastic, the results were fantastic and even the ground was being developed into something fantastic. But more than that, the chemistry was right. Our Manager was none other than Kevin Keegan. Who else could fill such a role in such a footballing fairytale then a returning hero and Tyneside legend? It had to be Keegan. And in turn Keegan made more magic and more chemistry.

Peter Beardsley returned home, just like Keegan had. Our team was almost entirely English, and there was plenty of Geordie in that too, especially in the kids that were coming through. The side gelled wonderfully and played a brand of football that made us the most popular 'second' team in the land. Fans had so many players to choose from to find a favourite player. There was Pav, Rob Lee, Barry Venison, Scott Sellars, Lee Clark and of course Beardsley and Cole. Everyone wanted to watch Kevin Keegan's Newcastle, our Newcastle.

There were countless memories, treasure trinkets that are captured by the heart and ignited every time an old season video is placed in the VCR or an old match programme is read once again.

There was the first win, over Everton, the first point, at Old Trafford, and the first away win at Villa in October. There was drubbing Chris Waddle's Sheffield Wednesday one spectacular Sky Monday Night Football Special where the black & whites famously had to wear blue at Gallowgate after the two teams shirts clashed. There was Liverpool – home and away – not least of all the emotional Hillsborough Anniversary trip to Anfield where I stood on the Anfield Road end and watched United win just like they did the last time they were at Anfield when my Dad came home and left us.

There was hammering Notts County 4-1 and 7-1 and hammering Villa 5-1 the night Andy Cole broke the clubs goalscoring record for one season. It was fairytale stuff; it was the stuff dreams are made of.

Things with Roxy were just the same. When autumn set in Roxy and I cuddled close together as the leaves fell from the trees around Gateshead College and Eldon Square. As winter set in I took her to Greggs for pasties and sausage rolls that gave you third degree burns unless you left them at least 20 minutes after you bought them. She took me to restaurants; little Italians during happy hours and she added a touch of sophistication to our love.

As winter set in we embarked on a *Pictures Marathon* where we went to the Cinema two or three times a week. Then Roxy moved in with her sister in Heaton and we spent countless nights cuddled up on the sofa watching classic films like HG Wells' *The Time Machine, It's A Wonderful Life* and Charles Dickens immortal classic, *A Christmas Carol*. Roxy introduced me to them all. I introduced her to *A Muppets Christmas Carol* and Pizza Hut. She taught me how to cook, how to love, and how to make love. I simply ordered pizza and taught her about Kermit The Frog.

We decorated Christmas Trees together, hung streamers across her sisters' pad while she was working nights at the hospital and then we'd collapse in a heap and make love there and then on the living room floor. We celebrated New Year with a loving kiss, we wore silly hats with mistletoe pinned to the front and we bounced in off the doorway with a champagne bottle still in our hands. When spring came in to bloom our love bloomed with it. Before we knew it, Newcastle were bearing down on a UEFA Cup place and we were bearing down on our first Anniversary.

When the 93 / 94 season closed and summer came along I had a massive amount of time off College waiting for the second year of my course to convene. Roxy left to go back home – which to her had been Sheffield for many years – and I spent the longest month of my life without her. The World Cup and the transfer rumours did little to appease my aching heart. She came back for one weekend, and I offered to go down for another, but she declined.

She came back in August – just as the 1994 / 95 season was about to get under way – and our love resumed where it left off. Although, for reasons I could never put my finger on, things were never quite the same. But the old one-two took off just like United's old one-two, with Roxy back in my arms and Cole & Beardsley back in the goals at Filbert Street on opening day. I was young, and in terms of love I was naive, but I was so very happy.

Beardsley broke his jaw that game, but the black & white machine rolled on regardless. The wins came and went, as did the goals. It was seven wins in a row before a 1-1 draw with Merseyside's least popular slowed Keegan's machine down. The goals rained in like a Wallsend September; the team kept chalking up victories, and the style in which they did it was phenomenal. The games were high paced, high tempo, pure football, all out attack, and play to win. Keegan only ever played to win.

But bad luck, bad timing, and maybe a squad that lacked in depth, and soon time and injuries took their toll. Rarely is something so beautiful so strong, in love, in life, and in football. Key players missed games: Albert, Venison, Beardsley and ultimately Cole. Newcastle's free-scoring number 9 had shin splints. Strangely enough his absence wasn't felt as keenly as that of Scott Sellars. If one thing undermined our season and even our chances of actually winning the title, it was the injury to Newcastle's wide left. Something as simple as Sellars injury had a knock on effect, something that unsettled the balance and the chemistry of the team, and something that ultimately sent Newcastle's Runaway Train off the track.

Sometimes the smallest of things can have the biggest of impacts.

Newcastle dropped points whilst Cole was out: the striker missing 5 games and probably only one win. He missed the first defeat of the season; ominously enough a 2-0 reverse at Old Trafford, where a young kid called Keith Gillespie scored the killer second.

After that result the sun seemed to set on the season as it did on the year. Something was wrong. The wins dried up, as did the points, and for Andy Cole so too did the goals.

Maybe it was my imagination; maybe it was fact, but either way, as Newcastle started to run aground, I couldn't help but feeling that Roxy and I were too.

There was something missing in our balance, something lacking in our chemistry, and after she went back home for a long weekend in the late autumn, we never quite clicked like we used to.

There was no pace to our relationship, the affection dried up, and of the two of us it seemed that I was the only one who wanted sex. We talked less, romanced less, and spent less time together. And the time we did spend together didn't have the spark we once had. We did all the same things, but the fire and the enthusiasm was no longer there. Roxy & I, just like Keegan's United, were misfiring.

Cole came back late in November… and duly scored. His late goal against Ipswich Town at St James Park looked like being the winner and all seemed right in the universe again. But Ipswich's last minute equaliser seemed to sum everything up. The game finished 1-1 and little did I or anyone who was there know, but we had witnessed the 68th and final goal that Andy Cole would ever score for us.

December, Christmas and New Year came and went; Fenwick's window was decorated and then undressed. Newcastle stuttered through and made it to FA Cup 3rd Round day to face Kenny Dalglish' Blackburn Rovers at Gallowgate. Rob Lee scored a late equaliser to earn a replay, but it would be a game that Cole would not see. By time United travelled to Ewood Park to dump Alan Shearer's Rovers out 2-1 in a replay Andy Cole was at Old Trafford and the Newcastle number 9 hung empty upon the St James' dressing room wall.

When news broke I was stunned. I was at college. It had been a funny day. Roxy wasn't herself and as always her mood or temperament could always unsettle mine. I sat in the refectory with my head in my hands, bemusing the clubs decision to sell my hero, when Roxy walked over.

"Can we talk?" she asked me sadly.

"Not now," I told her. She'd been moody for ages; now it was my time to sulk.

"But it's important," she said emotionally, regretfully.

"So is this!" I said coldly.

Minutes later I was off to St James to just see for myself if Cole had really left. Whatever Roxy wanted to talk about surely couldn't be more important than losing our number 9. When I got there I saw Keegan on the steps explaining to the fans. I admired him so much for respecting *us* enough to do that. I never asked him anything. I just absorbed the feeling that was going around Barrack Road like a black & white wake.

I was still numb when I went home. Roxy was there waiting for me. And this time we did talk. 670 days, 84 games and 68 goals after Andrew Cole walked into my life and became my favourite player he walked back out and joined Manchester United. 670 days after I saw Roxy's beautiful face in a crowd of strangers, a thousand kisses, a million cuddles and countless nights of making love, she walked out of my life and went back home to Sheffield to be with someone she'd met that summer. When she upped and packed she also ended up taking my heart with her.

And though I could never see it at the time, I am old enough and wise enough now to say thank you to both of them, for all the highs and all the lows, and for 670 days that I will never forget.

4. *Twelve Points, One Dream, And A Thousand Tears*

There's certain things in life that – no matter how brief they may be – you just have to sit back and enjoy. Van Halen should never have split with David Lee Roth; there *should* have been a new Ford Capri and Andy Cole should never have left St James Park.

But they did, there wasn't, and he did.

We could moan and complain and let bitterness linger on a pallet that once tasted such sweetness, or we could listen to the Gallagher brothers and simply don't look back in anger.

Me, well, I find it more satisfying to sing along to the anthemic *Jump*; to cherish the sight of Terry McCann or Bodie wheel-spinning a 2.8 Laser, and to sit back and reminisce over so many more than the 68 obvious reasons that Cole gave us to love him.

And of course, we must remember that life goes on. Sometimes things never are the same again: such as The Ford Probe or Paul Kitson. After all, could The Beatles ever go on without John, or Nirvana without Kurt…? I dare say not. But sometimes, other times, we move on, the world keeps turning and we learn to cherish the memories of what has been loved and lost or better still, we honour that memory by learning to love again.

After all, Van Halen found Sammy Hagar, Toyota brought out the Supra, and Newcastle eventually signed Les Ferdinand. And why couldn't that be love…? Well, to me, and every other Geordie faithful I know, when it came to Sir Les, it *was* love.

Cole departed Tyneside for Old Trafford in January 1995. The season petered out to a 6th place finish and a bit of an anti-climax. Ferdinand joined from QPR for £6 million in the summer of 1995. Keegan had long wanted the bulky, lightening quick, ferociously powerful striker. To many there was maybe only one striker better than Ferdinand in the entire country. We were delighted to sign him. Keegan was delighted to sign him! The grieving period for the loss of Andy Cole had been given and paid and time had come to once again fill the famous no. 9 that had been gathering dust since Cole's winter departure.

That summer Newcastle drew breath for a new challenge, a new assault on The Premiership – because of course 6th place was unacceptable – and new blood was added to the black & white veins. Along with Ferdinand, David Ginola, Warren Barton and Shaka Hislop were added – at great expense – as the club set about making a serious challenge for the 1995 / 96 League Title.

Those were halcyon days. I had a seat in the Leazes, tall and proud and towering over Tyneside like a monument. I was in row T, right near the back, in the third 'segment' if you will. I could see everywhere from up there; I could see far beyond St James Park and I could see almost every seat in it. And though I never seen him anymore, I knew the bairn was sitting somewhere nearby and that my customary glances would at some point, unwittingly, land upon him.

Newcastle kicked off season 95 / 96 like a train. An opening day win over Coventry City started a run that saw United top the table in no time at all. By time The lads hammered the original Wimbledon 6-1 at Gallowgate in October it made it 9 wins out of 10 in The Premiership summit. It was a remarkable game that summed up United's flamboyant, expressive, win-with-style start to the season. If a 6-1 score wasn't enough the game ended with Phillipe Albert curling a left-footer into the top corner past none other than Vinnie Jones in goal to seal the game.

I mean, think about it: that's your Centre-Half, outside of his left foot, passed stand-in Keeper-cum-actor Vinnie Jones to complete a six-goal hammering! Keegan – his team and his swagger – well it was all Hollywood really.

By time Newcastle travelled to Old Trafford just 2 days after Christmas the lead at the top was starting to look insurmountable. Only 2 defeats had fallen upon the side all season; goals were plentiful, and despite people telling us otherwise, the side had a decent defensive record. A first League Title since 1927 had started as a dream in August but by Christmas had become a real possibility.

The side went down 2-0 at Old Trafford and although the dream was very much alive, perhaps an undetected crack of something ominous had appeared. The thing is, we just weren't looking. A few days after that defeat Manchester United went down 4-1 at White Hart Lane to a Teddy Sheringham inspired Spurs side whilst on January 2nd Newcastle began the New Year by dismantling Arsenal 2-0 on Tyneside.

The lead was restored. The missing 3 points from Old Trafford were replenished, and the dream was very much alive and kicking. More victories came and went, and United went into February very much in the driving seat in the Title Race. It's hard to take that in, considering all that has happened since and our long trophyless drought. But take a minute and try and digest that fact: with only the final home straight of the season left Newcastle United looked certs to win The Premiership Title. It's mind-boggling.

But inside me, in that special place where dreams are kept and hopes are made, where fear creeps in and worry turns your feelings into butterflies that forever bounce around the ceilings and walls of your tummy, I struggled to let myself believe how close we were getting. The next game was against Bryan Robson's struggling Middlesborough. I had a nagging in my gut all week that the wheels were about to fall off, and what better a place for them to do so than Teesside.

At half time a John Beresford o.g. had left us trailing 1-0. My fears seemed well placed, my hopes and dreams ill-founded. Then – fresh from a 9-hour flight, so legend goes – from off the bench came the one, the only, the Colombian gunslinger himself, Faustino Asprilla.

He was mad, he was freezing, he was crazy and he was brilliant: he was Tino and he was ours and there at The Riverside he was our saviour. His crazy back heel nutmegs and such forth were decorations to sheer footballing genius. The South American turned the game, Newcastle did the 'Boro 2-1 and everything changed.

I wasn't at the match. For reasons I cannot now remember I was in The Three Bulls Heads with the lads, tossing back lagers, jumping on strangers, singing at the top of my voice, and watching the infamous 'foreign channel'. Things were good. I had settled well into my new life with my life's love, Rachel, and her two beautiful daughters. They had taken to me as I had to them and I had found a family that I never thought I would. All that was missing was the lad, the bairn, our Terry, who by now was leaving college for his first job, so his mother reliably kept me informed.

I missed the little bugger. The kid whose very first game had been none other than Kevin Keegan's debut was now a man. And he was now on the verge of being the envy of many a decade before

Knee High To A Grasshopper

him and watching the very same Kevin Keegan deliver Newcastle's first League Title in what was then 69 years.

Coming home not drunk but tipsy at not midnight but 8pm to Rachel and the bairns I was as happy as I had ever been.

The future was so bright that perhaps I let it blind my judgement. I forgot all about those good old kicks in the knackers of the past. Newcastle winning the title was so big and suddenly so possible that I got all wrapped up in the dream. And just as I began to believe the dream could actually come true the first steps of having that dream shattered right in front of mine – and countless other – black & white eyes began.

Newcastle travelled to West Ham for the second of three consecutive away tests. Having passed that first one gloriously at The Riverside Newcastle came unstuck in the second and third. A 2-0 defeat at Upton Park was followed by a 3-3 draw with Manchester City at Maine Road. They were tough examinations of United's title credentials. They were the types of games that could separate Champions from Runners-Up. Games like those, and Newcastle's faltering away form, ultimately would.

Champions are able to go get a beating at places like that and grind out a 1-0. Champions are able to play badly and win. Champions are able to rely on solid defending and nerves of steel, on inner belief and sheer determination. Runners-up go to places like that and score goals, leak goals, entertain, give a performance of drama and exhilaration, and ultimately lose. Runners-up find that when the 100mph football runs onto the hard shoulder there's no real substance and grit to hold the dream together.

Champions are able to go places like that and cling on for their lives. Runners-up can play someone off the park and somehow come away with nothing. These two mind-sets, these two personalities went head to head at Gallowgate on March 4th, on a Monday Night Sky Sports Football Special. Despite Sky's desperate attempts to convince the paying public that Liverpool were still part of the title race we all knew otherwise. This game was between Newcastle United and Manchester United, this game was between first and second, this game was between Champions and Runners-up. Sadly, all that makes a Champion a Champion, and all that makes a Runner-up a glorious loser all came to pass that fateful night.

Newcastle played the 100-mph football and Newcastle battered their opponent, but their opponent would not fall down. And midway through the second half their opponent swung a sucker-punch, in the shape of Eric Cantona and it landed smack on Newcastle's chin.

Manchester United played with the grit, the sheer determination, the nerves of steel and the inner belief that Newcastle didn't. Perhaps all it came down to was that Manchester United needed to win; Newcastle United simply wanted to. Maybe that's all that separated us after all is said and done. We thought we could afford to lose, we had points spare. They knew they couldn't… and hence they didn't.

Makes you wonder: how many times does desperation beat aspiration…

Cantona's goal silenced the St James Park faithful and an eerie, uneasy hush fell over Tyneside. I think that somewhere, deep down in all of us, we knew, right there and then where the Premiership Crown was going. I know that had we scored better results in the remaining games and weeks and even months we would have won the League Title but I think that night, that moment, when Cantona let out that beastly, medieval roar, we all knew who would win the title. And we all knew it wouldn't be the United we loved but the United we loathed.

Time went on to prove us right.

Time was aided by defeats at Arsenal, Liverpool and Blackburn. And Sky – for all I love them and what they've done for football – were there to capture it all. For every point dropped Sky were there to see it, and for every tear we cried Sky were there to watch it fall.

United – the United we love – their home form kept the dream alive. But as a 12-point lead became 9 points and nine points became 6 we all knew how it was going to end. Not that it was destined to I add, but because Newcastle didn't seem to believe that it wasn't.

Newcastle were second by time they lost that 7-goal spectacular at Anfield and they never regained that hallowed top spot. In the end the United we loath – as opposed to the United we love – finished just 4 points better off than we did.

I sometimes catch myself thinking about that match... and that season. I imagine a world where Albert's free-kick goes an inch lower and Man United crack; we win, and we win the title. If you wanted to you could argue that if that free-kick had gone in we'd have won the league. Instead it hit the bar and the dream has long since faded away. I imagine we go to Anfield, defend like buggery and come out with a smash & grab 1-0 in the worst game Sky has ever shown. Or maybe we go to Blackburn and boot Graeme Fenton 10ft up in the air before he's even touched the damn ball.

But then I remind myself, you can build a world on *ifs and Nicky Butt's* but they ain't worth shit in the cold light of day. The free kick didn't go in; we went down like Jesse James at Anfield and Graeme Fenton kicked our dreams 10 ft up in the air. And they broke when they fell.

I guess in a way the harsh lesson should be don't dare to dream. But I don't believe that. What is life without goals and dreams and aspirations? Don't get me wrong I would have loved it if we'd won that title (Jeez, I sound like Keegan here). But if it were a choice of consolidate, finish 6th and have none of that heartache and no chance of winning that title, or shoot for the moon, finish second and take a broken black & white heart to boot then I'd take the latter. Pennies are not for rainy days; they're for sunny days. Life is for living and dreams are there to be chased. Whether you catch them or miss them, always have the courage to run after them.

Sometimes you win; sometimes you lose, but as Kevin Keegan taught us always, always have the courage to play the game.

5. *I Don't Know What You Did Last Summer.*

There's certain things in life that – no matter how brief they may be – you just never seem to replace. As United crossed the finish line in second place on the 95 / 96 season I was as dejected as anyone. After losing Roxy – whom I still hadn't got over – I had a choice of throwing myself into my job or throwing myself into supporting Newcastle.

I opted for Newcastle.

I left college in June 95 and was soon working a poorly paid apprenticeship at Davies Garage in Benton. I was a mechanic; not a particularly great one, but I was a mechanic nonetheless.

With my first wages I bought Sky for my mam & me; with my second wages I bought the Adidas home shirt with the Brown Ale logo on that to this day remains my favourite. I wore it all season, home and away, as my lucky shirt. The luck didn't hold; it died with the twelve-point lead and a thousand tears.

I was still lost in my feelings for Roxy and in the time that passed between our splitting and Newcastle finishing Runners-up I was still single and still hung up. I found it hard to handle the thought of Roxy kissing, cuddling, undressing and making love to another man. How could she be so happy, so affectionate, so undressed and so in bed with me and then suddenly do all those things with another man? It was just like watching Andy Cole in the red of Manchester United. How could he bang the ball into the back of the net in our famous number 9 and run away celebrating, and then a week or so later be kissing the Red Devils badge and running off to The Stretford End?

Roxy and I did talk the January night that she – and Andy Cole – left my life. I didn't know what she'd done that last summer back home but it was costing me my girlfriend. In fairness to Roxy she was honest; she told me from the off that she'd met someone else.

"Have you slept with him?" I asked.

"No," she said – and I believed her.

"Are you going to," I asked.

"You already know that," she said.

She was right: I did; I just didn't want to believe it.

If my life had been a soap opera then *Two Out Of Three Ain't Bad* would have played in the background.

Nothing I said could change her mind. It was a bit like seeing the headlines on the back page of The Chronicle that a favourite player – like Andy Cole – was leaving. The deal isn't yet done and you still hope that the morning's Journal brings news that the deal has fallen through, but you know in your heart of hearts that it's not going to happen. Roxy was there in front of me, crying and even holding me. She could have changed her mind at any minute, and even though I hoped beyond hope that she would, I never believed it for a minute. And so that night Roxy – like Cole – was gone. The rest of that season, 94 / 95 pretty much just faded to black… and white.

Still, in time Cole was replaced, not by Paul Kitson, but by Les Ferdinand. In time Roxy was replaced too, by Angie.

Roxy left me in January 1995. Angie came into my life in the August of the same year. Coolio was in his Gangsta's Paradise, Bon

Jovi were telling us that their latest single wasn't a love song (which of course it was) and me, well, I was meeting the receptionist from Davies Garage and taking a shine to her. *This ain't a love song?* This ain't a rock band, more like. Anyway, Angie & I became friends right away and I guess on both sides the feelings were stronger, even if the words never were.

Angie was nice. It ain't often that a man falls for a woman because she's nice. He might fall for her passion, her allure, her charm and her wit, her stunning good looks or the sexuality that she emits like a light bulb to every man a moth. But rarely does a man fall for a woman because she's nice; unless of course that man is still nursing a broken heart.

Angie was about 5'8 and brunette. She was pretty. She had, how would you say… to hell with it, she had lovely boobs. But she kept them covered, when a different woman, a passionate, alluring, charming, more sexual, more confident woman would have maybe dressed to accent them. Roxy would have.

Angie was a little shy; she blushed when I talked to her, she wasn't the best at making conversation, but she tried. She was warm and friendly and caring and thoughtful. She was the kind of girl to wrap her loving arms around you and heal you within them. If Pat Benatar was right and love was indeed a battlefield then Angie would have been an Army Nurse.

She wasn't the kind to hurt you, to damage you, to suck you in and leave you stranded. She wasn't the kind to ever leave you for another man. Roxy was. Angie wasn't Roxy. And in that our love was both blessed and cursed.

We worked together for 2 years before the fire that Roxy had rained on was dry enough to re-light. We worked together throughout Newcastle missing out on the League Title by 4 miserly points. And we worked together throughout the wonderful Euro 96 held right here in England, and of course, right here in

Newcastle. We worked together that wonderful weekend when the 'papers said that Alan Shearer was allowed to talk to other clubs. We worked together that wonderful Monday that news broke and Kevin Keegan – sitting in Thailand somewhere told the worlds press "We have signed Alan Shearer" as nonchalantly as you'd say "Milk and two sugars please" or "Bottle of Brown Ale, Pet".

We worked together the Friday before the Charity Shield when me and the lads hired a Ford Transit to drive to London in, sleep in, and drive back from having left it too late to book any hotels or any trains. We were due to leave on the Saturday morning and I didn't have a sleeping bag. Angie went home and brought hers.

I slept in it that Saturday night after we joined thousands of other Geordies and turned Piccadilly black & white. At the time The Fugees were killing us softly, and standing in a car park in Stanmore on the Sunday morning my hangover was killing me surely. A few hours later Man United were killing us heavily. Newcastle – Shearer and all – went down 4-0 on my first ever trip to Wembley.

We drove home as the heavens opened and I sat trying to dry and warm myself in the back of our Transit Van wrapped in Angie's sleeping bag. I was sad, I was low and I was lonely. I had good friends but they all had girlfriends and slowly but surely I was seeing less and less of them. In such sentiments my feelings for Angie grew. Only people of a certain mentality get to 21 years old and worry about ending up alone. And so I wrestled with that all the way home, as Oasis played live on Radio One and dedicated *Slide Away* to the Mags.

I needed something, someone, in my life, and Angie more or less fit the bill when loneliness cast across me like a dark Wembley cloud. Hardly *Sleepless In Seattle* is it…?

The 1996 / 97 season proper got off to just as bad a start as that Wembley Sunday had. A 2-0 defeat at Goodison with Gary Speed on the score-sheet set the early tone. Shearer's first goal – a glorious free kick at The Leazes – was the highlight of August but Newcastle entered September with 2 defeats out of 3.

Next up was Sunderland at Roker Park. Away fans were banned but I travelled all the same. I wore an England top. I was offered a ticket but there were two of us there and neither was about to turn his back and go in without the other. Pals stick together. So we drove around in my old car and listed to the game on the radio, often parked right outside the main stand or in one of the streets to the side of the famous old shit-hole of a ground. With 10 minutes to go – and Newcastle having fought back from one down to another glorious Roker Park 2-1 lead – the gates were opened for the Roker faithful – fresh from the First Division promotion – to leave the ground.

In that moment the opportunity was opened up for me and one of my best mates, Woody, to run the other way, into the ground, up the steps and onto The Fulwell End. I guess it's not always full of shit! It wasn't that night. I'm not sure how many Geordies were left in there but my eyes were some of the last to ever see Newcastle United win at Roker Park. I still treasure the image of Alan Shearer dressed in the blue standing hands aloft milking victory as the final whistle went.

The results weren't bad after that. There was a good hammering of Boro at St James' and of course the *absolutely glorious* 5-0 hammering of Manchester United on what really was a super, super Sunday. But Keegan wasn't himself. He never quite recovered from his Elland road outburst and I guess the writing was on the wall for the wise to read in advance. I guess I wasn't one of the wise; I couldn't see a thing. Love is blind so they say. In my case it surely was. I never saw Andy Cole leaving; I never saw Roxy leaving. And I never for one black and white slap-me-in-the-face-with-a-blue-star moment saw Keegan leaving.

But that's exactly what he did. He stunned the football world. He stunned Tyneside. And he stunned me. In less time than a man needs to grieve Keegan was replaced. Terry Mac had one game in charge before the new appointment was made. Keegan was gone, and on a cold winters night in January 1997 Kenny Dalglish arrived.

I never took to Kenny Dalglish. On paper he was a great appointment and if I'd been responsible for making the appointment I might have went for him too. But he wasn't *ours*. Kenny Dalglish was *Liverpool's*. Kenny had no tie to the club, no link, no history and no connection. He had Liverpool in his veins, not Newcastle. Something felt wrong and ultimately the feeling would be proved right.

Dalglish's first 5 months in charge were impressive. The side – Keegan's side – steamrolled its way to a 2nd place finish in much different circumstances than 12 months before. As Newcastle clinched their first ever appearance in The Champions League, with Kirtsy MacColl's *Days* ringing in my ears I learned to let go of the past and look forward again. That song summed up everything I felt for Keegan and his time on Tyneside. *Thank you for the days, those endless days those sacred days you gave me.*

By the end of that melancholy season, in the summer of 1997, I grew up just a little. It didn't mean I didn't miss Keegan, I just learned to move on. It was the same with my Dad, and ultimately, I accepted it was the same with Roxy.

Hence that was the summer that Angie and I finally started dating, some 2 years after we'd first met. We 'got off' with each other at a works night out and soon after we went to the pictures. The first film we went to see was *'I Know What You Did Last*

Summer'. Angie kept her ticket as a keepsake. I've no idea where mine went.

We kept dating as the 1997 / 98 season turned into a catastrophe. As Sarah Michelle-Gellar and Freddie Prinze Junior were busy knocking over vagrants and running from serial killers Kenny was busy murdering Keegan's team. Favourite players left, such as Les Ferdinand, and foreigners such as Jon Dahl Tomasson and Temuri Ketsbia came in. Shearer's leg pretty much fell off in a pre-season came and before we knew it we had a team producing results that looked like they'd been written in binary.

I don't know what Kenny did that summer but losing the likes or Sir Les and Ginola and replacing them with John Barnes and Ian Rush left the side in ruins. Remember the Greek tragedy that was George Georgiadis? Good God. Rush, Dalglish insisted, knew where the goal was. So what? I knew where the goal was! I could see it quite clearly from the back of The Leazes, which is where most of Rushie's shots ended up. I'm sure Kenny's pal *did* know where the goal was; it was just his inability to put the ball within 30 yards of it that frustrated me.

Still, he netted the winner in a 1-0 at Goodison and it set Kenny's Newcastle on the way to a first FA Cup Final since 1974.

By the time I returned to Wembley, 2 years on from the Charity Shield debacle to see Newcastle face Arsenal my life had changed dramatically. I had a steady, if somewhat uneventful, relationship with my new girlfriend and I was a mechanic by then, fully trained and partially skilled. If a sports car had been brought in for a tune up I'd have done just that. A light tweak here and there and it'd be firing on all cylinders again. Using mechanics as a loose metaphor for football management Dalglish took a model that only needed but a tweak and a tune up but instead decided to strip it down and try and rebuild it. The new parts didn't work and it never ran the same again, including that FA Cup Final. A 2-0 reverse put paid to that.

Despite the deep disappointment of losing the Cup Final I took a philosophic approach to it. I wasn't angry anymore; I was defeated. I accepted that it really is better to have loved and lost then never to have loved at all. I wished we'd won the Cup Final but the semi-final at Old Trafford was something I'm glad I experienced. It was the same with Keegan. Yeah, I wished he'd have stayed, but it could have been worse; he might never have come in the first place.

What if Arthur Cox had never managed to sign him when I was just a bairn? Dad would never have came home drunk and happy that night in August 82; there'd have been no fish n chip supper and Geordie fairytale. Hell I might never have even been to a match!

Sitting at Wembley in 1998, watching another dream die dressed in its finest black and white, I resigned myself to the fact that Keegan just like Roxy was gone. I forced my heart towards Angie and Kenny and it dully went.

After all, it's one thing to learn to love and lose; it's another to learn to love again. And having lost that Cup Final there was nothing I would have loved more than to go back and win the damn thing next year.

6. Going Dutch

The world turns on a sixpence, let me tell you. Just like a team in a football match can be 2-1 down and then before you know it the lads are 3-2 up, life itself can turn on its head with equal aplomb. One minute you're hammering Man United 5-0 or Spurs 7-1 and singing *Walking In A Keegan Wonderland*, the next you're on a Sunday train from Kings Cross debating whether the shambles that Kenny Dalglish calls a first team should cost him his job. And all of that after our first appearance in a Wembley Cup Final since 1976.

The same can be said about life. One minute you're walking home from work to a loveless marriage and an equally loveless wife, the next you're getting off the train at Central Station to be greeted by the love of your life and the family you never thought you'd have. And all because they knew how disappointed I'd be with Newcastle's Cup Final defeat.

Now, at this time, I was 43-years-old. Rachel was mid thirties and her two little girls Emily and Millie were not so little anymore. They were pretty much pretty teenagers. They had grown up so very fast. One minute I was leaving Sheila back in October of '88 and before I knew where all the time had gone 10 years had passed and I was part of something wonderful that I thought would pass me by.

I can only speak for myself, of course, but for me everybody needs something to hold on to. I was fortunate; I had a family I was really happy with and a great group of friends.

Football had become a very passionate part of my life. For the bairn, for our Terry, now all of 23 years old, football was not part of his life; it *was* his life. He had nothing else in his life that he loved. Newcastle United had become his love, his obsession his pride and his joy. Sadly, as almost all of us have grown up to learn, no matter how much pride there is in our beloved club there is so very little joy.

I know how hard the lad took defeat in the Cup Final. Not because I was still in touch with him – hell I'd barely seen him in years – and not because he was my flesh and blood. It was because he was raised as I had been to stories of glory and FA Cup wins. I know that because I raised him. I tucked him in on oh so many nights to tales of the Crystal Palace, the early defeats and the victories of black & white Cup Finals of '10, '24 and '32. I watched him fall asleep to faded whispers of the fifties, when the Cup itself practically belonged to Newcastle United. It was a time when black and white sleeves dressed the arms that held the Cup aloft three times in just 5 years. And when he dozed and he drifted, I know that somewhere in his imagination he fell asleep to the fancy of black & white ribbons dressing silverware once again.

I know he treasured 3rd Round day as much as he treasured the festive season that preceded it. I remember one winter when the first January snow fell in Wallsend and the bairn wrapped himself up warm to watch FA Cup 3rd Round on Match of the Day. All of the other kids his age were just excited it was snowing; the bairn was just excited by the Cup. When he went to bed that night he didn't fall asleep to dragons and rainbows and dreams of Disneyland. No, he fell asleep to twin towers and Wembley and dreams of his beloved Newcastle bringing the Cup back home to an adoring Tyneside.

And on the very same day his boyhood dream came closest to reality, the last of the boy in him slipped away and all that was left for the man was the hard-bitten reality that dreams do not come true. Gladly, the man was wrong; sadly, it was a lesson his old man was unable to teach him.

The gulf between us had widened so very much it would have taken The Tyne Bridge to close it. You wouldn't have thought we lived, worked, drank and shopped just a handful of miles apart. You'd have thought it even less likely that every other Saturday we were seated just a few rows away.

The summer came with tempered optimism. Dalglish's first year had been a bad one: a 13th place finish with a totally changed team. Transition my arse; it was simply very bad management. But on the other hand, we had reached the FA Cup Final, and surely that could augur well for the future. We would spend, we would mend, and we would have a much better season. Hell, maybe we'd even be back at Wembley.

We did, we didn't, we didn't and we were....

It started in August, with the opening weekend of the '98 / '99 season. United faced Charlton Athletic at Gallowgate. Hopes were high, like the sun in the Tyneside summer, but they soon came crashing down to the grit and earth of our Tyneside streets. The opening day finished 0-0 against and United were booed off.

A 1-1 draw at Chelsea a week later and Kenny Dalglish – despite an unbeaten start to the season and the clubs financial backing all summer – was gone. A week later, before Newcastle could face Liverpool at St James' on a Sky Super Sunday Ruud Gullit was announced as the clubs new manager. He took to the pitch before the game with the Reds. He waved at the crowd and the crowd waved back generously. No one – however – in the whole ground that sunny day was quite as generous as our ageing back four. Michael Owen, none other, was literally rubbing his hands. Perhaps he'd seen the contract he'd sign some 7 years later. He scored a hat-trick, Newcastle went down 4-1 and the job's all yours Ruud.

A 1-0 reverse at Villa followed before Gullit took his team to Coventry City. We took about 18 Coaches from Slippery for a trip that we still talk about to this day. All the lads from work, all of our mates, all piled onto the Coaches and we drank and chatted and laughed and joked and sang all the way to the Midlands… and all the way back, with 3 points and a 5-1 win to boot.

A few more wins came and went but by and large Newcastle were crap. Of course, it was Kenny's fault, so we let Ruud be and we gave him time. We blamed Dalglish for the mess we were in, and in a way that distracted us from seeing that Gullit was only making it worse. The bairn was making similar mistakes. He wanted nothing to do with me by all accounts. He wasn't angry anymore; he was just distant, uninterested.

He blamed all of his unhappiness on his old college girlfriend and me, just like we blamed Newcastle's results on Dalglish. He didn't blame himself for anything, just like we didn't really blame Gullit.

Maybe that's why I handled Newcastle's rise and fall better than the bairn did: because I had Rachel, the love of my life, and he had Angie, someone to stop him from being alone.

Gullit took the reigns at a time when Celine Dion's heart seemed to be going on and on and when Aerosmith didn't want to miss a thing. Sadly, Gullit's revival didn't go on and on and Stephane G'uivarche – our £3.5million World Cup winning centre-forward – seemed intent on missing positively everything. By time Halloween came around West Ham were up at Gallowgate and in a real horror show the Londoners won 3-0. Most of the 36,744 crowd went home despondent. I'm sure the bairn was amongst them. But me, well I went home happy, and I'll tell you why…

I'd been with the Shipyards since I was a kid. I did my apprenticeship there, made my friends there, my shipyard family, and indirectly met the love of my life popping into the Newsagents on the walk to work there. I'd started putting on busses and coaches to away games back in the '80's and of course that had developed into *Slippery When What*. Those coach trips ran for a kick in the pants off ten years. In that time they grew in number and demand and popularity. Word of mouth had gotten around and the away day with the shipyard boys had gone from strength to strength. And it made me money, of that I won't lie nor dispute.

But I never did it for the money. I did for the love of it. I was the guy who put on the coaches, the rock n roll, good music, cold beer, damn good laugh, away day coaches. And I liked being that person. I did it because I enjoyed it; the money that came with it was a bonus not a reason.

Then, in autumn 1998 I decided to be brave and to follow my dreams. The Shipyards were struggling; there were lads in there who needed their jobs more than I did. Time had come to leave my steel castle and let younger men take up the tradition of the fading trade. So in autumn 1998 I decided to quit the shipyards and run *Slippery When What* as a full time going concern. I started my own business. Well, I didn't; I just did full time what I'd inadvertently been doing for the last ten years as a hobby.

Garry, Tom and Hopper joined me, not because they were great entrepreneurs, but because they were great football fans… and great friends. They were – they are – my pals. And pals tend to face their challenges together.

If we'd been on the very same Titanic that Kate Winslet had tried to jump off; the very same Titanic she sat watching sink from the safety of a bloody wardrobe door while the love of her life froze his bollocks off in the water (that's women for you), then we'd have drank one more beer and sank together. If we'd been in the trenches when the pipes of peace played the Christmas the great football match broke out then we'd have been in no mans land playing 1-2's and dribbling around minefields.

If we'd been born 150 years ago we'd have been Cowboys in the Wild West, sipping tequila and whiskey and stealing horses for fun. Whatever we'd have done, whenever a time we'd have been, we would have been pals and we would have done it together. Ain't nothing tougher than Pals.

So Garry, Hopper and Tom joined me and we set up SWW or simply 'Slippery Travel' for all and sundry. And we made it a success. Leaving the shipyard wasn't easy. For the Stephen King fans then imagine the Shipyard as Shawshank and imagine me and the lads as Andy and Red. You become institutionalised; you dream of leaving, of being free, of closing those cold iron gates behind you for the last time and never having to go back. But then what it happens and you've got to face the big wide world, it's scary.

There was sacrifice; there has to be for almost anything worthwhile. But ultimately there was success. As United & Gullit stuttered along our own little business, Slippery Travel, gathered momentum. Soon we were running coaches to not just away games but to all manner of private functions and day-trips. We were doing concert trips, weekends away, the lot. And in May of 1999 we did a very special trip: to Wembley for the 1999 FA Cup Final.

Victories over Crystal Palace, Bradford, Blackburn, Everton and finally Spurs on a glorious day at Old Trafford saw Ruud Gullit's Newcastle return to the twin towers just a year after defeat to Arsenal. The Gunners clinched the double by beating

Newcastle; to make life a little easier this time we faced Man United... who were going for the treble.

In fairness, despite all the hopes and all the dreams in the world, The Reds were never going to let an obstacle as small as Newcastle stop them winning an unprecedented treble of Premiership, FA Cup and of course Champions League. Basically we could have saved the money and simply bought a crate of Brown Ale and slammed the Arsenal final in the video. A 2-0 defeat, Newcastle never really a threat; been there, done that. But football isn't just about the result is it; it's about the people you share those results with, whether they be win, lose or draw.

Manchester United won the league a point ahead of Arsenal and 33 ahead of Newcastle who languished in 13th place as the season closed. Ominously for us, eight league places below us as the First Division winners were Sunderland. And suddenly old enemies were set for new battle; sadly a battle that with Gullit at the helm United were never ready for.

Once again the summer brought us a torrent of headlines and stories and out of the 4,000 players The Chronicle and its peers linked us with United eventually signed most notably two new Centre-Halves. Marcelino and Alain Goma came in at around £10million to shore up the now infamous leaky defence.

As the 1999 / 2000 season got under way Brad Pitt and Ed Norton were blowing up buildings and chinning Meatloaf in some New York basement, and Newcastle kicked off with 18 goals against in the first 6 games.

The 18 goals consisted of a 1-0 reverse to a Uriah Rennie inspired Aston Villa, a 3-1 reverse at Tottenham live on Sky Monday Night Special and an absolutely abject 4-2 thumping down at The Dell to Southampton. Wimbledon then rammed another three passed new £750,000 Dutch Keeper Jon Karelse who had been the biggest sinner against the Saints. Finally Andy

Cole put his name to four more that presented us with a 5-1 hiding at Old Trafford, but by then the club that had gone with a Dutchman had a Dutchman going.

Unluckily for Gullit – and dare I say luckily for us – it was the 13th goal of that ill-fated start to a season that saw the dreadlocks to the door. Newcastle versus Sunderland is to each and every one of us – from both black & white and red & white camps – the biggest game of the season. It's the game you dream of winning and have nightmares of losing.

To Gullit it was only a 'regional derby'.

His team selection underlined that he didn't understand the club, the game and most importantly, the supporters.

Gullit left Shearer and Duncan (I could pick a fight in an empty room) Ferguson on the bench. Paul Robinson, possibly the kid from Hartlepool or Darlington, possibly the guy from Neighbours who got off with one of the twins, started up front with Keiron Dyer.

As the rain came down and I stood on a roofless Leazes soaked to the bone, with rivers running down the concrete steps, Newcastle – with Tommy the Barman back in goal – went 1-0 up.

But the goal and the rain that continued to pour was not enough to wash my half time worries away. The second half was like a bad dream, with Tommy Wright in goal and Shearer and Ferguson on the bench adding to the sense of something surreal.

Ultimately those worries were justified. Sunderland levelled through Niall Quinn and then Kevin Phillips curled a chip over Tommy and The Wearsiders led 2-1. The boos at the end were deafening. And the floods that soaked St James Park and the Tyneside night could just as easy have been tears as they were rain.

There was no heart from United, no guts and ultimately no glory. Fight Club? Newcastle were anything but a club with fight.

Without that, most games will end in defeat; a local derby certainly will. First rule of Ruud Gullit; do not talk about Ruud Gullit. Second rule of Ruud Gullit; *do not talk about Ruud Gullit.*

In the end Gullit's teamsheet for that fateful Sunderland game had been his resignation. Before United could play again the Dutchman was gone.

7. *What I Liked About Ruud Gullit*

8. *The Bobfather*

When you're young years seem to last, well, years. When you get older the years seem to go by like months. I'd not yet been out of the Shipyard a year when we travelled to Old Trafford for that Andy Cole inspired mauling just weeks into the 99 / 2000 season. The next time we travelled, this time to Stamford Bridge, Bobby Robson was at the helm.

Appointing Bobby Robson felt good. It was like the feeling you get when you're on a train from London and it crosses the bridge over the Tyne just as you come home. It's looking out of the train window and seeing the Tyne Bridge, proud and strong, steel and emotion. It's like being without your loved ones or your girlfriend for a week and then finally feeling their arms around you holding you tight. It's your favourite armchair after days away from home; it's a nice cuppa in *your* cup. It's a home game back in your own seat after an arduous away trip to God-knows where.

Appointing Bobby Robson felt like that. For the first time in years I could go to sleep at night knowing the team were in safe hands.

For me that meant sleeping next to Rachel, holding her tight, and thanking my lucky stars that I had her. I was bearing down on my 45th birthday and not to sound too Kat Stevens but I was old but I was happy. Beside me was Rachel, still in her late thirties and looking better than most girls do in their late twenties. In the other rooms of our 3-bedroom home were Millie and Emily, now 14 and 16 respectively. Ten years had passed since I stepped into their lives.

The time I'd been in their lives, first as their friend and ultimately to them calling me Dad, was the same time I had been out of my son's. In the same ten years he had went from calling me Dad to simply not calling me at all.

And as much as I loved Millie and Emily I missed Terry a million times over.

You can call it what you like; maybe it was a mid-life crisis, maybe just a melancholy of the heart, but as Bobby Robson came home and was finally united with something he had always been emotionally tied to, I began longing to be reunited with the bairn.

The past is all around us. Most of the time we're unaware of it; sometimes we really start to feel it. After all the past is the road that lead us to the present; the present but a road that leads us to the future.

Sometimes we miss people. Sometimes we think about them, and we wish and maybe we even wonder about how to get them back into our lives. That's how it was for me when it came to the bairn.

I missed Terry so very much. I missed my son, my friend, and the kid I took to all those games all those years ago.

I kept tabs on him care of Sheila, which I have to give credit to her for. She became a friend again after we were divorced and strangely we get on better now than we did when we were married. Some people are born to be nothing more than friends. But some people are born united; none more so than a father & son. Terry of course was still my son – whether he ignored me or not, but he wasn't a kid anymore. Suddenly, out of seemingly nowhere, he was an adult. He was a 24-year-old man working in a garage and getting serious with his new girlfriend, Angie.

The world, let me tell you, is a wonderful thing. Life throws up more twists and turns, highs and lows than a Liverpool – Newcastle game live on Sky. There's so much that neither science nor religion can explain, but that somehow faith always can. For me, my aching to be a father again was ripe and set to come true. But just not in the way I had expected.

I hadn't seen him in years; we never really kept in touch except the odd Christmas card and birthday present. I never bought him much, but I'm sure that the gesture said more than any words ever could. Then suddenly the wheels of fate started rolling, and in a way that perhaps only fate could, a magical chain of events was forged and my life, and Terry's, began to re-entwine.

Under Sir Bobby Robson the dragons of relegation were slain and the Black & White Knight guided his hometown club to a respectable 11th place finish at the end of the 99 / 2000 season. The ship had been steadied, and in the process had beaten Manchester United 3-0, Arsenal 4-2 and maintained the unbeaten run on Wearside – stretching back to March 1980 – with a 2-2 draw on our first appearance at Sunderland's new stadium. It's called The Stadium of Light. As far as rhyming slang goes you've got to hand it to Bob Murray and his boys for giving us the easiest task in local rivalry.

The Lads even started by hammering Sheffield Wednesday 8-0 in Robson's first game. But perhaps the highlight of the season was the rebirth of Alan Shearer. For me, Shearer was awesome. He was powerful, strong, determined, world-class, excellent in the air, lethal on the deck and basically he was the best Centre-Forward I ever saw with my own two eyes, and there has been some wonderful competition for that mantle. One of Shearer's greatest qualities was the fact that he was a Geordie. He was one of us. He was a Newcastle fan. I don't doubt that if he *had* been just a sheet metal workers son with the same shifts as the rest of us working class he would have been sitting beside us at St James' watching the lads just like you & I do.

But he wasn't just a sheet metal workers son and he didn't work the shifts or the 9-5 like the rest of us; he was a footballer. He was a striker. He was our number 9. And didn't he just love it? Under Gullit his time looked to be up courtesy of a latter day version of the Gordon Lee v Malcolm Macdonald scenario. Tragically, back in 1976, Lee stayed and SuperMac left. That is one of the worst things to happen to this football club in all it's time. Fantastically, in 1999, Gullit left and Shearer stayed. That is one of the best things to happen to this football club in all its time.

And of course, Newcastle being Newcastle, they made it to Wembley for the third season in a row, and on each occasion with a different manager. This time Robson, Shearer and all faced Chelsea in an FA Cup *Semi*-Final. This time, with the right man at the helm, we fought and we attacked and we even scored a bloody goal. Sadly, the outcome was the same, and although a 2-1 defeat put paid to any hope of ending our silverware drought The Lads at least returned home with pride in tact.

It's not the result I'll remember about the day, not is it Rob Lee's header that brought us so much hope; hope that sadly lasted all of five minutes. No, for me, it was seeing the bairn. We'd taken the coaches down on the Saturday night and stayed over in the Travel Lodge near Westminster; it was the same one we'd used for both previous finals. On match day we took the coaches up to the coach park nice and early with a few bags of cans stashed away. We walked up to the stadium with cans in hand, soaking up Brown Ale, lager and atmosphere as much as possible.

We were right up next to Wembley herself, at the end of Wembley Way, just where the fans start to head towards the turnstiles. I was with a few of the lads and we went for a burger. The lad in front of me, all dressed in black & white was getting a hot-dog.

I got this sudden jolt of reminiscences down my memory and my body alike. I never realised that I had bought this lad his first ever match day hot-dog, when he was just a 7-year-old kid on his way to see Keegan's debut. Before he even turned around, somehow I knew.

"Hello son," I said as he took his hot-dog and made for the stadium.

He was dumbstruck. He just froze, with his mouth wide open. I don't know whether it was to bite the hot-dog or just surprise.

"Hello Dad," he said pensively.

"How's things?" I asked him. I can't remember what he said. "Reckon we'll win today then?" I asked him.

"We're due one," he told me.

"Good things come eh?" I quipped.

"I guess they do, Dad," he said as his friends grew impatient waiting for him.

"Go on," I told him, "Don't keep the lads waiting,"

He smiled at me. "It's good seeing you Dad," he told me.

My heart thawed so very much with those words. "We we're due one," I joked.

"Good things come eh?" he quipped.

"I guess they do, son," I told him, "I guess they do".

Now I don't want to incur the wrath of every Geordie world-wide but the result – a semi-final defeat – pretty much paled into insignificance compared to seeing the bairn. Don't get me wrong, I dreamed all game of winning the damn thing and celebrating with the kid outside, or coming back for the final with him and seeing us end our trophy-drought together. It wasn't to be. But family, friends – people – and loved ones should always come before football. That's my perspective and my opinion. If it isn't yours, then fair play.

The thaw I felt that day continued. As the 99 / 2000 season ended – with United in 11th place and trophyless – I felt the ice and the distance between Terry & me continue to melt. The summer seemed to melt it more. On August 23rd 2000 it was washed away.

Shaggy was telling us that it wasn't him, the Baja Men were wondering who let the dogs out and Britney Spears had done it again. And Newcastle United were opening the new top tier of both The Leazes and Milburn Stands. The capacity was a wonderful 52,000 and I was proud to be of them. The extension came at a cost; every body sitting in the back 5 rows of the 'old' Leazes had to give up their seat for the new family enclosure or corporate club or whatever. It also cost the club some more of its fading reputation with an ugly SOS Save Our Seats battle that was mostly conducted in the press.

I really wasn't arsed. Progress has a price and so what if my seat was part of it. I got first dibs on the new seats anyway. And so me, Tom and Garry took our places in the second row from the front, dead Centre of the new Leazes End, along with the other lads.

The first home game of the 2000 / 2001 season was against Derby County, following on from a 2-0 Andy Cole inspired reverse at Old Trafford on opening day. The new look stadium was daunting, impressive, awesome, add your own superlatives at will.

For the first time since 1978, when the old Leazes fell, when I was 23-years-old and when the bairn was just 3, St James Park could hold over 50,000 supporters. I was there in those seventies days and before, and I was as proud as anyone to be amongst those 51,327 that turned up for the midweek visit of Derby County.

Returning to the ground for the first home match of the season is always special, simply because you've missed the ground so very much over the summer. But anticipating new seats and such lavish development made the excitement and anticipation even greater.

I was standing by my new seat, marvelling at the new cantilever structure, as the seats began to fill. Row by row, isle by isle, stand by stand, St James Park began to heave, to breath, and to positively embrace the feeling of those who stood upon and within. As kick-off neared only a handful of seats remained empty. Three of those were just one row in front of me and just a little to my left.

The players had taken their places on the pitch before the last of those seats were filled. And imagine my surprise when, walking along the new Row A, top tier, Leazes End, came the bairn.

9. *You've Got To Hand It To The Box Office*

The world turns on a sixpence, let me tell you. When you're young years seem to last, well, years. When you get older the years seem to go by like months. One minute I was a kid at Gateshead College with a crush I couldn't have dreamt of and a hard-on that I didn't know what to do with, the next I was a 25-year-old mechanic getting engaged to a really canny lass I whom met at work.

One minute I was head over heels in love with a woman who blew my mind, the next my heart was safe and sound with a very nice, reliable lass who would never let me down.

One minute I was sitting in the back of The Leazes End, the next I was at the front of the new tier. Getting new seats is always a mix of worry and excitement. You wonder what the view will be like, what the banter will be like and who you'll be sitting with. But imagine my surprise when I walked to my seat with Dave & Adam, just minutes before kick off, to find my Dad sitting in the row behind me.

For years he had been my Dad. Then he left us to be with another woman. She had kids of her own and suddenly he wasn't just my Dad he was *their* Dad too. Then he told me I was a mistake, and that he and Mam had never intended to have me. Suddenly he was no longer my Dad anymore.

I remember that day vividly: December 29th 1990, a home game with Notts County. And there by the St James Park floodlights and the velvet blue winter sky I took off the scarf Dad bought me for my first home game in August 1982, threw it at him and walked away. Ten years had passed since then.

Seeing him standing there, clapping and shouting, eagerly awaiting kick off, well that threw me 7 ways from Sky Super Sunday. St James Park is so very special for so many people, and for Dad and me that is just the same. We were never close when I was a kid, until he dragged me to my first game back in August 82. We went to the match together for years, until around 1987 when Dad fazed me out and his mates and his beer in. We met there again by chance on the fateful night that United were relegated in 1989 and of course there was that incident in December 1990. But in all of the years that followed I can barely remember seeing him more than a handful of times, even though I knew we were both there.

From Ardiles to Keegan and Keegan to Dalglish, from Dalglish to Gullit and then Gullit to Robson, for all those days, weeks, months, seasons, and years we hardly ever met. And then bang, smack out of the blue star there he is, standing by his seat with Garry, Tom and Hopper.

I'm not sure if I was going to speak to him or not, but as I was shuffled impatiently to my new seat by those who didn't want to miss seeing kick off in favour of staring at my skinny arse, he turned and clocked me.

This is awkward because such a poignant moment should be written, recollected and replayed with poetry and emotion. But the truth is, I haven't got a clue what was said. The moment came and went with me standing still and feeling numb. You've got to hand it to the Box Office; they sure know how to screw up with style.

The same wonderful box office that had once sold all of the clubs tickets for Manchester United away in '93 to Travel Club members, forcing me to lead a rebellion from Barrack Road and reduce the Box Office Manageress to tears had come up trumps again. The same loveable box office that had over the years lost 2 of my season tickets, one of my Cup Final tickets, my Sunderland (Liam O'Brien up & over the wall) ticket and closed their counters on me selling Rotherham FA Cup replay tickets only to hand the guy to my right 7 tickets had done it again! The same beloved damn box office who had to open up at 5am to sell Blackburn away tickets after 3,000 of us queued from 10pm the night before to get one, had only gone and mixed up our surnames.

They actually tried to sit Dad and me together, but the row in front was as close as they could get us! Yeah, you've got to hand it to the box office.

Of course, at the time I was just standing dazed and perplexed, until bang, Carl Cort scored an early header and the place erupted. And in the celebrations I suddenly turned to see past the hugs and the cuddles from Dave & Adam, and without needing to see anything with my eyes, I knew the hand clinching mine was his.

United won 3-2 and with each goal the lads put away, through Daniel Cordone and a pearler from Stephen Glass, I found my arms around Dad and his around me. And as much as I resented and maybe even hated him, I loved him and loved that so very, very much. I wanted Newcastle to score 8 just to have the chance to get closer to him again and again. I felt 7 years old again.

When the match finished we shook hands, celebrated 3 league points and – like you would with any of the lads you sit with – we said "See you Saturday, mate".

And we did. And the Saturday after and the week after and the home game after that and so on and so forth. And we began building bridges, not as strong and as glorious as the Tyne, not as practical and as homely as the High Level, but bridges nonetheless. They were bridges with one simple condition: I let Dad cross over to my side; I never wanted to cross over to his. I know that a lot of water had passed under such bridges over oh so many years, but as much as I was willing to let Dad back into my life, I wanted nothing to do with his.

I know it was wrong, I know it was an over-reaction and I know I was being childish and petulant. But when all was said and done that was how I felt. And right or wrong we can't help how we feel. We can manage those feelings, try and grow and develop and be mature and forgive and forget but still, we can't help how we feel.

In the end I could forgive but I couldn't forget... or forgive. And as good as it was having my Dad back in my life, I just wasn't ready to be part of his.

After a few weeks he told me that he and the lads liked a few jars in The Telegraph on a Thursday night for a bit of pre-match banter and a bit of a wind-down. He invited me and the lads to join them.

Soon our Thursday nights were like our match days: off to The Telegraph, sitting at *our* table, the high chairs by the big screen and the fire exit, and just five steps from the bar. We'd throw a small fortune into the jukebox and twice as much behind the bar and we'd have a great night. And slowly but surely, we all became mates again.

The Telegraph: man I love that pub.

10. European Knights And New Baby Princes

That season, 2000 / 2001 was the start of three sensational seasons, each memorable for their own wonderful reasons. First off, Newcastle were crap that season, 00 / 01. Though United sat around 6th place by late January the side capitulated in what was nothing other than an ordinary Premiership to say the least. Only 3 wins out of the remaining 14 games saw the side plummet.

But it was a game in early May that will eternally spring to mind. We'd been to Liverpool for our annual drubbing. It's all very simple: we travel down around 8am with a tonne of cans and bottles and bags and bags of Greggs. We get to Merseyside early, we ditch the coaches and we pile into The Arkles. We quadruple the boozers' takings in one fell swoop, we have a good singsong – including the favourite *In Your Liverpool Slums* – and we get the party started.

We pile into Anfield in fine fettle around 20 minutes to kick off. We out-sing the Scousers all through the game; the players let us down – badly most years – and we hear the famous Anfield roar normally 2 or 3 times a game, most often with Kenny Dalglish, Ian Rush, and in latter years, Michael Owen running off gleefully to The Kop. With 2 minutes to go the Anfield faithful start a rousing course of *You'll Never Walk Alone*, which quite frankly makes me want to rip my arm off just to have something to throw at them. Then they take the piss, we laugh it off, and we go home a beaten team but brilliant supporters. And as much as we know that Liverpool are a better team than us, we know that we are far better fans than they are. And more than that, so do they.

Indeed that was again the case on May 5th 2001.

But for the second time in my life coming home from Anfield would prove to be life changing.

Now, on May 5th 2001 I was a 46-year-old man. My girlfriend Rachel – my partner to the politically correct here and now, Wor Lass to the ever affectionate 1980's – was just a little shy of forty. Her daughters (my Stepdaughters had Rachel & I ever bothered to marry) were 16 and 18 years old, and my son, my estranged bridge-building-still-yet-to-forgive-me-mechanic of a son was twenty-six. And my baby, my Kevin-H-Keegan-do-my-sperm-still-work baby was just seven months away.

Returning from Anfield still quite sober was nothing new. I came home, kissed Rachel, sat in my armchair like a king in a castle and took my rightful ownership of the remote control. Remote controls were designed for men. Remote controls are the rightful property of men. When a woman has possession of a remote control then there is imbalance in the universe. Bad things can happen. Shows like X-Factor and Nanny 911 somehow get watched; people like Jade Goody and Gareth Gates become famous. Jeez, if I wanted to watch talentless loudmouths on television every week I'd tune into Football League Review when the Mackem's came on.

Rachel came over with a cup of tea and kissed me on the cheek. She asked me about the match, told me she'd set the reminder for Match of the Day, and waved her magic wand by making the result fade away by the loving sparkle in her eyes. Part of why I loved her was her understanding of how much football – and

Newcastle – meant to me. She never jockeyed for my attention with it; she never battled with it or resented it, no. She embraced it, made herself part of it, and used her love like a bandage every time the useless bastards lost.

But that night, May 5th, fresh from Anfield and The Arkles and a 3-0 loss to boot, she was different. There was something heavy on her heart, large on her mind, that for some reason was shy to make its way to her lips. Then, over a conversation about how I didn't like The Rolling Stones when I was young but I did now, and how I never cared much for The Beatles when they were around, but was gradually warming to their unique mix of guitar-pop, she asked me about fatherhood… and told me she was pregnant.

Her logic was simple: something's you learn to appreciate more with time. I guess it was the same way Gary Speed appreciated every match he played and every training session he did because he knew his games were numbered as his 30's progressed. When I was a father the first time around I didn't really want it; now I was older I longed for it. And just liked handing Speed a new contract, Rachel falling pregnant was a chance to do it all again, but with the benefit of hindsight.

Was I scared? No. And by no I of course mean *hell yes*.

During the close season, and in the build up to the 2001 / 2002 season I turned the spare room into a nursery, I read loads of books on fatherhood, I pampered Rachel to the point that even though we weren't married we ended up talking divorce, and I basically spent the entire time preparing for my second swing of the fatherhood bat.

But of all the things I did, there was one crucial thing that I didn't: I didn't tell the bairn.

As Bobby Robson made wholesale changes and his squad ironically – took on a new and youthful look I neglected to tell

Terry that Rach' was pregnant. We saw each other a couple of times over the summer – Thursday nights in The Telegraph. But as happy as the lad was to share his life with me, he made it clear that he had no interested in hearing tales of Rachel and the girls, the people I left him to be with. It was like Peter Beardsley coming back to Tyneside in '93 and Newcastle being thrilled to have him, just as long as he shut the fuck up about his Anfield love-affair.

It was the same way you don't want your current partner telling you how wonderful sex was with their ex. And so low and behold although I'm no Freddie Spender I figured the kid probably didn't want to be regaled with tales of my new baby to be. So, I didn't tell him.

What a fucking idiot.

By time we were back in The Leazes End in August Rachel looked like she had a pillow up her jumper and Robson looked like he might have a trick up his sleeve. And just as I was wondering how to combine old and young, Terry and my baby-to-be, Robson was mastering it.

We were at Stamford Bridge on opening day – well, a Sunday – when a Laurent Robert inspired United came home with a 1-1 draw. New signing Craig Bellamy opened his account in the opening home game – a feisty 1-1 draw with Sunderland – and then the side hit the road for Teesside for the second derby in 2 weeks.

And as the young guns of Bellamy and Robert were settling in nicely, an old head returned to put the final touch to United's powerful punch. Alan Shearer returned from injury and against the Boro on September 8th 2001 he scored his first Premiership goal since November 4th 2000. It was his first goal in about 10 months. His second came about an hour later as Laurent Robert tormented a hapless Boro and Shearer bagged a belter, reminiscent to his strike against Holland in Euro 96. That game finished 4-

1... and so did this one. Newcastle absolutely hammered the Boro as the season got off to a successful start.

A week later United hit four again, this time to turn Manchester United over 4-3. That was just as magical. Life seemed brilliant. Everything seemed brilliant. The skies were blue again and suddenly the goals and attacking football returned. United had young players with pace and old players with experience and it gelled marvellously. Bobby Robson – one of our own – was in charge. I was just so, so happy. Newcastle 3 Manchester United 3, last few minutes, and then bang, Alan Shearer 4-3, I'm celebrating the winner... with the bairn... while the love of my life sits at home texting me and carrying my baby-to-be.

Life and football go so intrinsically and poetically hand in hand. For some of us life is a breeze. We're born rich, we have no worries, we barely have to work for a living and all that we desire seems to fall effortlessly into our lap. I guess that's a bit like being a Man United supporter; FA Cups and Premiership Titles and even Champions League Trophies come along in a steady stream. It's success after success all the way home. But for most of us, for you & me, life isn't like that. Most of us aren't so rich we don't have to work. Most of us aren't so lucky that whatever woman – or man – we so desire just falls at our feet, and most of us have to fight day after day just to keep on top of the game.

People like us are the majority. We're the other 80-odd league clubs who don't win trophy after trophy after trophy. But let me ask you, who would appreciate an FA Cup win the most, Man United or Aston Villa, Sunderland or Chelsea? Who would appreciate a Premiership Title the most, Arsenal or Everton, Middlesborough or Man United? And that's what it comes down to: appreciation.

Most of us aren't so fortunate that we're wonderful at everything we do. Most of us are still chasing our dreams. Most of us have to roll our sleeves up and scrap for the good things in life. And therefore when they come along, we appreciate them.

After all, what would an FA Cup win mean to us Newcastle fans...?

For me, at that point in my life, I was truly that happy and I truly appreciated it. And just when I thought I couldn't get any happier, I did.

As a bright summer full of life and hope eased naturally into autumn, and as autumn drifted magically into a frosty, icy winter, United hit some real form. And my son was born.

One of the most amazing weeks of my life began with a trip to Arsenal on a Tuesday night. Rachel was due any time and a trip to London on such a winter's day wasn't wise. So, as much as I love my football and love Newcastle, I made the simple decision that my family come first, and I settled for going to the boozer and watching the thing on Premier Plus. And if I ever needed any example to show you how much I love my friends then it came in the form of Garry & Tom turning down the trip to London to come to the boozer and watch the match. And Newcastle – with an absolutely awful record in the capital – went on to win 3-1. Seeing Alan Shearer smash home a last minute penalty to make it 2-1 was incredible. We did the conga around the bar. We barely got back to our bar stools and bang! It was 3-1! Robert broke away to seal the victory and Newcastle had stuffed the Gunners in their own back yard.

The following game was a trip to Leeds. Rachel insisted I honour my ticket. It was only an hour and a half down the road. She was safe and well. She insisted I go. And so me and The Lads did. But the night before – without warning – it snowed. It caught me by surprise, it caught most of us by surprise, but most of all it caught the council by surprise. Not a road was gritted for miles and what was a simple 90 minute trip to Leeds became a 4 hour treck just to ditch the car in someone's hedge and leg it to Elland Road right on kick off.

Some days there's just magic in the air from the off. That day at Leeds, Saturday December 22nd 2001 was one of those days. Despite an early goal from Craig Bellamy Newcastle soon found themselves 3-1 down. But the magic lingered in the frosty air.

And soon it was 3-2.

Then, with The Lads pouring towards the away end – an away end full of black & white – it was 3-3. With only minutes left on the clock a Keiron Dyer inspired Newcastle broke away and Nobby Solano – wearing the number 4 shirt – got in on the blind side of Ian Harte – wearing the number 3 shirt – and the game finished marvellously as the shirts summarised: Leeds 3-4 Newcastle.

It was amazing, incredible, astonishing, exhilarating: all that and more.

By time we had returned to reverse the car cautiously out of the hedge that we'd dumped it in our hearts were still thumping. By time we'd gotten the heating working and finally began to thaw out we were on the Leeds ring road and clocking the signs for the A1 North. By time we'd hit Wetherby the snow was teaming in the winter night. And then my phone rang. Rachel had went into labour…

The decision to take the car seemed a good one at that point. We couldn't have floored the bus and went for broke; we could with the car. But the snow begged otherwise. It was after 8pm when we finally arrived, all donned in black & white, to The Freeman Hospital. Garry & Tom made themselves comfortable in the waiting room, equipped with as much hot tea as they had 20p's for, and I dashed into the delivery room.

An hour or two later – just as the lads were settling down to The Premiership in the waiting room – Rachel gave birth to our son. He came out all pink and wrinkly, screaming and I'll admit it, ugly! But I loved him. As Rachel held him in her arms she asked if I was settled on his name. After that amazing afternoon at Elland Road I nearly named him Nobby. But the bairn, this little bundle of love and mess wrapped up in Rachel's arms, had really made a difference in my life. And somehow Keiron seemed the only name to give him. Well I didn't know he was going to be injured every week did I?

A few days later we had him home in time for Christmas. A day after that we walloped Boro for the second time that season. Defeats to Man United and Chelsea followed before Newcastle went on a decent run, unbeaten until March. That run included our first win at The Stadium of Light, 1-0 thanks to Nicos Dabizas. Wonderful stuff.

The 2001 / 2002 season finished with only 1 defeat in the final 9 and culminated with a wonderful trip to Ewood Park, Blackburn, last week in April. Newcastle were closing in on a place in the top 4 and that top four now carried a golden ticket to The Champions League. United grabbed it with a 2-2 at Ewood. Newcastle's goalscorer…? Alan Shearer of course.

The summer flew over. The 2002 / 2003 season came around in no time. As excited as I was at the prospect of potential Champions League football, the same that was ever so fleetingly danced with in 1998, I was absorbed by being a Dad again. I was smitten with Keiron, and whereby when Terry was born I was the young reluctant father forced into his duties, in Keiron's case I was the devoted mature Dad loving every minute of it. I never once dodged a nappy, (there's a 'shit hits the fan' joke in there somewhere but I won't be using it) I was the first one up during the night, and I was the one burping the little bugger while he puked all over my shoulder. Hell, I nearly bought a Sunderland scarf he threw up so much.

As Keiron took his first steps in our living room Newcastle took their first steps in The Group stages. Defeats to Dynamo Kiev, Feyenoord and then Juventus were stumbles that saw United flat on their arse and staring at the exit. But the magic that was still hanging high over Gallowgate was lit up in the way that only midweek floodlit European football can do. Newcastle fought back, magnificently.

Victories over Kiev and Juve' at Gallowgate brought the climax to the first group stage to a thrilling end. On November 12th 2002, a misty Tuesday night, I kissed my baby Prince goodbye and the lads and me made for North Shields and the misty ferry-port. Soon we were abroad the DFDS Prince of Scandinavia and heading for Holland and what was to be an unforgettable European night with our black and white Knight and our famous Toon Army.

11. When The Toon Hits Your Eye Like A Big Pizza Pie

You know you've made it when you're waiting for the Juventus score to decide your fate. That was the case in Feyenoord. It was one of the most amazing nights of my life. Me and the lads standing arms locked together in jubilant anticipation of what was to come.

After looking like we'd blown our European hopes with three straight defeats we pulled ourselves around with victories over Dynamo Kiev and Juve' themselves. Our final group came was away to Feyenoord. We stood on the ferry going over a bit like Denis, Neville, Oz and the lads coming back from Germany at the end of the first series of *Auf Wiedersehen Pet*.

And, Buds and Becks and Brown in hand, we rode the waves going up and down like our very hopes. Beat Feyenoord and we stay in The Champions League; draw with Feyenoord and we go into the UEFA Cup; lose to Feyenoord and we were out of Europe. This match marked one of the most significant times of my life. It summed up who I was, who I had become and more so, who I was set to stay forever more. I was engaged to Angie at the time. I liked her, I cared about her, I was fond of her, she had nice boobs and I trusted her. But I didn't love her. She didn't excite me, enthral me, make me crazy with passion and lust and take my heart off on a joyride.

It was at that time, going to and from Holland on the Ferry, that I took stock of my life. I think who were are, who we become is shaped by two things; one is the genes, the make-up, the characteristics and the chemicals we're born with; the cards we're dealt basically. I think the other is the things that happen in our lives, our experiences and how we handle them; the way we play the cards we're dealt, I guess.

For me, that trip to Holland gave me time and space to see things, things that perhaps I'd been too close to for me to really see before. I realised what the impact of my father – and Roxy – leaving me had on me. I was scared of getting hurt, which is why I got involved with someone like Angie, someone safe who would never hurt me. Worse than that I was scared of hurting someone else. If hopes, dreams and aspirations were bets and if emotions were money then I'd stopped gambling, because I didn't want to lose and I didn't want to emotional bankrupt anyone else either.

I don't think that's the way to live your life. But I guess that who I'd become was all summed up by my take on the Feyenoord game. Most of the lads were going gung-go and all guns blazing, glory or bust, Newcastle to win. Me, I'd mildly settle for a draw and stay in the UEFA Cup. And I hated that about myself.

Then a day later came the match and at 2-0 up – including a belting volley from Hugo Viana – I wished I'd had the convictions of the lads. In typical United style we threw away a couple of goals and at 2-2 I saw logic in my thinking. But what logic is there in romance? Absolutely Jack Shit none! With a minute to go, 2-2, Newcastle clinging on, my deal with fate to accept a place in the UEFA Cup looked a good deal.

Then United broke away…

…Suddenly Keiron Dyer was clean through. He finished the way Keiron always finishes… Dyer…

…But out of nowhere came Craig Bellamy. He struck the ball from on the goal-line, the Feyenoord goalie made a right arse of it and it nestled in the back of the net… and United had won 3-2.

You can jingle-bells all you like there is nothing quite like celebrating Newcastle scoring in another country. It was absolute magic. I reckon the roar could have been heard all the way back to Amsterdam, where me and the lads, Dad and his mates, and every other Geordie in the world seemed to be staying. Holland is a wonderful place, especially Amsterdam. But you've seen nothing until you're walking through the Red Light district, checking the beauties and the beasts in the windows, dodging a thousand crap bikes and then out of nowhere comes a rousing chorus of Blaydon Races.

We left the Old Sailor around midnight and a lad I recognised from home fell out of one of those magic doorways with the red light above it. He was refastening his pants and straightening his Toon shirt. He almost bumped into us as he stumbled back into the Amsterdam streets.

"You all right there mate?" one of the lads laughed as we steadied him.

"Never better mate" he said as he regained his balance. "The Toon have just won in Europe, I'm miles away from wor lass and I've just shagged a stunner!"

As he bounced up the cobbles to his own drunken chorus of 'One Bobby Robson' we glanced to the doorway he'd just left; the one with the red light and the blue tint. There in the window sat a foxy blonde with huge fake breasts, a little mini-skirt, a bikini top and a big pair of bollocks swinging between his or her legs.

It topped the night off brilliantly.

When we finally got tucked up in the hotel / hovel after the match and the beer and coffee shops I thought long and hard about the night. I loved the result, it was one of the best away games I had ever and have ever been to, and yet I hated myself for not having the balls to believe we could win the damn thing. I was so scared of us getting beat that I settled – head and heart – for the draw. That's not living; that's surviving, and there is so much more to life than just surviving, than just settling for the draw.

Those thoughts lingered with me the next day while we sat in The Black Tiger texting the lads at home and ensuring we got our flights and Hotels booked for our next Champions League trip: Inter Milan in the San Siro.

By time that journey came around it was March and I really needed the break. Newcastle had learned nothing from their first Group Stage results by proceeding to lose the first three matches from the 2nd Group phase. Again they rallied and when we set off for Milan our hopes were still faintly alive. But it was the fire in my heart that concerned me the most.

Angie and I had set a date for our wedding and suddenly it felt like the walls were closing in on me. Don't get me wrong, I'm not a commitment phobic or anything like that; I have no worries about getting married and settling down; I do however have deep-seated fears of committing to the wrong girl.

And in my heart of hearts I knew that was the case with Angie. The problem is, sometimes our heart is the scariest place to look.

I was terrified of what I'd see: that I didn't love Angie and that marrying her was a mistake. I mean, I loved her, I just didn't *love* her. God, how much sense does that make…?

She was pop music, not rock music. She was rhythm guitar, not lead. She was shy and quiet; I wanted loud and crazy. She was 4-5-1, I wanted 4-3-3. She was the 1.6 or the diesel, the miles per gallon and save the planet. I was fuck the planet give me a

2.8 injection, global warming and a sun tan. She was pass to a teammate; I wanted shoot from anywhere.

We were opposites – and not the kind that attract. I was into The 'Stones when she was into the roses.

She wore long skirts and jumpers, tights and sensible shoes; I wanted short skirts and stockings and blouses with tickets to tit-city, oh and with stiletto's to boot. She was take an umbrella in case it rained, I was jump in puddles and run off to the seaside and make love on the beach. I wanted passion and power and desire and lust. I wanted magic and excitement and Jesus Christ I just wanted to feel alive.

I hadn't felt that way since Roxy. Mind you, that's not to say I was still in love with Roxy, or even still wanted her. I just wanted to be as in love with someone the way I was once in love with her. The thing with Roxy was she was never dull. Foolishly, when she left me and cashed in the receipt on my heart I handed it to someone who I knew would never do the same. I was so scared of losing that I forgot to play to win. Nothing summed that up quite like that trip to Amsterdam & Feyenoord.

By time we'd hit the bar in Newcastle Airport I was running out of air I was so desperate for an escape. It was like having panic-attacks of the matrimonial kind. I was so messed up I was starting to connect to the lyrics from Ace of Base! Man, I saw the sign. Time had slipped away so quickly without me once raising my glass to yesterday. Angie kept on making plans and somehow I found myself caught up inside of all of her crazy dreams.

Just because I told her I loved her, promised I meant it, swore I'd never leave her, asked her to marry me, agreed to move in with her and bought a cat named Alfie she took that as carte blanche to start counting on me not to break her heart and to go booking churches and caterers.

Fuck me how did that happen…? Because I let it, that's why. I didn't have the stones to say 'no', or to be honest with her or me about my true feelings. And so the trickle became a stream, the stream became a river and the river became a damn ocean… and I started drowning in it. While I was busy looking for my *y* chromosome she was busy looking for dresses and falling in love. And fall as she did I didn't really want to be the one to catch her.

This might be a good time to reaffirm that I am not a commitment phobic. I just didn't want to commit to someone I didn't love. I wanted wedding bells and churches and rings on the finger and all that. I just wanted it with someone that made me feel like Tino not like Paul Kitson.

I tell you, I'm quoting Steven Tyler here but love is like the right dress on the wrong girl. At least that's how it was for Angie and me. The wedding bands were starting to feel like chains and the line "I do" like a sentence.

The trip to Milan was a Godsend to me. It came at a time when I needed it the most. It gave me a few more days away from Angie. Living together had been a good idea; living in each other's pockets had been stifling. By March 2003 and my first visit to Italy I was forced to look inside my heart and see the truth about my life and my love, or the lack of it for Angie.

I nipped of, away from the lads, for just half an hour on the first night we were there. I went to the bar downstairs and across the road while they were all getting ready in The Best Western. I picked up my thoughts where I'd left them on the DFDS Ferry. I realised that the implications of my Dad – and of Roxy – walking out on me and hurting me was that I didn't want to do that to anyone else. When they upped and left it damaged me to the extent that I was unable to break up with someone. I couldn't handle the guilt. The combination of them leaving was simple.

Because Roxy hurt me I picked a girl who would never do the same. But in doing that I picked a girl who didn't inspire me, or set my heart pounding. There were no highs but no lows. I picked a girl I didn't love. Because Dad had left I was unable to end a relationship. So I was stuck with Angie.

And perhaps the worst of it was that my self-esteem was so low that I got to thinking Angie would be my only hope, my only chance of finding someone. My mates were all settling down, my social circle was diminishing and even though I was way too young to rationally worry about it I basically gave up hope of meeting one of the other billion and odd women in the world and clung on to Angie to save me from being alone.

In hindsight – and hell even at the time but just many miles away – I could see it. But when it was right up close I couldn't.

Being in somewhere as beautiful and romantic as Milan helped too. It reminded me of what life should be like, as opposed to what I had let it become. I spent 3 days dreaming of being right there right then with a woman who *did* light my fuse, set my bull running, float my boat, fire my cannon or whatever euphemism you want to use. Being there in Milan, in The Champions League, clicking through the turnstiles into The San Siro to see The Lads and chant Blaydon Races was incredible. There was this sense of *we've arrived...I've arrived* about it all that made me realise how big and wonderful the world of love and football really is.

Newcastle – lead by 2 more Alan Shearer goals – earned a creditable if insufficient point against Inter Milan. And when we returned home a few days later I returned with a different perspective than the one I had taken to Italy with me.

There's little justice in the world, I find. Look at Buddy Holly, The Big Bopper and hell even John Denver; all died in a plain crash. And there's Westlife, jetting all over the world on tour and enjoying one save landing after another. No justice at all. If there'd been any footballing justice Newcastle would have won that game in the San Siro and the Champions League would have brought us yet more trips away in the remainder of the season. It didn't. But as we touched down at Newcastle Airport as safe as Westlife I finally accepted that Angie was not the one for me. However, what I gained in sight I was lacking in strength and although I knew I didn't love her I doubted that I would leave her.

Did I pucker up and take it on the chin? Did I set about setting both of us free to finally find and fall in love, no matter how hard it is on the knees? No, I threw myself into the Premiership Title Race and hoped with all of my heart that Robson's young side were capable of a miracle.

They weren't. A 6-2 home hammering by Manchester United taught us that. But we did clinch a return to The Champions League with a sweet, sweet 1-0 Nobby Solano penalty away win at Sunderland. The Stadium of Light was conquered once more. In the end we finished the 2002 / 2003 season in 3rd place and we qualified for The Champions League once again. Well, the problem was that we thought we qualified for The Champions League. We didn't. We qualified for the qualifiers.

As the 2003 / 2004 season was about to get under way I was away enjoying a weeks respite with the lads in Magaluf. At that time Newcastle crashed out of the qualifiers with a penalty shoot out against Partizan Belgrade. It was a weird time in my life. It was strange not being at the match and in a way that was typical of how I was feeling.

Angie worried about me going away with the lads; she insisted she trusted me but the thought of what I might get up to late at night with some bikini clad 18-30 girl gave her enough sleepless nights of her own. I'd have felt the same. We watched the match that night in a bar next to the beach, not far from BCM's and Bananabar. We were accompanied by Celtic and Rangers fans who watched their respective Teams win just in time to watch us lose in the shoot-out.

Ultimately that was the beginning of the end, for both United & Angie. Neither the season nor my relationship would recover from the results of that week. By the end of the 03 / 04 season the restlessness had multiplied in both cases and despite Robson guiding United to a highly respectable 5th place, and despite Angie guiding me through our wedding plans I knew that both were on borrowed time.

I tried to salvage something from the wreck I had let me life become: I changed jobs, leaving Davies in Benton, returning to Wallsend and TG's Garage. It was run by Kenny Goddard whose father, Tim, had a garage in Cordona Road, Easington, and had bought another in my hometown. When the chance to put some space between Angie & I arrived I grabbed it with both greasy, oily hands. I thought it might help, not seeing her every minute of every day. It did, for a while, but ultimately all it did was paper over the cracks. Not working together was good for us; it gave us some space. The problem was that the more space I got, the more I wanted.

Hurting the ones you love is such an awful part of life. Ending a relationship with someone who doesn't want it to end, someone who doesn't feel like you feel, who doesn't have the concerns you have is such a bitter pill. Some people say it's hard to tell someone that you love them; me, I say it's harder to tell someone that you don't.

I can hold my hand on my heart and say honestly that I cried the day Bobby Robson was sacked. The image of Sir Bobby standing by his car, leaving the training ground with the news of his sacking fresh upon his ears and crushing upon his heart reduced me to tears. And not just because I still believe it was sad and wrong to let The Bobfather go, but because I knew that I had to do the same to Angie.

But for all his faults and all his mistakes, where Freddie Shepherd had the bollocks to follow his convictions I sadly didn't. Freddie picked up the axe and wielded it; I simply went to the bar and tried to drink myself to surrender.

12. *From Harvey To Hollywood*

Some people are just born united. Some lovers are born to be together, some players born to wear a shirt, some captain's are born to wear the armband and some actors are born to play certain roles. To me, Bobby Robson falls into that category indubitably.

Robson, though never a United player, was always a United fan. The club was his club, as instilled in him by his father. And what greater way is there to inherit the honour of following a club than have it bestowed upon you by your father. He was a local lad; he grew up supporting Newcastle and always held the dream in his heart that one day he would manage *his* club. That dream came true when he replaced the ill-fated Ruud Gullit in 1999.

Robson was as destined for United as Jackie Milburn was to set records in the famous number 9 shirt, just as Alan Shearer was destined to break them. In the same way that Joe Harvey was destined to hold aloft the FA Cup, Bob Moncur was meant to hold aloft the Fairs Cup. And like Ant was meant to be with Dec, Robson was meant to be with Newcastle.

Some people are perfectly suited to certain roles. You can see it in the way that Jimmy Nail was born to play Oz. Or to go more Hollywood it's in the way that Connery was born to play Bond, Stallone born to play Rocky and Kermit was born to play the Frog in The Muppets Movies. It was the same way that Brando was born to play Don Vito Corleone. With destiny, grace and respect, that's how Robson was born to manage Newcastle United. The Bobfather.

Not only was Robson born to manage his hometown club, but he also did a bloody good job of it. Still, for too many of us, 3rd, 4th, and 5th place consecutive finishes in the toughest league in Europe wasn't enough. Despite taking a useless, relegation-threatened side of foreigners and misfits and giving us a team of young, predominantly English players who played the best football we had seen since the halcyon days of Kevin Keegan the cry went out for Robson's head.

Rumours abound that Robson and Shepherd, and even Robson and Shearer were at battle. Eventually the bullet was fired and The Bobfather fell. And I dare to say that is one of the worst decisions to be made at Leazes for many a long trophy-less year.

Don Vito Corleone was succeeded by his son, Michael. Alan Shearer, the one most thought would be groomed to replace Robson one day, was still too young, and somehow United opted incomprehensibly to replace Sir Bobby Robson with Graeme Souness… (See worst decisions, above). Replacing Robson with Souness was like replacing a flat tyre with a lemon-squeezer: it was clearly never going to work.

Since the birth of my second son, Keiron, in 2002 I have become more philosophic about life, love and football. I'm older and wiser now. Still, I often find myself wondering what would have happened if Arthur Cox had stayed, if United had gotten Bobby Robson instead of Jack Charlton; if Brian Clough, not Gordon Lee, had replaced Joe Harvey.

I often daydream that Ferdinand stayed, that Keegan didn't quit, that Alex Ferguson had to go to Middlesborough and get a Goddamn miracle, because Newcastle were already 3 points clear with just Spurs at home left to play. And I often daydream how I loved it when we beat them, loved it. And one day such notions got me pondering and wondering. Of course, so much of football is only a matter of opinion. But in the graceless and disrespectful dismissal of The Bobfather I got to thinking how only 3 managers since 1975 have been a success here on Tyneside.

Since Joe Harvey's sad departure in 1975 – after 13 years in charge – United have had no fewer than 14 managers in 32 years. I think it is fair to argue that of those fourteen only Arthur Cox, Kevin Keegan and Bobby Robson can be classed as successful. What did any of the others do?

Still, with the self-destruct button in danger of gathering dust United fired Robson just weeks into the 2004 / 2005 season. Perhaps replacing Robson with someone who could carry the club forward may have justified the decision. But replacing him with a man who systematically took the club back at least 5 years and God knows how many millions was insane. That kind of decision-making is why this club continues to under-achieve.

Yet still, as Souness took the reigns people continued to talk about expectation. I've followed this great club for most of my life and do I have unrealistic expectations? No I don't think that I do. This club has won nowt since 1969; do I expect to win a cup this year? No, no I don't. If the club finishes the season without a trophy will I be surprised? Like hell will I! No, the expectations on Tyneside are very reasonable ones.

I expect the club to punch its weight, that's all. I expect a club with such a massive support base, such massive commercial possibilities and such loyal followers to take all the goods at its disposal and manage them efficiently to make the club successful. Is that asking too much? I don't think it is.

If I had a 2.8 litre Ford Capri I'd expect it to be faster than a 1.4 Fiat Punto. If I had £40,000 to buy a new car I'd expect to get a better one than someone who only had £20,000. We get 52,000 week in week out. We spend our hard-earned money by the truckload on every bit of merchandise this club brings out. We buy the shirts, we buy the calendars and the training tops and the season videos and mostly we buy the damn tickets. Should we expect to achieve more with that resource than say someone like Bolton Wanderers or Wigan Athletic, Blackburn or Reading who have considerably less…? Yes, I think we should.

Is that an unreasonable expectation…? I'll let you be the judge.

I climbed onto my soapbox in the name of films and actors, of The Godfather and the Corleones. I will climb down the same way. We talk about expectation, but even Hollywood, wonderful Hollywood that brought us time machines, aliens fighting the President of America while Will Smith saves the day, Dinosaurs returning to life in mystic theme parks and cyborgs being sent through time to kill John Connor, even Hollywood could not bring us silverware. Santiago Munez, the hero of *Goal*, the Hollywood movie, came to Tyneside, scored a load of goals, won bugger all, Newcastle finished 4th and then he buggered off to Real Madrid!

That wasn't a movie script or a Hollywood classic! That was Jonathan bloody Woodgate!

Even Hollywood, with it's wild and wonderful stories and scripts, its Aliens and its Time Machines, found it too far fetched that Newcastle could finish higher than 4th!

But as in Hollywood, as on Tyneside, there's always another blockbuster around the corner. And no one – it turns out – writes better storylines that fate itself.

13. One Colour Champions League

Some people are just born united. Some people in life will just always, somehow, find their way to each other. Some people in life you just can't keep apart. But Beverley Knight was right: for every little thing you hold on to you've got to let something else go.

Truth is, you can't play both your Goalie's; and if Given's between the sticks then Harper – sadly – can't be. After all, only one person can wear the number 9 shirt. Now imagine that famous shirt is your heart. You might be unlucky and have no one to wear it; you might have a striker who just doesn't do the shirt justice (see previous Paul Kitson, Scott Sloan, Gary Brazil, Frank Pingel and Rob McDonald references). Or maybe you're really lucky and you find someone who is destined to wear that shirt (see Andy Cole, Mick Quinn and David Kelly references). That's how it was when Keegan signed Alan Shearer: but what about poor Les Ferdinand whom we had to take the shirt off…?

If you're in a relationship with one person it's pretty hard to have one with someone else. People do, mind you, and affairs and the like are hardly a surprise in these days of disposable marriages and photocopier tans. Not that I'm judging mind you: although there was a time when I did. After all, I sat as judge, jury and executioner on my own father when he took the number 9 shirt off my Mam and gave it to Rachel, the girl from the Newsagents down our street.

It was a mistake to judge my father that way. But I was too young to know better, too blind to see the truth. But I would see. And I would know better. And that lesson would come soon. Because some people are just born united. Some people in life will just always, somehow, find their way to each other. Some people in life you just can't keep apart. I would however repeat my mistake before class was dismissed.

After a disappointing season with Sir Bobby whereby we only finished 5th in one of Europe's toughest leagues – where the hell was my perspective – I started to become disillusioned with football as I was with life. From getting back from Magaluf I would work all week, go to the pub on Friday night with the lads to discuss the weekend's match, and then go out all day Saturday and Sunday to watch the matches. I stopped going to away games as much as I used to and my weekends were pub, lager, football, cider, lads, vodka, the home game, more lager, live Sky games, Tequila, jukebox, cigarette's and Goals on Sunday. I was so unhappy at home that before long I was pioneering the lads Sunday La Liga Specials which normally ended well passed midnight if they saw so much as kick off.

That was how I spent the 2003 / 2004 season: pissed.

I was using alcohol as an escape; it soon became a trap.

The crux of the matter wasn't that I loved the taste of the lager or whiskey or vodka I was swilling around my mouth. It wasn't that I loved waking up in the morning feeling like shit with a head that sounded like the away end when Newcastle conceded at Gallowgate. It wasn't checking my wallet and seeing I was broke and it wasn't the dull cloud that hung over me as I danced around the edges of sobriety.

No, the crux of the matter was simple: I had problems in my life and I wasn't ready to deal with them. So I drank. And ultimately that only made all of my problems worse.

My relationship with Angie was suffocating the life out of me. I desperately wanted to break up with Angie but I simply didn't want to break the lass' heart. I'd had it done to me and I didn't want to do that to her. I thought I was protecting her by never seeing her, spending all of my time with my mates and basically living in the pubs and clubs of Newcastle and Wallsend. I wasn't protecting her at all; I was preventing her from having a chance of finding someone who could love her the way I never could.

My Dad was aware of what was going on, but before I could lean on him, I cut him off completely… again.

The 2003 / 2004 season drew to a strangely bitter end, despite Newcastle's lofty position. We didn't see how well we'd done to finish 5th; we just saw how badly we'd done to slip out of the top four. I think a lot of fans hadn't forgiven the players for having missed out on Champions League qualification back in August. With 4th place and Champions League qualification slipping away by May the bitterness drew to a head. The Lads won only 2 away games all season, the last of which was way back in October. By time the final league game of the campaign came around – Liverpool away – the season was over.

Ultimately and for the second time in my life a game at Anfield would prove to be life changing.

I'm not talking about either of the 4-3's that Sky somehow manage to show at least once a week. I'm talking about 1989 when my Dad came back from Anfield and left us to be with another woman. The second time – this time – May 2004 – it was finding out that my Dad was also someone else's Dad too. He'd had a kid, back in 2002, and hadn't bothered to tell me. One misplaced sentence, a word uttered in the wrong company, 2+2 didn't add up to 5 and the cat was out of the bag.

Standing in Stanley Park after a 1-1 draw whilst a 44,000 mix of red and black & white streamed away – one colour to the Champions League, two more to the UEFA Cup – my Dad – his Dad – tried to explain. I'm not sure I even heard him. I was miles away; not in Stanley Park with the towering Anfield stands peering over the summers day trees; not lost beneath the sounds of match-day traffic and the smell of hot-dogs; no, I was back in a Gallowgate car park in winter 1990. I felt as if I was 15 again.

I was tired, hoarse, worn out and exhausted. If Arsene Wenger had been my Dad he would have mollycoddled me and given me a few weeks off to recharge my batteries. If Brian Clough had been my Dad he would have given me a clip around the earhole and told me to buck up and get on with. The thing was, I had nothing left. Even the anger and the frustrations I had been suffering were gone. I was just beaten. I turned into the Merseyside sunshine and I walked away, shaking my head while my Dad shouted "Terry, Terry, Te-rr-y" across the Scouse tinted teatime.

I felt hurt and betrayed. Worse still, I felt foolish. My pride was as dented as a row of cars parked in Vic Reeves street. But I didn't have enough left in the tank to fight, to argue or to get upset. I just had enough left to walk away.

Dad had a 2-year-old son. But that summer I *acted* like a 2-year-old. I spat my dummy and I threw my toys out of the pram in a way I'm sure the brother I'd never met would have been proud. I cut off ties with my Dad – his Dad – once again, and I went back to drink, drink and a little more drink. Dad had hurt me so badly and I guess I wanted to hurt him back.

All in all it was a very bitter summer.

The club had let me down; the players were overpaid premadonnas who cared more for the wages, the Ferrari, the Pop-star Girlfriend and the 'Crib' than they ever did for the support, the history and the shirt. I wanted a way to hit back at them both. And when the season ticket renewal landed through my door I knew exactly how to do it.

14. *Things I Miss About Football*

It was August 21st 2004. Jet wanted to know if we'd be their girl, Maroon 5 told us that she would be loved and somebody had told The Killers. Newcastle faced Tottenham Hotspur in the first home game of the new season and I was paying the price for holding onto my secret about Keiron by letting go of Terry.

The season had started with a 2-2 draw on Teesside. I don't think the bairn was there. The season continued with a 1-0 home defeat to Spurs. The bairn wasn't there. Next was a midweek game with Norwich. The game ended 2-2. The bairn wasn't there either. It turned out to be Bobby Robson's last home match. And as I left The Leazes End that night I couldn't help but wonder if the bairn had seen his last home match too.

He wanted to hurt me, but he was speechless. He knew the empty seat would say more than his words ever could. It was a worrying time. A few days later and a 4-2 defeat at Aston Villa put paid to Robson's tenure.

My heart was bruised in seeing Sir Bobby asked to leave; it cracked the following home game when, like The Bobfather, the bairn wasn't there to take his seat. Newcastle beat a hapless Blackburn Rovers side 3-0 in early September. Rovers had just released their struggling manager Graeme Souness. But he was at the game anyway, and sadly, we all knew why.

After the match I was afraid to think of what a future with Souness would mean. Instead I got to thinking about the past and how much football has changed. And I got to thinking of all the things that I miss about football.

I miss short shorts, like the little Umbro ones the lads wore all through the '80's. I miss terracing, I miss singing Blaydon Races and bouncing down The Gallowgate End. I miss the old Leazes End, just like the bairn misses The Corner. I miss games kicking off at 3 o'clock Saturday and I miss the Blue Star on the front of the black & white shirt. And I miss red numbers on the back of those shirts.

I miss Goalie's wearing green; I miss players not afraid to get mud on their shirts but who try to stay on their feet. I miss singing at home games. I miss having a decent atmosphere at St James'. I miss players who got a decent wage not an astronomical one. I miss the England players being the best in the country, rather than some Premiership reserve. I miss players who can tackle and players who can dribble because both, believe me, is an art.

It's easy to wish the world were different; it's a lot harder trying to change it. I guess, like Hooberstank, you just have to trust that things happen for a reason. You can't live your life on ifs and Nicky Butt's. Hey, when Joe Harvey left I would have loved him to be replaced by Brian Clough. In similar fashion I would have loved to see what fortunes would have been had Bob Moncur replaced Gordon Lee or if Kevin Keegan had been replaced with Bobby Robson. What if Arthur Cox had been replaced with Malcolm Macdonald instead of Jack Charlton…?

What would the history of the club be had Malcolm Macdonald brought the flair and talent of his Fulham side back to Tyneside instead of Jack Charlton's more rugged approach…? Would

SuperMac have lost Waddle, disillusioned Beardsley and did both of those things to the fans…? Or maybe the club would have gone forward, and forward in style.

And can you imagine how different the history of both Newcastle and Sunderland might have been had Bob Stokoe, one of best Centre-Halves Newcastle ever had, had left Blackpool in 1972 for Tyneside and not Wearside…? Or what if the fans had gotten the big name they so craved in the late 70's early 80's and Lawrie McMenemy had taken over at St James Park instead of Roker Park?

I wish I'd never been through a divorce, I wish I'd never let the bairn down and I wish I'd never chosen not to tell him about Keiron. I've made mistakes; who hasn't? But I don't do regrets. After all, if I hadn't got Sheila up the Damien Duff then – devastate me as it did – I wouldn't have the bairn. And if I hadn't left Sheila and the bairn – devastate him as it did – I would never have been with Rachel and I'd never have had Keiron. In the end I guess you've just got to accept it, make the best of it, and maybe even wonder if it all happened for a reason. And it's just the same with the football.

If Gordon Lee hadn't quit when he did, maybe we'd never have ended up in turmoil. And if we hadn't ended up in turmoil maybe Bill McGarry would never have been here to be sacked and maybe Arthur Cox would never have been appointed. And without Arthur Cox there'd be no Kevin Keegan; and without Kevin Keegan we would have been deprived of so very much.

Still – for all the twists and turns that took us where we were – there was nothing I missed about football more than being there with Terry. Without him beside me football just wasn't the same anymore and his absence seemed to sum up the lack of emotion and chemistry around a loveless Barrack Road.

That first season without him, 2004 / 2005, drew to a close with United slumping headlong into 14th place. The following August was filled with *desperation* for better things rather than hope for them.

Expectation, well expectation had caught the last train out of dodge long before the 2005 / 2006 season got under way.

James Blunt was telling us we were beautiful (every 5 minutes if I remember right) Green Day wanted us to wake them up when September ended and Hard-Fi were hard to beat. Sadly Newcastle – with Graeme Souness in charge – were anything but hard to beat. And as for most supporters watching Newcastle did require someone to wake us up not only when September ended but pretty much after each match the lads played.

Record signing Michael Owen brought rays of sunshine to late August but with more injuries than goals it was left to a rousing 3-2 win over Sunderland to bring us to life. Owen scored 7 goals before Christmas but then injury robbed us of his talents. After Christmas the darkness descended implacably. Still, it was not our new record signing who would make the year special, but the old.

Suddenly – from out of the blue – the team's fortunes would turn around and end on a high. Football and life have so often gone hand in hand for me and in both cases something wonderful from the past was about to step up and make the present – and the future – so much brighter.

And aren't heroes always more wonderful when they are ones from our past…

15. Objects In The Rear View Mirror

Some things in life just belong together, such as Ant & Dec, Shearer & Ferdinand, or Jim Steinman and Meatloaf. Some things you just can't keep apart. And sometimes today reveals cards that fate was holding all along.

Some people tell you not to go back; some people tell you it's poetic when you do. Sometimes it works, such as in 1992 when Keegan returned or when he brought back Peter Beardsley. Other times it fails, like when The Bobfather brought back Robbie Elliott. The way we defended it was more like having Billy Elliott at left-back.

I loved Newcastle United and it hurt turning away from them. I toyed with the idea, the urge, and the desire to go back. But I was disillusioned, disappointed, and felt deeply let down by a club I barely recognised as my own. Under performing, overpaid players driving around in huge Yankee-doodle-dandy-mobiles without a care for the shirt and what it meant. A brand of football that was as poor as the punters had seen since the days of Jim Smith, and a Manager in Graeme Souness that was taking the club backwards at the speed of light. But worse still, there was a distance between the club and its players and the supporter that made me feel cold.

So as much as I loved football, I cut my nose off to spite my face and I turned away from it all because it hurt me.

And of course, I had done the very same thing with my Dad. Did I love him? Of course I did. Did I miss him? Hell yes. But did I bridge the gap between us? No, I was far too spiteful to do that. It was daft: I loved Newcastle and I loved my Father but I chucked in my season ticket, refused to renew it, and lost touch with my own Dad. And all the while I was drawing ever nearer to a summer wedding to a woman I didn't love one jot.

As February 2006 came along and my wedding was no more than 5 months away I guess I was resigned to defeat. But then one more defeat came along for Graeme Souness and the man that nobody wanted for the St James' hot-seat was finally asked to get out of it. With that a ray of sunshine came flooding into both my world and United's.

A 3-0 midweek reverse to an average Man City side was Souness' last in charge of a club I thought he was never qualified to be at. For right or wrong, and regardless of the mess it may cause, the club acted to end our unhappiness and cut our losses before things got any worse. Souness replacement for the next 12 games was a surprise, but a welcome one at that. Glenn Roeder – one of our own – stepped up from the Academy and took the club into his safe hands. And for the first time in months I felt warm again.

I liked Roeder; he had been part of the first Newcastle team I had ever fallen in love with, the promotion side of 1984. Glenn Roeder brought back memories of sunny Tyneside days, the old West Stand basked in blue skies, Keegan's last game v Brighton, laps of honour, silver strips and NUFC badges. He brought back memories of The Gallowgate End, surges, atmosphere and the rite of passage that is the guy behind you peeing on your leg. Glenn Roeder reminded me of happy times.

Having Roeder in charge was a blast from the past, and although it was totally out of the blue, I revelled in its novelty and its nostalgia.

And it had the desired effect. In his first game in charge Newcastle grabbed a vital 2-0 win over Portsmouth on Tyneside, on a day when Tyneside's favourite son grabbed all the headlines. Alan Shearer's goal was United's second of the afternoon and his 200th for the club. The great Jackie Milburn had sat on 199 for pretty much half a century; Shearer's goal took him clear as Newcastle United's record goal-scorer of all time. All in all, it was a pretty special day at Gallowgate. Unfortunately for me, I wasn't there to see it. I had cut my nose off to spite my face and it meant my eyes were on Jeff Stelling instead of Alan Shearer.

Glenn Roeder's short-term appointment was successful. The up-turn in form continued: United lost only 3 of his 14 games in charge, winning no fewer than 9. Still, as skies got brighter over Tyneside it was a day on Wearside that will live longest with Newcastle fans. A 4-1 win over the auld enemy with Shearer's last ever goal, last ever game for the club, will forever reverberate around black & white hearts. It also added muscle to the Glenn Roeder CV when the managers' job was decided on a permanent basis.

And true to form, as things picked up for United they inevitably pick up for me. In the clubs case an old favourite came to the rescue; in my case it was very much the same.

I was at work just a few days before that wonderful Newcastle victory at The Stadium of Light. It was cold but it was sunny. The heaters were fighting the Wallsend chill and the garage doors were wide open to the world outside. I had grease and oil all over my hands and my concentration was deep in someone's engine just as the inkling for a cuppa came to play. I hollered to one of the lads to put the kettle on as I tightened the bolts on one more cylinder head. I wiped my hands with a cloth rag and made to the doorway to catch a sight of the wintry blue sky.

To my left was a blond lass dressed in jeans, a roll neck jumper and a brown leather jacket. My eyes fixed on her and something inside clicked. Sometimes the eyes are just a fuse and with one glance at the right person the fuse is lit and moments later the heart goes off like dynamite. Seeing this lass was just like that. My mind was stirring: *Roeder, Keegan, Arthur Cox, The old West Stand, Wallsend...* And she was asking Jed Peterson – our gaffer – if he could take a quick look at her car. *Wallsend, Chalk Goals, my Dad, fish n chips and Geordie fairytales...* I smiled at the cute way that she said 'pretty please' as she tried to charm Jed into helping her out.

We were stowed under and fully booked. Jed was explaining as much and asking her to bring it in later in the week, but she was persistent, explaining it was just something with her headlights, something that she was adamant would only take 5 minutes. *Knocky-nine-doors, kicky the can, and hide & seek...* And Jed maintained he couldn't help her out.

My gaze stayed upon her as my memory tried to kick-start like half of the motors in the garage behind me. Then she turned around, and I could see she was beautiful. I'm not talking just her looks; I'm not talking supermodel one stick of celery and an eating disorder; I'm talking real beauty and girl next-door beauty. And how did I know? Because she was the girl next door. Or at least she had been when I was just a bairn. She was Mandy.

I remember standing there with grease and oil all over me, and Jed's spanner under my arm. I had a thousand words hammering around my heart and head but none would organise themselves into a sentence that I could form in my mouth.

"I'll take a look at it, Jed", I said, trying to fight the smile that was bursting to get on to my face.

Jed just shrugged and walked away. And my smile sneaked out.

In her best I-could-have-been-in-Friends manner her eyes went wide, she put her hands on her pretty face and word for word mouthed "Oh-My-God!"

We lit up like fireflies. She made towards me to give me a hug and then we stopped short for my oily overalls and used-to-be-white T-shirt. Still, she eased forward and gave me a kiss on the cheek. And bang! My heart fired up like a big old V8. I had this rush of feeling that I hadn't seen the likes of since the days of Andy Cole. My eyes sparkled when they fell on her, my heart raced; my pulse 'thadumped' and my tongue did its best to tie itself in a million knots.

We exchanged starry-eyed pleasantries. And right from the first glance, right from the kick off there was chemistry. Suddenly I couldn't have picked Angie – or even Roxy – out of a line up and I remembered what it felt like when a man loves a woman. All I wanted to do was to kiss her, take her in my arms and go dancing until 4am to some good old music like Ben E King, Percy Sledge or Otis Redding.

I made changing two light-bulbs last 20 minutes as we tried to cram in 18-years of catching up. I got the gist for Mandy. She moved away to study nursing in Nottingham and had been working in Chesterfield then Leeds ever since. She moved home just a few months ago and was now settling back on Tyneside, back in Wallsend.

When her car was fixed she asked me how much she owed. Oh boy was I her gallant hero!

"Divvin't worry about it," I told her heroically. "If you want to bring it back in on Thursday I can take a look at it, give it a service and all," I offered.

My heart was thumping so loud I swear you could hear it.

"Yeah, sure", she said. "'Bout 11.30...?"

It's a date," I said, wishing it was one.

"I look forward to it," she said, and I prayed she meant the date.

The rest of the day is a blur. I was on cloud nine. I felt alive. I felt awake. All the dust and the cobwebs that had gathered on my heart were suddenly blown away. I couldn't get her off my mind all day, all week.

Thursday couldn't come quick enough.

I filled in the gap with the build up to the derby. When a Newcastle – Sunderland game is the distraction to the main even then that main even must be something special. To me it was. To me it was Mandy.

All those years ago she was the first girl I ever fell for, whether was it was crush, puppy love or the real thing. Either way she was the first. And I let her slip through my teenage fingers. And even though Mandy made me feel like a little boy I was a man now, and this man would not be making the same mistake again… no matter what it cost me.

I knew what I had to do: I had to leave Angie, break her heart, cancel our wedding, lose a fortune and become the villain of the peace. The money and the bad-guy status didn't bother me; breaking Angie's heart did. But after Mandy made two more unnecessary trips to TG's Garage to get her car fixed I knew it was a price I was ready to pay.

On that third occasion – when Mandy brought her Clio in for an MOT – we finally took the step we both knew we wanted. It's too easy to wait, to become Ross & Rachel, to let opportunities pass you by. But Alan Shearer didn't get where he was by passing up chances. If you want to be successful in life you have to grab those chances and make them count. Life is not always about those who get opportunities and those who don't; it's often about those who are not prepared to let those opportunities slip away.

I did Mandy's MOT for free, in my lunch hour. I played it cool as usual.

"Divvin't worry about it," I told her heroically. "Look, if you want to bring it back in…" I added before Mandy cut me short.

She smiled. "I only came in for new bulbs for my headlights and I've already been back twice more for services I didn't need. Terry, I just got an MOT 6 weeks before mine runs out… you're going to have to ask me out soon or it's going to bankrupt me coming back here until you do…"

I smiled back. We had out first date two days later.

Nothing happened between us that night other than words and feelings, but when you think about it, in relationship terms, words and feelings are pretty damn important. Whatever it was, something was struck between us that night which was strong.

I told her about Angie. I didn't want to spoil what we might have by lying.

"Won't you get in trouble," Mandy asked, "for being out with someone else?"

I just smiled. "Some people are worth getting in trouble for," I told her nostalgically.

All I had to now to be happy was to make someone else miserably unhappy. All I had to do was break off my relationship with Angie. That, however, was easier dreamt than done. I toyed with the notion every minute of every day. I labelled it as carefulness, thoughtfulness, consideration and kindness. It would have been a misleading label. In truth it was indecision, albeit indecision for all the right reasons.

I thought about the cowardly way out; I thought about coercing Angie into an argument that she wasn't looking for, blowing it out of proportion, and using it as a way of getting out. But the Gods or fate or destiny had been good to me and I didn't want to fly in the face of that. I'm a big believer in karma. Don't piss heaven off, Steve Tyler wrote; you'll have hell to pay.

Now I have my religion and that is of course Newcastle United. And though I ain't ever been one for church I guess I do believe in God. Some call him Jehovah, some call him Allah and some call him Howard, like in the Lord's Prayer, you know, 'Our Father who art in heaven, Howard be thy name'. To me he's the same guy. Just like some call the guy who picks the team *Coach*, some call him *Manager* and some call him *Director of Football*. Same job, different title, as in football, as in religion.

While caretaker Glenn Roeder was leading United into a race for a European berth, and I was struggling to decide what to do with my love life (yeah, two women wanted to be with me, ain't live a bitch) I prayed just a little for strength. I told God that if he wanted me to stay with Angie and sacrifice my own happiness for hers then give me a sign by letting Newcastle win the Champions League. Alas God wanted me to be with Mandy.

Then a day after that prayer something remarkable happened.

A family in our old street in Wallsend, where I grew up with my mother & father until my father left us for Rachel the girl from the newsagents, were moving house. The new family moving in wanted to use the garage next to ours. The garages were only half used these days and in the row of about 8 garages the one next to us had been spare for something like twenty years. Hell, ours had been empty since I moved in with Angie.

My mother explained all this to me when she phoned my mobile that afternoon at work.

"Look," she said, "It's complicated. Just come down as soon as, will you?"

"Yeah, sure", I said getting more and more nervous by the second. My Mam made it sound like something horrible had happened.

I bunked off a little before 3:30pm and drove my Astra back 'home'. I parked up at the front door and then realising my Mam would be out I drove round the corner to the garages.

I couldn't kill the engine and get the hand-break on quick enough. I couldn't believe my eyes. There, parked exactly where my father had left it almost twenty years ago, was a pristine white Ford Capri. The car – a 2.8 – had been Dad's pride and joy after the success of Slippery When What. It also coincided with Dad's drinking, drink-driving and imminent separation from my Mam. He had the car for one solitary day if I remember right. He drove it to the club one December night in 1987 and the next day he reported it missing.

The police took it as stolen, but truth was that it was simply *missing*. And reason being: well not because some toe-rag had half-inched it from the club or even home, but because in his drunken state Dad had put the damn thing in the wrong garage. Hence next morning when he and his hangover went to get it, it wasn't there. And despite his best efforts, those of Northumbria Police and PC John Goddard in particular, the car never showed up. That's because for the last 20 years it had been sitting in next doors empty garage.

I was stunned when I saw it. The tyres where flat, there was a whole load of dust – which inadvertently had protected from rust – and we had no idea where the keys might be.

"Do you want to go tell your Dad?" Mam asked.

"No, no not yet," I told her, still fascinated, still intrigued. It was like a little bit of the past had somehow travelled in time to the present.

"Where do we stand with insurance?" Mam asked.

"I don't know", I told her honestly, "but if you leave it with me I'd love to take care of all of this."

Mam just shrugged her shoulders and asked if I wanted the kettle popping on now that I was here. I agreed, but the tea was long gone cold when I finally left the side of the prestigious car.

Spring of 2006 was a special time for me. The winter faded and passed away and the world came to bloom. Days got brighter, sunshine returned, the nights stayed lighter later and everything was just warmer and coming life. Coats were replaced with jackets, jackets were replaced with T-shirts and soon the days were so bright that shades were more than just fashion, they were necessary.

Glenn Roeder's Newcastle were winning football matches again – including a 2-1 win on Teesside – and climbing the league table. We followed a 3-1 win over Spurs with a 3-1 win over Wigan, and we followed that with a 4-1 win away at Sunderland. We followed that up with a 3-0 win over West Brom, a 0-0 at Birmingham that sent Steve Bruce's side down and even Michael Owen returned to first team picture.

As Shearer's testimonial beckoned I was still wrestling with my moral, emotional dilemma regarding Mandy and Angie. I needed somewhere to go to think. I needed somewhere to clear my head, to listen to my heart, somewhere to be alone with my thoughts. All through that Spring, and all through that Newcastle United revival, as Alan Shearer clocked up 206 goals in the famous number 9 shirt I found my solace in the past as I wondered what to do with my future. I took Dad's old Capri to work thanks to Jed and his tow-truck and I went about restoring it.

Jed kindly let me have the keys to the TG's and while everybody else clocked off and went home between 4 and 5 o'clock I stayed back and made use of the garage and all of her tools. And slowly and surely I went about bringing the 19-year-old Ford Capri with only 24 miles on the clock back to life.

While The Frattelli's whistled for the choir, the final whistle went on Alan Shearer's playing career and I went about working on the old Capri. Restoring her allowed me time to think and to contemplate. Never was that so great as when I emptied Dad's old glove box. In there I found a letter, addressed to one of his Shipyard brothers. It was a simple keep in touch letter to Gary Robinson, one of the old lads from Dad's crew and one of Dad's closest friends.

Curiosity is a tempting mistress. I pondered for little more than 20 seconds before reading it. In the letter Dad wrote how his marriage was on the verge of breaking. He wrote how he didn't love Sheila, my Mam, and probably never had. In his unmistakable and remarkably eloquent penmanship Dad talked about how he only married Sheila because he had gotten her pregnant and he wanted to do right by her, and right by his son… me.

In fact Dad went on to say how he only ever stayed with Mam because of me and that the only good thing that his marriage had brought him, the only warm thing to come home to from the factory each night was his son, Terry.

And I cried.

Not for myself or how touched I was for what my father was able to say in written words to a friend what I never let him say in spoken ones to his son, but because when he finally had the courage to follow his heart I threw stones at it like a spoiled little bastard.

Dad's letter described how much he loved Rachel and ached to be free to be with her. He described how Sheila made no attempt to make him happy, and hadn't done so for so long. I know he was quoting Meatloaf but *his* words perhaps said it better than Dad's ever could: *She's been cold to me so long I'm crying icicles instead of tears.*

Sitting in Dad's old Capri, the car that had once – for one solitary day – been his pride and his joy I thought about how hard it must have been for him. My Mother had treated him like crap for years but for years he stayed with her… for me.

And there was me, with no kids to worry about, feeling just like Dad did all those years ago. He had Sheila whom he didn't love just like I had Angie. He had Rachel whom he did love just like I had Mandy. All he did was what I was about to do myself anyway and I never forgave him for it. I felt like such a hypocrite. He hadn't been guilty; he hadn't walked out on us, or deserted us or left me because he didn't love me. He was miserably unhappy and he stayed as long as he could because of me, because he loved me. All he wanted was to be with the woman he loved, just like I did with Mandy, and I held him to a 20-year grudge because of it.

I dried my eyes, folded away the letter, and began working harder than ever on that car. I knew I couldn't give Dad back the past, but in giving back just a bit of it maybe I could start giving him back a future.

Shearer hung up his boots in a testimonial with Celtic. I listened to the game on the car radio. And when the final lacquer was laid and the Capri was primed and ready to roar I locked it away in TG's Garage and I went home to break up with Angie.

16. *All You Need Is Love*

I've never had a woman treat me as bad as Newcastle United treats me. If I ever had a relationship with a woman who treat me as bad as my football club did I'd up and leave. Hell, I did up and leave Sheila. But still, through thick & thin, I remain in a loyal and loving relationship with a club whom I know really couldn't give a damn about me.

So why do I stay? Because I love Newcastle United.

And that's what makes us football supporters special. I know that by and large football divides us as we go team v team, club v club, week after week, season after season. But what we so often overlook is that our love of football unites us. It doesn't matter whether you follow Newcastle, Sunderland or Middlesbrough. It doesn't matter whether you follow Chesterfield or Leeds, Hartlepool or Liverpool, Darlington, Accrington or Manchester United. The love and the loyalty we show our clubs – often when we are being treat like crap in return – makes us very similar, very special people.

In marriage we stand up in front of our friends and family and often in front of a God that half of us don't believe in and we make our vows. We vow to stay together for better or worse, for richer or poorer, in sickness and in health and forsaking all other. And as time goes by, more and more of these vows are broken and more and more of these marriages end in divorce.

Take me as an example: I vowed to stay with Sheila 'til death do us part. I'm with Rachel now, and as far as I know nobody died.

Yet we make no such vow to our football club and does anyone ever divorce the team they support? I don't think many do. I promised Newcastle United nothing, yet after over 40-years of nothing I'm still as loyal as I ever was. We've had richer and poorer, thick and thin, ups and downs, and for every better we've had so very much worse. But did I ever leave? Did I ever cheat on my football club? Was I ever unfaithful? I never was.

That's the beauty with football. There's no loyalty anywhere in the world greater than that between a football supporter and their club. Players come and go, marriages start and end, Managers are hired and fired and lads and lasses cheat on each other time and time again. But does a football supporter ever have a one-night stand behind their clubs back? When did you ever hear of a Newcastle fan having a one-nighter at Anfield or Old Trafford? It wouldn't happen!

How many times has a man or woman argued over infidelity and said "It meant nothing to me, it was just sex". Can you imagine a football supporter saying to his club "It meant nothing, it was just trophies!"

I've known of people who have had blazing rows with a partner and then either split up with them or just went out and slept with someone else. Yet no matter how many times we roll out of a match dejected and let down we don't hit back by sneaking off to The Riverside or Goodison Park for a quick home game.

Even in the most severe cases when we hurt so much or become so disillusioned that we throw in our tickets and don't go back, we never find another love. Supporting a club is timeless. For example, our lovers almost always have history, a past, and previous partners. Football fans – God Bless them – have no such thing.

Football supporters have one love and one love only. My first game was in 1963; Terry's first game was of course 1982. In all those years I never went to see anyone else play. From that day Newcastle were my team and I have been with them ever since. You don't find football supporters who used to be Liverpool fans, had a season ticket at Sheffield Wednesday for a few years, then spent a few years single before going to watch Spurs and then after a couple of crazy one nighters with Halifax and Torquay ended up settling down at Newcastle. Football fans never wake up after a drunken night out and think 'Good God I can't believe I watched them'. Well...

You know the old joke: what's the difference between a fox and a pig: about 8 pints. People get drunk and pull an 8-pinter for a one-night stand. Football supporters would never do that. For example, you'd never find a Newcastle fan getting drunk and going off to watch Barnsley or Rotherham because they were gagging for a match. Football fans are different. We find our club, we stay with our club and we'll support them ever more. If love were as true as football support then the world would be a much better place.

If I'd loved my wife like I love Newcastle United I'd still be with her. And why? Because I love Newcastle United. And as much as we may fight or we may argue the fact is football supporters, true ones, real ones, are the most wonderful people on God's earth, regardless of the team they support.

There are morals in supporting a football club; morals that are shared by all true supporters regardless of which team they support. I know people who have been divorced; hell, I've been divorced. I've had more than one sexual partner. Maybe God or the Church would look down on that, but as football supporters do any of us care? No, not at all. But on the rare occasion when we meet someone who has changed their allegiances from one club to another, we frown upon them. And rightly so. Hell, I've got difficulty finding time of day for people born and raised up here in the North East who support Man United or Liverpool for example.

That's not all.

When you love something you look after it. And when you love something – or someone – you stay with them, you don't leave them, and you don't cheat on them. Football supporters show a dignity and a loyalty that is missing in so many other aspects of life.

That's true in romance and relationships too.

The couples that make it and the couples that don't, they all go through the same crap. The difference is that the couples that make it love each other enough to take the defeats and come back for more, just like we as football supporters do.

I guess what I'm getting at is that if you're with someone who you don't love enough to be faithful to then let them go. Go find someone you are *that* in love with, and give *them* the chance to find someone who'll love them the way they desire to be loved. If you *are* with someone you love that much, then treat them like you would your own club. *I* learned that when I left Sheila for Rachel. I found out in the summer of 2006, after Glenn Roeder's Newcastle finished a commendable 7th, that the bairn – our Terry – had learned the same.

Word gets around; it always does. People close to the lad told me he had changed, mellowed, become more worldly wise and dried some of that water behind his ears. I thought a lot about him that summer; I thought a lot about both of my sons. And watching Keiron run around the street kicking a penny-floater off the garden wall and screaming 'Shearer' I knew it was time.

I brought him home his supper one night – fish n chips and dandelion & burdock – and I told him all about Newcastle

United. There was no euphoria, there was no Kevin Keegan and I guess there was no hero. But there would be. This club is too magnificent to slide away. It's always darkest just before the dawn. I knew things would get worse before they got better, but somewhere there was a hero waiting to come make this wonderful club great again. This giant will always awaken. And whenever that happens I wanted the bairn to be there.

I thought I'd give him an idea of what was to come with a trip to Portland Park to see the Reserves play Ashington in a July pre-season. I know I was clutching at straws but dreams are there to be chased not feared, and as scared as I was of a rejection still I asked Terry if he would come and join us. His phone was off, so I settled for text. I told him where we would be – me & Keiron – and I left it with him.

It was one of those football summer nights where you can close your eyes and all your senses just tell you that you're at a match.

There was the smell of hot-dogs and Bovril, the sound of banter and debate and turnstiles clicking in the background. And it was warm banter; wrapped in the dialect you know and love. I love the sound of the Geordie accent in a football ground, especially one like Portland Park. There was the pleasant warm July night with the cool Ashington breeze rolling down the terracing, not seats, terracing.

Keiron and I stood in the warm summer night. It was important to me to take him to a game like that at a place like that. I wanted him to understand what real football, grass roots football was all about. Keiron was busy munching crisps, look for hot-dogs and poring his pop all over his Newcastle shirt. I was in a world of my own, somewhere around 1982. I was so lost in thought I didn't even hear his voice.

"This is the bairn then?"

"Aye, this is Keiron," I said, roughing the lad's hair a little.

"Keiron?" he asked me with raised eyebrows.

"Well I didn't know he was going to be injured every week did I? Besides," I smiled, "it could have been worse; I nearly called him Nobby."

I laughed a little in the warm pre-season Ashington night.

"Then I thought about the Hall's that lived in our street when you were just a bairn", I said. "Remember them? And their poor soon Albert? He's gay now you know. No bloody wonder if you ask me. Your Mam used to call him the catheter kid he had so much piss taken out of him."

"Dad!" he said, making the word last three syllables, "The bairn," he added as if I'd said something wrong.

I just smiled; I guess I liked it that he was already looking out for the kid.

I looked at the poor lad, standing on a terrace at Ashington FC but still in a world of his own. He was knee high to a grasshopper when I first took him to a match, and now there he stood as large as life a fully gown man. But still, no matter how old they are they're always still just bairns to us parent's aren't they?

I chuckled as he blew upon my Bovril.

"If Keegan hadn't walloped a couple past him back in '74 you'd be called Willie. Can you imagine that: two sons called Nobby & Willie!"

I'm not sure whether he was going to laugh or to cry, but looking at the little blond bairn smiling up at him I'm sure he felt *something*. Keiron put one arm above his eyes to protect from the setting northern sun and with the other he jutted his salt & vinegar upwards and offered Terry a crisp.

"No thanks, Keiron," Terry told him through a lump in his throat as he spoke to his brother for the very first time.

For a moment time stood still.

My eyes welled up; I had to look away and so I began staring at my match programme. Terry seemed to be looking somewhere only the memory can see, and Keiron was checking where the smell of hot-dogs was coming from.

I picked Keiron up and sat him on the barrier we were stood in front of. A million memories came flooding back like the Tyne along the Quayside. Watching the way my son perched himself eagerly upon the barrier, watching him smile at me and watching his eyes widen as his heroes (Newcastle United's Reserves – God the kid was in for a long few years) took to the field I could have been looking through a window in time and seeing Terry himself.

I looked at Keiron's excited face and I couldn't help but wonder what the next 25 years would bring him now he was enlisted in the ToonArmy. What games would he talk about twenty years from now? What would be his highs and lows? Who would be his favourite players? And would we ever win a damned trophy.

Though I hoped his years would be blessed with more silverware than mine I doubted they could be filled with better memories.

Then one of those awkward silences drifted over us. We were making small talk but there was a big talk looming and little way of avoiding it.

"I'm glad you turned up tonight," I said, not looking at my eldest, just looking at the pitch. "He's useless," I added as a sub-commentary to our tentative family reunion.

"Yeah," Terry said, in reference to neither and both of his previous statements.

"I didn't think you would, you know. I thought maybe you'd be stuck at work, or didn't fancy the traffic, or maybe you just weren't ready to meet the little 'un," I added as a stray pass made its way into the stand. "Seriously, what do they do on the training ground all week?"

"It's hardly his fault is it?" Terry said.

"I blame Roeder. His job, his backroom staff, his fault."

"No, I mean the bairn! It's hardly his fault is it?"

"Aye, you're right," I said, as a Linesman missed a blatant offside.

I hadn't seen Terry in years. Well, with the odd exception of Service Stations, Central Station, Wembley, Milan and Stanley Park. That was a weird one. I hadn't seen him in ages and then bang; he turns up at the same Burger Van as me yards from the San Siro just like he did on Wembley Way.

Then he found out about me becoming a father again and he did what it took to cut the ties completely. The empty seat at St. James Park said more than his words ever would. I know it hurt; it was meant to. It's hard to describe how I felt about what Terry did. To me at least, football mirrors life in so many, many ways. The best I can do is to say that I never gave up.

Basically I knocked his mother up when we were just kids and I did the honourable thing and I stuck with her. We could have had an abortion, but no matter how bad things turned out between Sheila and me, and even Terry & me, I never once regretted keeping the kid. Fall out's can be made up, bridges can be rebuilt; abortions are permanent. After that there's nothing to build a bridge to but a void. I did the right thing. I hoped it would turn out better but it didn't.

I never loved his mother, but I put up with all the coldness she gave me and I stayed in a loveless marriage because I wanted to be with the bairn. Then one day, out of the blue, I met a girl and I fell in love. And so – wrangle with the decision as I did – I eventually left the woman I married for the woman I loved. I never regretted that either, for what it's worth; I just wish the bairn could have understood.

Instead he took it really badly and it cost us our relationship. He never forgave me for walking out on him, when all a long he'd been the only thing stopping me from walking out on his mother for years.

But I never lost faith. I never gave up hope that one day we would be re-united. It's a tricky thing, faith. I guess it comes down to believing in something that you just can't see. Hell, I've never seen an ice-cream van at a petrol station but I know that they sure don't run on fresh air. I couldn't see Terry forgiving me, but I kept the faith that one day he would. I kept trying to bridge the gap between us, and on a few occasions I came close.

That night at Ashington I thought perhaps my determination and refusal to accept defeat might – just might – be about to pay off.

"I've bought him a season ticket," I told the bairn.

"Poor little bugger. What did he do to deserve that? Couldn't you have just grounded him or stopped his pocket money?"

I didn't respond; I just resumed. "I've bought you one too," I told me hopefully.

Silence.

"Will you come back?"

"Jeez, Fatha" he said slipping into his broadest Geordie, the same that he'd picked up by my side all those years ago. "I don't know."

"Will you think about it?" I asked him fairly.

He said nothing. He just stood there jangling a set of car keys.

I ruffled Keiron's hair and the bairn turned and smiled at me. "You enjoying it son?" I asked.

Keiron answered in big eyes and wide smiles: he was loving it.

"Wigan will be his first game," I told Terry. "Remember your first game, son? Jeez, you were just knee high to a grasshopper," I said.

And did he remember my first game? Hell, he's a football romantic. Your first game is like your first kiss; if you love the beautiful game it's something you should never forget.

"Yeah," he said, "I remember my first game. I remember it like it was yesterday…"

We didn't talk much after that. Terry was somewhere down memory lane, and jingling those car keys in his hand it looked like he'd driven there. Me, well I wasn't so fussed about his first game; I was just wondering when his next one would be.

17. Wigan

It was August 2006. It wasn't as hot as summers used to be. Maybe summers are always hotter in our memories. I lived in Wallsend, alone. Angie kept our old place; I bought somewhere new. Mandy stayed over quite a bit. She made me feel like I was seven years old. We watched DVD's, romantic films, cooked Italian meals and sat in the garden just as soon as we got in from work until ten o'clock every night when the sun went down.

But she didn't stay over that Friday night, the Friday before the new season started. Perhaps one of the reasons we love football is the redemption in it. No matter how badly you get beat one week the next game always starts nil-nil. No matter how low down the league you finish the next season always starts even. I think it's nice that at least once a year all of our mistakes are wiped out and we get a clean slate to start all over again.

Those were my thoughts as I read The Journal, waited for my bacon sandwich to cook and watched Socceram on Sky. Dad had been delighted with the Capri that I returned to him after that pre-season friendly at Ashington. He'd used it as a means of keeping in touch almost every day. He didn't ask about me returning to St James' with him and I didn't give any insight into what I'd decided. Truth was, I guess I hadn't made my mind up. Bucks Fizz would be turning in their grave.

Still, all morning I had the match-day buzz inside me. The season didn't promise that much in terms of optimism but since when did we support Newcastle United for the trophies and the success…? I guess I just wanted to be part of it again.

I was just banging on the bottom of the HP Sauce when I heard the letterbox go. I made my way for the post only to find that the postman had not been. Lying on my welcome mat was my new season ticket… and a Fruit & Nut. From out in the street I could hear a familiar engine driving away.

My friends are very dear to me, always have been and always will be. Sometimes they just know without words that you need them, and sometimes without words you just know they're there for you. Around 12noon, just as Jeff Stelling was introducing Gillette Soccer Saturday, there was a loud knock at the door.

I was upstairs at the time. I looked out of the window, opened it and saw all of the lads were standing at my door.

"Terry!" one of them yelled, "Get a shift on!"

I looked at them bemused, Fruit & Nut in my hand.

"Well are you coming or what?"

"Where?" I asked puzzled.

"For trombone lessons you plonker!"

"What?" I asked, my stupidity testing their patience to the yield.

"To the match you daft bugger!"

For a moment time stood still and 24 years flew past my eyes.

"Yeah," I said, "I'll be down in a minute."

The camaraderie between us was as strong as ever it had been. Soon we were in The Telegraph, though part of my heart was somewhere in The Farmers, God rest its long gone bricks, its long gone soul.

As we reached our turnstile at about 2 minutes to three the lads all stopped.

"I think you should go in first," they offered poignantly.

"Thanks Lads," I said as I closed my eyes and walked through turnstile 16, hearing its click welcome me home.

A few flights of stairs later and I was back in the theatre that is St James Park. It's changed so much, but after all of these years I am still part of it. The lads ushered me forward. I took one look at my season ticket and knowing that ground like the back of my hand I made my way to our row with not so much as a second glance. I stood at the beginning of row F in the Sir John Hall Stand, north-west corner. To me it will always be The Leazes End. And there, about 7 seats away, were my Dad and my brother.

Keiron saw me and waved. I was surprised he recognised me. Dave & Adam ushered me forward as my Dad turned to his right to see me. I don't know who patted me on the back, Dave or Adam, but it meant the world. They knew just how big a moment that was for me.

The game had kicked off just about a minute before.

Dad didn't know what to say. He understated it in his own immutable style.

"You haven't missed much," he said, smiling with a tear in his eye.

"I think I've missed about enough, don't you?" I told him as I ruffled Keiron's hair and then offered it forward to shake hands with my Dad. "But I won't be missing anymore, Dad, I won't be missing anymore".

There must have been about 10 of us grown men in that row and the only one not welling up was the bairn. Dave broke the moment before one us embarrassed ourselves and actually cried.

"So what do you fancy today then Jackie," Dave asked.

"2-1," Dad said.

"And what about you Keiron," Adam asked. "What do you think the score will be?"

"Hmm… 10-0!" Keiron smiled enthusiastically.

We all chuckled. "What does he know," I said, "He's barely knee high to a grasshopper"…

In truth it didn't matter whether it was 10-0 or 2-1. All that mattered was that we were United again.

18. Caffeine For The Giant

I guess that would have been a pretty good place to put this story to bed. My long journey through fatherhood had reached its happy ending. Terry and I were finally able to bury the hatchet and the lad was finally able to forgive me for leaving the woman I could never love for the woman I could never leave. It took a similar event in his own life to show him the way, but with a little help from a 20-year-old letter and the mystery of what happened to my old Ford Capri, he was able to get there.

As for Terry, well his journey reached a pretty happy conclusion too, with finding his soulmate, his meant-to-be, his written-in-the-stars. But I'll let him tell you about that for himself. In August 1982 I took him to his – and Kevin Keegan's – first ever Newcastle game. 25 years later I took his kid brother to his first ever match. And after all we had been through Terry was there beside us when I did. With that I thought our story was complete. But destiny holds cards that she doesn't always wish to reveal and no one can write better stories than the hand of fate itself. With such thoughts in mind our story had one more reunion to go.

By time Newcastle had beaten Wigan 2-1 on opening day of the 2006 / 2007 season I'd been hanging off United's results for nigh on 40-odd years. In that time I had witnessed 1 Trophy won, 3 promotions, 2 relegations, Fairs Cup football, UEFA Cup football, Cup-Winners-Cup football and Champions League football. I'd seen 2 stands pulled down and 4 stands and an extension rise from the ground. I'd also borne witness to 15 Managers and some of the best and worst players to ever grace and disgrace the famous black & white stripes.

After all of that somehow Wigan at home didn't seem like it would shape the destiny of the club a great deal in either direction. What it did do was cement my family back together once and for all. And that's why Wigan at home will always be special to me.

I'm a simple man by all accounts with pretty simple pleasures. I like my beers cold, my guitars loud and my satellite TV on the biggest screen that I can fit in my living room. I like honest people and if I'm honest myself I'll admit that I still get a kick out of watching a teenager fall of a skateboard or someone getting hit in the nuts with a football. I like old cars and big boobs. And I like good football played on the deck; the Arthur Cox way as opposed to the Big Jack way, for want of better definition.

That season was a pretty abysmal one. Under Glenn Roeder's stewardship Newcastle again struggled, again underachieved and again disappointed. But there beside me was my youngest son Keiron and my oldest son Terry. Of course our football family was complete with the entourage of friends that came with us. Terry had his mates alongside him and I had mine. In total there was a gang of about 20 of us in all, including the lads we met just by sitting alongside them.

It might have been dour on the pitch, but it was magical in the stands.

I'm not sure supporting Newcastle has ever been about winning trophies. You could hardly call the Toon Army glory hunters. But for all the shortcomings of the team and for all we crave that success and those trophies, Geordies have an undeniable ability to take the hard times with the greatest of wit and humour. Some of my best times following this club have been when the team has been basically bollocks. But no matter how bad the players have been they can never detract from the quality of the fans.

Those wonderful fans watched Newcastle trundle to a miserable 13th place. A 2-1 victory of Liverpool was the last home win noted. Alan Shearer was replaced with Obafemi Martins and seeing the famous number 9 shirt on someone else's back took some getting used to. Martins, for his flaws, packed away 11 goals in it. Those were rare highlights – like his goal and the game at Spurs or the home draw with Manchester United – that decorated a season of failure.

I wanted Roeder to succeed; I really did. He was one of our own; he loved the club, had played for the club and had worn the armband with great pride. Things like that matter to me. I don't like strangers or outsiders sitting in the Managers chair. I think that job is best reserved for someone who already has an understanding of the club, an affinity for it, and a rapport with its most important asset: its supporters. But Roeder just didn't seem big enough for the job; he never seemed to make the Manager's chair his own. After the 5-1 FA Cup replay humiliation to Championship side Birmingham in front of the Gallowgate faithful I knew that the next FA Cup tie the club faced they would face it with another man at the helm.

But with my football family re-united, somehow not even the continued shambles that I like to call my favourite club could stop me from smiling. Following Newcastle United is a drama, a rollercoaster. There have been many times when the cars were nose-diving towards the ground; there will be many more. But there will always be another high at some point. We're lucky at this club: night will always follow day up here, just like sun will follow rain. It's yin and yang; it's black and white. For me, I was just enjoying the company of those I was riding the rollercoaster with.

My real family were going pretty well too. Things with Rachel were wonderful. We were happy and we were secure and I don't think a man can ask for much more than that. My would-be stepdaughters, Emily and Millie who only ever called me Dad were blossoming young ladies who had grown up the right way. They grew up that way because that's how we raised them. It's rare these days but I think those girls really do respect Rach' and me, their parents.

Terry and I rebuilt our bridges and I was finally able to be a father to him too. We talked about relationships, about Angie and Mandy, Sheila and Rachel, about loyalty and fidelity and most of all we talked about growing up. To me, what I think I enjoyed the most was being part of his life. I was involved in his decisions, consulted about his dilemmas, and he shared with me his thoughts and feelings, hopes and fears.

In April 2007, with the season drawing to its anti-climax, I offered him a job. Slippery Travel, or Slipper When What had grown into a hugely successful business. We owned over a dozen coaches and minibuses. These coaches and minibuses needed upkeep, maintenance and servicing. Who better, I thought, than the bairn to do it. We shook on the deal over a pint in The Telegraph on a Thursday night. I pay him fair and he works hard. If he wants a bonus he keeps tabs on the Capri. I think that one is a labour of love to him.

I stood one day, at the yard, watching him covered in oil and grease working on one of the Coaches. Keiron was to his right, in dungarees and an SMB cap. The bairn – the young 'un – was holding a ratchet and 2 spanners for him. Keiron idolises his big brother; and I dare say that the feeling is mutual.

Standing at the yard, watching Terry fix one of my coaches, watching Keiron idolising Terry, knowing that Rachel was sat in the office behind me and tallying up the books, well that day – as strange a road as I had taken – I knew I had arrived exactly where I was destined to be. God, fate, destiny or something had been good to me, not least with the second chance to be Terry's father and certainly not least with the chance to be a father a second time. When Rachel told me she was pregnant I was stunned. I just presumed that by that stage of my life – I was 45 years old when she conceived – I'd have Shola-nuts: basically firing blanks. I never thought I'd hit the target again.

Standing at the yard that day, watching my bairns, hearing Rachel mention something about a cuppa from her office in our business I flicked my cigarette onto the gravel and I stumped it out with my boot. I quit smoking, right there and then. I didn't do it because anyone told me to, or because of the ban but because I wanted to reduce my chances of getting cancer. My life was good and I didn't want it coming to a premature end. I didn't want to look to the touchline of life and see fate holding up my number. This was a good game and I had no intention of not lasting the 90 minutes.

Cigarettes are like Titus Bramble: the lad can play for 80-odd minutes and not make a mistake. Hell he might not even be the reason you lose the game. But if you keep playing him then sooner or later he's going to screw up and cost you a goal. The fags are the same. You can probably smoke for 30 years and not get cancer. And they might not even be the reason you die. But if you keep on smoking them then sooner or later they'll catch up with you.

For me I just wanted to quit them before they got me. Just like most of us kept hoping Titus would be dropped / sold / shot before he cost us another goal.

As the rollercoaster that is being in the Toon Army continued it's downward plummet there was one thing that disturbed me more than the ride: the lack of screams.

Somewhere between Bon Jovi and Sigmund Freud it's said that all men are hero's... in dreams. My dreams of ever pulling on the black and white shirt in a more official capacity faded away a long time ago. I dare say I'll never Manage the team's affairs and the likelihood of Slippery Travel making me into a Geordie-Abramovic are slim to none. With that I have to accept that I will probably never awaken the sleeping giant that is Newcastle United. But that doesn't mean I'm not important and it doesn't mean I don't have my part to play.

Much has been made of how long we've gone without winning a trophy. And there are many people who love to see this great club, our great club struggle. Some are people of supposed power, such as the press; some are just idiots from our own back yard. Hell, some are even both. But that season I was not so disturbed by what was happening *on* the pitch but by what was happening *off* it.

For example, the atmosphere at the ground was almost non-existent. Now I could accept that, I could moan about it, or I could do something about it. And so now, every home game I get up off my arse and I sing, and I chant, and I back the lads from first kick to last. That's the way I used to do it on the terraces; that's the way I used to do it on the famous old Leazes End. But since the terraces died and seats came to pass it's not how we do it anymore. Sadly, in that way I am in the minority. If you're the guy behind me who spent £400 and odd quid that year to see my arse then I apologise but there is a greater good at stake here.

Against Blackburn in the final home game the crowd turned against Roeder. United foolishly did a lap of 'honour'. The vast majority of fans had left by then; they left with scathing criticism of Chairman, Manager and players still echoing in the ground behind them. A few days later and Glenn Roeder was sacked.

Now if 50 odd thousand had stayed for that lap of honour, if the crowd had backed Roeder and voiced their understanding that his injury-plagued side could be excused then – rightly or wrongly – I'm sure he would have been given another season to try and crack it. But the crowd didn't back Roeder, or Freddie Shepherd. Hence Roeder was soon gone. And though we may never have the casting vote in the St James Park boardroom I still believe we have the power to get any Manager here sacked. And to some extent any Manager here appointed.

I knew the good times would come again; I had faith that this darkness would turn to light. Maybe one day that will be the trophy we crave; maybe it will just be a return to good football and a regular Champions League football. The club is a sleeping giant, but I have no doubt that it will one day awaken.

The point I'm getting at is that I know we – the supporters – will never revive the club, hire its Manager or select its team; I know that we will never pull on the famous black & white and force our way into the starting 11. But we still have a massive part to play here. For one we can keep turning up at the games and keep this place sold out. For two we can sing. We can recreate an atmosphere at St James'. We can help make this place a fortress; we can be the famous 'twelfth man'. We can get there before kick off and back the lads as they warm up, just like we used to all those years ago. All it takes is one of us to get up off our seat and start a song. And if the guy next to you does that then get off *your* arse and help him. And if there's a group fifty seats away singing then you guys get up and join them. And so on and so on. And if you don't know the words then go to a bloody away game and learn them. Away from home the support is loyal, vocal and intelligent by and large. It's the cream of the clubs support. We need those who follow this club away from home to turn and relight the home support too. If you don't follow the lads away, then why not give it a go. And if travelling the length and breadth of the country to watch the same crap that's served up on the doorstep every other weekend is too much to ask then at least follow the away support's example and back the lads back home.

It's important that we do these things, make that extra effort and continue this little labour of love. We have seen with Kevin Keegan in the mid 90's what this club is capable of. So far it's potential remains untapped. Sitting in the emptying Leazes after that end of season home defeat to Blackburn Rovers I knew that one day a hero would come and save us. I also realised that until that time we – as supporters – need to keep on turning up, keep on singing and keep the faith. And though flexing the muscle of our support will never wake the club from it's 40 year slumber it's still vital that we re-enforce our tradition and our reputation, even if it is just caffeine for the giant.

19. Goodbye Mr A

Nickelback were standing in line for clubs they'd never get in, Rihanna was under her umbrella and our love alone was not enough for the Manic Street Preachers.

It was May 2007.

Dad stayed and watched the lap of 'honour' against Blackburn. He didn't clap; he didn't boo. But he refused to leave. I think he understands that when you don't love something you can walk away; when you do love something you see it through 'til the end. As Mandy and I celebrated our first anniversary I think I understood it too.

I'd like to say that everything worked out and that everything had a happy ending. But it didn't. I'd like to tell you that Angie was as relieved to be free from our relationship as I was; I'd like to tell you that she met *her* meant-to-be and fell head over heels. She didn't. Angie took the split pretty bad. It broke her heart; *I* broke her heart. I felt like a complete bastard for doing it and it's something I will live with everyday. But the cards had been good to me and to be with my Queen I had to let Angie go. The hardest part for her was trying to understand that she wasn't my Queen.

I guess the best way I can describe it is to ask you to think of Alan Shearer. When we think of Alan all we think of is Newcastle United. But what about the Blackburn fans whose hearts he broke when he left them to come to us? There was a time when he was their cherished number 9 before he was ours. I guess, like Mandy and me, Shearer and Newcastle were destined to be together. That doesn't mean that destiny comes without sacrifice. In a way we as football supporters have it lucky: we only ever have one love. There's no sad farewell's between a fan and their club.

But apart from Angie I guess my story did have a happy ending. I've been lucky, I know that much. It took me so long to realise that life was for living. More to the point it took me so long to have the courage to play the way I always knew I should. I lost a lot of time, a lot of opportunities, and I played the hand God gave me pretty poorly. To be cashing in a happy ending is testimony to the remarkable good fortune shown to me by whatever higher power it is that deals those cards.

I'll take what I know now and I'll help raise Keiron the right way. That's what big brothers do isn't it? When he grows up he'll talk to a stranger in the street, have a beer with his breakfast, take the ugliest girl home from the disco and dance with all of the married women that wish they weren't married. He'll live life like a cup-tie not a league game. He'll enjoy whatever good things come his way. I'll make sure of that. And when he's made a boatload of memories and he's ready to settle down I'll help him toe the line and hang on to the love that's sure to come his way.

I think that relationships are inherently fragile. It only takes the slightest bit thing to crack them and sometimes when that happens it snowballs until you and every valentine card you ever bought is smack-dab at the bottom of the mountain. And a lot of that is because half the people that are together aren't right for each other. But they're so scared they'll end up a lone that they try and ride it out rather than take the chance that the hand of fate will write the right person into their stories.

But somewhere amongst all of that I believe that love lasts forever. Call me a sucker if you like but that's how I feel. Maybe there *is* someone for everyone; maybe some people just don't find their person. Every time I flick on the TV or pick up a 'paper there's a whole load of lonely people who'd support that school of thought. Hell, take Angie for one of them. I jumped ship and shot the hell out of Dodge when the altar and the finishing line were in sight, and I took all of the lass' hopes and dreams with me when I did.

Maybe life really is like a great big game of football. We all face an opponent. Maybe that opponent is just bad luck; maybe it's bad decisions. Hell, maybe it's even the devil himself. But just like in football, regardless of the opponent you've just got to go out there and play. I'm all for tactics and organisation and knowing your strengths and weaknesses. But I'm not one for going anywhere and playing for the draw, or just hoping to survive anymore. Life and football do have that in common at least; neither is there to be survived; both are there to be played… and won.

I got my victory and it came with more than it's fair share of the rub of the green. I got lucky; the hand of fate wrote my meant-to-be into my story. Maybe it will for you too.

When the 2007 close season came it closed more than a chapter in my life. To be honest the big family reunion and the boy-gets-girl of it all could quite easily have closed this very story. But the hand of fate held on to its pen and wrote one more twist in the tale. Sometimes fact really is stranger than fiction.

That summer, a few weeks after a draw at Watford had closed the curtain on our season we went on a week's holiday for my birthday. When I say 'we' I mean almost everyone. Mandy and I went, as did Dave and Adam. Dad and Rachel went, along with Garry, Tom and Hopper. Splodge, Rob, Neil, Woody, Ian, Tony, Stu, everyone! Keiron came along, and although they were invited and would have been hugely welcome, Millie & Emily were young ladies now set for their own holiday in Spain.

We all went to Magaluf. We met other people there, too, such as Steve & Julie, David & Ali from Wallsend. We met a couple from Birtley – Ben & Jenny Thomas – who we shared a cab with when we thought we were going to miss our plane. I didn't even have enough money on me to pair for the fair. Luckily Ben pulled out a huge wad of £20 notes and got us from the pub to Newcastle International just on time.

Newcastle United were manager-less at that time and in a way that added to the excitement. We'd be up early every morning, roll off to a Tom Brown's, grab a paper, have a breakfast in the Spanish sunshine and then sit around the pool debating who the new boss should be. By time we came home we all knew it was Sam Allardyce.

The flight home was full of optimism, hope and new beginnings. There were quirky little moments that filled the moment, the occasion and the heart with encouragement. One was my Dad just thanking us for coming; another was watching Rachel and Mandy becoming good friends. The one I will perhaps treasure most was a little lad in a red & white Sunderland shirt running up and down the aisle on the plane as he went to and from the toilet. The kid must have had the bladder of a walnut. Each time he ran by us, Keiron – dressed in his finest black & white – turned his nose up. After about the sixth time there was a loud thump and the poor little Mackem was face down on the carpet. I looked at Keiron who was slowly pulling his leg back in. He raised his eyebrows and did his best Tony Adams 'dive' gesture.

I don't think I'd ever felt closer to him.

When we got home we were no sooner back at work when more good news filtered through: Freddie Shepherd had been bought out and a new owner was to take control of Newcastle United. I think that the vast majority of us preferred a complete stranger to the devil we knew says much about the regard Freddie was held in. There was a certain air of sympathy from me towards Freddie but I dare say that'd be a rare sentiment. Don't get me wrong, I was delighted he was going. But I dare say he did more and cared more for the club than perhaps we ever realised. Sadly – though some of his piss-poor decision-making should not go without mention – he was forever undone by showing us, the fans, the people, what he really felt about us via the News of the World. Freddie was a millionaire; we were but a product of the working class. How poetic that I now sit at every home game and Freddie is banned from St James Park by Mike Ashley.

In the end what Freddie possessed in money he lacked in class. The same can probably be said in reverse about the working class people of Tyneside.

The new regime started well, with a 3-1 win at Allardyce's former club Bolton on opening day. Two league wins and two league draws set up the opening 4 matches. However, defeat to little Derby County showed the cracks in the Newcastle set up and suggested that nothing had really changed from the frailties of the past. Still, victories over West Ham, Everton and Spurs kept results at a higher level than the performances were at.

Those cracks reappeared with defeat at Reading. In hindsight it was the visit of Harry Redknapp's Portsmouth that turned out to be a death-knell for Big Sam. As summer turned to autumn and autumn prepared for winter Newcastle turned out to be very ill prepared for Pompey. The south-coast side humbled Newcastle 4-1 in front of the Gallowgate faithful. Newcastle never seemed to recover from that. A 1-1 draw at Sunderland where surely all 3 points were up for grabs only made matters worse.

Newcastle went there to defend and sit back and grab a point of their own. The auld enemy lacked in ability and in confidence. And although Sam's mistake was not on a par with Ruud Gullit's a decade ago it showed the difference in footballing beliefs between the man picking the team and the thousands supporting it. That's a tricky one to get out of in a part of the world where those beliefs are almost on a par with religion. A James Milner goal salvaged a point for Sam's side.

United followed that Stadium of Light draw with an absolutely abject throwing in of the towel against Rafa Benitez Liverpool. Poor performances can be excused; bad days at the office are forgivable. But to roll over and die in front of 52,000 paying customers is a sin. Incredibly, despite being in the job only a matter of months talk of Allardyce being in danger of losing it began to leak out.

The stories persisted in November and December and Newcastle's footballing Christmas was not a particularly merry one. January brought a new year but not a new season and as the FA Cup was once again up for grabs I couldn't help but feel that black and white sleeves would be a long way from catching it.

I think that the patience around Newcastle had worn thin. The club were still lovesick for Kevin Keegan, some would say. I think it's simpler than that: I just think that as fans we're getting sick of people making an arse of our club. If the heart harks back to a time when we had something to be proud of for a change is that so hard to accept?

Such thoughts drifted around the Tyneside streets like litter. Old memories of happier times, of flowing football, of players who did the shirt justice, of players who earned their wages. It doesn't have to be about overpaid underachieving starts. Was Les Ferdinand cheap? Or did we pay him a fortune every week…? The guy must have been loaded, but it didn't stop him working his bollocks off and giving 100% week in week out. Alan Shearer, Rob Lee, David Batty, John Beresford, Peter Beardsley; I bet they all earned a tidy buck but not one of them ever went out there and let the shirt down by refusing to break sweat in it.

Sam Allardyce is probably not a bad manager; his track record before Tyneside proves that and I dare say that he'll go on to do well somewhere else. But at Newcastle it just wasn't working and restless Geordie hearts grew collectively colder at his brand of football and his lack of results. There was always an undercurrent of animosity between the two, I felt. For me, for reasons I just couldn't put my finger on, Big Sam just rubbed me up the wrong way. I didn't like Graeme Souness as a Manager but I respect him as a man. With Sam there was always something about him I just couldn't get around.

Some people seem to understand Newcastle United and the people that really make this club special: the fans. Some people don't seem to get it. Sam, sadly, was the latter. Some people understand that we want to be entertained and more importantly that we want to have a go. We don't want to go to places like bloody Wigan and try to hang on for a point. Some people, no matter how much they want to succeed here, just don't seem to click with the Geordie faithful. Others understand that it's just as important to give us, the paying customer, whose hearts go into the club along with their money, something to be proud of. Some people don't understand that we work hard up here and we play hard too. Some people do. And some people know how to provide a product *for* the working class.

In January 2008 I was at the yard working on one of the Slippery Coaches. It was around twenty past four in the afternoon. I had the radio on. Timbaland and One Republic had just told us it was too late to apologise, Nickelback told us that we all just wanted to be big rockstars and then they played The Hoosiers 'Goodbye Mr A'. Before the song had finished my mobile went: and so too had Sam Allardyce.

20. *Trading Hero's For Ghosts*

Hell I'm not one to question the logic of Forrest Gump but I'm not sure that life is like a box of chocolates. Chocolates are sweet, enjoyable and full of creamy tasty fillings. To me life is more like a trip to the hairdressers: you always spend more than you intend to, you rarely get what you ask for, and even though the sign says 'facials' you really shouldn't get your hopes up. And in the end although you leave riddled with self-doubt, if you're lucky someone nice will have rubbed their boobs against you and it'll all feel worthwhile.

Life is hard and if something is worth having then it's up to you to go out and get it. And if you're really lucky your hard work will be matched with good luck and you might just end up happy. I did. And as a parent an integral part of my happiness is essentially that my family are happy too. And they were. Emily & Millie, Keiron and Terry, Rachel and me.

Newcastle had just been hammered 6-0 at Old Trafford and were due to face Stoke City in an FA Cup 3rd round replay. I'd been away all afternoon looking at a new house in Wallsend. Maybe it was just the way that things were going with the family but it felt like it was time to go back to my spiritual home. That's where I was born and raised; more importantly it was where I belonged. Part of the reason I had stayed away was because of Terry. Now he was the very same reason for moving back.

Leaving is part of life, but so too is coming home. And a man should always return to where he belongs. If he doesn't know where that is then his heart will one day tell him.

I was on my way back to the yard with Rachel. Terry was 'babysitting' his spanner-holding, oil covered assistant and working on one last engine before clocking off. He'd get changed at work and then we'd head to the match and Rachel would take Keiron home. He had school in the morning and was yet to be kept up late for a midweek match. He grumbled about it but hell, it wasn't like he was missing much.

We were just coming through the city centre when news began to break. I did a quick U-turn in the Capri, Rachel clung on for dear life, and I spun off in a way that would have made Terry McCann proud. We made a beeline for Gallowgate, whipped along Strawberry Place and past David Craig, the guy from Sky Sports and screeched to a halt just opposite Shearer's. People were gathering at pace, horns were honking, people were shouting, the crowds began to swell and not to sound too Jagger & Bowie but there actually were outbreaks of dancing in the streets.

I jumped out of the car, ran across the road and left Rachel to park up. Minutes later I was heading out of the ticket office and urging Rach' to get us home before we got stuck in the traffic.

Finally, with the promise of queues growing ever larger around the club, Rachel and I got out of the city centre and made our way home. We traded dashboard light for kitchen light and called into the Chip Shop around the corner from the Slippery When What coach yard. We arrived around 5 o'clock, with a swagger and a stagger, a song and a smile, and four packets of fish n' chips wrapped in the early edition of the days Chronicle.

Even though Terry was still arms deep in a coach engine when we pulled up he knew that something special had happened. Moments later he whisked Keiron off in his merry arms and rushed him inside for tea. I never really thought about it at the time, but Terry used to be a bit special when he was excited. He always had a knack of bringing out the excitement in others too. That teatime he was magic. He was a happy man. He sat Keiron down while Rachel poured us Dandelion & Burdock and handed out our fish n' chips. I'd kept him in suspense long enough so I finally asked him if he'd heard the news.

Then I reeled off my Geordie fairytale, told a Geordie way: fish n' chips, Dandelion and Burdock, an oily, greasy garage and hero coming home to save us and make us proud once again.

I told Keiron how the barren years were over, the sleeping giant was awakening, and we'd all be there to see it.

Newcastle had signed Kevin Keegan as Manager.

Terry was checking his mobile; I was checking the rumblings in my heart that carried back almost twenty-six years, and Keiron was checking to see which packet had the most chips in.

All of a sudden the coach yard was a tickertape parade. The ringtones went off, the calls came through in droves from Terry's first text.

"Is it true? Is it true?" they all asked like kids wondering if Santa has been on Christmas morning.

I just smiled and hugged my family like we were right there on the terracing. It was true: Keegan was back.

When I handed Keiron his match ticket he was so excited that he couldn't sit still. Then Terry stood up and took him by the hand.

"Come on Keiron," he said. "There's another bus ride about to go off and we've got tickets to ride".

Where's it going?" Keiron asked, unaware of a metaphor that had started in August 1982.

Terry just smiled at him. He was already lost in thought. His mind, his memory and his heart were at European night's at SJP, hammering Man United 5-0, thanking Sunderland very much for the six-points and watching the lads come in 6-0 up at half-time as they returned to the top flight. He was watching helicopters leave the St James Park pitch, watching Chris Waddle drop the shoulder or Peter Beardsley do a shuffle. He was watching David Kelly, Andy Cole, Alan Shearer, Les Ferdinand and Tino Asprilla. He was at Grimsby one wonderful night in 1993, at Antwerp one wonderful night in 1994 and at Roker Park & Ayresome Park two magical days one October of 1992.

Then Terry thought of the future; I could see it in his eyes. The sparkle began to flicker as the ghosts of Dalglish, Gullit, Souness and Allardyce began to fade away. Suddenly he could see The Champions League, The Nou Camp and Milan and suddenly maybe they could be more than just memories.

Keiron tugged his brothers sleeve and innocently repeated the question: "Where's the bus going, Terry?"

Terry smiled and pictured Kevin Keegan at the wheel. He was about to say 'Where we belong Keiron, where we belong'. Then he thought of the self-destruct button that sat somewhere in the St James Park boardroom. He considered Mike Ashley, Chris Mort and the new regime. He prayed that button would be allowed to gather dust. He understood that such matters were out of his hands. Then he looked at Keiron and he realised that the things in life that really mattered *were* in his hands.

He checked his answer. "I don't know where the bus is going, Keiron", Terry said, "but no matter where it goes I know we'll travel together."

Printed in the United Kingdom
by Lightning Source UK Ltd.
135199UK00001B/259-279/P